BLACK HORIZON

'Where do I belong then?'

'You belong,' she said, 'with me.'

The mists were beginning to boil around them now, a dark and turgid stew of movement.

'I died, giving you life ... and I gave you something more.' Her voice was earnest, but her features, behind the mist, were unclear. 'I gave you a piece of my spirit, Jack – a piece of my life ... and a piece of my death.'

The fog around them grew even denser and more agitated, and he suddenly became afraid of losing his way in it. He clutched again at her hand, and this time she let him grasp her fingers. He felt himself drawn, with extraordinary power, into her embrace; her eyes were blazing green with delight, and her teeth sparkled white as she laughed. Over her shoulder, far behind, but growing closer all the time, he could now make out a churning bank of thick black cloud, rolling in place like a monstrous wave, seething like a storm held in check on the horizon . . .

About the Author

Robert Masello is a graduate of Princeton University, and has written both fiction and non-fiction works. He is a freelance writer for several magazines and newspapers, including *The Washington Post*, has lectured on writing and appears often on both radio and television. He lives in New York City.

ROBERT MASELLO

BLACK HORIZON

NEW ENGLISH LIBRARY
Hodder and Stoughton

First published in the USA in 1989 by Berkley Publishing Group

First published in Great Britain in 1990 by New English Library paperbacks

A New English Library paperback original

Printed and bound in Great Britain for Hodder and Stoughton paperbacks, a division of Hodder and Stoughton Ltd., Mill Road, Dunton Green, Sevenoaks, Kent TN13 2YA (Editorial Office: 47 Bedford Square, London WC18 3DP) by Richard Clay Ltd., Bungay, Suffolk.

British Library C.I.P.

Masello, Robert
  Black horizon.
  I. Title
  813'.54[F]

ISBN 0-450-51110-3

For Laurie—
my reward

In fields of light, a shadow plays,
That men heed not, nor change their ways,
Till Death's lean finger, jewel bedizened,
Beckons them cross that black horizon.

Anonymous, eighteenth century

BLACK HORIZON

Prologue

February 6, 1967

Weehawken, New Jersey

"JESUS, HOW OLD is she?"

"I don't know. Eighteen, nineteen." His fingers quickly adjusted the transfusion bag on the rod above her arm. "Auto accident. The driver's already dead."

A nurse hurried in with another bag of blood, type A negative.

"How's heart function?"

"So far, okay. It's a miracle, considering."

"Considering what?"

Mehta stopped to wipe his glasses. "Considering what she had in her—marijuana, alcohol, possibly LSD. Even without the accident, it's a miracle she's alive."

Prescott shook his head. He'd worked the Emergency Room long enough to take nearly anything in stride—but not so long that he was inured to the horrors. He surveyed the body laid out on the table—a tall, slender young woman, barely breathing under the white sheet. She might have been pretty, too—but that he couldn't say. Her face had gone straight through the windshield.

Above her head, the monitors recorded her pulse, breathing rate, brain activity. It was the EEG that worried Prescott the most—her brain was very close to shutting down all function.

"I know what you're thinking," Mehta said. "She's gonna flat-line on us any time now."

Prescott didn't answer.

"There's just one other thing that I think you ought to

know," said Mehta, stepping back from the table and thrusting his hands into the pockets of his lab coat. "According to her friend in the waiting room—"

"The girl wearing the beaded headband?"

"Right. According to her, this one here is pregnant, around ten weeks gone."

The EEG monitor beeped rapidly, signaling a sudden shut-down of all electrical brain activity. A flat white line coursed across the blue data screen.

"Heart and lungs?" Prescott asked urgently, scanning the monitors. But he could see for himself.

"They're both still pumping," Mehta said. "She's still alive, if you can call it that." He paused, chewing on his lip. "For that matter, they're both still alive—the mother and the baby."

Are they? Prescott thought, looking down at the breathing body, grimly festooned with needles and tubes, catheters and suction cups. Is this life? Or just some screwed-up kind of death? Where is she now, this faceless girl, with the beating heart and the unborn child?

Where, he corrected himself, are *they* now?

Part
One

chapter ∼ one

The Present Day

AS SOON AS the members of the cast had taken their last bow, the musicians, crammed into the orchestra pit just below the stage, started packing up their gear. Jack Logan unplugged his guitar from the amp and lifted the strap from around his neck. Vinnie bent over to tie his shoes; he always kept them untied during a performance, claiming they interfered with his breath control.

"Think it's a hit?" he asked Logan, over the last of the applause.

"You never can tell from an opening night," Logan said. "Half of the people out there are investors, and the rest are relatives of the cast."

Vinnie sat up again, flushed just from having bent over. He was so overweight that the fold-up chair he sat on was completely obscured. "God, I hope it's a hit," he said, tucking his trumpet under one arm. "I need this job to last. I owe about two thousand on my Mastercard and Barbara's expecting pearl earrings for Christmas. If this show closes, I'm gonna be back doing the bar mitzvah circuit."

It was every musician's nightmare—winding up as one of those guys in a ruffled shirt and tuxedo, playing "Moon River" for the millionth time in a rented hall on Long Island. Logan had done it, too; in fact, the night before he'd landed the job as guitarist in this show, he'd been playing a wedding in Moonachie, New Jersey. But for four months now the show had been in rehearsal, and every week the score had changed —numbers had been dropped, replaced by new ones, which were dropped themselves the next week. Logan hoped, as much as Vinnie, that the end result was a hit. Broadway paid a lot better than bar mitzvahs.

In the musicians' locker room, Logan stashed his sheet music and put on his overcoat and gloves. Vinnie locked his trumpet away—the other brass players were too paranoid to leave their instruments in the theater overnight—and pulled on the light windbreaker the producers had provided to everyone involved in the show. Across the back, in the same distinctive script used on the marquee and in the ads, was stenciled *Steamroller.*

"That all you're wearing?" Logan asked.

"I want to advertise," Vinnie replied. "Maybe I'll sell some tickets."

"At forty-five bucks a pop, you've got your work cut out for you."

"That what they're charging for orchestra?"

Logan nodded, zipping his Fender Strato-caster, a vintage '59, into its black carrying case. "Even the mezzanine's going for thirty-eight fifty."

They checked out with the backstage door manager, and followed several of the other players into the narrow alleyway leading to West Forty-fifth Street. In front of the theater they could see a huge crowd of milling people, all trying to hail cabs or find the limousines they came in. Two enormous white searchlights had been set up on a flatbed truck across the street, their rotating beams crisscrossing in the night sky. Logan recognized a local reporter—she appeared on the eleven o'clock news—preparing to do a remote. She was clutching a white-and-yellow *Playbill* while one of the camera crew moved her into position.

"Catch this," he said to Vinnie. "Channel 4 is about to decide our fate."

"She's smiling," Vinnie said. "That's a good sign."

Her camera director asked her for a voice level.

"Has Broadway finally got a hit on its hands?" she said. "Tonight, *Steamroller* opened, under the direction of the man who first—"

"Enough," he said, without looking up at her. She stopped instantly, the smile fading from her face, replaced by a look of infinite boredom.

"Bad sign," Vinnie muttered.

"We're on in one minute," the director said.

Logan and Vinnie moved toward the curb, where they could hear what she had to say without blocking the crowd still leaving the theater. As on most opening nights, there were a lot of diamonds, Rolex watches, fur coats. Logan had bought his own overcoat, a long raglan tweed, off a second-hand rack on Canal Street, for twenty-five dollars. He slipped the neck of his guitar up under it, while resting the base on his foot. He didn't want anybody banging into his most prized possession.

"Excuse me," the director was calling, "but could you people—yes, you there—please clear away. You're blocking our shot."

He was talking to an elderly couple—very Cartier and Palm Beach—who had inadvertently strayed into his shot. The woman understood the problem before her husband did, and pulled him gently to one side.

"No, dear, the hotel's that way," he said, resisting.

"I know that. But you're standing in the way of a camera."

He looked around, a little confused, then saw the TV crew. "Oh, I'm *so* sorry," and he began to back up more than he had to.

"Adolph, that's far enough," said his wife, with a laugh.

But he had already stepped on someone's toe, turned to apologize, tripped, and before anyone knew what was happening, had slipped off the curb. He fell flat on his back in the street.

"Watch my guitar," Logan said to Vinnie. "I'm gonna do a good deed."

The old man had rolled over to one side: his wife was anxiously waiting for someone to help him up. Suddenly a limo driver who'd seen the empty spot at the curb, but not the old man, gunned the engine and started to pull in.

"No! Stop!" his wife cried.

The old man threw up his hand, catching the grill of the car just as it hit him. He was knocked back against the curb; the car jounced to a halt. It was all over in an instant.

"Adolph!" His wife threw herself down beside him. "Adolph!" She was clutching his hand, staring into his face.

He didn't answer. She looked up wildly. "A doctor! Is there a doctor? We need a doctor!"

No one moved. Jesus, Logan thought, a crowd like this and not one doctor? The limo driver was out of the car, telling anyone who'd listen that it wasn't his fault. "The guy was already down—how could I see him there?"

"Please, please, he's not breathing," his wife was saying. A man took off his overcoat and wrapped it around him. "Keep him warm," he said, "I'll call an ambulance."

Instinctively, Logan knew it would be too late. The old man hadn't been hit hard, but he must have had a heart attack from the shock. Somebody, Logan figured, had better do something fast—maybe what he'd seen on all those medical TV shows. Pump his chest, get him breathing.

Pressing through the circle of onlookers, Logan knelt across from the man's wife. "I'm not a doctor," he said. "But we've got to do something."

He pulled the extra overcoat away, straddled him, then pressed hard on his chest cavity. Nothing. He put his ear to the old man's chest. There wasn't any heartbeat he could detect. He pressed again. Should he be trying artificial resuscitation? His mind raced—wasn't that only for drowning? He leaned back, then forward again with all his might. Someone said "Pound him—pound him right above the heart." Logan tried it, first tentatively, then hard.

"You'll kill him!" his wife said, trying to restrain Logan's fist.

Honey, he's already dead, Logan thought bitterly. At least give me a chance to save him.

He bent forward and listened again.

"Adolph, Adolph," his wife was crying, wringing one of her husband's limp hands.

Logan heard no heartbeat, only the rustle of the old man's shirt brushing against his cheek; the shirt smelled of pipe tobacco. Logan squeezed his eyes shut, and pressed the old man's shoulders between his hands. He could feel the fragile bones, and even hear them creak. You're not gonna die, he thought. That's just not going to happen here. In his mind's eye, unexpectedly, he saw a sand hill, on a hot summer day, with a red steel scaffolding all around it. I'm coming with you, he thought. I'm coming. The summer sun became brighter and brighter, and Logan felt himself traveling, as he had done once before, a long time ago, right up into its blaze. *Through* it, for that matter. But without any feeling of exertion, or even speed. Everything around him was white, and white hot, but the heat didn't matter, nothing did. He was traveling like an arrow shot from an unimaginable bow, hurtling toward a target he couldn't see. Coming . . . coming . . . coming, he thought, and then remembered nothing more until he found himself rolled over onto his back, thinking of sand again, mountains of gritty dun-colored sand, and looking up into Vinnie's anxious face.

"You okay, man? Are you okay?"

He heard sobbing, but it seemed happy somehow. There was joy in it, relief. He turned his head on the pavement. Adolph's wife was hugging her husband in her arms, rocking him, soothing him. Adolph was *answering* her, one of his own arms feebly draped around her waist. From down the block, Logan heard the wail of the ambulance siren, stuck in traffic.

"Logan, can you hear me?" Vinnie was drawing him up into a sitting position. *"Talk* to me, man."

Logan nodded his head to indicate he was okay. Over her husband's shoulder, Adolph's wife caught his eye. "Thank you," she mouthed, "thank you." Tears were streaming down her face.

Logan suddenly felt colder than he'd ever felt before, and shivered violently. Vinnie helped him pull his twenty-five-dollar overcoat closed. Leaning on Vinnie, he got to his feet. "Jesus, I'm freezing," he said.

"Come on, we'll go over to Charlie's and have a drink."

A medic had fought his way through the crowd and was trying to disengage Adolph and his wife. Logan suddenly panicked.

"Where's my guitar?"

"It's okay," Vinnie said, but not convincingly enough. "I told those TV guys to watch it."

"Where are they?" Logan said, spinning around.

"We're right here." The director waggled one hand over the heads of some people standing between them.

Logan unsteadily made his way through the crowd.

"You know, you're some kind of a hero," the director said.

Logan gripped the handle of the guitar case.

The reporter materialized in front of him. "What did you do just now? That was incredible," she said. "Are you a paramedic or something?" She took in the guitar. "Are you in the band for this show?" she added, sounding even more amazed.

Logan said, "No, I'm not a paramedic. But I am in the band." He turned to go. "You'll have to excuse me—I've got a hot date." Vinnie plowed a path through the crowd, and Logan followed in his wake. Traffic was stopped dead; they crossed the street between two taxi bumpers. Everything around them flashed white, then red, then white again, in the alternating beams of the spotlights and the ambulance beacon.

At the door to Charlie's, the maître d' asked what was going on outside.

"Guy had an accident," Vinnie replied. "And this guy," he said, clapping Logan on the shoulder, "brought him back from the dead."

chapter two

THE NEXT DAY, Logan awoke at his usual hour—one o'clock in the afternoon—and started the water boiling before even opening his eyes all the way. By the time he'd shaved and showered, the water was ready to be poured through the coffee filter and into the same mug he drank from every morning. He took his coffee black, not because he especially liked it that way, but because he couldn't be bothered to keep fresh milk in the fridge. Sitting at the card table he'd set up at one end of the studio apartment, he sipped at the coffee, while idly surveying the windows of the apartments across the way.

The writer, a heavyset woman with short hair and glasses, was already at her desk, typing away. She would stay there until five o'clock sharp, then flick off her desk lamp and disappear into the inner recesses of her apartment.

The gay dancer, wearing nothing but jockey shorts, was flinging himself around the room, to an apparently relentless beat.

The elderly sisters, twins who wore identical clothes whenever Logan saw them together on the street, were watching TV.

Gradually, the events of the night before were returning to him. In the shower he'd noticed the soreness in his knees—from kneeling in the street. On the kitchen counter, he'd found a matchbook from Charlie's—where he'd had three drinks he could recall, and possibly more. On the table in front of him was a copy of the *Playbill* for *Steamroller*, which he'd taken just in case there wasn't any second performance. He'd have to buy the papers to find out.

As for the rest, the stuff that had actually gone on with the injured old man, he couldn't really recall a lot of it. Nor did he want to. It was something he didn't want to think about.

Not now. Maybe never.

On the answering machine, the message light was flashing three times. He rolled back the tape, and turned up the volume on the voice monitor.

"I hope I'm not disturbing you." His grandmother—she always started out that way. "I just wanted to wish you good luck—that show you're in is opening tonight, isn't it?" A day late: also the usual. "I hope it's a great success . . . give me a call and tell me all about it. I hope you're feeling well . . . Give my best to Stephanie."

He hadn't told her the latest about Stephanie. They'd broken up three weeks ago.

The second message was from one of his guitar students, canceling a lesson.

The third was Stephanie. "Listen, I need to come over this afternoon to pick up some stuff. Specifically, I need the sheet music for the Trout Quintets. I've got a job at some P.R. reception at Wave Hill. Anyway, if you don't want to see me, don't worry about it—I've still got your keys and I can let myself in. See you—or not—later . . . Bye."

Jack checked the clock on his bookcase. Twenty of two. Should he quickly clear out, to avoid seeing Stephanie? It seemed sort of ridiculous, to have to run away from his own home. But on the other hand, he hated scenes, and this could easily turn into one. He also wanted to go out and see how the newspapers had reviewed the show.

He was already into his shoes and just about ready to go when his buzzer went off.

"Damn," he said, then, "Yes?" into the intercom.

"Oh, you're home. It's me . . . can I come up for my stuff?"

Jack didn't answer, but just buzzed her through. He heard the downstairs door swing shut, then her footsteps on the stairs. He opened his own door and stood back to let her pass.

She was wearing a black-and-white scarf wrapped around her head. She looked at him a little apprehensively. "I wouldn't have come so early, but I needed to start practicing that music."

"Come on in," he said, gesturing her out of the doorway. "I'm not gonna bite you."

She walked over to the side of the bed, which took up the center of the studio, and unknotted her scarf. "Whew—is it cold outside. The wind on Riverside Drive is enough to blow you over."

Jack gave her a look, and she suddenly realized what she'd said. Her new boyfriend—Kurt, of the penthouse apartment and the house in Easthampton—lived on Riverside.

"So how is he?" Jack asked. "Raid any companies this morning?"

"Not that I know of," Stephanie said, looking around the room for something else to talk about. The *Steamroller Play-bill* caught her eye. "So how'd the show go?" she asked. "I haven't seen the papers yet today."

"Neither have I. Nobody forgot their lines. The audience seemed to like it."

"Be great if it's a hit," Stephanie said encouragingly.

"Yeah," Jack replied, "great." He pulled a white plastic bag out from under the card table. "I've been putting your stuff in here," he said. "Leg warmers, stopwatch, leotard, lens solution. I don't know where the Schubert score is."

"I do," Stephanie said, going to the record rack and squatting down. "I stuck it in here," she said, and slid it out from between the Rolling Stones and Stravinsky. "I didn't even disrupt your alphabetical order with it." Stephanie knew that in many things Jack didn't care about order or neatness—but when it came to anything having to do with his music or his instruments, he was as compulsive as they come. "I've got a gig at Wave Hill, some sort of reception."

"So you said on the machine."

She tried again. "How's Vinnie doing? Is he sticking to his diet?"

"Not so you'd notice."

A pause fell. Stephanie said, "I guess you don't want to do this, huh?"

"What?"

"Stay friends, keep in touch."

"Sure, sure I do," Jack replied, walking over to the window and wedging his hands in the back pockets of his jeans. "You and me and Kurt, whenever he can find the time. I was thinking of renting a summer place near his, so we could all go boating together. If the show's still running, I'll just get somebody to sub for me. That way I won't ever have to leave the beach. We could all have a really great time, don't you think?"

Stephanie got up from the floor, put the Schubert into the plastic shopping bag. She took her scarf off the bed and knotted it under her chin again. "The thing is," she said, "you'd probably have liked him, under other circumstances. I know what you think—and he's not just another investment banker."

Jack turned to face her. "Jesus, you're not going to start telling me what a great guy he is, are you? I mean, what do I have to do—be his friend now?"

"No," Stephanie said, walking to the door. "I just wanted you to still be mine." She stopped, fumbling in the pocket of her coat for something.

"Give me some time," Jack said softly. "It's too soon. Just give me some time, okay?" He hated this to be happening.

"Okay." She pulled the keys to his apartment out of her pocket, and placed them gently in the tray of loose change that he kept by the door. "Good luck with the show," she said. "See you around."

After she left, Jack stood where he was, wondering what to do next. Finally, he remembered that he hadn't seen the newspapers yet. It didn't seem to matter so much anymore, but at least it was something to do. He grabbed a handful of change and went out to see if he still had a job.

chapter three

DR. SPRAGUE WAS studying some preliminary lab reports when his assistant, Nancy Liu, tapped on his open door.

"Yes?" he said, irritably. So what if he'd left the door open —she should know by now that he hated to have his concentration broken.

"I'm sorry to interrupt, but there's something I thought you'd want to see." She produced a copy of the *New York Post*, open to an inside page, and put it on the desk in front of him. There was an ad for Jack LaLanne, some item about Angie Dickinson, and a review that was headlined "*Steamroller* Rolls Over." He looked up at her questioningly.

"What the hell is this?"

"Under the review, there's a short note, right at the end." His eye dropped down the page, to just below the review.

After the opening-night performance, Mr. Adolph Zakin, founder and chairman of Zakin Theatrical Properties, one of the largest theater management chains in America, was struck by a car directly outside the theater. He was rushed to St. Luke's–Roosevelt Hospital Center where a hospital spokesman said he remains in serious but stable condition. According to Mrs. Zakin, who was with her husband at the time of the accident, "His life was saved through the intervention of some young passerby. Adolph himself believes he died, and was returned to life. Whatever that young man did, it was a miracle; he must have been an angel from God."

Now Sprague knew why she'd shown him the paper.

"Zakin I can talk to anytime," he said, "provided he lives. For now, find me that fucking angel."

The minute she'd seen the story, Nancy had known Sprague would go for it; maybe, she'd figured, it would even earn her some brownie points—though with Sprague you could never tell. He could just as easily have balled her out for reading the paper on office time and threatened to dock her a day's pay. How, she wondered not for the first time, had she wound up doing such stuff? With a master's in psychology from NYU, and a good shot at her PhD, she was now about to blow the rest of the day tracking down "an angel from God," at the behest of a boss she'd already decided was halfway around the bend.

Maybe even three-quarters.

She sipped the last of her tea from the cup, and called information for the number of the *Post*. At the switchboard, she asked for Murray Spiegel, the name on the *Steamroller* review, and was instantly connected to someone who answered "Entertainment." When she asked for Murray Spiegel, the voice, female, impatiently said, "What's it about?"

"It's about the note at the end of the review in today's paper. About the theater owner, Adolph Zakin. I'm calling from the Institute of Abnormal Psychology, here in New York—"

"Murray didn't write that," the voice interrupted. "I did; I work with him. What do you want to know?"

Nancy was taken aback by the woman's peremptory tone, and had to quickly collect her thoughts. "First, I'd like to know who actually witnessed the incident. Was it you?"

"No."

"Then where did you get the story?"

"From a friend of mine, a TV reporter, who did. Why?" She suddenly sounded wary. "Do you know something about it?"

"Only what I read in the papers," Nancy replied. "The case interests us, for clinical and experimental reasons. Could you tell me the name of the TV reporter?"

There was a pause. "Not till I check with her first."

"Fine." Doubtful she'd be of much interest to Sprague,

anyway. "How about the name of the young passerby who saved Zakin's life?"

"Don't know. I don't think my friend does either."

"Could she find out?"

Exasperated sigh at the other end of the line. "Maybe. I don't know. Call me—ask for Arlette—tomorrow, after ten. I'll see what I can do."

Nancy was about to thank her, but she'd already hung up.

chapter
four

THE MOOD IN the orchestra pit that night was predictably schizoid. The reviews had been mixed, to say the least; half the musicians thought they were going to be out of work again, and the other half thought the show could make a run of it. Everybody had seen the item about Adolph Zakin in the *Post*, and thanks to Vinnie they now knew the true identity of the "angel from God." When Logan entered the locker room with his guitar, Haywood, the black percussionist, did a drum roll on the metal bench and shouted, "Hallelujah! The angel of the Lord has come!" Veronica Berghoffer, the flautist, looked up at Logan with her pale, lashless eyes and said, "That was a wonderful thing you did." Vinnie, sensing that Logan might not be pleased with the publicity, busied himself with emptying the valves on his trumpet. Logan stashed his coat and guitar case.

"You really did that?" Haywood asked, sitting down beside Logan. He drew two mint-flavored toothpicks out of his breast pocket, handed one to Jack. Haywood went through about a hundred every night.

"I guess so," said Jack. "Anything, you know, to help the show."

"Seriously, man, this show could use it." Haywood was one of the pessimists. "You see that line in the *Post*, about the band being as flat as the sets?" he asked of the room in general.

Several of the players laughed, and nodded.

"Shit, I know *I* was in tune," Haywood said. "I think it was

Vinnie could use some help pickin' out a key."

"Yeah?" Vinnie replied, smiling; he was glad they were already off the angel topic. "I *carry* you guys. Catalano was playing about six bars behind all night."

Catalano, the sax player, threw a split reed at him, which, somehow, landed in Veronica's hair.

"Thanks very much, guys," she said, gingerly untangling it. "As if I don't have enough problems already."

That brought them all down on her, insisting she tell them her other problems. Veronica, not a girl who'd ever excited much masculine attention, was falling all over herself with embarrassment and delight when Burt, the house contractor, came in. An affable piano player in his fifties, Burt had hired most of the musicians for the show, and now acted as sort of a camp counselor. "Okay, okay," he said, clapping his hands together to get their attention, "time to go to work, folks!"

"Saved by the clap," Veronica said, without thinking.

Haywood nearly fell over laughing. Catalano rolled his eyes and played a scorching three-second solo on his saxophone.

"Why can't you play like that when you're in the pit?" Burt kidded him. "Now let's get cookin'. Five-minute call was ten minutes ago."

Like a cowboy, he rounded them up and herded them out of the locker room. In single file, trading wisecracks, they marched through the narrow passageway, lighted by a red sixty-watt bulb, and into the orchestra pit. While setting up, Logan shot a glance at Vinnie, who sat directly across from him, and Vinnie, knowing exactly what it meant, said, "*Basta*. No more of the angel stuff, I swear."

But that wasn't to be the end of it. When Logan was leaving after the performance, Gus, the backstage doorman, said, "There's a Jap in a black suit, waiting for you outside."

"What?"

"Just what I said. He said you was to see him right after the show."

Logan tucked his scarf into his coat, and stepped into the narrow alley that led to the street. At the end of it, there was indeed a Japanese guy, wearing a chauffeur's cap and uniform. A light snow, wet as rain, was blowing in the air.

"You are Mr. Logan?" he said, and Jack nodded, warily. "I

am from Mrs. Zakin. She asks to see you tonight."

"Now?"

"Yes," the chauffeur replied, with a quick nod of his head. "If it is convenient."

"Well, to tell you the truth . . ."

"The car is right here," he said, gesturing at a huge black sedan—a Rolls, Jack noted—parked at the curb. "Only take a few minutes." He opened the back door of the car and held it. Inside, Jack could see maroon leather upholstery, and glass decanters shimmering on a small bar.

"Only take a few minutes," the chauffeur repeated. "And straight home afterwards. Please." He waited, still holding the door open.

"Where *is* Mrs. Zakin?" Jack thought to ask. He wasn't about to go tooling out to Westchester or Connecticut just now.

"Five minutes," the chauffeur said. "Carlyle Hotel."

Good enough. Sliding his guitar across the seat first, Jack climbed in; the door shut with a gentle but firm thump. As the car pulled out, Jack saw Vinnie and Haywood coming out of the backstage alley together, laughing about something and slapping palms.

The ride to the Carlyle was actually too quick. Jack was just beginning to acclimate himself to the plush interior; he'd poured himself two fingers of Scotch, and was reclining in the corner directly behind the chauffeur's cap. If only Stephanie could see him now, he thought. Stephanie and Kurt. What a hoot if they were standing on some street corner trying to hail a cab while he sailed by in this; Stephanie wouldn't believe it. For that matter, Jack was finding it pretty hard to believe himself.

The chauffeur got to the car door before the hotel doorman, and said, "Go right up, please. Suite nine-twelve. You can leave that in the car," he said, referring to Jack's guitar. But Jack said he'd just as soon take it with him.

Crossing the lobby, he felt that his guitar and secondhand overcoat were drawing the stares of the desk clerk and an idle bellhop. He did his best to radiate rock-star vibes while waiting for the elevator. At the door to suite 912, he was greeted by Mrs. Zakin herself, who took one long look at him first, as if to make sure this was the man she wanted, then smiled and said, "Please do come in, Mr. Logan. I'm so glad to see you."

The room wasn't what he'd expected; it was surprisingly spare, with an old-fashioned sofa, a couple of armchairs, a small cherrywood desk by the window. Mrs. Zakin asked if Jack would like anything to drink, and he declined.

"To eat? I can call downstairs."

"No, thanks very much anyway." He leaned the guitar up against the sofa, then sat down beside it. Mrs. Zakin took the armchair nearest him.

"I know I don't have to tell you why I wanted to see you tonight," she said, her fingers lightly resting on the pearl necklace she wore. Her hands were thin, and looked as if they'd been tan so long they could never change back. Jack could see she'd been a beauty in her day. "If you hadn't been there last night, I don't believe Adolph would be alive today." She frowned. "What am I saying? Adolph would *not* be alive today. Not if you hadn't been there. You saved his life." And suddenly there were tears forming in her eyes, and she leaned forward, taking Jack's hand between her own. "You saved his life. I can never, ever thank you enough for that."

Jack didn't know what to say. *No problem* would have sounded a little ridiculous. *You're welcome*? *Anytime*?

"It was Adolph himself who insisted I track you down," she said, releasing his hand. "He's in the theater business too —it wasn't hard finding you . . . As soon as he's better, he wants to see you himself. You know, Mr. Logan—"

"Please, just call me Jack."

"Jack," she continued, lowering her eyes, "my husband believes that he did die last night, that his soul had actually left his body and that you somehow managed to . . . reclaim it." She looked up at him now, fixedly. Her eyes were a pale, watery blue. "He believes that you have some extraordinary power in you, some ability no one else has." She paused, as if waiting for him to confirm it, to admit that yes, he could, when he felt like it, bring back the dead. Jack shifted uncomfortably on the couch.

"Mrs. Zakin, all I did last night was some stuff I'd seen on 'St. Elsewhere.' TV. Your husband has just imagined all the rest."

"Did he imagine you?"

"Pardon me?"

"Did he imagine *you*? In the hospital last night, he was able to describe you—right down to that coat you're wearing. 'A young man, tall, black hair,' he said, 'in a long overcoat. Deep green eyes.' He said you touched him, that your hands were as hot as a stove. That you covered his eyes with them, protecting him from a terribly bright light he couldn't bear to look at anymore. That the heat from your hands went through him like electricity. That you—and this is exactly how Adolph put it—soldered him back together again."

There was a large window behind Mrs. Zakin; a wet snow was coming down hard now, sticking to the glass. "He must have seen me when he came to," Jack said. If he'd wanted to, he could dimly recall some of what she was describing. But he didn't want to—just as he didn't want to think too long about the darkness, or the storm blowing outside. He knew, if he did, he could lose himself too easily, get swallowed up in the wind and the night.

"No, that's not it," Mrs. Zakin said, dismissively. "What Adolph has said is true—he didn't just imagine all this; he wouldn't be capable of it. Especially not in his present state."

"But isn't it possible," Jack ventured, "that his present state is precisely why he's imagined it?"

Now he could see he'd ticked her off. She sat bolt upright in her chair and looked at him as if she couldn't understand why he was refusing to cooperate. "Mr. Logan, I'm telling you what I know—and what I believe you know, too. Something happened last night that you are refusing to acknowledge—why, I couldn't say. I should think you'd be proud to. But I'm not going to interrogate you. You still have my gratitude, and you always will." She got up abruptly and turned to the desk behind her. She picked up a white envelope and handed it to him. "This is to thank you for what you did," she said, though her voice was still cold. Jack took it without thinking. Then it dawned on him that it must be a check.

"This is money?"

"Just a token," she said. "If you'd like more, you can have it."

Jack stood up, laying the envelope down on the sofa. The tips of his fingers, where he'd held the envelope, tingled as if he'd been given a shock; he rubbed them together to get rid of

the sensation. Mrs. Zakin noticed, and looked at h
even greater puzzlement.

"I didn't do it for money," he said.

"I didn't say you had," she replied. "But that's n
not to accept something for it. Take the check."

"I can't," he said, picking up the guitar case.

She followed him to the door, and when he sa
night, she urged him again to accept the envelope.

"I can't," he repeated, turning away. "Give it to some
ity. But not to me." He went down the corridor and pre
the button for the elevator.

Standing in the open doorway of her room, she dropped th
hand still holding the check. "Any in particular?" she asked,
dryly.

"Up to you," Jack said. "Maybe an old-age home for musicians."

On the way downstairs, he noted, with relief, that his
fingers had returned to normal.

chapter five

IT LOOKED, FOR all the world, like some sort of crock-pot —a squat ceramic jug, the color of dirt, with a curved metal handle. Sprague had been waiting three days to get it. After scrubbing his hands in the laboratory sink, he loosened the clamps that held the lid down, and then peered inside at the contents.

The inside of the container being black, it was difficult at first to see what he was looking for, half-submerged there in the solution of ionized water and formaldehyde. But Sprague reached in, his hand cupped as if to cradle a baby's bottom, and lifted it out and into the light. Its weight was even less than that of a baby—approximately three pounds, possibly a few ounces more because of the saturation. Its color, he was pleased to see, was good—the cerebrum a mottled but pearly gray, the pons and cerebellum the rosy pink of underdone lamb. Where it had been severed from the spinal cord, just below the ventral bulge of the medulla, the cut was clean and at the correct diagonal; it appeared to be, as far as he could tell, a perfect specimen. And well worth the wait.

Quillerman, whose brain it had been, had served twenty-four years of his life sentence, before being murdered himself —for reasons unknown—in the prison yard at Attica. Quillerman's crimes had been well documented a quarter of a century earlier in papers all over the United States. For six months, he'd gone on a random killing spree, from Maine to Maryland; four victims were found, all of them bludgeoned to death and then dumped in the nearest body of water (once a swimming pool). He claimed that there'd been two more, but he couldn't remember enough details of who they were or where he'd killed them to offer any proof. The four documented cases, however, were sufficient to put him away for life.

Sprague had interviewed him often, as part of his clinical research. What were the deep-seated psychological factors that led a person to commit serial murders? Was there a particular behavioral matrix from which such killers emerged? Could such aberrant development be predicted, or in any way guarded against? Sprague had studied dozens of murderers over the years, and asked them all the same questions, given them all the same batteries of tests, testified as an authority in several of the more celebrated cases. He was well known for his work in the field. But he still didn't feel any closer to the ultimate truths.

More and more, he'd become convinced that the answers lay in the physical brain itself, somewhere in that spongy lump of twelve billion nerve cells, of reptile stem and primate cortex. Everything else was too subjective, too vague, too contradictory: for every killer who had inordinately loved his mother, there was another who'd hated his; for every one who'd been abused in childhood, there was another who'd been spoiled and pampered. Sprague wanted answers now—*hard* answers, verifiable, observable—to the big questions. And those he felt he could find in only one place—the brain—and in its astonishing capabilities.

Placing Quillerman's brain in a shallow glass dish, he weighed it (subtracting the standard ten ounces for the dish); measured it (just slightly above the average circumference); took several Polaroids to record color and anything else he might have overlooked in his preliminary examination. With a pair of stainless-steel calipers, he lifted the brain and fixed it in place on his dissecting table, then drew up his stool.

The moment of truth—that was how he always thought of it. The moment when, with scalpel in hand, he would begin to uncover the inner structures, the secret compartments, the telling anomalies of the single most complex mechanism in the known universe. He punched the red button on the portable tape recorder he kept on the shelf above the table.

"December 7, 1988," he said. "Dissection of the brain of

Theodore Quillerman." He simply left the tape running; there was a two-hour cassette in it.

"Statistical information." He recited the measurements he'd taken. "Composition and hue, good. Approximately eighty hours since Quillerman's death, by violent misadventure."

Now then. He placed the scalpel at the back of the brain, just where the deep midline groove began. Humming the theme from Mozart's "Jupiter" Symphony, he drew the blade forward, gently but firmly, along the groove, splitting the cerebrum into two neat hemispheres. Residual blood oozed up and out of the gray outer layer, two-millimeters-thick, and from the whiter mass of nerve fibers clustered just below. The corpus callosum, still partially integrated, he pried apart with his fingertips; the severed strands dangled like spaghetti hanging through the bottom of a colander. Completing the separation, Sprague lifted the right hemisphere up and away from the rest of the brain, then set it down on an examination tray nestled by his elbow.

"Sagittal cross-section," he said, "reveals intact, though marginally hypertrophied, cerebellum and pituitary. Hypothalamus appears normal."

He leaned back on his stool for a moment, to observe his handiwork. A clean job of it, done, he confirmed with a glance at his wristwatch, in less than fifteen minutes. He should have had observers; skills like his should not go unapplauded. He leaned forward again, eagerly, his face hovering just above the now halved brain.

There it all was, he thought, laid out before his eyes, just *waiting* to be probed, cultured, subjected to microscopic exploration. It excited him just to think of it. Because somewhere in there, tucked away among the hundreds of thousands of gyri—folds—and sulci—furrows—were the reasons for everything, the motivations, the memories, the mechanisms of self. The amygdala hung like a glistening acorn from the front of the specimen—that, Sprague thought, is where Quillerman first felt the need to commit aggression, the blind compulsion to arm himself and kill.

And here, just anterior to it, was the thalamus, shaped like two tiny footballs, but acting as a relay center for those murderous impulses.

Behind that, the mesencephalon, or midbrain, with its four distinctive bumps—these were the visual and auditory nuclei. Courtesy of these, Quillerman had seen his victims try to flee and struggle to defend themselves; one woman, he had boasted in his confession, had spontaneously stripped off her clothes, hoping to distract him from murder with rape. Courtesy of these innocent-looking bumps, Quillerman had listened to his victims' final pleas, and the subsequent crunch of the bludgeon. (A steel pipe, from a refrigeration assembly, had been his weapon of choice.)

And here below them, roughly the size and shape of a clenched fist, was the cerebellum, one of the brain's oldest—in evolutionary terms—components. This was the sensory-motor hub, the primary switchboard where information was processed, and actions ordered. From its fissures, heavily convoluted and compressed, came the delicate manipulations Quillerman had gone through to break into his victims' homes and apartments, as well as the tight grip on the pipe, the frenzied swing of it through the air, the careful mopping up of the blood. It was all here, Sprague thought, surveying the brain, all of it, somewhere in this collection of glands and fibers and porous tissue . . .

For several hours, he worked on, oblivious to the time, completing his dissections along the coronal and horizontal planes. He made slides of cellular structures at thirty-six sites, recited copious observations into supplementary cassettes, sectioned and labeled and preserved, for later study, samples of everything from the basal ganglia to the optic tract. When he'd finally finished, and the brain lay, like a disassembled engine, on the table before him, he sat back again, his back aching, his hands shaking from the intense control he'd had to exert. He'd made a thorough and precise dissection; nothing had been overlooked or neglected. There were weeks of work ahead, just examining and analyzing the cultures and slides he'd prepared tonight. He could only congratulate himself on a job well done . . . and yet there was something else that he felt as well.

Sprague was familiar with the sensation—he'd experienced it many times before. That nagging sense of missing something, of not fully comprehending, of not seeing the forest for the trees. He'd done it all, every step, by the book—

but the book left out what he most wanted to know. Where, in all this bloody clutter before him, were the elusive intangibles —grief and happiness, fury and lust? Where, precisely, was personality? Where was Quillerman in all this carnage? The heart, of course, pumped the blood—but this, the brain, housed the secrets, of thought and emotion and, possibly, mortality. How much of Quillerman was now contained in Sprague's slides and vials and tubes? Did it all die in the prison yard at Attica—or was it still, some essence of individual life, distilled in these tissues, latent but undiscovered?

Did Quillerman, to come to the point, have a soul? If so, Sprague wondered, where had it gone? That question, more than any other, virtually consumed him. If people indeed had something called souls, then what precisely were they? And why couldn't he, Sprague, a man who'd tried the soft humanistic approach, and now the hard facts-and-physiology tack, why couldn't he be the one to find out? There had to be an answer, some way of knowing once and for all what really happened at the moment of death. Transcendence or extinction? Sprague had his suspicions, but suspicions weren't enough. No one had ever won a Nobel Prize for his suspicions. Sprague needed to know for sure . . . so he could then be the one to tell the whole, waiting world.

chapter
six

BECAUSE BROADWAY CLOSES down on Monday night, Jack called his grandparents' place in New Jersey that afternoon, and said he'd come out for dinner. His grandmother said she'd make his favorite—roast leg of lamb with mint jelly—and his grandfather said, as usual, not much. "That hell-hole"—meaning New York—"getting to be too much for you?" They lived ten minutes outside of the city, in Weehawken, New Jersey, but treated New York as if it were the capital of some dangerous third-world country. Growing up in their house, and looking across the Hudson at the shimmering Manhattan skyline, Jack had always both feared, and been secretly drawn to, whatever it was that lay on that far shore.

Their house was nearly identical to dozens of others that lined both sides of the street—it was two stories high, in need of a fresh coat of white paint, with a front porch just large enough to accommodate in summertime two aluminum lawn chairs; at this time of year, it was barren except for a dented snow shovel and a brown-bristle doormat.

"That's the same snow shovel I used to use when I was a kid," said Jack when his grandfather answered the door.

His grandfather glanced at it, said nothing, stepped back to let Jack pass.

"Is Mam upstairs?" For some reason long since forgotten, his grandmother had always been called Mam, by both of them; his grandfather was Clancy, to everyone.

"She's resting," the old man replied. He was shorter and heavier set than Jack, but had the same deep green eyes; the cardigan sweater he was wearing bore traces of cigarette ash all down its front.

"Asleep?"

"Nah, just resting." The TV was on in the front parlor (Mam had dubbed it that, resolutely refusing to say "living room") and Jack could hear a game-show host exhorting a contestant to take a chance on something. "Go on up," Clancy said, heading for his recliner. "Tell her the timer went off on the stove."

Nothing had changed, Jack reflected, as he once again hung his overcoat on the peg in the hall: the house had the same still and vaguely unwelcoming air to it that he remembered from his boyhood. He had always avoided bringing his friends home from school with him, because he knew that they felt it, too. It was as if Clancy's dour attitude had colored the very walls.

Just outside the door to his grandmother's bedroom— Clancy slept in his own room, at the end of the upstairs hall —stood an antique grandfather clock, made of burnished oak from County Cork. For over 150 years, the weighted gold rods had swung back and forth beneath the beveled glass front: at the top, a pale yellow moon had endlessly waxed and waned above a painted panel of an old stone church and graveyard. Tonight, the moon was three-quarters full.

"Jackie?" Her voice was thin and breathy.

"Me, Mam," and he went into her room.

She was sitting up in bed, against a pile of white lace pillows. The table at her elbow was littered with tissues, plastic prescription bottles, a copy of *Catholic Golden Age Digest*.

"Clancy told me to tell you the timer went off." He kissed her on the cheek; her skin was dry and brittle as parchment, and smelled faintly of Johnson's Baby Powder.

"We'll give it a few more minutes," she said, patting the bed for him to sit down. "You always liked it a bit crispy."

"How're you feeling?"

She waved the question away with the back of her hand. "Same as always. Tell me about that show you're in. Has it started?" Mam had always been foggy about dates and details.

Jack told her it had opened the week before, that the reviews had been mixed, that for as long as it lasted he'd be making a good salary. Mam listened, with what passed for rapt attention, her eyes fixed on him, one hand resting on his. But Jack knew most of what he said was just vanishing on the air, that even what she did take in would soon be forgotten. She was happy just to see him, to have him sitting on the bed beside her; all of her attention was concentrated on that, and what he had to say, regardless of its importance, was purely incidental.

"That's good to hear," she said, patting his hand (he had just explained that the show's advance sale was comparatively *low*). "And what about Stephanie? You should have brought her with you. She sent me a very nice card after you were out here the last time."

"I've been meaning to tell you," Jack said, thinking now was as good a time as any, "Stephanie and I aren't seeing each other anymore. We broke up a few weeks ago."

Things like breaking up, things having to do with dating, had never made much sense to Mam; she continued to look at Jack expectantly, as if still waiting to hear when he would next be bringing Stephanie to Weehawken.

"We aren't going out anymore," Jack repeated. "She met somebody else, and she and I split up. I don't even really talk to her anymore."

Not strictly true, he thought; in his mind, he talked to her all the time. There was no end to the things he said to her in his mind. "That relationship's all over." *Relationship*—another word Mam had never fully grasped. For that matter, Jack thought ruefully, neither had he.

But this time Mam had indeed heard him. "Oh," she said, "I'm sorry. I thought she seemed like such a nice girl. I hate to think of you always living all alone over there in New York. I want to know somebody's taking care of you there."

"I can take care of myself," Jack assured her. "I even learned how to roll my socks last week." She smiled. "But I'm gonna starve if I don't get some dinner soon. What do you say?"

He got up from the bed; Mam pulled the coverlet away from her legs. She was wearing one of her housecoats—this one a burnt orange—and a pair of woolen socks. Balancing herself with one hand on Jack's shoulder, she stepped into her backless slippers, and then followed him down the stairs.

Clancy had the evening news on now. Whenever a commercial came on, he used the remote-control to switch the station.

"Timer went off half an hour ago," he grumbled as they passed through the parlor.

"Oh, it did not," Mam shot back. "It's been no more than ten minutes."

The kitchen table was already set. Clancy lumbered in when he heard the oven door close: he was carrying his favorite beer mug, the glass one that had printed on it "What a beautiful day! Now watch some bastard go and louse it up." It was one of the novelty gifts he'd been given at his retirement dinner, by the guys on his shift at the plant. Their big gift had been the color TV—which stayed on all through dinner, even though it was in the next room and out of sight.

Jack remembered these dinners well; there used to be a portable TV on the counter right behind where he sat. Clancy would watch it over his shoulder, while Mam passed the dishes around and asked him about his day at school. Clancy had only wanted to know if he'd made the football team; Jack, who couldn't have been less interested in football, was a constant disappointment to him.

"Makin' any money yet?" Clancy asked him now, ladling a smooth coat of mint jelly over his slab of lamb.

"Some," Jack replied.

"Not what you'd have made if you'd come into the union."

"I am in the union."

"Musicians' union. That doesn't mean a damn thing."

Jack knew better than to argue the point. Mam put another boiled potato on his plate.

"Jack's in a new show that's doing very well," she said.

Shows didn't interest Clancy; in his book, they weren't proper work for a man.

"Christ, did you hear that?" he said; he was referring to a report on the TV news. Something about Vietnam veterans, victims of Agent Orange, protesting in Washington. "What the hell else do they want? My best buddy got both his legs shot off at Normandy Beach—and he wasn't out protesting for the rest of his life. What do they want? Some kind of guarantee —you go to war and you won't get hurt? What the hell did they think they were doing over there?"

This, too, was a familiar diatribe. Anything that smacked

of the sixties, Vietnam, drugs, and political protest seemed to touch a special nerve in Clancy; Jack figured it was somehow connected to his mother. From a couple of snapshots he'd seen, and from what Mam had said over the years, Jack gathered that his mother had been involved in all that. In one shot, taken on the boardwalk in Asbury Park, she was wearing a tie-dyed T-shirt and flashing two fingers, in the shape of a V, at the camera. Jack remembered asking his grandmother what that gesture had meant.

"It meant peace," Mam said, and her fingers had lightly touched the border of the picture.

"I'd have loved her a lot, wouldn't I, Mam?"

"Yes, you would have," she had said, before turning the page in the photo album, "very much."

Clancy refused ever to speak of her.

Dinner ended when Dan Rather signed off. Jack helped Mam clear the table. Later, they joined Clancy in the front parlor to watch a couple of sitcoms. Clancy had calmed down now; he was, for Clancy, sociable, laughing once or twice at the shows, offering Jack possession of the remote control. When he decided to step outside for a cigarette—smoking around Mam had been strictly forbidden by her doctors—Jack said he ought to catch the next bus back, and kissed Mam good night.

"Find yourself a nice girl," she said, as he pulled on his overcoat. "You shouldn't always be living alone like that."

"I'll walk you down to the bus stop," Clancy volunteered unexpectedly: he took his own coat from the hall closet.

They descended the front steps, Clancy holding the wooden railing. At the bottom, he lighted a Marlboro.

"So how's Mam?" Jack asked, now that they were out of earshot.

Clancy drew on the cigarette. "She had a bad spell last week; I had to run her over to the clinic."

"What'd they say?"

"The usual." They turned down the street, toward Boulevard East. "She's not getting enough oxygen. Needs to rest. Keep taking the goddamned pills. All the usual." For ten years, the emphysema had gradually been getting worse, and Clancy had taken it as a personal affront. There was nothing he could do about it, and he resented that deeply. It was one of the things that made him so irascible—not that there was ever any shortage of such things.

"How's the lung?" The other had already been removed. "Is it functioning okay?"

"Yeah, okay," Clancy replied, "that's about all."

They walked in silence, past one after another of the small frame houses. Occasionally, a car crawled past them, looking for a parking place. Other than that, their footsteps were the only sound on the street.

At the corner, they crossed over to the gas station and stood in front of the sign that listed the prices for regular and un-leaded. The buses to New York made a stop here.

"It could be a while till the next one," Jack said. "You don't have to wait."

"I'll wait," Clancy said. "What else have I got to do?"

Jack had known that would be his answer. There was very little about Clancy that he couldn't predict—not because he was so easy to read, but because Jack had known and ob-served him all his life. When it came right down to it, Clancy was a much more complicated character than he first ap-peared. Jack could see beneath all the off-putting stuff, the anger, the bitterness, the coldness. What lay beneath it wasn't exactly a heart of gold, or even a very forgiving nature. But there were reasons down there, below the surface, for all that unpleasantness. For one, all his life he'd worked grueling hours in a machine-tool plant, and now he was finding retire-ment even harder to take than the job. His only child, Jack's mother, had been killed, as he once put it, "before she'd even had a chance to stop being a teenage jackass." And now his wife, of forty-six years, was slowly being consumed by some-thing he was powerless to stop. Clancy wasn't the kind of man to articulate his feelings—even his love for Mam. Or his fear of losing her. Instead, he bottled everything up inside, where it all curdled and turned sour. He was, in the end, someone who'd been frustrated and confused by life. And Jack felt sorry for him.

Which still didn't make him any easier to be around.

With relief, Jack saw the bus make the turn at the top of the hill and wait for the light.

"Here it comes," he said.

Clancy took one last pull on his cigarette, then flicked the butt into the street. "Mam said to ask if you need any money." He was already reaching into his trouser pocket, where he carried his money clip.

Jack stopped him. "Hey, I'm working these days, remember?" He held out one arm to signal the bus to stop. "And it's union wages, too." After he got on board, he raised one hand to wave good-bye, but through the tinted glass Clancy couldn't see him.

chapter
seven

"I STILL DON'T get it."

Nancy was used to this; once again, she patiently explained what the institute was, how long it had been around, what the purpose of their research was. "And we will pay you for your time," she reiterated. This Logan guy was a hard sell—first she'd had to go through all the hoops at the *Post* just to ferret out his name, and now that she'd found him she had to convince him to cooperate. He still sounded dubious.

"Dr. Sprague will simply interview you about your experience outside the theater that night, and possibly conduct some tests—none of which will cause you any pain or discomfort. I promise you. People we've interviewed in the past have actually said they enjoyed it." There was still a silence on the line. "Trust me."

"I've never even laid eyes on you."

"One more reason to come in," she said, with a laugh. She didn't normally do this, flirt with a prospective subject, but Sprague would have her head if she didn't get Logan to come in. And besides, she had to admit, there was something about his voice that she did sort of like.

"When would you want to do this?" he asked, still sounding uncommitted.

"Anytime," Nancy assured him. "Even this afternoon, if you're free. You could be in at three and out by four. With a hundred dollars for your trouble." What else could she say to convince him? "It would really be a big help to us here if you could manage it."

He was silent again, then said, "Let me get a pencil."

Victory! she thought. And she gave him the address and whom to ask for when he got there.

This was dumb, Jack thought, and maybe even larcenous. He was going to take these people's money and waste their time, answering a lot of questions he knew nothing about. The incident with Zakin was getting completely out of hand—he'd take these tests, or whatever they were, pocket the hundred, and let the whole thing drop. Today would be an end of it.

At York Avenue and Eighty-sixth Street, he got off the bus and walked down to the institute, a nondescript block of gray stone, five or six stories high, with black wire mesh criss-crossing every window. Jack found that a tad disturbing.

Inside, it wasn't much better. A uniformed security guard, with a face like a bulldog's, sat behind a semicircular counter that had several small video screens built into it.

"What do you want?" he snapped.

"I'm here to see Nancy Liu. She's expecting me."

Scowling, he pushed a clipboard at Jack to sign in on. Then he studied the signature as if he were sure this was some kind of fraud. Finally, he called her extension. "Yeah, I'll send him up." He jerked one thumb toward the single elevator at the back of the entry hall. "Top floor, laboratory C. As in cat." He said it as if it were a profanity.

The elevator itself was small and rickety, and as it slowly went up past the first five floors, Jack wondered exactly what went on in here. Abnormal psychology. Were they interviewing chronic nail-biters, or teenage arsonists? Were there people in here getting electro-shock therapy, the way Jack Nicholson had gotten it in *One Flew over the Cuckoo's Nest*? Were there dogs and monkeys, in rows of cages, with electrodes in their brains and levers they had to push if they wanted to get food or water? He strained to hear some sound as the elevator passed each floor, but there was nothing. Not even Muzak.

At six, it bumped to a halt. Nancy was waiting for him when the door slid open.

She was black and white—that was the first impression to cross Jack's mind. Her hair was jet black and shone like a dark frame around her face; everything else was white—her pants, her shoes, the lab coat.

No, not everything. Her eyes were black, too. And luminous.

"You met Tulley downstairs?"

"The guard?"

"Yes."

"Nice guy," Jack said. "I liked him a lot."

"Everyone does." She smiled. "This is the only job he's had since his parole . . . for armed robbery and assault."

"Really?" Jack said, incredulously.

"Really. Dr. Sprague had originally seen him as a patient. When he was up for parole, Sprague arranged for him to get this job. I just thought you should know that we do good works here."

"I'm impressed."

"I was hoping you would be." She led him down a short corridor and in past a steel-plated door. "Before you meet Dr. Sprague, I need to get some information."

"Shoot." Jack was surprised at how comfortable he already felt with her. She was very pretty, and probably the first Chinese girl he'd ever met who didn't play the violin . . . so far as he knew. Every string section he'd ever seen looked as though it had just come in from Hong Kong.

He sat down in the contoured plastic chair across from the desk—whose contours ever fit these chairs? he wondered—and answered the questions she read to him from a printed form. So far, they were easy. Name, address, place of birth—stuff like that. At marital status, he said single, and while jotting it down, she nodded, almost imperceptibly.

"Is that the right answer?"

She blushed, and tried to cover by saying sententiously, "At the institute, there are no right answers—only right questions."

Then she ran down a list of diseases, asking if he'd had everything from mumps and chicken pox—yes—to serious afflictions like heart disease and tuberculosis—no. When she asked about his mother's medical history, it got tricky.

"I don't know," he said. "She died soon after I was born."

"Oh gosh," Nancy said, looking up from the form, "I'm sorry." Her pen slid down the page. "What about your father?"

"I'm afraid that's a blank, too. I don't know who he was."
He said it as matter-of-factly as he could.

Nancy, without comment, made some notation on the form.

Over the years, Jack had gone through a lot of changes when it came to that last question. As a little boy, it hadn't mattered at all—as far as he was concerned, Clancy was his father. When he got a little older, and learned the truth—or what was known of it—it had gotten harder. For a while, he went through a phase in which he imagined all sorts of men, men he passed on the street or sat across from on the bus, to be his father, and half-expected any one of them suddenly to rise up in front of him, clasp him in an embrace, and declare himself. Of course it had never happened, and now, as a grown-up, he took some grim satisfaction from dealing with the question as bluntly as possible. There was some sort of retribution in it.

"I think we're done with the background information," Nancy said, in subdued tones.

That was the only drawback to his brutal honesty—it made other people embarrassed for him.

"So what happens next? You tie me down and perform the lobotomy?"

"Close, but not that bad. Have you ever had an EKG—electrocardiogram—or an EEG—electroencephalogram—done?"

"No." Nor did he want to now.

"They're really very simple, and totally painless."

"Trust you?" Jack said, recalling their phone conversation. She laughed. "Trust me."

In an adjoining room, Jack found an examination table covered with the standard white paper, and surrounded by the usual paraphernalia of a doctor's office. "You want me on the table?"

"Please." She was wheeling away from the wall a wide metal trolley, with two blue machines roughly the size of typewriters resting on its top shelf; both machines had strips of paper, about six inches wide, fitted into their top surface. On the shelf below them, between a jar of tongue depressors and a box of rubber gloves, Jack thought he spotted a Sony Walkman.

"You'll have to remove your shirt, your shoes, and your socks."

"Isn't this a bit kinky?" Jack said, starting to unlace his sneakers.

"You ain't seen nothin' yet."

He wedged his socks into his shoes, and let them fall to the floor. When he'd taken his shirt off, Nancy folded it and put it on the counter behind her, then cranked the top of the table to a slightly elevated position. "Now if you'll just lean back," she said, rolling the cuffs of his jeans up above his ankles. Taking one of the tongue depressors from the lower shelf, she dipped it into a jar of Vaseline and spread the petroleum jelly in smooth patches on the inside of both ankles.

"You weren't kidding."

"It gets better." Over the skin she'd just coated, she strapped two thin bands of black rubber, which were themselves attached to wires that fed into the machine on the left. Then she came to Jack's side, and spread more of the Vaseline on either side of his chest, just above the nipples. Her hair, cut straight across at shoulder level, fell forward as she worked.

"This part you're gonna love." Squeezing two hollow suction cups between her fingers, she stuck them to the spots she had daubed on his chest, and gave them each a little twist to make them stay.

"Almost done." Quickly and expertly, she anointed each of his temples, two spots on his forehead, and another at the base of his skull in back; to each of these spots, she attached a small, sticky electrode, all of which were wired back to the blue machine on the right.

"Don't I at least get a last cigarette?" Jack said.

"Nope. The whole building is a no-smoking zone. But you do get headphones." With this, she produced the Walkman Jack had seen earlier. "These are just going to play a relaxation tape for you. After you put them on, I'm going to start both machines, simultaneously, and let them run for about ten minutes. All you have to do is lie here and think about anything you want. Just don't try to get up or do anything. . . . Any questions?"

"What's the tape?"

"Heavy metal." She slipped them onto his head, adjusted

some dials on the machines, then said, the way an emcee might, "You're on."

Over the headphones, he heard nothing but a little static, and then, far off, what sounded like the plaintive cry of a sea gull. It was, because the next thing he heard were waves, breaking gently against a shore. Ebbing, and flowing, breaking, and retreating. He smiled and closed his eyes. This was a piece of cake, for a hundred bucks. The machines gave him no sensation at all; there was only a slight tugging on his chest where the suction cups were attached.

Think about anything . . . anything at all. At first that meant the crackly feeling of the paper sheet beneath him, and the slight chill where the Vaseline wasn't sufficiently covered by the cups or electrodes. The table itself was pretty comfortable; he wriggled his toes and felt the constriction of the ankle bands. He cracked one eye open; Nancy was jotting something down on a clipboard. He liked the way, with her head bent forward, her hair curved inward around her face. She caught his look, put the clipboard down, raised ten fingers to indicate how long she'd be gone, and left the room; when she closed the door behind her, a draft blew across his bare feet.

He closed his eyes again. Stephanie came to mind, unbidden, unwanted. He thought about the last afternoon he'd seen her, when she came to pick up that Schubert score. She'd looked good; she always looked good. Maybe too good; maybe that's why he'd wanted her so badly, and why it hurt as much as it did to lose her. If she'd been the right person for him, they'd have gotten along better than they did—right? And she wouldn't have felt the need to go looking for a Kurt . . . Kurt and Stephanie. Together. Stephanie and Kurt. Before he could stop himself, he was envisioning the two of them going to dinner, browsing through the flea market on Columbus Avenue, taking a drive in the country. Waking up in the morning. Making love . . . He saw Stephanie, tilting her chin up, the way she did just before coming; and Kurt, whom he'd seen only once in his life, bearing down on her, staring down into her eyes the way Jack had liked to do. Involuntarily his eyes squeezed harder shut, to banish the image: *himself*, he thought, think of himself instead, the first time that *he* had made love to her. Think of that. In his studio, that summer afternoon; they'd been out walking in the boat basin. Stephanie was wearing jogging shorts and a "Mostly Mozart" T-shirt. He gave her a glass of orange juice, with ice. She had gulped it down so fast a trickle of juice had run down her chin. He had wiped it away with one finger, then licked the finger. Then her. He remembered taking the bottom of the T-shirt, and lifting it up over her head. She was full-breasted, but never, as he would learn, wore a bra. He had dipped his finger in the orange juice remaining in the glass, then touched it to her nipples. "It's a good way to prevent colds," she had said, as he cupped each breast, licking away the juice. "Vitamin C."

He felt now a certain tension in his crotch, and thought, for one awful moment, that the machines might somehow have recorded what he'd been thinking about, or his physical response. No, no, nothing like that could have been done, he told himself—these machines couldn't read his mind, they could only record . . . what? Ups and downs, fluctuations of his heartbeat, the frequency of his alpha waves, whatever . . . but nothing concrete, specific.

Still, he didn't *want* to think about Stephanie and all that anymore. Something *else*, he thought, think about something else. He concentrated again on the sound of the waves playing softly over the headphones. The waves made him think of the beach, and the boardwalk at Asbury Park. Mam and Clancy had taken him there many times when he was a kid. He remembered walking over the wooden slats, worried that his foot would slip and get wedged between them. And riding the Ferris wheel with Mam, the car they were in swaying as it finally lurched to the very top and stayed for what seemed an eternity. The ocean in the distance, just beyond the lighted strip of beach, had looked to Jack like the night sky—black, boundless, but with moonlight, and the occasional boat beacon, speckling it like stars.

He had played on the beach many summer days over the years—with a red pail when he was very young, with a transistor radio when he was older. He'd always been a builder, of sand castles, moats, tunnels to China. But eventually the tide would rise like eager fingers, to pull down the walls of his fortress, or fill the hole he was still busily excavating . . . a hole in the sand that got darker and colder the deeper he went, and that he couldn't ever keep from crumbling inward . . . as it had that morning, that hot summer morning, with Freddy Nunemaker.

Mam had warned him, stay away; the cyclone fence had a sign saying DANGER. But Freddy said come on, and Jack followed—over the fence, and into the deserted construction site. A huge yellow crane towered, like a slumbering dinosaur, high above his head. "The Desert Fox!" Freddy cried, bobbing and weaving across the site as if avoiding gunfire, his toy bazooka mounted on one shoulder. "Cover me!" He was wearing a G.I. Joe helmet made of green plastic, and a pair of Keds with one long, white lace untied; it trailed after him as he scrambled up a mountain of sand, hot and dry on the surface, still damp, from the night's rain, below. Jack said, "I don't think you should try that," but Freddy was already halfway to the top. Behind him loomed a red steel scaffolding, ten or twelve stories high—an addition to the office complex being built. "King of the mountain!" Freddy shouted. He aimed his bazooka at Jack, standing far below him, and fired; a blue plastic shell popped out of the muzzle, and tumbled harmlessly through the air.

"Return fire!" Jack cried, pointing his black pea-shooting pistol up at Freddy. Though he knew the pellet would never travel that far, he shot anyway, and Freddy, pretending to be hit, clutched at his stomach, then crumpled, hard, to his knees. "Ya got me!" The sand beneath his knees began to run, in tiny rivulets, down the side of the hill. Freddy threw his head back, and groaned theatrically. His helmet tilted backward, held on only by the chin strap. The sand began to stream down the hill now; to Jack, Freddy looked as though he was sinking. "I think you should come down off of there," he said, but Freddy was too absorbed in his own dramatic finish to hear him. His knees disappeared into the sand heap, and Jack could see, from below, that the whole top of the mountain was shivering, sand cascading down the sides. "Freddy!" he shouted, and Freddy did suddenly stop in the middle of his death throes—that had always been his favorite part of playing war—and fix his helmet on his head. He glanced, a little startled, down at Jack, and tried to get up. More of the sand gave way beneath him. "Hey, Jack," he said, his voice uncertain. "Hey, Jack." The whole mountain now appeared to be coming alive, quaking, the dried-up sand on top streaming down the sides, revealing the darker, wetter sand below it. Freddy was still struggling to get to his feet, the sand continually giving way beneath him. He slid, buried almost to his waist now, a few feet down the hill. His bazooka, which had fallen from his hand, had already been swallowed up. The sand swirled like a whirlpool around him; the harder he scrabbled at it, trying to break free, the faster it whirled—and the deeper he sank. "Jack!" he was screaming. "Help me! Jack! Help me!"

Jack ran to the foot of the hill; the sand was pouring down around him, over his shoes, spreading across the ground like a dun-colored tide. Freddy was covered up to his chest now, screaming for help; Jack looked frantically around the site, for a rope, or a plank, something to throw him. The sand was tumbling down now in great wet clods, as Freddy was sucked deeper into the hill's heaving vortex. Only his head and shoulders were still visible as he thrashed around: his helmet had slipped forward, over his face, muffling his cries. There was nothing for Jack to throw him—how would Freddy even see it if he did?—and there was no way to climb the crumbling hill. The sand kept falling. Freddy was up to his neck; Jack was knocked backward by another sudden avalanche. When he looked up the hill again, only one hand and the helmet were showing; the hand waved, the helmet twisted, shining like a reflector in the hot summer sunlight. The sand rumbled, and gave off a dank, strong odor . . . the helmet settled flatly into the slope, as if it had suddenly been yanked from below . . . the hand kept waving, back and forth, back and forth, in an ever-diminishing arc . . . back and forth, with less and less vigor . . . waving, it struck Jack, even as he stood horrified and helpless below it, like a windshield wiper on a day with no rain.

He awoke with a jolt, not knowing where he was. Everything seemed bathed in light; he shut his eyes against it. The waves were still ebbing and flowing over the headphones. Someone was touching his elbow again, more insistently than before. He felt exhausted, utterly drained, and suddenly very cold. He shivered, in one violent paroxysm, and felt the hand abruptly leave his elbow.

He opened his eyes. Looming above him, in the harsh fluorescent light, was a man—at first all Jack could make out were his steel-rimmed spectacles and a nimbus of frizzy gray hair. He was wearing a white lab coat, like Nancy's—where was she?—and saying something Jack couldn't hear. Hesitantly, his fingers feeling numbed, he slid the headphones away from his ears.

"—all right? Your skin's quite cold."

"Pardon?"

"I said, are you feeling all right? From the way you jumped when I touched you, you must have been having a nightmare." He was tall and gaunt, and his eyes behind the spectacles appeared pale and pink-rimmed, like a rabbit's. "Were you?"

"What?"

"Having a nightmare."

Was he? Jack could hardly remember what he'd been thinking about. He could recall a sensation of flight, and terrific heat, but not much more than that. On awakening, he'd felt cold, and vaguely panicked. Seeing Nancy now, standing to one side, attending to the still clicking machines, he felt a little better.

"Am I still recording?" Jack asked, blearily.

The man glanced at the machines. "No, the printout is always just a few minutes behind the actual recording of the data. When I checked five minutes ago, you were fine."

"Good to hear," Jack said, rubbing his eyes—his hands felt like ice on his face—and shivering again. "Is it okay if I get dressed now?"

"Miss Liu," Sprague said, and she left the machines, still unfurling their data, and detached the electrodes, the suction cups, the black bands from his ankles. When she'd finished wiping away the traces of Vaseline, the man handed him his shirt.

"I'm Dr. Sprague, in case you were wondering. Orson Sprague."

"Jack Logan."

"The angel from God."

"Right," Jack said, hastily pulling on his shirt. "I keep forgetting about that."

"I don't." Sprague gave him a smile that was as icy as Jack's fingers; his teeth were small and gray. He waited till

Jack was buttoning his cuffs, then asked again, "So what *were* you dreaming about?"

No let-up, Jack thought. More alert now, he remembered thinking about Mam and Clancy, and the beach at Asbury Park. And yes, Freddy Nunemaker. "A friend of mine, from when I was seven or eight years old. We used to play together."

"That's what you were thinking about when I disturbed you?"

"Yes."

Sprague wheeled around, clearly no longer interested, and picked up the clipboard Nancy had taken her notes on in the office. She was returning to the machines when Sprague said, "Let them go—I'll look at the printouts later. Go back to the lab and finish staining those Quillerman slides."

Jack sensed he was just getting rid of her. Before leaving, she gave him his shoes and socks and, while Sprague was flipping through the sheets on the clipboard, a quick, almost conspiratorial smile. When the door had closed behind her, Sprague, without preface or apology, said, "What did your mother die of?"

"An auto accident."

Sprague made a note of it, and no comment. "And your father, I see, is a total cipher. Who raised you?"

"My grandparents," Jack said, lacing up his sneakers.

"Is there anything this medical history might have missed that I should know about?"

"I don't think so; I don't know what it is you should know about."

"Neither do I, until I hear it." He had a funny way of speaking—very fast, accusatory, as if he didn't trust words to get at what he wanted anyway. "What's here," he said, brandishing the clipboard, "is commonplace. What happened outside that theater the other night is not. I need to find the proper avenue into that event."

Jack didn't know quite how to help him. "Why don't you ask Zakin?"

"I plan to, just as soon as his medication decreases enough to assure his lucidity. In the meantime, I have you. And the accounts Miss Liu has taken from that television reporter who was there that night, and the newspaper person she told it to."

So that's how the story found its way into the paper, Jack thought.

"They were both next to useless." He looked fixedly at Jack; his expression was not very hopeful. "I need to know if there's something unusual about you, Mr. Logan."

Jack shrugged. "My hair parts naturally on either side."

Sprague ignored it. "*Is* there something? The routine tests probably wouldn't show it, even if there were. The paranormal tests might."

More tests? Jack glanced at the clock on the wall; he'd already been there well over an hour. "Sorry, Doctor, but I've got a show to do. I've got to go."

Sprague looked at him blankly. "Now?"

"Yes." Jack got off the examining table. He and Sprague were almost exactly the same height—about six feet two.

"Then you'll have to come back again. I haven't got what I want yet."

Jack didn't say yes or no; he just pulled on his overcoat, shook hands, and headed for the door. Sprague was standing with the clipboard in his hand. "Miss Liu will call you tomorrow, to set up another appointment." Jack waved good-bye, still not committing himself, and quickly made for the slowest elevator on the East Side.

It wasn't until ten o'clock that night that Sprague went back to check the EEG and EKG data. When Logan had left, he'd gone straight to the lab to make sure the Quillerman specimens were completed properly. That, as usual, took longer than expected. And Miss Liu had insisted on leaving at eight-thirty. God damn these assistants; no one wanted to work anymore.

The paper sheet on the examining table still showed the wrinkles Jack had left on it. Sprague ripped it off and tossed it into the wastebasket. The printouts from the two machines had curled all the way to the floor; Sprague recovered them without much enthusiasm. This was all going to be another exercise in futility—he was going to interview all these people, and conduct all these tests, and wind up knowing nothing more than he had to begin with. Logan, he felt, was a young buffoon; he was as likely as Tulley, the petty criminal downstairs, to have extraordinary powers.

Since he'd already reviewed the early portions of each printout while Logan was still being monitored, he skipped to the last three or four minutes' worth of data. He pulled the narrow strip of the electrocardiogram through his fingers; the heartbeat was regular, regular, then perhaps a bit faster, but nothing out of the ordinary, nothing too far beyond the normal range. When, Sprague wondered, was he going to find a subject worthy of his attention?

He dropped the EKG sheet on the examination table, and took up the EEG data. Again, he looked at only the last few minutes, the moments that it had recorded before he had touched Logan on the elbow and made him jump like that. And suddenly his heart sank. With all the other problems attending his research, now this: the electroencephalograph had apparently broken down. Three or four minutes before the end of the printout, the line, which until then had recorded all the usual brain-wave variations, had suddenly dipped precipitously and then flattened out altogether. It couldn't have been a power shortage, because both machines drew from the same source and the EKG had worked perfectly the whole time.

What would *this* cost to repair? Sprague thought; his funding was already low. Maybe, he prayed, it was something he could fix on his own, some minor glitch that just needed adjusting. Quickly he fastened two electrodes to his own forehead, and turned on the machine. He let it run for a minute, then waited for the printout to complete itself. The data that appeared looked, to his surprise and relief, fine. The machine was working fine.

But what about this Logan stuff then? He studied the earlier printout again, with greater concentration. At the very end, yes, after the flat-line there *was* a slight upturn. Was that the moment he'd touched Logan for the first time, while telling Liu to shut off the recording mechanism? And wouldn't that indicate that the machine had been functioning correctly all along, right up until that second?

But it couldn't have been, it simply couldn't. Because the flat-line that preceded the upturn, and lasted for what had to have been a space of two or three minutes, indicated one thing and one thing only: the person being monitored had suffered a sudden and sustained brain death. Sprague felt his breath catch in his throat. Either the machine had malfunctioned, which seemed increasingly unlikely, or Jack Logan, who'd walked out of this very room only hours before, looking like just another of the cocky young fools who jostled Sprague on the street everyday, had been for several minutes—and the very thought made Sprague's heart surge with unaccustomed hope —a dead man.

chapter eight

ALL THROUGH THE show that night, Jack was thinking about his session at the institute, and his meeting with Sprague. Would he go back again, to get his paranormal abilities tested? What would that entail? What would it prove? Would Nancy Liu be the one to conduct the tests?

After the last round of tepid applause—when he stood up in the pit, Jack could make out a lot of empty seats in the balcony—he took the subway up to the Olympia Coffee Shop, a Greek diner a few blocks from his apartment. Vinnie and Haywood came along, which was not unusual, and so did the flautist Veronica Berghoffer, which was. She'd heard them agree to go, and asked if she could come along. "My room-mate defrosted the fridge without telling me, and my yogurt was more fermented than it's supposed to be. I'm starved."

"Sure," Jack had said. "But just don't try to order anything healthy at the Olympia. They'll get offended."

They took their usual booth, with the red vinyl seats, in back; it commanded the best view of the dessert carousel, packed with lemon meringue pies, blueberry cheesecakes, cream puffs, and eclairs. "The amazing thing," observed Vinnie, "is how they can get that stuff to look so good, and taste so bad."

"What are you gonna have tonight?" Haywood asked.

"Lemon meringue."

Jack ordered the cheeseburger deluxe; Haywood said make it two "but extra grease with mine, please"; and Veronica, her pale blond head bent over the menu, looked stumped. The waiter, pencil poised, waited.

"What'll it be?" Vinnie prompted her.

"I don't know," she said, biting her lip. Jack wondered if she'd ever worn any lipstick. "What's the soup du jour?"

Haywood laughed, and Vinnie rolled his eyes.

"Vegetable barley, Manhattan clam." He started to turn away.

"Vegetable barley," she said quickly.

"Cup or bowl?" He was already halfway to the kitchen.

"Bowl."

"That a way," Vinnie said. "Go for it."

"You guys eat here all the time?" Veronica asked, neatly replacing her menu in the metal clip on the edge of the table.

"No more than once a day," Vinnie said.

"That's how come we always look so good," Haywood added.

"I knew there was some secret." She was smiling, and looking directly across the table at Jack. This is a big night for her, he thought—three guys, even if they are all just friends. She looked very happy to be there; she had a nice smile. Jack asked what she'd heard about the show's advance sale.

"I heard it's all right, but not great. At least they won't be posting the notice for a while."

"Posting the notice" was what musicians dreaded; it was the announcement from the producers, usually tacked without warning to the locker room bulletin board, advising that the show would be closed in fourteen, and sometimes fewer, days.

"I heard they're planning to make a TV commercial," Vinnie said, "to show in the 'burbs, to try to get the bridge-and-tunnel traffic coming in. Very low budget."

"I don't care how low budget it is," Haywood said. "If they use music—and they're gonna have to use music—we ought to be cut in for something." He looked to Jack for confirmation.

"Probably," Jack said. "If you want, I'll talk to Burt about it tomorrow."

"You do that. 'Cause you're the most diplo*matic* person we've got."

When the food came, it came all at once, a jumble of plates

and bowls and glasses that there wasn't really enough room for. Veronica delicately crumbled one saltine into her soup, and left the other in the pack.

"You sure you're not gonna overeat?" Vinnie asked.

"Why," Haywood interjected, "you want her other cracker?"

"Who you calling a cracker?"

"Oh, excuse me," Haywood replied, shaking the salt and pepper with one hand over his french fries. "Guinea."

"That's better. Spook."

"No problem, wop."

Veronica looked baffled, and a little appalled.

"Racial slurs are a form of male bonding," Jack explained.

"You got it, mick," said Vinnie, with a mouthful of lemon pie.

Around one o'clock, Vinnie said his wife was expecting him home early that night, and caught a cab across Eighty-sixth Street. Haywood, who lived twenty-five blocks farther uptown, took a bus.

"You're over on West End, right?" Jack asked Veronica.

"Yes," she said, "at Ninety-third."

"Come on, I'll walk you home."

Even at that hour, and on a cold night, the street was fairly busy—the Korean grocers were still polishing their fruit, the bars were crowded, the panhandlers were hustling change. Veronica walked close to Jack's side, clutching her thin cloth coat around her.

"You cold?"

"A little," she admitted.

He put his arm around her in a companionable way, and rubbed her arm.

"I just figured out what's wrong," she said, fitting herself neatly under his arm.

"What?"

"Where's your guitar?"

For one split second, even Jack panicked—then he remembered. "My Fender's at home; I'm using it to do some demos. I'm playing one of my back-up guitars in the show this week, so I left it in the locker room."

She laughed. "I just don't think I've ever seen you without it."

"Yeah. Have guitar, will travel."

Her building was one of the huge, gray prewar slabs that take up half a city block. Jack waited while she unlocked the door to the deserted lobby—"The doorman's off after midnight," she said—and then walked to the elevators with her.

"Jesus, it's cold out tonight," he said, readjusting his scarf.

Veronica appeared to be studying her shoes. "I think the apartment's a mess, but if you'd like to come up for a minute to warm up, I could offer you coffee, or some brandy."

Jack considered. Would this be wise? He hadn't been with any woman since the break-up with Stephanie. And he wasn't sure Veronica was offering, anyway.

The elevator arrived, and Veronica stepped inside enough to hold the doors open. "I guess it *is* kind of late," she started to say, when Jack said "Sure," and got in with her. They rode up the seven floors without saying anything else.

She was right about the place being a mess. The living room floor was covered with newspapers and album covers; the blinds had fallen out of one window and lay draped across the hissing radiator. There was an empty pizza box and a can of Diet Coke, lying on its side, on the rug in front of the sofa.

"My roommate," Veronica said, almost as if introducing her. "I've basically ceded the entire apartment to her, with the exception of my room." ·

Veronica's room, at the end of a long, narrow hallway, was more what Jack had expected: very neat and tidy, with framed prints—Vermeer—from the Frick Museum, and a white iron day-bed, made up to serve as a sofa with plumped-up cushions in a flowery fabric, against the far wall.

"I keep the brandy in here," Veronica said, "or Connie would have it with her pizza." She was taking the bottle and two glasses off a tray on the windowsill. "Oh—is brandy what you want? I forgot to ask."

"That's fine," Jack said, folding his overcoat across the back of the desk chair. Veronica was fluttering around the room—depositing the bottle and glasses on the end table beside the bed; hanging her coat in the closet; flicking on the radio, tuned to WNCN, the classical music station; closing the one drawer of her dresser that was an inch ajar. She was nervous, and now that she had him up there, Jack could tell that she didn't know what to do next.

For that matter, neither did he; he was pretty unused to this stuff. For the past three years, he'd been with Stephanie, and only Stephanie. It was odd to find himself again in a woman's bedroom, late at night, pouring out a nightcap, preparing for . . . whatever. He wasn't sure what was going to happen, and he wasn't even sure what he *wanted* to happen. He poured very liberal portions of the brandy.

"To *Steamroller*," he said, when Veronica had finally, demurely, seated herself beside him on the bed. She was wearing the long, simple black dress that the producers liked the women in the orchestra to wear. "Long may it run."

They clinked glasses, and listened to the radio—a chamber orchestra, playing some eighteenth-century symphony.

"Mozart?" Jack said.

Veronica cocked her head to one side, listened to a few more bars. "I think it's Haydn. One of the Paris symphonies."

"Is it gonna wake your roommate?" he asked, even though the door was firmly closed.

"No. Hers is the room across the hall, and I'm not even sure she's in there. Sometimes she spends the night at her boyfriend's."

"You don't sound like you like her very much."

"I don't, but she's the one who holds the lease on the apartment, and at least she's not around very much." She unbuckled her shoes and let them fall to the floor. There was a hole in the toe of one stocking. "Oops," she said, covering one foot with the other.

"I've got a pair of socks at home just like that," Jack said.

"You live on Eighty-seventh Street?"

"Between Broadway and Amsterdam."

She took a sip of her brandy. "By yourself?"

"Yep. It's a studio."

The symphony ended, and the announcer came on. "Did you notice that clucking woodwind phrase in the first movement?" he asked his listeners. "That's what gives the symphony its name, 'The Hen.' Otherwise, it's simply Number Eighty-three, in G Minor." There was a silence, and it appeared he would leave the air without naming the composer.

"Who's it *by*?" Jack said aloud.

"And when we come back, another of the late symphonies, also named after an animal, this one dubbed 'The Bear.'" And then he *was* gone, supplanted by a commercial for the Russian Tea Room.

"I guess we'll have to wait," Jack said.

"I'm not going anywhere," Veronica replied, softly.

Jack swirled the brandy in his glass, watching it catch and reflect the warm glow from the bedside lamp. The colors were beautiful—golden, and amber, and orange—and as he gently moved the glass, they changed, fading or darkening, or flowing together, in a soothing, almost hypnotic fashion. What was he doing here? In all those weeks of rehearsal and performance, he'd never even considered fooling around with Veronica. She was a nice girl, yes, and a damn good musician, but that's about all he'd ever thought of her. Even now, if he were to be brutally honest, he wasn't really attracted to her; there was something too pale, too unemphatic, about her. She bit her lip, she had no eyelashes to speak of, her ankles were thick . . . and she wasn't Stephanie.

That was the real clincher, and he knew it. It wasn't so much that he wanted Stephanie back—things had been bad long before Kurt had come along to make them worse—but Stephanie was the body he knew, the body that his own had become accustomed to, attuned to. He'd forgotten about all this uncertainty, this preliminary stuff, and he wasn't yet sure that he wanted to remember.

The commercials ended, and the announcer returned. "We've heard 'The Hen'; now it's the turn of 'The Bear,' so called because if you listen carefully to the melody in the finale, you'll be hearing the sort of tune performing bears were once made to dance to. The English Chamber Orchestra, conducted by Daniel Barenboim, in Symphony Number Eighty-two in C Major—"

"*By?*" Jack asked.

"—by the 'Father of the Symphony,' our special guest tonight, Franz Joseph Haydn."

Veronica clapped her hands together, in victory, as the strings and woodwinds, in the opening fanfare, charged up the C Major triad.

"But is it one of the Paris symphonies?"

"Yes, it is," she said, nodding her head, sure of herself now. "I studied a lot of late eighteenth-century orchestral works at Juilliard, and this is one of the mature symphonies

Haydn composed in Paris. He purposely opened it with a bang because the French really liked it that way."

"I'm impressed," Jack said, genuinely so. He leaned forward to adjust the pillow behind his back, before realizing Veronica was leaning against it, too. He gave it a tug, and she was pulled suddenly against him. Her drink spilled across his lap.

"Oh, sorry," he said.

"No, no, that's okay. But I've got brandy all over your pants, maybe I should get a wet cloth—"

"Forget it, they're blue jeans, it doesn't matter."

"You sure? I could easily get a cloth—"

Their faces were just a few inches apart, her hand still resting on his thigh; he took her chin—smaller than Stephanie's, more fragile feeling—and held it as he kissed her. Her lips were dry, and a little ragged. He wet his own lips with his tongue, then kissed her again. Her hand stirred, tightening on his thigh. He groped for the bedside table, to put his brandy glass down, and heard something fall over. When he looked, he saw that he'd toppled a small silver picture frame. Veronica leaned back against the cushions, catching her breath.

"Your family?" Jack said, turning the frame right side up and self-consciously studying the photo it held. Did he want to go through with this thing with Veronica? He angled the picture toward the bed.

"Yes," Veronica replied, softly. "That's my parents, and my two older sisters."

They looked very stolid and blond, smiling at the camera in what appeared to be a suburban backyard. Her father, a big beefy man with a high forehead, was wearing a barbecue apron.

"What's your dad do?"

"He worked for an insurance company. He died last year, of liver cancer."

Jack stroked the back of her hand.

"My sisters both work at the same company now."

He let his fingers trail up her arm, and watched them as if they weren't his own. His body was proceeding on automatic pilot, while his mind remained at some remove.

"Where do they live?" he asked, almost in a whisper.

"Outside Boston." Her eyes were closed, her head thrown

back. Jack leaned over her, and kissed her throat. There was a slightly alkaline taste to her skin. He felt like an interested observer, and nothing more.

When he unfastened the hook at the back of her dress, and slipped the dress off her shoulders, she shivered. "Are you cold?"

"A little," she said. "Maybe we should get under the covers."

Jack took another large swallow of the brandy, hoping it would help him to get in the mood, and slipped under the comforter with her. Gradually, their clothes came off, and were shed on the floor beside the bed. Before discarding his pants, Jack took out of his wallet the condom he'd been carrying since . . . since whenever he'd stopped making love to Stephanie. Now that was a depressing thought. When he tore a strip off the wrapper to take it out, Veronica became very still.

"Do you not want to?" Jack asked, gently.

Veronica paused, her head turned to one side, toward the framed photo on the bedside table. "Yes . . . no, I want to." She faced him again. "I want to."

He kissed her again, passionately this time, trying to will himself into the act, trying to feel himself entirely *there*; Veronica's body beneath him was warm and soft and smooth. He let his own body rub against her, up and down, until he felt himself grow sufficiently excited.

But even then, as he moved inside her, his mind was only partially engaged; one minute he was seeing Veronica's pale, lashless eyes, staring up at him with pleasure and yearning, and the next he was back on Orson Sprague's examination table, drifting back down into that afternoon's interrupted reverie. . . .

Veronica could sense it, too, his intermittent ardor. At times she was able to lock eyes with him, and feel a strong connection, their bodies moving in rhythm; but at others he seemed to have traveled a million miles away, leaving only some shell of himself to embrace her in the creaking iron day-bed. She held him tighter, her hands spread across his back, hoping to retrieve him to the here-and-now. His body was heavy, and hard, on top of her. But she liked it, every second of it, even having the breath crushed out of her. She'd wanted Jack since the first day of orchestra rehearsal; she could hardly believe that she had him now.

Which made her want *all* of him, all of him *there*, there with her *now*. She looked deeply into his eyes, the deepest green she'd ever seen, and whispered his name. He was looking right down at her, his arms planted beside her shoulders, but what he was seeing she could only guess. There was something unfathomable, and almost hypnotic, about his absent gaze, something that made it impossible to reclaim him, and almost as hard to look away. The skin on his back, exposed to the air, was cool, and she drew the comforter up toward his shoulder blades.

"Jack . . ." and as if he'd been asked some mundane favor, he bent his head, and pressed his open mouth to hers. His eyes remained open, and so did hers; she felt herself pinned, like a butterfly to a mat, and slowly transfixed by his open, blank stare. She thought, for whatever reason, of that photo of her family . . . and of her father, flipping hamburgers on the backyard barbecue. She felt as though she was falling asleep, with her eyes wide open, and with Jack still embedded in her; she felt everything around her growing whiter, and warmer, except for Jack, whose skin, even under the cover, was getting colder all the time. She could hardly bear to have his chest touch hers.

Her father had never been a demonstrative man, but his affection had never been in doubt. In her mind's eye, she could see him now, driving the family station wagon, raking the leaves, mowing the lawn. She felt so weary, her legs were like lead . . . she wished that Jack would simply get it over with, and come.

But how strange it was to see her father like this, so clearly, and under such bizarre circumstances. She hadn't had such sharp images of him since the funeral, and even then it had been hard to shake the way he looked at the very end—shrunken, emaciated, his cheeks hollowed out and gray. Seeing him now, hale and hearty, made her want to cry and hug him against her.

Jack felt like a block of chilled marble.

It almost seemed that her father could see her too. He swam, a kaleidoscope of images, into her vision, gradually taking on more and more definition. He seemed, without ex-

actly moving, to be closing the distance between them. Was
she the one moving? She could make out now the entire top
half of his body; he was wearing a plaid flannel shirt she'd
once given him for Christmas, and his arms were outstretched
toward her. He had his wristwatch on, with the face turned in,
the way he'd always worn it; as a little girl, she'd liked to play
with him by turning it around the other way. She reached for it
now, happy, wanting to play that childhood game again. But
as she did, his hands went back in protest, the fingers outspread. She looked at his face, and saw that he was furious,
and horrified at something. At her? What had she done? He
was shouting something, and pushing her away. And his face,
as he did so, seemed to dissolve, the flesh melting away from
the skull, the lips narrowing, the cheeks drawing in. He
looked, all of a sudden, as he had when he died—or worse
yet, as he'd looked *after* he'd died. He drew his head back—
the hair was almost entirely gone, and the tendons in his neck
stood out like cables—and let out a scream that Veronica
could suddenly *hear*, as clearly as the Haydn symphony on the
radio, *hear* piercing her very marrow, *hear* echoing in her
head and around the walls of her little bedroom.

She was screaming herself now, thrashing her head on the
pillow; Jack was grunting, coming inside her. He was colder
than anything she'd ever felt in her life. She couldn't stop
screaming, nor did she want to; it was the only way to drown
out the sound of her father. She put her hands to Jack's icy
chest and heaved him off of her, then threw the quilt away
from her legs; on all fours, she scrambled naked across the
floor. She fumbled with the doorknob, and lurched into the
hall. Connie, her roommate, was standing there in her purple
down coat.

"What the—?"

Veronica bolted past her, panting with terror, and into the
bathroom, slamming the door behind her.

"What the hell is going on?" Connie planted herself in the
open doorway to Veronica's room, and watched as Jack grog-
gily drew the quilt around his loins.

"What the hell did you do to her? And who are you anyway?"

chapter nine

ONE OF THE nice things about the newspaper business—one of the *few* nice things, as far as Arlette could tell—was that nobody kept track of your hours. You could pretty much pop in and out of the newsroom anytime you wanted, and no one asked any questions; it was assumed you were tracking down a story, or following up a lead. Arlette wasn't actually a reporter yet—she'd been on staff for less than a year—but the way she looked at it, how was she ever going to get to *be* a reporter if she stayed roped to her desk all day doing everybody else's drudge work?

At twelve o'clock sharp, when Murray Spiegel, her boss, left for his usual three-hour lunch, Arlette counted off four minutes on the clock—enough time for Murray to get out of the building—then stuck her note pad in her purse and headed for the elevators. Even though it was freezing outside, a cab, in midtown traffic, would make too much of a dent in her weekly budget, so she scurried to the Lexington Avenue IRT. At Seventy-seventh Street, she got off and walked the three blocks to the Carlyle Hotel.

Before knocking on the door of suite 912, she pulled her jacket straight, and taking the Dentyne from her mouth, dropped it in the standing ashtray in the hall. A woman who introduced herself as Mrs. Zakin answered the door, then ushered her into a spacious bedroom in back.

"Adolph," she said to the frail old man propped up in the bed, "this is Arlette Stein, the reporter from the *Post* who called earlier. Are you still feeling up to talking with her?"

Arlette could tell that if he wasn't, Mrs. Zakin would have her out of there in two seconds flat.

Fortunately, he nodded twice, and gestured toward the brocade chair that was drawn up beside the bed. Mrs. Zakin plumped his pillows, and drew the lapels of his smoking jacket closed over his chest, while Arlette sat down. "I'm going to make some phone calls, Adolph; if you get tired, or need anything, ring." Arlette saw a silver dinner bell on the night table. She figured she had until that bell rang to get the story, if there was one here.

"I appreciate your seeing me," she said. "How are you feeling?"

He looked at her with watery eyes; his white hair was brushed neatly against the sides of his head. "I feel like I got hit by a car. And had a heart attack. And died."

Arlette's hand was shaking—beginner's nerves—but she hurriedly jotted down what he'd said in the shorthand she'd learned at Katharine Gibbs.

"Is that what you think happened?"

Zakin looked away, at a heavy oil painting—flowers in a vase—on the opposite wall. Arlette wondered if she should make a note of it. To set the scene?

"That's what I've been asking myself, ever since that night. I keep thinking, it couldn't have happened; I couldn't have died. If I had, I wouldn't be here now, talking to you. I must be imagining things." He paused. "But that's why I told my wife I would talk to you."

"Why?"

"Because," he said, turning toward her again, "it did happen. I died, and that Logan person—my wife has met him—came after me and brought me back. My wife says he denies it." He shrugged. "That's his business. I know what I know."

Arlette was scribbling down every word. "Could I ask you to be more specific? I mean, what exactly happened after you were hit by the car outside the theater?"

Zakin looked off into space as he recounted what he could remember. He told her about the sensation of leaving his body, and the sadness he felt: then the strange sense of freedom, and flight. He described the white-hot passage he seemed to be traveling through, and the blinding light he could neither look into nor look away from. How he seemed somehow to have shed all weight and gravity, to have become pure—pure *essence*—somehow. How he might almost have begun to welcome the sensation, when a tall figure in a long coat was suddenly beside him, covering his eyes, *incorporating* him again. Arlette struggled to keep up with every word.

"I'm not a religious man," he said, "never was. My idea was, you die, that's it—you're dust. Now I know that's not so. Something else happens, afterward: you go on, in some state. Whether you see the face of God or whatever, I don't know. What I wanted to say—what I guess I wanted to tell the world—was that you do go on. There's something else, *after*." He looked at Arlette's pen, dashing across the notebook page. When it stopped, he repeated, slowly, "There's something else, after." She drew a quick underline beneath the last sentence.

Mrs. Zakin poked her head in the doorway. "How are you doing, Adolph?"

"Another minute."

She withdrew.

"Mr. Zakin, I write for the *Post*, as you know, but also for several other publications." She hoped he wouldn't ask which ones. "I wonder if I could have your permission to use these quotes—which are really quite wonderful—in whatever forum I can place them." She had worked out the wording of that last request before coming over.

"Why did you think I was telling you all this?" he said. "I've made a lot of money in my time; I haven't made a lot of discoveries. This one I thought I should share. As far as I can tell, it's good news."

And *very* good copy, Arlette thought, flipping her notebook closed. Maybe even good enough to help her make a name for herself.

Next stop, that institute.

Nancy had apparently hit the jackpot with this Logan guy. Although Sprague hadn't been all that excited when she left the lab the night before—in fact, he'd been his usual gloomy self—by the next morning he was jumping all over her. "Call Jack Logan," he'd said, the second she'd come through the door from her Tuesday morning seminar. "Call him and tell him we need him to come in for further testing. Tell him the tests we did were mechanically flawed. Tell him anything you need to—promise him another hundred bucks."

From Sprague, perpetually short of funds, this was a big concession.

"I'll try him this afternoon," Nancy said, wondering why all the urgency.

"Try him *now*," Sprague shot back. "And if he gives you trouble, promise him two hundred bucks."

Two hundred? If Nancy hadn't thought Sprague was already crazy, she'd have definitely thought so now.

As she went back to her desk and located Logan's phone number on the appointment calendar, she wondered what had happened, hours after Logan had left the lab, to get Sprague so excited. The only thing it could be, she thought, as she dialed Logan's number, was something to do with the printouts. Sprague had intended to look them over after the Quillerman slides had been stained and labeled.

"Hello, this is Jack Logan." An answering machine. "You can leave a message for me here, or with Radio Registry, at 555-4242. I'll get back to you as soon as I can." At the beep, Nancy left the message. Then went looking for the EKG and EEG readings.

They weren't where they should have been—in the examination room, or in Sprague's lab, or in the files; in fact, the manila folder that should have been in the file cabinet, to hold Logan's medical history forms, was missing altogether. Sprague must have been keeping the whole thing under lock and key in his own office.

At two o'clock, just as she was unwrapping her tuna fish sandwich, Tulley buzzed her from the security desk downstairs.

"I got a reporter down here, says she wants to talk to you. Stein."

"Who?" Nancy heard him ask for the name again.

"Stein. Arlette Stein. Says she's from the *Post*."

Nancy racked her brain; she remembered who she was, but had she made an appointment with her?

"So what do you want to do?" Tulley said over the intercom. Nancy knew he liked nothing better than to refuse people admission.

"It's okay," Nancy replied. "Send her up."

There was an abrupt click.

Stein came out of the elevator as though it were the starting gate at the Kentucky Derby. Suddenly, she was a lot friendlier than she'd been on the phone, giving Nancy a firm handshake and a big warm smile. She was small, smaller even than Nancy, and had curly red hair that bobbed as she talked.

"Hope this isn't a bad time for you, but I thought, since we've been working together, it might be a good idea to meet in person."

Working together?

"Your call last week really got me thinking. I mean, Adolph Zakin is an important person, so whatever happens to him is important to begin with, but this whole business of returning to life makes it kind of special, I think. Something worth following up on. That's why I came by." Nancy ushered her into her office. "I wanted to know what you've managed to find out about Jack Logan and what really happened that night—from your angle."

Angle? Nancy was having a very hard time keeping up with this woman.

"I was just over at Zakin's place at the Carlyle"—Arlette wondered for a second if she should be giving that away yet—"and I had a great, exclusive interview with him. He hasn't talked to any other media people yet, so for the time being he's still entirely our story. I got some very good stuff," she said, taking her note pad from her purse, "about his feelings of leaving his body and all that. But it would be super if some of the research or whatever you're doing here corroborated what I got over there." She looked up expectantly, with her pen poised over the pad. "What have you guys been up to here?"

"We guys," Nancy said, with great deliberation, "haven't been up to all that much yet." She wondered what, if anything, she should admit to. "We have done a preliminary interview with Mr. Logan—"

"Which uncovered what?" The pen hovered.

"It would be much too early to say. And whatever we did find out, would have to come to you from the director of the program, Dr. Sprague."

"I see." The pen dropped. "Is Dr. Sprague around? Can you buzz him or something?"

Where did this woman get her nerve? "Dr. Sprague is a very busy man. It might make more sense—"

"Oh sure, I understand that," Arlette burst in. "But I do want to break this story as soon as possible, and I don't have a lot of time. Could you just try to round him up now, while I'm here?" She cocked her head to one side, curls bobbing, and gave Nancy a hopeful smile.

Nancy said, "Wait here," and went in search of Sprague.

She found him in his back laboratory, the one he used to conduct, in relative secrecy, his paranormal investigations. He was tinkering with the random-number generator.

"What?" he said, not even bothering to look at her.

"You have an unexpected caller."

"Logan?" Now he looked up.

"No, but it's related to that. It's the reporter from the *Post*, the one who wrote about Zakin."

"What's he want?"

"*She* wants to talk to you. She seems to think we're all working together on a big story. She's already spoken to Zakin himself; he's apparently out of the hospital."

"Did she say what he said?"

"According to Ms. Stein, 'I got a lot of good stuff about leaving his body and all that.' She wants to know what we're up to over here." Sprague sat back in his chair. Nancy could see he was dealing with his warring instincts: on the one hand, he hated people and he hated intrusions; on the other, he loved attention, particularly from the press. In the end, his ego won out.

"I'll talk to her in my office."

Nancy performed the introductions, then, knowing Sprague would want the whole show to himself, left. Arlette was sorry to see her go; this Dr. Sprague was a sort of creepy-looking guy, so pale and so white, almost an albino. Thinking of the rabbit in *Alice in Wonderland*, she jotted down "March Hare" in her note pad.

And at first, he wasn't easy to interview, either. When she asked him about the general purpose of the Institute for Abnormal Psychology, he went off on such a tear, talking about schizophrenic chemical imbalances, deviant socialization patterns, cortical and neural anomalies, that she could hardly get it all down, even in shorthand and skipping the stuff that made no sense at all to her. But it did eventually dawn on her that none of what he was saying had much to do with the sort of thing that had happened to Zakin that night and that he was supposed to be investigating. So she asked him why that was.

He stopped for a second, and pressed the tips of his long, bony fingers together, making a kind of steeple in front of his face. "I was saving that," he said. "You see, the research that I've been describing so far is what the institute understands, funds, and sanctions. I, personally, have ancillary interests. These I pursue," he added, with a nod toward her pen, "on my own time, and with separately acquired grants."

"Got that," Arlette said. "And these other interests, they include stuff like the Adolph Zakin episode?"

"They include a wide range of paranormal phenomena, everything from psychokinesis to astral projection. But yes, I am most interested in questions of mortality, of soul, if you will."

"Like reincarnation?"

"Reincarnation is, by and large, a lot of claptrap, a theological shell-game that only idiots like Shirley MacLaine would fall for. If human beings do have an incorporeal essence, and specifically an essence that survives in some manner after the death of the physical body, I see no reason or logic for believing that that essence should willingly, karmically, much less repeatedly, enter into a dairy cow, sea slug, or another human being. That's just some sort of wishful thinking, on the part of people who are none too careful about what they wish for.

"I believe," he continued, leaning forward and laying his palms flat against the desktop, "that there may indeed be some such essence commonly denoted as soul, but that if there is, it is immutable, and possibly immortal. I also believe that if it does exist, then there must be some way of verifying, even quantifying, its existence. There must be a way of locating it, observing its particular dimensions and peculiarities, *tracking* it, if only by inference. We don't *see* quarks and neutrinos, but we know they exist because we have found ways to detect their presence and their migrations. Imagine if we could do the same for the soul! Imagine if we could prove in some manner that emotions are only the everyday ingredients of what we now think of as personality—and that personality is only the simplistic catch-all for something much greater and more mysterious! Imagine the revolutionary consequences, in every realm of human thought and endeavor, if some separate entity, operating along lines entirely its own, was empirically established once and for all."

Arlette had long since given up getting it all down. She was wrapped up in what Sprague was saying, and the almost mesmerizing fashion in which he spoke. This could be a big story, after all—as big as they come, if there was anything to back up all the conjecture. All she had to do was stay on Sprague's good side long enough to find out.

"Your assistant," she ventured, "told me that you'd interviewed Jack Logan."

"Did she?" he replied. "She told me you had interviewed Adolph Zakin."

A silence fell, during which they studied each other across the desk. Arlette spoke first.

"I wonder if you found anything interesting?"

The corners of Sprague's mouth turned up in a wintry sort of smile. "Nothing I want to broadcast just yet. But the early results, I will say, are promising. Very promising." He paused. "Perhaps if you could share with me whatever you learned earlier today, I could keep you apprised of whatever progress I make here. I will need, ultimately, a vehicle with which to communicate my discoveries to the greater public."

The terms of the bargain were perfectly clear: in return for her help now and in the future, Arlette could become the privileged vehicle to which he referred. Which seemed more than fair. She wouldn't have much of a story without Sprague's help—and with it, she could have a whopper. Without so much as blinking, she flipped her note pad to her Zakin notes, and began to read them aloud.

chapter ten

"ALL RIGHT, GUYS, SETTLE down. We're gonna do another take—and let's try to make it crisper this time." Burt, the contractor, was sitting up in the control booth, enjoying his power; Jack and the other members of the *Steamroller* rhythm section—Haywood on drums, Van Nostrand on bass, and Gardiner on keyboards—were laying down the basic track over which the rest of the orchestra, and later the vocals, would all be dubbed. It was all for the thirty-second TV spot that the producers hoped would save the show.

"Wait a second," Haywood said, adjusting his headphones. "I got a bad mix in these cans."

"What's wrong with it?" Burt said from the booth.

"For one thing, not enough click."

Burt told the engineer to turn up the metronome volume.

"And for another, the piano's too hot."

"Hey man, I can hardly hear myself," said Gardiner, glissing up the keyboard with the back of his hand.

The engineer turned down Haywood's keyboard level. Haywood, encased in a Plexiglas booth toward the rear of the studio, tilted the snare drum to an angle he preferred.

"We all set?" Burt asked the musicians in general.

Jack looked around, then said, "All set down here."

"Then let's put down another one."

The metronome, set at 140 beats per minute, started clicking over his headphones again; Jack gave a two-measure count-in, and the rhythm section swung into action. Jack was being recorded "direct," the microphone set on a stand right in front of his amplifier; so was Van Nostrand, a guy with the biggest hands Jack had ever seen, on bass. He played with his head down, his long brown hair hanging over his face and his fingers plucking the strings with casual precision. Haywood, of course, was sucking on a toothpick while his sticks flew across the surfaces of the cymbals and drums. In thirty seconds, they abruptly stopped and sat very still until the last reverberation of the last note had faded. Burt's voice, sounding pleased, came over the intercom.

"I think we got it. We're gonna do a playback." The tape was rolled back, and played for everyone to hear. When it was done, Gardiner, lost behind his mountain of keyboards, said, "I could do that middle riff better. Wanna try one more?"

"Not today," Burt cut in. "We're only budgeted for twelve to two, with a possible twenty. There's not enough time. We've got to start laying down the rest of the band."

"Then that's it, gang," Jack said, lifting his shoulder strap over his head. Van Nostrand threw back his hair, and packed up his instrument. Just past the padded door to the control booth, there was a large waiting room where the other musicians were killing time until it was their turn to record; Vinnie was sipping a Dr Pepper. "How'd it go?" he asked as Jack emerged.

"Smokin'," Jack said, "we was absolutely smokin'."

"You gonna stick around for the overdubs?"

"I don't know. I'm gonna check my messages first." There were three pay phones mounted on the wall, and Jack had already put in his quarter and dialed before he realized that Veronica Berghoffer, her back turned, was on the one next to his. He beeped his machine, and it played back his messages: one from Mam, with a touch of the usual confusion, and another—the third he'd gotten in two days—from Nancy Liu at the Institute of Abnormal Psychology. Only this time she upped the ante, to two hundred dollars. At the end of her message, he used his beeper again, to signal the machine to rewind, and this time the sound made Veronica turn. The half-smile on her face froze the moment she saw who it was; the phone cradled on her shoulder started to slip, and Jack instinctively reached to catch it. Veronica recoiled, so suddenly that she bashed into Catalano, talking on the phone behind her.

"Hey, what gives," he said, turning in place.

"Sorry," Jack said, "my fault."

"No, mine," Veronica said, to Catalano.

"You guys playin' dominoes or something?"

Veronica mumbled something quickly into the phone, and tried to move away. Jack caught her sleeve. "Aren't you ever going to talk to me again?"

"Sure," she said, not looking at him, and still trying to leave.

"Whatever happened that night, I'm really sorry. Whatever went wrong for you, it wasn't intentional on my part."

"Yeah. Okay. Understood." She flashed him a glance, meant to make it convincing.

"You know, we ought to at least be friends again—we may have to be looking at each other in that orchestra pit for a long time."

"Not from what I hear," she said, before abruptly breaking away. Jack watched her make a beeline for the ladies' room; then he went and joined Vinnie.

"So what did you do," Vinnie said, "not call her the next day?"

"What?"

"Haywood and I figured you took her home, and you went to bed with her. Now she runs the other way every time she sees you. You either did something terrible, or you are the worst lay she's ever had." He sucked up the last drops of Dr Pepper with the straw. "Haywood says it's you stink in the sack, but I stuck up for you—I said you'd probably just treated her like shit."

"Thanks for the vote of confidence."

Vinnie made a face, as if to say "Don't mention it."

"Let's just say it didn't work out."

"No foolin'."

"She did say something just now about how she didn't think we'd be seeing each other in the pit for a whole lot longer—you hear anything like that?"

"You mean about the show closing? I hear something every five minutes—Catalano's a basket case over it." He slipped the empty soda can under the sofa. "But this spot we're doin' today could be the last gasp. I asked Burt what was up, and he couldn't even look me in the eye."

"They're not going to keep the show running through Christmas?"

"They're gonna try," Vinnie said, "but who knows?"

Burt's voice came up over the room speaker. "All right, boys and girls, the rhythm section is done. The rest of you can come in now. And please, park the munchies in the waiting room."

Vinnie got up off the sofa, his rumpled shirt hanging loose in back.

"Don't forget to untie your laces," Jack said.

"Never do. You sticking around?"

Jack gave it a moment's thought, then said, "No. If this show's in that much trouble, I better start hustling up some alternative sources of income."

"If it's drugs, I don't want to know. See you tonight." He shuffled off through the padded door, just behind the panic-stricken Catalano.

Jack went back to the pay phones, to claim a fast two hundred dollars.

chapter eleven

THIS TIME SPRAGUE studied Jack with a special intensity. The way he walked, the way his eyes moved around the room, the way he smiled at Miss Liu when she asked him to sit at the table with the random-number generator on it. Was there anything about this man, Sprague kept asking himself, that he might have missed the first time, that should have jumped right out at him and declared "Here's the one you've been waiting for, the one with that hidden reservoir of special powers and abilities"? He was tall, he was dark, he was, Sprague supposed, good-looking; but even now—knowing what he knew, and paying attention to every nuance—he was damned if he could see anything out of the ordinary about this guy.

"Is this a paranormal machine?" Jack asked, somewhat facetiously, and Sprague replied, "It's a machine we use to measure paranormal abilities." It was a rectangular metal box, with a circle of ten red lights on its upper surface: in the center of the circle, there was a little counter with two spaces, both of which now read "0."

"Inside this box," Sprague said, tapping it with his fingernail, "there's a small quantity of a radioactive substance called strontium ninety. The subatomic particles of this strontium are constantly deteriorating in a random fashion. This machine acts like a Geiger counter; every time a particle decays, these here," he said, pointing now to the two zeroes, "will read either one or two, depending on the split second the particle has arrived. A one will make the red lights flash, one each time, in a clockwise direction; a two will reverse the pattern, and the next red light in a counterclockwise direction will flash. Do you understand so far?"

"I guess so," Jack said, "but I sure hope you're not going to test me on this stuff."

"No; in fact, you don't really need to know any of this. I explain it as a courtesy. We call this a random-number generator because it guarantees us a mathematically reliable source of absolutely random events. What I want you to do, once we start the machine, is simply try to influence, with the powers of your mind alone, the flashing of the lights: I want you to try to make them flash, one at a time, in a clockwise direction."

"You're joking."

"Not at all."

Jack glanced at Nancy; with Sprague sitting right next to her, she remained impassive.

"How am I supposed to do this?"

"By concentrating on either the lights themselves, or on the counter in the center; every time it stops at number one, you'll get the result you want. It's up to you. For that matter, you can actually try to influence the decay of the particles inside the box. Just so you get the lights to flash clockwise."

Jack considered this utterly ridiculous, but reminded himself of the two hundred dollars.

"Are you ready?"

"As I'll ever be."

"Then we'll begin." Sprague paused, to let Jack focus on the machine, then flicked a small switch on its base. A few seconds later, the light at the top of the circle flashed; a few seconds after that, the light to its right—the clockwise light —also flashed. Nancy made a notation. Jack stared down at the lights, his fingers resting on his temples. A third light flashed, also clockwise.

"Guess I've got it knocked," Jack said.

"I suggest you not talk."

A fourth light flashed; again clockwise. Nancy noted it on the tally sheet. And glanced at Jack.

The next red light took a step back; then there were three more flashes in a clockwise direction. Sprague was pleased. Jack bent closer to the machine. *Was* he actually influencing the lights?

Nancy's data sheet was numbered one to one hundred, and split into two columns: Clockwise and Counter. She would record one hundred flashes in all, and the order in which they came. She'd done it several times before, with different subjects; it was very boring, and not once had the results been statistically significant. So far at least, this Logan was the most promising she'd seen.

But then he missed the next three flashes—or at least they were all counterclockwise. He leaned back a little, as if to try a different angle; two clockwise flashes followed. Then two counterclockwise. Sprague was looking less pleased. Nancy could see that the early pattern was probably going to prove to be a fluke; the flashes were coming in no discernible sequence now, and the numbers in both columns were starting to even out. Jack shifted in his chair, his eyes still on the machine. Nancy wondered again what had made Logan so especially interesting to Sprague. After a few more minutes, the run of one hundred had been completed and she announced that Jack had totaled fifty-three flashes in a clockwise direction, and forty-seven against. Not, she knew, a significant score.

"Shall we do another run?" she asked Sprague: they generally did.

"Yes," he said, "just to be sure. Then we'll try the Zener cards."

The second run went even worse than the first; Jack seemed to be earnestly applying himself, hunkering down over the machine, but the final score was forty-five clockwise, fifty-five against. Sprague appeared unaffected by the bad result. He pushed the machine to one side of the table, and laid down a deck of oversized cards.

"These are called Zener cards," he said. "There are twenty-five in a deck, and they show five different symbols." He put one of each faceup in front of Jack. "The star, the circle, the square, the cross, and this last one we call 'wavy lines.' As I draw each card and look at it, I want you to tell me what it is. We'll go through the entire deck once, reshuffle, and then do it again, just to improve our statistical base. Have you got it?"

"I guess so."

"Repeat to me the five symbols."

Jack did, and Sprague grunted. Nancy pulled her chair back, so she could see each card as Sprague pulled it. He quickly shuffled the deck between his long, bony fingers, then drew the one from the top—a square.

"Circle," Jack guessed.

Sprague, expressionless, put the card down and lifted the next.

"Wavy lines."

It was a cross.

As the run progressed, Sprague studied Jack across the table. He was clearly trying to exercise some sort of intuitive power, but it was equally clear he had none to draw on—at least in this context. Nor did this cause Sprague any undue alarm or disappointment; he was administering these standard paranormal tests more to be thorough than anything else. He had already decided that whatever abilities Logan did possess would only show up later, during the EMG and hypnosis experiments. Logan could do *something*, he felt, but it wasn't likely to be some simple ESP stunt. It was almost gratifying, when the two runs had finally been completed, to find that Logan had managed only nine hits in all.

"Is that good?" he asked.

"The laws of probability," Sprague explained, "would dictate ten. You scored one less than you should have done by luck alone."

Jack, though he hadn't expected to do well, felt deflated nonetheless.

"We could do more tests like these, of your clairvoyant or psychokinetic abilities, but I don't at the moment see the point. There are other avenues I'd prefer to pursue. Have you ever been hypnotized, Mr. Logan?"

"No."

"Do you feel any apprehension at the prospect of being hypnotized?"

"You mean, would I mind?"

"I mean, do you feel any internal, visceral resistance to it?"

Jack checked himself internally, and said he didn't think so.

"Then we will."

Jack suspected that even if he had felt apprehensive, it wouldn't have made the slightest bit of difference. Sprague had just wanted to know in advance if Jack was going to throw up any obstacles.

They returned to the room where Jack had undergone the EEG and EKG—only now the examination table was cranked up so that Jack would be half sitting on it. When Sprague asked him to remove his shirt and shoes as he had done before, Jack said, "I thought this was going to be hypnosis."

"It is," Sprague said, "but at the same time I want to refine some of the earlier tests. We'll be doing what's called an EMG this time; we'll get some measurements of respiration rate, blood volume, skin temperature, and resistance. You won't feel anything more than you did the last time."

For two hundred dollars, Jack figured they could measure whatever they wanted. Nancy attached the suction cups and electrodes, and then, to Jack's surprise, another sensor—this one to his chin—and placed three of his fingers into little silver thimbles, which were wired back to another blue metal machine.

"Let's see, first of all, how susceptible you are," Sprague said. He sat down on a stool so that his eyes were exactly level with Jack's. Reaching out, he pressed his index finger to the very top of Jack's skull. "Not now," he said, "but on the count of one, I will want you to inhale, and then look up toward this finger—without moving your head. On the count of two, and with your eyes still raised, I will want you to slowly, as slowly as you can, lower your lids. On the count of three, I will want you to exhale slowly, and beneath your closed lids let your eyes fall to the normal position. Is this understood? Good." He pressed his finger harder to the top of Jack's head. "We'll begin. One: inhale—and look up toward the finger."

Jack's green eyes rolled up in his head, toward the finger it would be impossible to see. Sprague watched intently as the irises rose higher and higher, so high in fact that they disappeared completely under the lids; Logan's eyes showed nothing but white.

"Upgaze, extreme four," Sprague whispered to Nancy. Then said to Logan, "Now I want you, without looking down, to slowly lower your lids."

Jack's lids fluttered a moment, then smoothly came down. Not a trace of the iris had shown itself again—a very rare feat.

"Eye-roll, extreme four." He took his finger away from

Jack's skull. "Now I want you to exhale, and keeping your eyes closed, let them return, slowly, to the normal position."

Nancy knew, from the two scores she had just recorded and what she had herself observed, that Jack's ability to enter the trance state was virtually off the scale. He would be the best subject Sprague had ever had. She waited now for Sprague to tell him to open his eyes, as was customary after this quick susceptibility test, but Sprague remained silent, studying Jack and deliberating. Still without saying anything, he lifted his chin and indicated to Nancy that she should turn on the various recording devices. But she hesitated—Jack hadn't been told he was going to be put under yet; the usual advice and instructions hadn't been given to him. It didn't seem ethical to just go ahead with it. Sprague threw a furious glance at her, reached over the top of the EEG machine, and flicked the switch. Then he turned on the other machines, too. Jack continued to breathe evenly, his eyes closed.

"Mr. Logan, I want you to remain relaxed," said Sprague, in what was for him an unusually calm and conciliatory tone. "I want you to breathe slowly, and deeply, and to listen only to the sound of my voice. I don't want you to speak yet—only to listen to me and to do as I say." Sprague had silently moved his stool closer to Jack's side, so that now he was almost whispering in his ear. "I want you to imagine yourself falling into a deep, deep, but dreamless sleep. I want you to feel utterly relaxed, utterly restful. Your limbs are tired, and very heavy. Your legs are tired, as if you'd been climbing, climbing stairs, all day long; your arms are heavy, as if you'd been lifting heavy boxes, all day long. Your whole body feels tired, and heavy, and heavy, and tired. You want only to rest, and to listen to my voice. Only to rest, and to listen to my voice." His words were coming in a low singsong, purposely lulling and repetitious. From the early results of the machines she was monitoring, Nancy could see they were already having some effect; Jack was indeed in a calm and restful state. Sprague must have assumed, after Logan had scored a double-four on the upgaze and eye-roll tests, that he would approach and enter the trance state effortlessly. He was right so far, though Nancy still didn't approve of his methodology.

"While you are in this deep, and restful, and pleasant state," Sprague was saying, "I want you to concentrate only on my voice, and listen only to what I'm saying. I want you to answer whatever I ask you as truthfully and as fully as you can. I want you now, for instance, to tell me your full Christian name. What is your full Christian name?"

"Jack Patrick Logan." He spoke in a low, sober monotone.

"On what street do you live?"

"West Eighty-seventh Street, in New York."

"What do you do for a living?"

"I play guitar."

Sprague was apparently satisfied with the manner of his replies. He asked him next some slightly less perfunctory questions. How long had he been playing the guitar? What kind of music did he most enjoy? Were his friends chiefly other musicians? Nancy knew he wasn't particularly interested in any of the answers yet; so far he was just drawing Logan into a thoughtful and receptive state of mind. Gradually, he would lead him, indirectly, to what he really wanted to know.

In the meantime, Nancy kept a close watch on the machines ranged in front of her. The EKG and EEG were functioning fine, and within the normal parameters; the other measurements, of skin temperature, blood flow, respiration, were also unexceptional. She knew that if anything sudden or unexpected occurred, she was to immediately alert Sprague, though never in such a way as to make the subject aware or alarmed. She saw Sprague adjust his glasses and lean in even closer to Jack. Now, she thought, he's about to introduce the Adolph Zakin episode. But instead, to her surprise, he asked Jack if he'd had what he considered a happy childhood. Odd he should turn the dialogue in that direction.

As if Jack, even in the trance, thought so too, he paused before answering. "It was," he said, haltingly, "not really typical."

"How was it not typical?"

Again, a pause. "I didn't have real parents; Mam and Clancy, who raised me, were my grandparents; they were older than my friends' parents. Our house wasn't the same as my friends' houses."

"Why wasn't it the same?"

"It was older, and quieter. It wasn't a place my friends felt really welcome. It wasn't," he added, in that same hushed, reflective tone, "a place that I ever felt I completely belonged."

"Did you feel you belonged at some friend's house?"

"No, I didn't feel that," Jack said. "But I did feel their houses were more normal somehow."

"Whose houses were these?"

"A few different people's. Jeff Morrison's, Dana Schaeffer's, Freddy Nunemaker's . . ."

"I want you to think back, to the last time you were here, Jack."

Nancy noticed that Sprague was now using his first name.

"You said then that you had been thinking about a friend of yours, from your boyhood. Was that friend one of the people you just mentioned?"

"Yes."

"Which one?"

"Freddy Nunemaker."

"Freddy was a good friend of yours?"

"He was my best friend, when I was seven or eight years old."

"What sorts of things did you do together?"

"All sorts." Jack had a semblance of a smile on his face. "Rode our bikes together. Played tetherball. Shot squirt guns at girls in the neighborhood."

"Was it one of those things you were thinking about last week?"

"No," Jack replied. "Something else." The faint smile flickered, then died. He didn't elaborate.

"I want you to think again about what you were thinking about last week," Sprague said. "And I want you to tell me about it. What were you and Freddy doing?"

Jack was silent at first. Then he said, "Playing war."

"And what did that consist of?"

Jack described their weapons and gear, and the television shows they drew their inspiration from.

"And you played this game often?"

"Yes."

"And in all the times you played war together, did anything unusual ever happen, something in particular that might have been in your thoughts last week?"

"Yes . . . once."

"Tell me about that."

Nancy noticed a slight blip, not yet worth alerting Sprague to, on a couple of the meters. It could have been an electrical short.

"Once, we climbed the fence at a construction site, on a Sunday morning." He was speaking very slowly, as if he were reluctant to speak at all. "We weren't supposed to be there."

"Who said so?"

"Freddy's parents, and Mam and Clancy."

"But you did anyway."

"Yes."

"And you got into some trouble there?"

Jack hesitated again, then said, "Yes." Nancy could see him visibly stiffening. "Freddy was pretending to be Rommel, the Desert Fox. He was carrying his toy bazooka. He was running all over the site . . ."

Jack fell silent, and again, Sprague had to prompt him. "And something happened then, to you or to Freddy?"

Jack's face had assumed an increasingly cold and distant expression. Nancy glanced down at the thermistor reading; his skin temperature had declined by half a degree, in just the last few seconds. Hurriedly, she scanned the other instruments; his heartbeat was steady, but the brain activity showed a slight decline, too. She tapped Sprague lightly on the shoulder. He turned swiftly on his stool, craned his neck over the instrument display. "Make a note of every change," he whispered urgently. Then turned back to Jack.

"What happened," he repeated, "to you or to Freddy?"

"There was a mountain of sand," Jack said. Even his voice, to Nancy's ear, sounded as if it had just dropped a register. "It had rained heavily the night before. The sand was dangerous."

"And one of you climbed onto that sand?"

"Freddy did. He climbed to the top. And the sand gave way."

To Nancy's amazement, Jack's skin temperature was dropping before her very eyes—three full degrees already. The blood volume to his extremities was also decreasing. His EEG showed a steady diminishment. She had never seen anything like this.

"When you say the sand gave way," Sprague asked, with soft, slow deliberation, "what do you mean? Did Freddy fall off the mountain of sand?"

"No . . . he was swallowed up by it. He sank in, like quicksand."

Unless these machines were going completely haywire, Jack's skin temperature had just dropped another two degrees; he should be shivering like mad. And the EEG was registering only minimal consciousness. Nancy began to grow frightened; she touched Sprague on the shoulder again, but he shrugged her hand away and continued to bore in on Jack.

"Stay there, Jack. Stay there with Freddy. Stay where you are, and tell me what's happening. *Exactly* what's happening."

Logan looked like a death mask of himself. His voice, when at last he spoke again, was positively sepulchral. "Freddy disappeared . . . under the sand. When the sand stopped moving, I found a board, a long wooden board, and laid it against the sand."

Nancy made frantic notes of the plummeting measurements.

"I shimmied up the board to where he was buried. His helmet still showed. I dug down to his shoulders. I was able to pull him out, after a lot of work . . ."

"Yes? And then?"

". . . then I pulled him down, headfirst, off the mountain . . . I put him on the ground. He wasn't breathing . . . I put my fingers in his mouth, and took out gobs of sand . . ."

Nancy didn't know what to make of any of this anymore. His heartbeat was perceptibly slowed, but still regular. As for the other measurements . . . if he weren't right in front of her, talking even, she'd have sworn he was a goner.

"I blew into his mouth, the way I'd once seen a lifeguard do it. Nothing happened. I kept doing it. He still didn't breathe . . . he still didn't breathe . . ." There was a long silence, punctuated only by the barely audible clacking of the machines. Jack looked as if rigor mortis were setting in; his body was so stiff his back hardly touched the table anymore. Sprague waited anxiously, afraid to break the silence; he rose from the stool, perspiring, and ran his eyes across Nancy's instruments. He seemed unsurprised by what he saw. He'd *expected* these results? Nancy thought.

"You must talk to me, Jack," Sprague finally said, resuming his seat. "You must tell me where you are right now, and just what's happening."

Jack's face remained immobile, his eyes closed, his jaws clenched.

"Where are you, Jack?"

"With Freddy."

Another long pause; his skin temperature was glacial.

"Freddy's ahead of me, but I can catch him." A slight, incongruous smile came to his face. "Because I already know the way..."

"The way where?"

"Where you go after."

Was he just speaking more softly, or had his voice actually grown more distant somehow? Nancy had to strain to hear him.

"Hold on, Freddy. Hold on." He was clearly talking to his friend now, reliving the experience. "Let's go back. No one will ever know this happened. Let's go back..."

"But where *are* you?" Sprague insisted, unable to keep the note of frustration out of his voice.

Jack's improving spirits were not to be dampened. "Hold on, Freddy. Don't look at the light. You can do it. Hold on."

"Jack—*tell me where you are.*"

Still smiling, Jack did not reply. Nancy's EEG meter showed next to no electrical brain activity; the printout would undoubtedly reveal a simple, but impossible, flat-line. And though she was probably imagining it, the chill from his skin seemed to have permeated the entire room; she pulled the lapels of her lab coat closed across her chest.

"Breathe," Jack was saying now, "breathe, Freddy. Breathe."

Sprague had given up, for the moment, trying to reach him.

"That's right—good." Jack laughed, tilting his head back; the electrode wires stretched and shivered around his face. "Yes, it's me, it's me, Freddy. Yes." He laughed again, as if with enormous relief. "Yes."

His whole body seemed suddenly to relax, his chin coming forward again, his arms dangling loosely at his sides. The three fingers encased in the silver thimbles, part of the thermistor apparatus, rattled against the side of the examination table. Nancy glanced again at the instruments in front of her: the skin temperature and blood volume measurements were rapidly returning to the usual range. His heartbeat had increased again, to what it should have been all along. The brain-wave scan had jumped from nil to normal, in a matter of no more than seconds. None of it made any sense at all to her. Sprague would have to figure it out later; she simply made notes of all the changes.

"Jack . . . do you hear me? It's Dr. Sprague."

"I hear you."

Even the room seemed to be getting warmer.

"Jack, I want to bring you out of the trance state now. I want you to do exactly as I say, as I say it. All right?"

"Yes."

Sprague repeated the procedure he had used to put Jack under, only this time in reverse order; first, he had Jack deeply inhale and lift his eyes under closed lids, then lower them again while exhaling. "When you feel me stroke the back of your left hand," he said, "you will slowly open your eyes, and feel fully awake and aware. Do you understand?"

Jack nodded, as if he were already almost there, and Sprague touched the back of his hand. His eyes opened, staring straight ahead, then slowly shifted to his left, where Sprague was sitting with Nancy right behind him. He shivered, suddenly, and said, "Whew! You got a draft in here?"

Sprague said nothing, but Nancy came around the machines to remove the various probes. She handed Jack his shirt, while Sprague sedulously cleaned his glasses with the hem of his lab coat. Jack, not sure how he'd done, asked Sprague if it all had been a wash.

"No," Sprague admitted. "Not at all." Slipping his steel-rimmed spectacles back on, he looked Jack in the eye. "You remember nothing, I assume, of what transpired in the trance state?"

"Should I?"

"No. It's just as well that you don't . . . for the time being."

Still wondering what had happened, Jack looked to Nancy for help. But after all that she'd just seen, she didn't know what to think, or how to deal with him, either. She gave him his socks and shoes, and after Sprague had abruptly left the room, escorted him as far as the elevator.

To her own surprise, this time she was vaguely relieved to see him go.

Part
Two

chapter twelve

SPRAGUE HAD TULLEY bring the car around. It was a Chevy Cavalier, the two-door model, and since Sprague was too tall to sit comfortably in back, he had to share the front with Tulley. It was annoying, but not as much of a problem as it might have been—Tulley had no more interest in talking to Sprague than Sprague did in talking to Tulley. They drove down the FDR Drive in perfect, sullen silence.

Traffic, as usual, was lousy. Sprague sat with his battered leather satchel—crammed with drugs, papers, and medical instruments—wedged between his legs. He was on his way to another routine, court-appointed psychiatric evaluation; one Ruben Garcia, on trial for the murder of his wife and her putative lover, and under a twenty-four-hour suicide watch since he was found trying to swallow a plastic spoon in a holding cell. Sprague's job was to ascertain, among other things, how sincere the attempt had been.

But Garcia wasn't what Sprague was thinking about; Logan was. Logan was all he'd thought about for the past three days. Ever since he'd conducted the second battery of tests, he'd been obsessed with the results. The baffling, and in several ways impossible, results. Whether he was aware of it or not, this Logan creature was able to defy the physiological laws; he was able to do something Sprague could not yet fathom—though he had his suspicions. And if those suspicions were correct, Jack Logan could be the key to unlocking the greatest single mystery of life.

But how, Sprague wondered yet again, could Logan have

come by such powers? And how could they be properly tested, verified, and documented?

Tulley, his jaw set like a boxer's, blasted the horn, and a Volkswagen bug inched away from the curb.

"How long?" Tulley said, pulling into the empty spot.

"An hour, maybe more."

"You want me to wait?"

"Yes. I want you to wait." Gratitude, Sprague thought; every week I keep the parole officer off his back, and still I get an argument.

Clipping the I.D. badge to his collar, Sprague got out of the car and walked past the guard house to the hospital annex; inside, the city and state housed their ill, or insane, criminal suspects until they could be tried and shipped off to the proper jail or asylum. An outside camera picked him up as he approached the door, and another picked him up as he entered the building. The nurse at the front desk recognized him, checked her log, and handed over a green folder with what Sprague was sure would be the same information he'd already been sent.

"I'll have Garcia sent to the consulting room," she said, picking up her phone.

Sprague passed through the electronic security check, and allowed the cop on duty to inspect his satchel for firearms, explosives, and God knows what else. Only Sprague knew the extraordinary damage that his little stoppered vials could inflict if properly—or improperly—administered. The cop closed the bag and buzzed him through the steel-plated doors.

The consulting room was no more than a barren room with a Formica table, half a dozen chairs, and foam padding on all the walls. Five minutes after Sprague sat down, a cop brought in Garcia, his hands cuffed in front of him. In all his years of professional practice, Sprague still hadn't gotten over how placid, how seemingly harmless his murderers, rapists, arsonists, could appear when removed from opportunity, or the source of their rage. Garcia was a spindly little man, in his late forties, unshaven, wearing the standard-issue gray shirt and sweat pants. He alighted on the chair that the cop pulled out for him as if he had already left this earth, saying nothing, staring into space. When the cop had left them alone together, Sprague offered him a cigarette—he didn't smoke himself, but had learned his subjects invariably did. Garcia nodded, and Sprague put the cigarette between his lips, then lighted it.

While Garcia smoked, holding the cigarette between the fingers of his manacled left hand, Sprague explained who he was and why he was there. He slapped his leather case onto the table, and removed the examination forms. Garcia never looked at him, but through squinted eyes studied the interior of the case. The bottles, vials, and instruments appeared to interest him, Sprague noted.

"I want to ask you to answer some questions for me, Mr. Garcia. There aren't any right or wrong answers. There is only what you think, and what you want to say." Garcia listened to the rest of the instructions without saying anything, or even giving any indication he understood. Tulley looked gregarious by comparison. But when Sprague began the actual tests, Garcia complied, and answered each question as it was put to him. If it hadn't already been obvious to Sprague, it soon became quite clear that Garcia was a genuinely suicidal man—clinically depressed, despairing, without hope or the will to go on. In the blot tests, he described, in English that was heavily accented but better than Sprague expected, only scenes of dismemberment and disjunction; in free-association, he revealed enormous guilt and self-loathing; in the personal interview/analysis, his detachment from daily life was exceeded only by his compelling desire for obscurity and annihilation. He was a man biding his time, patiently awaiting a suitable means to his own self-destruction.

His eyes, when he thought Sprague was unaware, repeatedly flicked to the leather satchel and its store of stoppered vials.

"When you say that you like things to be very, very quiet, do you mean also that you like there to be no other people around? That you like to be left entirely alone?"

"Yes. Alone. Nobody else." He dropped his cigarette butt, the third, into the blue foil ashtray at his elbow.

"You must find it very hard here, with people around, doctors and nurses and policemen, all the time."

Garcia let the statement stand.

Sprague asked a few follow-up questions, not because he really needed to know anything more, but because he needed time to consider something that had occurred to him about halfway through the session. It was just after he'd written "disassociative: suicidal" on one of the district attorney's forms that the thought had first come to him; he'd immediately rejected it, but it had returned moments later. Here was Garcia, a man who *wanted* to die, whom no one would miss, whose best prospect was a lifetime of incarceration in a state facility for the criminally insane. And here was Jack Logan, a man who possessed—assuming, of course, that Sprague was right—a gift that was at once an untold boon to all mankind, and virtually untestable under the usual rules of scientific inquiry and experimentation. If, Sprague told himself, he was clever enough, he could gamble, with almost total impunity, an otherwise irredeemable burden on the tax rolls—and Garcia looked to have at least another fifteen or twenty years in him—for a discovery the likes of which the world had never seen.

Garcia was sitting back in his chair now, his manacled hands resting in his lap.

Sprague leaned forward, to speak in lowered tones. "Will you believe me," he said, "if I tell you I want to help you? That I know what you want—what you *truly* want—and that I can help you to achieve it?"

Garcia studied him, not sure what he was getting at.

With his elbow, Sprague nudged the open satchel closer to Garcia.

"But you will have to do exactly what I say, exactly the way that I tell you to. *Entiende, amigo?*"

Garcia nodded, slowly, his eyes darting to the plastic vials, then listened closely to Sprague's instructions.

chapter thirteen

IN THE PAPER that morning, Nancy had seen another of those full-page Saks Fifth Avenue ads counting down the shopping days till Christmas. Just eighteen of them left, and she hadn't bought a single present yet. At five-fifteen, she told Sprague she had a class downtown—he never kept track of her actual schedule—and set off in the direction of Bloomingdale's.

She wasn't more than a block from the institute when she heard footsteps hurrying up behind her. She glanced over her shoulder, instinctively clutching her purse with both hands, and saw Jack Logan, flipping up his collar against the wind and smiling tentatively.

"I thought I'd get lucky," he said, drawing up alongside her. "Where are you headed?"

"Bloomie's." Where had he come from? "This is lucky?"

"Yes. I've been standing in that pizza joint across from the institute for the last forty-five minutes, waiting for you to come out."

"Why didn't you come in?"

"I didn't want to see Dr. Sprague. I wanted to see you." He gestured down the street. "I can walk and talk at the same time, and I don't want to hold you up."

They turned down York Avenue. As Jack said nothing further, Nancy asked, "How are you doing?"

"Fine," he replied, then said, "No, not exactly." He looked over at her as they walked. "I'm not exactly fine."

"What's wrong?" Nancy could think of several things herself, such as the bizarre results of the last lab session. Even now, she wasn't sure how she felt about being in his company; he'd seemed like a nice enough guy, and she did like those dark green eyes of his, but ever since that session, she'd been a little, well, leery of him.

"Something's been off for a couple of weeks now," he said, "ever since opening night of the show. That was the night that thing happened with Zakin."

As if she didn't know.

"Coming to the institute is making it worse. Or else it's just getting worse on its own, and the institute has nothing to do with it. I really don't know anymore." He did indeed sound very confused.

"What is the 'it' you're referring to? You don't feel well?"

"Physically I'm okay. I'm not running a fever or anything." They stopped to wait for the light. "But I feel like something's happened to me, or is still happening. I can't sleep at night anymore," he said, knowing he had to offer her something specific. "I go to bed late, after the show, but I was always able to sleep like a log. Now I feel like I never really go under, never really dream; it's as if something is holding me back. Some defense mechanism."

"Why wouldn't your body want you to get a good night's sleep?"

The light changed and they crossed.

"Beats me. Why would my body, or I guess I should say my nose, want me to smell something like cold metal off and on during the day?"

Nancy looked up at him now. Olfactory hallucinations sometimes preceded things like epileptic seizures. Was Jack the victim of some rare seizure disorder?

He noticed her intense expression, and laughed self-consciously. "I know it sounds weird. And I can hardly describe what cold metal smells like. But every once in a while, I get this whiff of it, right out of nowhere."

"At any particular time?"

He glanced into the window of a liquor store, strung with colored Christmas-tree bulbs. "When the spotlights suddenly go on at the opening of the show. And once in this Greek coffee shop I go to."

"Watch it." A delivery man pushed a dolly, crated with Jack Daniel's, between them.

"Maybe you should start eating somewhere else," she said, trying to sound less concerned than she was.

"There's this dessert carousel," he explained, "usually filled with all kinds of glop. Last week, they were cleaning it out late one night, and it was just a white cabinet, with empty white shelves, turning around and around under a bright, white light. I started staring at it, and before I knew it, I went into some kind of a trance almost, and the smell of that cold metal came to me again. If the waiter hadn't slapped my cheeseburger down in front of me, I'd probably still be sitting there, staring at it."

His mention of a trance interested her enormously; it would interest Sprague, she knew, even more. "I'm not sure I'm the one you should be telling all this to," she said. "Dr. Sprague is—"

"Exactly—what *is* Dr. Sprague? Oh, I know about his credentials and all that. But what does he want with me? And what has he found out so far? Half the time I'm at the institute, I'm completely out of it, with headphones on, or wires stuck all over me. I leave there feeling like I've been put through a wringer, and I don't even know why." He took her by the elbow, steering her around three teenage boys sharing a boom box, and into the sheltered doorway of a closed antiques shop.

"I'll go to Sprague if I have to. He's strange, but I don't have anything against him. I just thought I'd have a better chance with you of finding out . . . what's going on with me." He looked at her imploringly, his collar turned up around his face.

And what could she tell him? That under hypnosis, his heartbeat slowed and his brain stopped dead? That his blood volume altered, and his body temperature dropped so low the whole room took on a chill? That he relived saving a little boy's life, and in so doing seemed to lose his own? How could she explain to him these inexplicable things? And would she, even if she tried, be putting him, somehow, at some greater risk? She remembered something one of her psych professors had said: "The last thing you tell someone with an inferiority complex is that they have one. It just gives them something else to feel inferior about." Maybe this was the same sort of thing: maybe the last thing to tell Jack Logan was that he seemed to be capable of slipping between two worlds, of operating in this one by all the usual rules and in some other by God knew what laws. Maybe he needed, at least for now, to be protected from just such news. Her brain reeled with all the permutations while Jack's green eyes, almost black in the dim doorway, bored into her; his hand still held her elbow.

"Jack," she said, shaking her head slowly, "there *is* something going on. But honestly, I don't understand it. In the trance state you're able to do some surprising things—"

"Like what?" he interjected, his hand squeezing her arm.

"Physiological things, like moving the blood around to different parts of your body. Stuff like that, that only Sprague could really explain. But everything you've told me sounds very important, and I know that Sprague would want to pursue it. I agree with you that he's pretty odd"—she offered him a small smile, which she was relieved to see him return—"but he's also, believe it or not, quite brilliant in his way." And unscrupulous—she couldn't help remembering how he'd put Jack under hypnosis without fair warning. "But he'll help you"—for his own purposes—"if you let him." He dropped his hand away from her elbow. "And for what it's worth, I'll watch him like a hawk."

"My guardian angel?"

"Oh no—you're the angel, remember?"

He laughed, and for a moment she thought he was going to give her a hug. From the look on his face, he thought so, too. Instead he just guided her out of the doorway and back in the direction they'd been going.

"You wouldn't be one of the few New Yorkers who hasn't seen *Steamroller* yet?" he asked.

"That's the show you're in? No, I only see what I can get at the half-price booth."

"Come tonight, after you've done whatever you have to do at Bloomingdale's. I'll leave a house seat for you at the box office."

She was taken completely off-guard.

"And afterward, you can tell me how the orchestra sounds. I still think they've miked the brass too high."

* * *

At the box office, Nancy found an envelope waiting, with a ticket and a note inside. The note said to go around to the backstage entrance after the show.

Her seat was on the aisle, in the orchestra section; the stub said $45.00 on it. Even at the half-price booth, Nancy always asked for mezzanine or balcony. She sat down with the shopping bag between her knees; the only thing she'd found at Bloomingdale's that she could afford was an argyle sweater for her brother. He was seventeen and very label conscious. The other gifts in the bag—some gloves for her sister, a scarf for her father, placemats for her mother—she'd bought at smaller stores in the area. She was, at once, excited to be occupying a great seat at a recently opened Broadway show, and unsure if she should be there at all. When she'd called to say she wouldn't be home for dinner, she'd just said she would be working very late; that, her parents would never argue with.

When the show began, with a blaring overture, she listened hard, to try to separate the guitar from the rest of the instruments. But everything was so loud, it was difficult; maybe Jack was right and the brass *were* miked too high. The show itself was about a rich young man whose family tries to pressure him into a society marriage and a lifetime of privileged indolence. But he won't have it; he runs away to work among the common people, as a construction worker, and eventually writes a smash hit musical about his experiences, entitled, not surprisingly, *Steamroller*. To Nancy, the stuff about it being a hit seemed like wishful thinking; the show was pretty slow going, and more than once she found her thoughts wandering back to Jack Logan and . . . and what she was doing there.

This was not, she felt, a very good idea; Logan was one of Dr. Sprague's, her employer's, clinical subjects, and a highly unusual one at that. She ought not to be consorting with someone currently under scrutiny at the institute. She should have declined his offer to see the show, and simply encouraged him to contact Sprague about his problems.

But maybe this was one way to keep him in contact with the institute; maybe in cultivating some sort of social acquaintance with him, she was cementing the professional relationship, and even possibly learning something that would be of vital use to Sprague later. Even as she thought about it, she knew she was only rationalizing what she'd done, coming up with excuses for what she still suspected was unwise behavior. In her heart, she knew the real reason she was there; and that, she also knew, was neither logical nor smart. But she'd done it, she *was* there, and as she settled into her chair for the last act, she told herself that if she just watched her step for the rest of the evening, no harm would have to come of it.

When the show ended, to a round of tepid applause, she asked an usher to show her the way to the backstage entrance; he only knew how to get there by going outside the building through a side door, and then back in again from the narrow alleyway that ran alongside the theater. At the stage door, she gave her name to an old man working a crossword puzzle, and he waved her down the hall. She walked toward the sound of voices and laughter, and found herself at the threshold of what looked like a high school locker room: there were rows of dull-green lockers, and wooden benches running between them. The floor was bare cement, and what wall space there was was covered with wrinkled old theater posters. A black guy with a toothpick in his mouth said, "What have we here? An autograph hound?"

"I'm looking for Jack Logan," Nancy said.

"Just my luck. Hey, Logan—"

Jack appeared from behind a row of lockers. "You made good time," he said. Then, sweeping his arm around the locker room, added, "I thought you might like to see the glamorous backstage scene at a Broadway theater."

A light fixture just above his head suddenly sputtered and died. The black guy laughed and said, "Gonna have to work harder, man."

"This is Xavier Haywood," Jack explained. "No one knows why he comes here every night."

"He's one of the homeless. We take care of him. He's sort of a mascot." This from a fat guy who squeezed past Nancy and out the door. Several others followed him.

"Let me get my coat," Jack said, and disappeared again. Nancy noticed a pale blond woman lacing up her boots, and furtively glancing her way; Nancy smiled and the woman dropped her eyes.

"Successful mission?" Jack said, coming around the other side of the lockers.

Nancy didn't know what he was referring to.

"Your Christmas shopping," he said, tapping the paper bag she was carrying. "You get everything you wanted?"

"Oh. Yes—pretty much." On the way out, the old man asked Jack for a five-letter word for swamp.

Jack paused.

"Marsh," Nancy said.

The old man studied the puzzle, said, "It fits," and went right on working.

"You're forever in his good books," Jack said when they got outside. "Where to now?"

"Well, I have to get home pretty soon. I live down in Chinatown."

"Perfect. I'm starved. Take me to some place that's only known to the locals. Come on." He led her toward Ninth Avenue, and hailed a cab. When they got downtown, Nancy had to give the cabbie directions through the winding streets. They pulled up outside a tiny restaurant, with a red and yellow screen in the window.

"This one's open all night," she said, "and only Chinese are allowed in."

Jack stopped with his hand on the restaurant door.

"It's okay—you're with me."

Inside, there were no more than eight or nine tables; at one of them, four Chinese men were playing a game with what looked like ivory dominoes. Jack and Nancy took a small booth toward the rear. The waiter appeared with a pot of tea, but no menus.

"The menu is on the walls," Nancy said, indicating the brown paper sheets, covered with Chinese characters, stuck helter-skelter around the room. "Shall I order?"

"I'm at your mercy."

She rattled off something in Chinese. The waiter seemed to argue a point, but Nancy prevailed.

"What was that all about?" Jack asked, pouring out two cups of tea.

"He said he had no more octopus heads; I said check again." Seeing the look on Jack's face, she laughed and said, "Kidding. Just kidding."

"Promise?"

"Scout's honor." She held up two fingers in the scout salute.

"Actually, it's kind of a relief to see that the waiters in Chinatown are as rude to Chinese as they are to us gringos. Where'd you learn to speak the language?"

"Right here, in New York." She told him a little about her family, her father's job at a firm that imported shoes from Taiwan, her sister's addiction to MTV, her brother's ambition to own a computer company.

He listened politely, then said, "But what about *your* plans? How'd you come to work for a guy like Sprague?"

"That's another story . . . I'm working on a PhD at NYU, but the money for grad students is really tight. I needed the job at the institute just to make ends meet."

"But Sprague?" Jack repeated.

"Yeah, well, he has a huge reputation in the field, and though I could do without some of the mental torture, I really do learn a lot from him. Besides," she added, "it looks good on the résumé."

The waiter arrived and clattered the dishes down on the table. Nancy explained what each one was: hot soup made from minced chicken and corn, baby prawns with bean curd, a saucer of steamed dumplings. She was surprised herself at how easily and openly she was talking with him; it was something she didn't do with most people—especially those she knew as superficially as she knew Jack.

But there was something about his eyes, the way they seemed to take in everything about you while you talked, that made her feel that she did know him well—and that he knew her.

She heard her inner voice telling her to get a grip on herself.

"What made you decide to be a musician?" she asked.

"A lack of any other talents."

"Now you're just being modest."

"No, I'm just being truthful. I can't add or subtract, I can't stand the sight of blood, I can't get myself out of bed in the morning—playing guitar seemed like a great way to make a living."

And then he told her about his first rock 'n' roll band—the Ravens—formed when he was in eighth grade. And the first official gig they had, playing at a friend's neighborhood party. "It was the sweetest five dollars I ever made." He told her about Mam and Clancy, and growing up in Weehawken. "New York was just across the river but to me it felt like Oz—some mythical, faraway kingdom that I'd never get to know."

"So how's it feel to be the wizard now?"

"Not me. I'm just one of the Munchkins." Then, smiling at her over the rim of the teacup, he said, "You know who the real wizard is."

She knew, and smiled too. "But I wouldn't depend on his kindliness."

"I may have to. I can't take too many more sleepless nights."

The check came, slapped onto the edge of the table along with two fortune cookies on a dish.

"Choose," Jack said, pushing the dish toward Nancy.

She broke one open. And blushed.

"What's it say?"

"'Tall dark stranger will bring you much love.'"

Jack laughed, but found himself secretly gratified. He broke open the other cookie.

"So?" Nancy said when he didn't read the fortune aloud. "What's yours?"

"Weird," he replied, still studying the little paper strip. When he let go, she picked it up and read it herself.

"'Your mother says hello.'"

"Sort of weird for a fortune, isn't it?" Jack asked.

"Yes." Unfortunate, too, in light of what she knew of his background. How did he say his mother had died? "Maybe we each picked up the wrong cookie."

They paid the check, Nancy insisting they split it. Outside, the wind had kicked up, but otherwise the night wasn't too cold. "I'll take you home," Jack said, "then you can point me to the nearest subway."

"I'm just a block away." They walked down the street, past a couple of Chinese groceries and a fish market with empty boxes of ice awaiting the next day's catch. Around the corner Nancy stopped in front of a huge, featureless box of a building that Jack figured could only be subsidized housing; it had that distinctively spiritless, monolithic look to it.

"Home sweet home." It dawned on her that somehow she'd

made it through the whole evening without ever telling him what she thought of the show. "And thanks for getting me into *Steamroller*. I really enjoyed it."

He gave her a skeptical look.

"No, really, I don't know how I forgot to say something sooner." The wind blew her shopping bag around between them, up against her legs. "But maybe the brass section *was* miked a little high."

He smiled, and before she could react, had bent forward and kissed her lightly on the cheek. "Glad you were free." His breath was warm on her ear. He straightened up, and looked around. "And now, that subway stop?"

She gave him the directions, and as he turned to go, he called back, "See you at the wizard's."

chapter fourteen

"IT'S BEST, I think, if you say as little as possible."

Arlette nodded.

"That way he'll speak more freely. We can clear up any confusion later on."

"Maybe I should wear a white coat or something, to make it look like I'm staff here?"

High ethical standards, Sprague could see, were not going to be a problem with this woman. "I don't think so. You may need his trust later on; he shouldn't feel duped from the outset."

"You're right," she conceded.

Of course he was right—everything he'd planned was going right. He hadn't even had to pursue Logan anymore— Logan had called in on his own, sounding hesitant and unsure, wanting to talk about some problems he was having. It had been easy as pie to persuade him to come down to the hospital annex. "I may have to attend to a patient or two," Sprague had said, "but there should still be plenty of time for us to discuss your situation."

And for Sprague to determine, beyond a shadow of a doubt, just what Logan was capable of.

He arrived right on schedule. Sprague retrieved him from the reception area, and ushered him back to the consulting room. Arlette he simply introduced as an associate. Jack didn't question it, but he didn't look anxious to unburden himself in front of her, either. Instead, he made aimless small talk, asking Sprague what this place was all about.

"The patients here are involved, one way or another, in the criminal justice system," Sprague replied, remaining purposely vague. He expatiated on the kinds of maladies presented by the current inmate population, touching, as if by chance, on the case of Ruben Garcia, whom he characterized as a man rendered suicidally depressed by the brutal murder of his wife; more specific details he failed to mention.

"In fact," he said, glancing at his watch to make sure he was proceeding according to plan, "it might make sense for me to make my rounds now, and consult with you, Jack, afterward. That way," he said, with one of his glacial smiles, "we won't have to worry about being interrupted. You have the time, I hope?"

"No problem," Jack said, glancing again at the gum-chewing Arlette; this was a scientist, or a doctor? "It's a Monday night, my night off." He didn't add that no matter what time he got home, he'd be up until dawn anyway, staring at the ceiling or practicing chord progressions on his guitar.

"Then that's what we'll do," Sprague said, abruptly standing. Arlette stood too; Jack remained seated.

"I'll have to lock the consulting room after us," Sprague said. "It would be easier if you simply came along on the rounds."

Jack was surprised, but also fairly curious. He'd always wondered what doctors did when they went on their famous "rounds"; now he'd have a chance to see for himself.

With a clipboard clamped under one arm, Sprague led the way out of the room, up two flights of stairs, and through another set of swinging steel doors guarded by another city cop. The hallway beyond was preternaturally quiet—just a straight, wide expanse of green linoleum and fluorescent light. Both sides of the corridor were lined, at ten-foot intervals, with identical pale green doors; each one had a small window in it, no doubt of some unbreakable glass, mounted at eye level. Sprague, after consulting his watch again, hesitated, then said, "I think I'll look in on my arsonist first. Gilbert Hoster."

Hoster was laid out on his bunk, reading a tome entitled *Treasures of the Vatican*. In the past six months, Sprague had explained in the corridor outside, Hoster had fire-bombed three abortion clinics in New York and New Jersey; he did it, he claimed, at the behest of Saint Jude. During his brief consultation with Sprague, he was unfailingly polite and mild-mannered, and when they turned to leave, he insisted that Arlette and Jack accept copies of a religious tract headlined "Armageddon—Armies of Light Versus Armies of Night."

"Please read it—it's important."

Jack promised he would, and Hoster returned to his bunk looking relieved.

Three doors down, Sprague stopped and peered in through another of the glass panels. "Mr. Garcia appears to be sleeping," he said. He knocked loudly on the door, then used his pass key to unlock it. While Sprague approached the bed, Jack and Arlette waited at the threshold. "Come in already," he barked at them, while shaking Garcia by the shoulder, "and pull the door closed behind you." As in Hoster's cell, there was just barely enough room for them all to stand.

Garcia, in gray sweat clothes, was turned toward the wall, his knees drawn up toward his chest. Sprague hastily turned him over, glanced for some reason at the wall clock set into a recessed space above the door, then shook Garcia again. His limbs appeared slack, his muscles uncontrolled. His eyes, to Jack, looked as though they had rolled up into his head. Sprague suddenly crouched down beside him, clutching his wrist to feel for a pulse; he placed his ear against Garcia's chest. "Nothing. Not a thing." He said it with urgency, but nothing more. "But he's still warm." He looked around the room, as if trying to locate something.

"You mean he's dead?" Arlette's gum simply tumbled from her open mouth. She shrank back toward the door.

"I'll get help," Jack volunteered.

Sprague snatched something off the floor near the foot of the bed, examined it in his open palm. "It's too late for that," he said, holding the empty plastic vial out toward Jack. "He must have taken this"—there was a label Jack couldn't read—"and he must have done it, judging from the state of the body, within the last five minutes." He was staring directly into Jack's eyes, almost as if he were issuing a challenge of some sort. "There's not time to get the proper resuscitation equipment up here."

Jack returned Sprague's stare; inside, he felt a swirl of emotions. Shock, and confusion, even sorrow—this, after all, was the man who'd already seen his wife brutally killed. Now he'd taken his own life; too much sadness, too much to bear. But he shouldn't have done it; life was too precious. It could have been made right again—if only he'd held on.

Sprague's gaze never wavered.

But what does he want from me?

"Can you help him?"

Could he? God, it was just like with Zakin. But that's what had started all his trouble. That's what he'd come to have Sprague explain—and help him get rid of. Now he was being asked to start it all up again.

"Can you do it?" Sprague was insisting now. "Can you save this man's life, Jack?"

He looked over at the bed, at Garcia's slack face; beard stubble covered his jaw. Could he save him? He moved closer, Sprague stepping aside.

Who are you? I never even saw you alive. He bent down, placing one hand flat against Garcia's chest. The sweatshirt was warm and slightly damp.

Do you want this? Will you want to come back?

There was just enough room to sit beside him on the bunk. Jack was embarrassed at the strange intimacy of it, and frightened by what he was about to do... or try to do. He felt Sprague, and now Arlette, staring at his back, and wondered if under such conditions it would even be possible. He closed his eyes and tried to forget they were there. All his thoughts he focused on Garcia, all his energies; he tried to feel, in his very bones, who Garcia was, what had propelled him to such a desperate act. Without knowing why, he bent at the waist, until his chest was lightly touching Garcia's; he smelled sweat, the faint odor of starch from the sheet, the cold metal of the iron bedframe.

In his head, there was a bewildering chorus of voices—he heard Sprague saying "Can you save this man?" and Arlette's "You mean he's dead?" He heard the sound of Mrs. Zakin sobbing, and the wail of a siren stuck in traffic. He heard his own voice telling him not to do this, not to take the chance he was taking, and beneath that, like a second conversation accidentally audible on a long-distance line, a woman whose voice was indistinct but oddly, achingly familiar. What was she saying? Was she talking to someone else—or to him? He strained to hear her words; it seemed so important to make out what she was saying, but her voice alternately rose and fell, and the most he could gather was the sense that, yes, she *was* talking to him. He heard his name, and trilling laughter, laughter that flattened out instantly as if borne away by a gust of wind on a vast, empty plain. Where was she? Who was she?

His hands were gripping Garcia's shoulders; he had drawn his legs up onto the bed, too. At first, he thought his eyes were open again, staring into the whiteness of the crisp, starchy sheet. But they weren't; he was traveling through a landscape of bleak, white light, traveling as if he were a leaf carried by that same gusting wind. He could see in all directions at once; behind him, a red steel scaffolding, receding fast; before him a burning sun that shimmered with heat and grew larger all the time. Its perimeter seemed to pulse with light, beating like a great white, shapeless heart. The voices in his head had faded or gone—all but the one, the young woman he could not make out. Her voice, if anything, had grown louder, though her words were still swallowed up by the rushing wind and a vague, distant commotion.

The heat was growing more intense by the second; Jack raised his hand before his eyes. He could no longer look at the beating light; he could only hurtle toward it, bracing himself for the scorching shock of collision. And then it came, with a burst like hitting a swimming pool from the high dive: he reeled in light, his skin abraded by a dry, invisible fire. He felt scrubbed, inside and out, by a flaming wind, which was at once painful beyond measure and more keenly satisfying than anything he had ever imagined. Part of him wanted to escape screaming, and part wanted to remain, and endure it, forever. Had he not known now wasn't the time, that he was only a pilgrim in these holy precincts, he would have stayed, would have given himself over to the engulfing light, would have let it do with him whatever it willed. But now was not that time; he did not yet belong there, and the light, he felt, knew it as well as he did. He was rolled and buffeted and spun, like clothes in a dryer, and as the heat abated, so did the light.

He felt in his heart a gaping loneliness. He felt rejected, and terrifyingly lost—though he sensed, all around him now, the presence of others. Among them, he knew, and very near, was Garcia, whom he had almost forgotten, as he had almost forgotten himself. He breathed his name, and as if that alone were enough to incarnate him, Garcia appeared, in the clothes he had died in; he looked, as Jack himself felt, lost and confused. His face floated uneasily in front of Jack's eyes, and it was then Jack realized the face was strangely transparent; like a clear plastic mask; it could be seen, and seen through, at the same time. So could his body; when Jack looked at Garcia he could see him—his arms, his legs, his chest—and see also a limitless expanse of gray . . . it could not be called terrain, because there were no apparent features to it, but a vast barren plain of gray shadow and haze, which spread away in all directions, growing darker and more clouded toward the far horizons. Garcia, he sensed, was headed toward that darkness.

"Not yet," Jack said, his voice sounding oddly muted and flat. "Not yet." His hands, without reaching out, were clutching Garcia's shoulders; it was possible to hold him, Jack discovered, without actually feeling anything. Like touching your own jaw after a shot of Novocaine. Garcia neither welcomed, nor resisted, the embrace; he seemed not to understand what was expected of him. It was only when Jack subtly urged him back, in the direction of the light, that his expression became one of fear and reluctance. *"Eres un ángel? Eres un muerto?"* Jack understood no Spanish; he merely held Garcia tighter, said, "Come with me." Garcia tried, but hesitantly, to free himself. His expression turned to utter terror. *"Eres el diablo? Sí eres el diablo!"* This much Jack was able to grasp; he smiled and said, "No, I am not the devil. No *diablo*," he repeated, shaking his head. But Garcia wasn't convinced. *"Diablo!"* he cried, his whole body quaking with fear now. *"El diablo lleva los asesinos al infierno!"* He fell to his knees, screaming in terror, but no longer trying to escape.

Jack knelt down and wrapped him in his arms. He could feel no flesh, but the coldness was extraordinary. He held him closer, hoping to warm him; Garcia's head slumped, as if he had died again, against Jack's chest.

Without having to rise, Jack felt them both moving, back toward the light, away from the plains; as they did, he sensed, without seeing them, that he was passing among multitudes, that he could, if he desired, summon up any one of them. The air around him seemed to swarm with voices, all of them vying for his attention and his ear. But there were so very many, and they were so hopelessly jumbled together, with dozens of accents, hundreds of languages, that in the end it became a noise with no more meaning than the rushing wind. The light grew brighter, and the heat more intense, the voices fading, until only one, only one, could still be faintly, distantly heard. Jack *knew* that voice, it was so familiar, it was as much a part of him as his own blood. He strained to see, in the blinding light, where it was coming from, and who was calling to him.

Garcia began to grow heavy in his arms; to hold him better, Jack clasped his hands behind Garcia's back. And stared, over his shoulder, into the white void. That voice, the voice of a young woman, echoed in his head and coursed through his veins. He needed to hear it again, and more desperately, needed to *answer* it; it was as thrilling as a jolt of adrenaline, and as soothing as mother's milk . . . it was . . .

"Mother!" he screamed, and a pale white face, its features unclear, suddenly carved itself from the greater whiteness. Long, dark hair flowed to either side.

"Mother!" The shock made him tighten his grip on Garcia.

The face was speaking to him; he could see the mouth opening and closing. But she was falling away, farther and farther away, as if drawn backward by an irresistible force. He thought, just before she disappeared, that he saw a hand, a thin white hand with a bracelet of blue stones, reaching out toward him, and he screamed again . . . and again . . . and again . . . and—

"Logan! Logan! Let him go or you'll kill him. Let go!"

He opened his eyes; he was kneeling on the floor; there were voices again, shouting all around him.

"Diablo!"

"Logan, let go!"

Garcia was squirming and pushing away. Sprague was trying to pry Jack's arms loose.

Jack broke his grip. Garcia scrambled backwards, his eyes wide with fear, up onto the bunk and flat against the corner wall. *"Diablo!"* he shrieked, first at Jack, then at Sprague. *"Diablo! Monstruos! Mentiroso!"*

Jack fell back, shivering, against the foot of the bed.

"What's going on?" A cop had thrown the door open. A

nurse stood behind him. Someone else, another white coat, skidded to a halt outside.

"Straitjacket," Sprague said. "We need a straitjacket."

Garcia knew the word, started screaming even louder. Two black orderlies, big as bulls, elbowed their way into the cell, stepped over Jack without a second glance, and wrestled Garcia's arms into the loose white sleeves of the jacket.

"Sedation?" the nurse suggested.

"No."

She looked surprised.

"No sedation," Sprague repeated.

Garcia was lying facedown on the bed, panting fiercely into the blanket. The orderlies looked to Sprague for further instructions, got none, and sauntered out of the room.

Sprague wanted Garcia to remember every second of the past few minutes; he wanted him to lie there, awake and aware, trussed and terrified, in a widening pool of his own spittle. And then, when he was finally calm enough, and there was no one else around to hear his secrets, Sprague wanted him to describe exactly what had happened, where he'd gone and how Jack had found him. He wanted to hear, from someone who had been there and had just returned, an account of life beyond the grave. If he resisted, if he felt cheated and refused to cooperate, Sprague would guarantee him a long, well-guarded life, full of sedation and padding and straitjackets. If he went along, and told Sprague everything he wanted to know, Sprague would promise him no further foulups. Sprague would promise him a lasting death—and this time Sprague would deliver.

chapter
fifteen

On Wednesday, the article ran on an inside page of the entertainment and leisure section.

ADOLPH ZAKIN, THEATER OWNER, BACK TO WORK—AND BACK TO LIFE

It wasn't very long, just a few hundred words, but it was the first time Arlette had seen her own byline in the paper. Her boss, Murray Spiegel, hadn't liked the idea much—"sounds too *Enquirer* to me"—but it was a slow news day and he could see how badly she wanted it; he'd initialed her copy and told her to make him a lunch reservation at Caravelle.

And now, here it was, in black and white.

Adolph Zakin, owner of one of the most successful theatrical property chains in America, returned to his West 57th Street office today, looking none the worse for having died, in front of one of his own theaters, on November 17 of this year.

What a great lead! She clapped her hands together after reading it over. A reporter at a nearby desk looked up from his work and scowled. Arlette mouthed "sorry" and went on reading. She tried to pretend she hadn't written it, that she was just an average reader leafing through the paper on the morning train. Would she have been grabbed by now? Would she be eagerly reading the rest?

Yes, she thought—she would. The piece went on to explain what had happened outside the theater, and how Zakin had later described it from his suite at the Carlyle:

Looking off at the expensive oil painting that adorned one wall, he repeated, "There's something else—*after*."

Arlette still got a chill from that.

The end of the piece was a quick summary of the work currently being done on Jack Logan, "the young musician with the mysterious talents," under the supervision of Dr. Orson Sprague at the Institute of Abnormal Psychology. Sprague was even quoted to the effect that his early results were "very promising."

Arlette folded the paper with satisfaction. It wasn't a headline story yet, but it was a start—and after what she'd seen with Garcia at the hospital annex, there'd be a lot more to come. Sprague had sworn her to secrecy over the Garcia episode, saying he needed to do follow-up studies before any word was released. "If this incident becomes common knowledge," he'd said, "my access to Garcia will be terribly restricted, and I'll never be able to uncover what went on." Arlette, though she was chaffing at the bit, had agreed to hold off . . . for the time being.

The phone rang; Arlette picked it up without looking, cradled it on her shoulder. "Murray Spiegel's line."

"Hi, Arlette. I just read your story in today's paper. Wow."

It was her friend, Bonnie Robb, the TV reporter who'd first given her the tip.

"Did you like it? How about that lead?"

"The lead?" Bonnie said. "Oh, yeah, it opened great. And I love that spooky stuff about something coming after. In fact, I was wondering if there's anything in it for the local news, the five P.M. broadcast. I wanted to ask you a couple of things."

"Sure."

Even as Arlette answered Bonnie's questions, about what kind of interview subjects Zakin, or Sprague, or Logan would be, her mind was racing to stay one step ahead: how much of her info should she be handing out—even to a friend? Would a TV report strengthen or diminish her own ongoing story?

How could she capitalize on Robb's sudden interest, and on any other attention the story received? She felt that she was riding the crest of a wave, and if she could just manage to keep her balance, she'd be able to ride it right onto the front page.

Or at the very least, a guest appearance on the Geraldo Rivera show.

chapter sixteen

JUDGING FROM THE crowd around the bulletin board, Jack figured the dreaded "notice" had been posted. But when Vinnie spotted him and said "It wasn't me," with his palms raised as if to show he was clean, Jack knew it had to do with what he'd come to think of as "the Sprague stuff."

When he stepped up to read the newspaper clipping tacked to the board, the other musicians instinctively drew back. Veronica glared at him, and stalked away.

Had she posted it?

Bad as it was, in a way he was relieved; at least it didn't mention anything about what had happened with Ruben Garcia. It was still just Adolph Zakin. And the byline, Jack noticed, was Arlette Stein. Hadn't that been the name of the woman Sprague had introduced simply as an "associate"? An associate from the press, apparently.

Jack was too wrung out to care.

For the past two nights, he'd had maybe three hours of sleep. And if Sprague had had his way, he wouldn't have had even that. Sprague wanted him virtually to live at the institute, to be available for study and observation around the clock. Sprague was like a man obsessed, measuring Jack in every way he could, checking his blood count, monitoring his blood pressure, peering into his eyes and down his throat; Jack had been scoped and scanned and sampled until there was simply nothing left to do.

Except to ask questions. And Sprague never seemed to run out of those. What had he felt when he first put his hand to

Garcia's chest? What did he see when he closed his eyes? Where had he gone? How had he traveled there? What had those voices seemed to be saying? How could the white light have been painful and pleasurable, at the same time? What did the woman, the one who called to him, look like? How could he tell that she was his mother? (Jack could only say that he *knew.*) And finally, again and again, phrased a hundred different ways, how *exactly* did he do what he had done—Sprague had seen the results, but not yet understood the process—and *where* had he learned to do it?

Those answers, even Jack didn't know.

But Sprague was determined that, together, they find out.

Coming to play the show was like taking a breather. He was among friends, and doing something that he didn't even have to think about; he knew the score inside out, and even if he wasn't playing as sharply as he should have been (Vinnie had kidded him that he was dropping so many notes, they needed a vacuum cleaner in the pit) he was getting by. Once he got some rest, and straightened out some of the other stuff, his playing would get back in shape, too. Between this performance, the matinee, and the evening show, maybe he'd even manage to go home and take a nap.

"Move it," Burt hollered from the locker room doorway. Jack and the few remaining players grabbed their instruments and hurried past him, down the narrow passageway, lighted with bare red bulbs, that led to the pit. Setting up, he saw Haywood, behind his drums, fluttering his hands like little wings: another "angel" joke. Jack shook his head, like "enough, already," and Haywood picked up his drumsticks.

Consuela, the conductor, kicked off the overture; Haywood's job was to hit a cowbell three times, then the rest of the orchestra, in unison, had to come in. They did, with Jack half a beat behind. Vinnie, his cheeks puffed, raised his eyebrows at Jack. *Shit.* Jack adjusted the guitar strap around his neck; he was afraid to look at Consuela. *Concentrate*, he told himself; *concentrate*. He knew the score by heart, but he made himself study it, follow it along measure by measure, as if he were some alternate "subbing" for just this one performance. He made it through the rest of the act with only one major flub that he knew of—hitting the overdrive instead of the chorus pedal—and breathed a sigh of relief when the curtain came down for intermission.

Instead of going back to the locker room, and risking a lecture from Burt or Consuela, he stayed in the pit. With the stagelights off, and the house lights on, he could gauge the turnout—which looked passable for a matinee. A lot of old people, a smattering of tourists, several larger groups from those suburban theater clubs. Winter coats were draped unceremoniously across the mezzanine and balcony rails—a flouting of the house rules—but it at least made the auditorium look more crowded than it was. Hell, these people weren't even getting to see the star of the show; he'd come down with the flu and been replaced, according to the little slip of paper inserted in all the programs, by someone with the unlikely name of Templeton True. And True, Jack comforted himself, had made some bloopers of his own in the first act. Maybe that would take the heat off of him.

It didn't though; before giving the downbeat for the next act, Consuela muttered "Wake up" to Jack. That threw the fear of God into him, and for the next half hour or so he played a lot better than he had been. He paid close attention to the score, and watched the conductor's baton carefully.

Until something else, something slightly off, caught his eye.

At first he didn't know what it was. A low black curtain rimmed the pit, concealing most of the front row seats from view. Aside from some shoes poking below the curtain here and there, all that could be seen of the people in those seats was the top half of their face, or the crown of their skull; it depended on how tall they were, and how they were sitting. More to the point, Jack knew—without even thinking about it—exactly how far those seats extended around the pit; there were fourteen in the row and the aisle cut in, on the left-hand side, just behind Veronica Berghoffer's shoulder. Today, there was one seat too many.

And in it, there was a shadowy figure, a woman, who seemed to fade in and out of view.

At moments when the stagelights were on full, Jack strained to get a clear view of her, but no sooner had he seemed to get her in focus than the lighting would change and she would appear to vanish. Nor could he understand why or how an extra seat had been added to that row. Wouldn't the fire regulations prohibit such things?

He missed another cue, while staring off over Veronica's shoulder.

He caught up two bars later.

When the next lull came, he looked again, this time at the bottom of the pit curtain. Unless he was mistaken, and it wasn't easy to tell for sure, there were the tips of two feet poking through—but *feet*, not shoes. Or boots. Bare feet. In December weather.

The toes of one foot wriggled.

His eyes jumped up, to try to catch a glimpse of her face. But she must have been sitting back in her seat; all he could see was the top of her head—dark, straight hair, parted in the middle.

Still, it was enough to make him shiver.

Van Nostrand, who played bass right behind him, kicked the bottom of his chair, and Jack jumped. The next tune had started; Jack fingered the first chord wrong.

Consuela just shook her head, without even looking over at him.

Jesus, Jack thought. He played the rest of the number with his hands shaking, his eyes resolutely on the music stand in front of him. When it ended, to a round of applause—this was the show-stopper number, and if it didn't get a hand, nothing would—he still didn't look up. He didn't dare. He played the rest of the show that way, like a drone, staring at the score, watching for his cues, listening to the stage action. He was never so grateful to swing into the grand finale, when Templeton True belted out a reprise of the "Steamroller" theme, than he was this time. The curtain came down, the applause came up, the curtain call followed, with the orchestra repeating the signature theme from the overture, and Jack allowed himself, finally, to look up, and out of the pit again.

The face, with the houselights on now, was visible to him, leaning forward over the pit curtain.

And it was a face he had seen, a thousand times, in his dreams.

Her skin was pale, her cheekbones high, framed on either side by a straight fall of long, dark, shining hair. Her lips were parted, in an open smile, and her eyes . . . her eyes were as large and deeply green as they had appeared in the photos Mam kept in the parlor. As wide and large and deeply green as his own.

They studied him now with yearning, and recognition, and a measure of joy . . . claiming him, as it were.

Declaring him *her son*.

Jack's heart felt as if it had stopped beating. The applause died down. The other musicians were already packing up. But she alone kept clapping, rapping the rolled-up program against one hand. He looked wildly around, to see if anyone else was even aware of her. But no one seemed to be. Vinnie was avoiding his gaze, Catalano was already gone. Veronica—and God, the woman was sitting right behind her—was folding up her score with complete aplomb. Just one more performance, over and done.

The rapping of the program echoed around the walls of the theater, a steady, brisk, unending beat. But no one else seemed aware of that, either. The face was still smiling, and nodding now, as if to say "Yes, yes, you're not imagining this." But he had to be, he had to be; no one else was even paying any attention. It had to be all going on in his head, inside his head, and only there. The rapping went on and on and on, over the usual sounds of the audience leaving—seats springing up, chatter, coughing, bags rustling, the distant noise of the street outside wafting in through the open front doors. Nearly everyone was out of the pit now. Still, the hollow clapping went on. A blue and silver bracelet danced around her wrist.

Jack, transfixed, stared at the bracelet.

"Hey, man—"

Jack convulsed at Haywood's touch, as if he'd been jolted with a cattle prod.

"What the *fuck*!" Haywood jumped back. "What is wrong with you?"

Jack shivered again.

"What is *wrong* with you?"

Jack glanced at Haywood, then back toward the clapping specter.

She was gone.

The extra seat was gone.

The pit, except for the two of them now, was empty.

"You going mental on me or what? First you play like shit, now you want to hang out here till it's time for the next show? What's your problem?"

Jack swallowed, hard. There was nothing to see anymore; what could he show Haywood? "Did you see a woman, right about there"—he pointed where the extra seat had been —"looking into the pit just now, clapping?"

"What? If she was clapping, that's good news. But no, that row's cleared out." He took a gentler tone, replacing his hand on Jack's shoulder. "Time you cleared out, too. You're not lookin' very good."

Jack took a deep breath. "Yeah, you're right—I've got to get some sleep before the next show."

"Yeah—you do that. Come on." Haywood moved a music stand out of the way, as if for an invalid, and led Jack back toward the locker room.

In the hall outside, Consuela, already wearing her overcoat, was conferring, animatedly, with Burt; they both looked over as Jack approached. Consuela said one thing more, then stalked off. Burt said, "Jack, I gotta talk to you."

Jack didn't have to guess what it would be about.

But Burt started out talking about the newspaper clipping on the bulletin board instead, asking Jack a little about that institute it mentioned, and saying how tiring it must be to undergo tests and all. Still, Jack knew where he was headed, and soon enough he got there. "I think you're wearing yourself out," he said, not unkindly, "and today it showed. I know you're good; I knew that when I hired you. But Consuela's ticked off, and even I think you need to take a break. I'm gonna use a sub for the next few days. Get some rest, and give me a call next week."

The ax had fallen. Haywood and Vinnie were waiting for him in the locker room. He told them.

"Hell, take a vacation," Vinnie said. "Leave it to us—we'll make sure the sub sounds like he can't read music. You'll be back on Monday."

"I were you," said Haywood, "I'd stay gone for two weeks. I'd head for one of those Club Meds and get me a real good tan."

"You've got a tan," Vinnie said.

"I didn't mean *mine*," Haywood replied.

Jack smiled wanly; he appreciated their staying, but just

now he really wanted to be alone, to think through what had just happened. They offered to go to the Olympia Coffee Shop with him, but he said no, he was just going to go home and veg out.

"See you in a few days then," Vinnie insisted on adding.

"Yeah—next week," Haywood said.

Yeah, Jack thought, in a few days. I'll be seeing you guys again in a few days.

Purposely, he left his second-string guitar and some other stuff—extra picks, an old strap, a dog-eared copy of a book by Ned Rorem—in his locker. No use making any more of this than it was. Just a short, and temporary, leave of absence.

That's what he told himself, over and over, on the subway home, reciting it like a mantra. A short, and temporary, leave of absence. Much as he hated to dwell on it, it was still easier to deal with than what had happened earlier—his mother's face smiling at him in the pit. What the hell would he say to Sprague about *that*?

At his apartment, he turned on the TV and flopped onto the bed with a bottle of Heineken. Maybe I'd better cut back to Old Milwaukee, he thought. "The People's Court," Judge Wapner presiding, came on after the commercials.

Sometime during the show, which seemed to involve some carpeting that had been installed upside down, he drifted off to sleep. He awoke with the phone ringing, and the apartment dark. His machine picked up before he could find the phone.

"Hi, it's Nancy. Dr. Sprague wants to know what time you can come in tomorrow. He also wants you to bring—"

"I'm here," Jack said, cutting in. The machine clicked off and rewound.

"—your birth certificate," she said, completing her thought. "I didn't think you'd be home. Why aren't you at the show?"

He looked at the fluorescent face of the alarm clock. It was ten after eight.

"You don't want to know."

"I do." Then, "It didn't close, did it?"

"No, but it's gonna run for a few days without me . . . I missed half my cues and the contractor told me to take off for a few days."

Nancy paused, as if trying to assess the importance of what

he'd just said. "So it's just a temporary thing—"

"A leave of absence," Jack put in.

"—until you're back on track." She could hear how depressed he was. "Is there anything I can do?"

"I don't suppose you could get me some amphetamines," he said, only half joking.

"Gee, I'm afraid I just ran out." She was thinking something over. "But I was just about to leave the institute, and if you wanted me to"—here goes—"I could come over for a while." She held her breath, wondering what she'd just done.

Jack wondered too. But his heart had lifted the moment she'd suggested it. He sat up in the bed now, rubbing his face; he'd have to shave again. And straighten up the joint.

"Sure," he said, "I'd like that. What time?"

"Depends on the crosstown bus. But I'll be leaving here in a couple of minutes; otherwise, Sprague'll find something else for me to do."

The moment they hung up, he stumbled into the bathroom, tossed his shirt on the towel rack, and lathered up his face. He noticed himself putting a fresh blade in the razor, and humming a few bars of vintage Springsteen.

He was happy about this; he was looking forward to it. And only a few hours earlier he was at absolute ground zero. Funny. It made him think he liked this Nancy even more than he knew.

He made sure not to cut himself shaving, put on a fresh shirt, and spent the rest of the time smoothing out the comforter on the bed, drawing the heavy curtains that he used to keep out the daylight when he slept late, stacking some Joe Pass records on the stereo; he had a CD player, but almost all the music he liked he'd accumulated over the years on albums. And most of it wasn't likely to be reissued on CD; his favorites were an acquired taste, which few people had ever acquired. Next to his Strato-caster guitar, his records were his most prized possessions.

Nancy arrived just as he was scanning the barren shelves of his refrigerator for something to serve. "Before you take off your coat," he said, "I should warn you that the only thing I can offer you is a bag of stale Chips Ahoy and a beer."

She looked unenthused; she also looked great, a bright red scarf tied loosely around her throat, her purse—more of a canvas knapsack, really—tossed over one shoulder.

"Are you hungry? I know a place not far from here where we can get some great octopus heads."

She smiled.

"Come on."

He knew it was officially a date when he didn't take her to the Olympia. This made it their second, though it didn't really feel that way. He'd seen so much of her at the institute, ever since the Garcia episode, that he felt, already . . . well, something more for her than he would have expected. They went to a relatively upscale place, and drank Amstel Lights while waiting for a table.

Dinner itself was overpriced and not especially good, but the way Jack looked at it, you went to these loud and crowded restaurants not to eat but to see and be seen. Being seen with Nancy was very pleasant; the guy at the next table, there on what was apparently a blind date that wasn't going so well, kept looking over at her, and Jack couldn't blame him. She was dressed casually, in fitted trousers and a soft-mushroom-colored sweater, nothing particularly showy or glamorous. But she was so damned pretty—her skin so pale and smooth, her black hair so thick and glossy, her features so delicate—that she was arresting nonetheless. Jack wondered just how beautiful she'd be if she pulled out all the stops. And hoped he'd have a chance to see one day.

Afterward, they went back to his apartment, Nancy hesitating for a second outside the building. "It *is* a school night," she said, and Jack said, "I'll write you a note." When she still hesitated, he added, "Besides, I just got fired."

"*Furloughed*," she corrected.

"That's a good word."

Upstairs, he gave her another beer, since it was all he had, and then gestured toward the bed.

Nancy looked stunned.

"Sorry, but we either have to sit at that card table by the window, or on the bed."

"Strategic planning," she said.

"Men are all alike." He turned on the Joe Pass records, then joined her on the bed; they pushed the pillows against the wall and used them as backrests.

At first they talked the same way they had at the restaurant

—in high, bright tones, about movies and music and their least favorite TV commercials. But as they relaxed, and the gentle strains of the acoustic guitar played on around them, they found themselves getting quieter, and more introspective, and sliding by degrees lower and lower against the pillows. And Jack found himself, now that he was away from the noise and commotion, remembering all that had happened earlier in the day—the bad news from Burt, and the terrible shock he'd gotten in the pit. That was the one thing—the sight of his mother—that he hadn't confessed to Nancy. Even after everything she already knew about him, he was afraid that if he told her about what he thought he'd seen that afternoon, he'd sound totally off the wall. Bad enough that he was temporarily out of work; he didn't want her thinking she was in bed—or more precisely, *on* the bed—with a complete basket case.

"You're getting gloomy again, aren't you?"

"Huh?"

"Getting gloomy. Thinking bad thoughts."

"Oh. Yeah." He rolled over onto his stomach, bunching a pillow under his chin and folding his arms around it. "I just realized it's after eleven. I'd be leaving the theater around now."

"And then what?" She rolled over on one side, to face him.

"Then I'd probably be going to the Olympia. With Vinnie, or Haywood." He put his head down, into the pillow. His hair curled in black tendrils over the back of his collar. He didn't say anything else, and Nancy wasn't sure what to say, either. She put out one hand and gently rubbed his shoulder.

"That feels good," he mumbled into the pillow.

"Ancient Oriental art."

He dropped his shoulders more, and Nancy let her hand graze across his upper back. Under his thin flannel shirt, his body felt hard and muscular. And massive; only once had she dated anyone as tall and broad as Jack. A football player who'd spent every second trying to get her into bed. Without success. "You don't know what you're missing," he'd said, after throwing in the towel. "I'll live with it," Nancy'd replied.

The record ended, and Nancy heard another one drop.

"Hope you like Joe Pass," Jack said, softly.

"If that's who this is, I do."

She leaned up on one elbow, and massaged his shoulders more firmly. He exhaled, contentedly. Should she go on, she wondered? It was clear she'd get no argument from Jack. She glanced across him, at the clock on the bedside table. It was eleven-thirty now. If she kept this up much longer, it would lead to a foregone conclusion. Was that what she wanted? Damn. Why were these things always so complicated?

He fidgeted on the bed, pulling his shirttails loose from his pants. No trouble reading that message. She snaked one hand under the shirt, and brushed slowly up and down his back. He sighed.

Damn. Damn. Damn.

"Nails," he whispered.

And she turned her hand so that her fingernails lightly scored his back.

With one arm, he reached out and flicked off the bedside lamp. The room was plunged into total darkness.

For Jack, it felt like an actual fall, a sudden immersion into soothing blackness. With the killing of the light that had been falling on the head of the bed, there came an end to the images and thoughts that had continued to plague his conscious mind. He let himself drift now to a deeper, darker, more sensual level, let himself revel in the feel of Nancy's hand—and then both of her hands, as she straddled him—lifting his shirt up and over his shoulders, kneading his flesh between her fingers, lightly raking her nails along his spine. He felt her sitting—perching, really—on the back of his thighs, leaning forward to press his shoulder blades, leaning back to trail her fingers down his rib cage. He could feel her knees clamped to the outside of his legs, and when she ran one fingertip in a horizontal line across his lower back, he longed to feel her reach around and under him and with those fine white fingers, with the sharp, attentive nails, unfasten his belt. He longed to roll over, lift that tawny sweater up and over her head, and take her naked body between his hands.

But even as he dreamed of taking her in his arms, of rolling over and making love to her, he felt himself falling ever closer to sleep, felt his energy ebbing into the mattress. The nap he'd taken after the matinee was the first deep sleep he'd had in days; it had whetted his appetite, refreshed his taste for that necessary oblivion. Now he was torn between desire and exhaustion, Nancy's ministrations at once exciting his ardor and driving him deeper into that torpor his body craved. He willed himself to awaken and make love to her, but willing and doing were not the same. Or were they? He was no longer sure what he was actually doing and what he was only imagining, what was real and what was fantasy. His body and mind felt so numbed with pleasure, with simple sensation. Had he in fact rolled over? Was he holding Nancy's breasts, unseen in the dark but small and soft, in the palms of his hands? He didn't recall taking her clothes off her, but now she was naked; he didn't recall undressing himself, but he was naked too. Time seemed to have stood still. The room, with the heavy curtains drawn, was pitch black. Everything seemed to be moving in slow motion, sometimes even replaying itself. He saw himself lifting the sweater over her head, as if it hadn't already been done; he felt her hands fumbling at his belt buckle, as if his pants weren't already off. He felt as if several hours had passed, and he had started and stopped many times. He wondered why she wasn't speaking to him, and when he asked, he was surprised to see she was kneeling in the middle of a yellow spiral, surrounded by little white houses with roofs like mushroom caps. "Ask the wizard," she was saying, and all around him he heard a confused babble of voices, laughing, mocking him, urging him on. He wanted her desperately, but whose voices were these? How could he take her with these invisible witnesses watching his every move? "Don't worry about them," Nancy was saying, "they're all dead anyway."

Jack was appalled—was she telling him the truth?—but relieved too. If Nancy didn't care, why should he? If they were dead anyway, what did it matter? Nancy took his hands and drew him down to his knees; still, he loomed above her. He cradled the back of her head, his fingers entwined in the shiny black hair, as she kissed his neck, and then his chest. Her shoulders, bare, were so white and delicate. He watched the play of the bone beneath the smooth, white skin, watched it flex and settle and roll. He spread one hand across her back, nearly spanning the width of her body, and pressed her closer against him. Her cheek was flat against his chest now; he could feel her breath on one nipple. And then her tongue, flicking at it. The voices of the dead people whispered in his ear. But he shook his head fiercely, to discourage them from

talking. Nancy slid herself beneath him, laying her head down
on the sparklingly clean yellow brick. It makes a sort of halo,
Jack thought. "Oh, no, you're the angel," Nancy said, reading
his mind. He smiled—God, how good it felt to be so understood—and bent down to kiss her. At first her lips were
closed against him, then they parted and he tasted her hot
breath entering his own mouth. With it came a flood of pictures, writhing dragons in green and gold, snow falling on a
field of poppies, red steel girders raised in the shape of a
pagoda. *So this is what it's like to kiss a Chinese girl.* She
wriggled her hips beneath him, and opened her legs. He put
one hand between them. My God, how he wanted her! He
watched as she licked the palm of her own hand, from heel to
fingers, and then reached down to hold and stroke his shaft.
This was no dream, this was real; he could feel each finger as
it wrapped itself around him, teasing him, provoking him,
making him wet. He thrust his tongue deeply into her mouth,
fetching up a moan that reverberated in his own throat. She
pumped his shaft, stiffening it, and he suddenly couldn't wait
any longer; lowering himself on top of her, he pulled back his
hips, then pressed forward, forward to enter her.

But he was rubbing against something granular and dry and
ungiving—the spotless bricks—no, the sheet. He could feel
the wrinkles abrading his skin. He pulled back again, afraid he
would come before he had entered her, and tried again. But
again he was caught in twists of bedding, pressing himself
into folds of cotton. "Guide me," he whispered, "guide me."
Her fingers enclosed him, gently but firmly, and he slid forward, smoothly, effortlessly, as if forever. He slid forward,
fully extended, into the warmth and buried darkness. He
ground his hips down, hard against her, and before he could
stop, before he could prolong it, felt himself coming, in one
long, low, shuddering spasm. His whole body froze, became
rigid for twenty or thirty seconds; then, a sudden shiver
coursed the length of his spine. "Jesus," he sighed, and found
the sound of his own voice oddly intrusive, as if it had come
from somewhere else. Nancy's arms were coiled loosely
around his shoulders. On his loins he felt the sticky heat of his
own semen; on his back, a faint, cool breeze . . . that gradually
chilled him. He wished that Nancy would rub some warmth
into him. Wasn't she getting cold, he wondered? He tried to

embrace her more closely, but all he felt was the sheet again —and a tightly packed clump of pillow. Where had she gone? What had happened to her? The wet patch around his groin was growing slightly uncomfortable; he rolled over, but the dampness clung to him. Was the sheet stuck to his skin? He reached down to free it, and collided with his belt buckle, hanging loose. And his pants, unzipped, and pushed only partway down. When he reached for Nancy's arm, still resting under his head, he found only his own unbuttoned shirt, hopelessly knotted up. What the hell was . . . He turned to the clock; the fluorescent dial said 3:45. Only the faintest silhouettes of his dresser and chair, stereo cabinet and card table, were discernible in the darkness. He fumbled, back-hand, for the light, and blinked when it came on.

He was alone. The bed was a mess.

"Nancy?" He knew there was no one in the room.

But he had felt, so strongly, that someone was there . . . until only moments ago.

He rubbed his eyes, and threw his legs over the side of the bed. His shirt began to untangle itself, and slowly slip down his back.

He must have fallen asleep during the massage; Nancy must have tiptoed out; he must have just now had his first wet dream in years.

Jesus. It had all been *so real*.

He undid his wristwatch—man, he'd never even gotten that off—and put it on the bedside table. Right beside a rolled-up *Steamroller* program.

Nancy's, he thought, before remembering that Nancy hadn't seen the show that night.

He unrolled it, curious, and a slip of paper fluttered out and onto the floor. He picked it up.

Management regrets to announce that Gregory Wheelwright will not appear in this afternoon's performance.

His role will be played instead by Templeton True.

chapter seventeen

OF COURSE IT would be the one morning she came in late that all hell would break loose at the institute. There were three slide packets waiting for her at the security desk, her own desk upstairs was covered with loose mail and several pink "While You Were Out" slips, the phone was ringing persistently the whole time she hung up her coat, and from Sprague's inner office—and this was the most surprising thing—she heard several voices in earnest conversation. Sprague never made appointments at this hour. He never made them at all if he could avoid it.

"That you, Liu?" he hollered.

"Yes," she said, poking her head in the doorway. Two women turned—one was Arlette Stein, red curls bobbing; the other was a pretty blonde who looked vaguely familiar.

"Get the damn phone. And three coffees, all black."

He went back to what he'd been saying to the two women.

Nancy returned to her desk, fuming, and grabbed the phone.

It was Jack. "Geez, bite my head off why don't you?" he said.

"Oh, God, I'm sorry." She lowered her voice. "I got in late, and Sprague's being an asshole."

"I got your note." He'd found it stuck to the metal rim of the medicine chest. "You can tell the asshole I'll be in, as requested, this afternoon."

"Good—that's one thing going right."

"And I'm sorry too—about zonking out on you last night."

"Yeah," she said, laughing softly, "some testimonial to my charms."

He tried to laugh along. "What happened anyway? Did I just fall asleep while you were rubbing my back?"

"If sleep is what you want to call it," she said. "You acted like you were knocked out."

"And nothing happened?"

"You mean between us? Not while I was there . . . I just tiptoed out, making sure the door was locked behind me."

From his silence, it seemed like he was unconvinced.

"Why?" she asked. "Are you pregnant?" He laughed, thank God, and suddenly Sprague was hollering something about the coffee. "I've gotta run," she whispered. "See you later."

She brewed the coffee in the lab across the hall, using a Bunsen burner, and carried the cups in on a stainless-steel dissection tray. This was just the sort of menial chore she had sworn to herself she would never do. As a token protest, she didn't stop to offer the tray around, but simply pushed it onto Sprague's littered desk and turned to leave the room.

"Hi, Nance," said Arlette, reaching past her to claim one of the foam cups. "I'd like you to meet a friend of mine, Bonnie Robb. Maybe you've seen her on channel four."

So that's why the blonde had looked familiar. Nancy offered her hand.

"Have you been assisting on the Logan case?" Robb asked, hanging on to Nancy's hand. Maybe this was something they taught reporters, Nancy thought—hang on to your quarry any way you can.

"Miss Liu helps me with my research and recordkeeping," Sprague inserted. He managed to make it sound like washing the floors. "Several calls came in earlier," he said to Nancy. "Call them back and see what they were about."

Robb relinquished her hand, and Nancy excused herself. Damn him, she thought; he had no right to treat her like that. She yanked out her desk chair, sat down, and started combing through the packages, mail, and finally, the phone slips, that had accumulated. The calls were all recorded in Sprague's own inimitable scrawl. "Baldwin," and a phone number; "Merck," and another; neither name rang any bells. The third slip said "Investigator—Mansfield." Investigator? What kind of investigator?

And what, now that she had a moment to collect herself and think, was that TV reporter doing up here? Why had she asked if Nancy had assisted on "the Logan case"? Good God, was Sprague angling for a guest shot on some TV show? And was he planning to drag Jack into it?

She pretended to be attending to the slide packets she'd brought up, while listening through the open doorway to the conversation in Sprague's office. It had a kind of summary tone to it, as if they'd already agreed on most of the major premises and were now just confirming the details. Arlette was saying something about Adolph Zakin, that she was reasonably confident she could persuade him to cooperate: "His whole thing was that this was good news, as far as he could tell, and that the world ought to know about it. I think I can talk him into it." There was some discussion of his health, and lucidity, and Arlette again said she could "deliver the goods." Bonnie Robb, and now Nancy recognized even her voice, that clipped no-nonsense cadence from the evening news, was reciting dates and times, and Sprague was yeaing and naying. Tuesday, at five-thirty, was eventually agreed upon. For what, exactly? But that had apparently already been discussed. There was the sound of notebooks being closed and stuffed in bags. Bonnie Robb was saying, "Mind if I take this coffee along with me?" and then, standing near the open doorway, asking Sprague if he was sure about Logan.

"I'll be seeing him this afternoon," Sprague replied. "No problem."

On the way out, Robb stopped to give Nancy another of her resolute handshakes—she wasn't quite as good-looking as she appeared on television, but still, not bad—and Arlette unwrapped a fresh stick of gum and tossed the wrapper in the wastebasket.

"Want one?" she said, offering the Dentyne pack to Nancy.

"No thanks."

"See ya." And she scurried out after her friend.

Nancy was just reaching for the phone slips when Sprague bellowed "What about those calls?" from his desk.

"I'm answering them now." Then, before she could stop

herself, added, "You took the messages—why didn't you find out why they were calling?"

"Because," he said, and she could hear the wheels on his desk chair rolling back, "I was busy." He came through the door and plopped an open copy of the *Post* on her desk. "I was attending to this."

There was an article circled with a red magic marker. "Adolph Zakin—Back to Work and Back to Life."

"Yesterday's paper," Sprague said. "Tulley had to show it to me."

Nancy was quickly scanning the piece.

"Call back the *Investigator* first. See what kind of story they're planning."

"You mean it's the tabloid?" Nancy saw it on the supermarket check-out rack: usually the headline had something to do with UFOs or miracle diets. "You're not planning to talk to them about Jack, are you?"

Sprague pursed his lips and looked as if he were giving it some thought. "Perhaps you're right," he said. "But call them back anyway."

She wished she hadn't reacted so vehemently—and said Jack instead of Logan.

"I am going to have to watch how I channel all this publicity from now on. The institute can stand to gain a lot, from the *right* kinds of stories. And of course," he said, with a sly smile, "we'll want to run these ideas by Jack."

So he hadn't missed her little slip.

"When is Jack coming in today?"

"At two."

"Good. I'll be in the front lab till then. Another brain came in . . . before you got here."

He whirled out, his white lab coat flapping behind him, and Nancy slumped in her chair with relief. She'd really been skating on some thin ice this morning. She'd have to cool it for a while.

Much as she hated to do it, she dutifully returned the call to the *Investigator* and asked for Mansfield. The voice, a man's with a slight English accent, said, "Speaking." When she identified herself, he thanked her profusely for returning his call, mentioned the *Post* piece, and went rattling on about what a great story it would be for the *Investigator* and when could he interview the principals, and what kind of exclusive could they give him and was there someplace particularly "evocative, a hospice or even a nearby cemetery," that could be used for the accompanying photos? It wasn't that he wouldn't take "no" for an answer: he didn't leave time for a "no," a "yes," or even a "maybe." When he did, finally, pause to catch his breath, Nancy said, sounding as much like a dull-witted functionary as possible, that she would give the information to Dr. Sprague and he would get back to him. That didn't satisfy Mansfield at all, and he was off and running again, trying to pin down a time that very day he could come in and "get the ball rolling." Nancy said she would give the information to Dr. Sprague and he would get back to him.

"Listen, dear," Mansfield said, in a confidential but slightly sinister manner, "there are other sources, and other ways, of going about getting this story. I'd prefer, you understand, to get it straight from the horse's mouth, as it were, but if the horse won't talk . . . well, others will."

Nancy wondered who these others might be, but refrained from asking. "I'll give the information to Dr. Sprague and he'll get back to you."

Mansfield didn't exactly hang up on her, but it was close.

Which made returning the other two calls an even less appealing prospect. The Merck number turned out to be the switchboard at a nursing home, and Nancy found herself transferred to the head nurse. When she explained who she was, the nurse clucked her tongue and said, "Mrs. Merck isn't authorized to make outside calls like that. But somehow she always manages. She's here with Alzheimer's. Please ignore the call."

With some misgivings, Nancy did. Poor Mrs. Merck. Nancy dialed the third number, and after eight or nine rings, was about to hang up when a woman answered, breathlessly, with a baby crying in the background.

Nancy went through her spiel again, and the woman hesitated for a moment. "My husband must have called you," she said. The baby started bawling even louder. "I'm sorry, can you hang on for a minute?"

When she returned, making soothing sounds to the baby, she apologized again and said, "Why did they have to discover breast-feeding is better?" She laughed, and said, "Smiling in the face of adversity."

"Is this a bad time to talk?" Nancy asked.

"No, it's okay—though it's Adam I suppose you should really be talking to." There was a rustling sound, as if she were adjusting the phone on her shoulder and the baby at her breast. "He showed me the clipping last night. But he didn't tell me he'd called. Basically—and after six months of knowing, I still don't know how to say this—my husband's dying." Her voice caught for a second. "He's twenty-eight, he has an inoperable brain tumor, and we don't know what to do anymore. He's off chasing some other doctor right now, with a cure made from apricot pits or peanut butter or a secret mixture of ancient herbs...I shouldn't sound so cynical and above it all: I encourage him to go."

"And you're sure he can't be helped with the...usual methods?"

"No, we've been down all those roads, and the answer is always the same. 'Six months to a year, six months to a year.' We've already used up four of the months."

"I'm sorry." Nancy already knew why Baldwin had placed the original call, but felt she had to ask anyway.

"Because he thought this guy mentioned in the article, Jack Logan, might be able to help him. It says he has these mysterious powers. Mysterious powers is what we need right now."

"But Logan isn't a *healer*," Nancy said, as gently as she could. "So far we're not really sure what he is, or what he can do. I'm very sorry about your husband, but honestly, I think your best bet would be to—"

"Betting is all we *can* do," the woman interjected. "Don't you see that? At this point, we can gamble everything, because there's nothing left to lose. So what if this guy doesn't turn out to be Jesus Christ? We've already been through half a dozen guys who claimed to be—and none of them were. And we're no worse off, except for the cash of course, than we were before. We've just got a lot less time left to find the right answer." The baby cried, as if understanding its mother's anguish. Nancy heard her quietly shushing it, and when she came back on the line, she was more composed again. "All we're asking for is a chance. Maybe this Logan guy—or the Dr. Sprague who's studying him—knows something that can help. Maybe they can cure Adam—or maybe they can just bring him back from the dead, when that time comes."

Nancy felt herself shudder.

" 'Maybe' isn't much, but it's better than 'no' . . . Will you help us?"

Nancy was still reeling from the matter-of-fact mention of resurrection. What was happening here? The call from Mrs. Merck, and the *Investigator*, the conference with Bonnie Robb and Arlette—and now this, a straightforward appeal to be *brought back from the dead*. For the first time, Nancy could see a whole confluence of forces emerging, a meshing of motives and needs, of some people's ambition and others' desperation. Was this the first shot in a bombardment yet to come?

And how would Jack, the target of it all, be able to survive?

"I'll speak to Dr. Sprague," Nancy assured her, "and I'm sure he'll discuss your situation with Mr. Logan, too. That's all I can promise you at the moment. Please tell your husband we'll be in touch, whatever happens."

"Thanks. I will." The baby let out a sudden squall. "Time to switch breasts. Thanks for your help—I appreciate it."

Nancy put the phone down and stared off into space. She hadn't begun the day with the clearest head, and now she felt in an absolute fog, genuinely troubled and uneasy. What would she tell Sprague about the Baldwin case? What would he tell Jack? What would *happen*? Again, she saw, opening before them all, an endless panorama of pain and suffering, a world of woe, now beating its way to the court of last resort . . . to the Institute of Abnormal Psychology, where miracles were performed by "the guy with mysterious powers."

The phone on her desk rang, but she didn't have the heart to pick it up. She simply looked at it, with vague apprehension, the way one might a snake in a cage.

At two o'clock sharp, Jack checked in at the downstairs security desk. As he scribbled his name in the register, something he'd done a dozen times, he noticed that Tulley, who usually paid no attention to him, today was watching him closely.

"How are you doing?" Jack said.

"Can't complain."

This was about as sociable as he'd ever been.

"You know, I read something about you in the paper the other day."

Jack slid the pen and clipboard back across the desk to him.

"Said you brought this rich guy back to life. That why you're here?"

"Yeah. I guess it is."

"It true?"

That one Jack didn't have such an easy answer for. "Did I bring a guy back to life?" he said, buying a little time. "What do you think?"

"I don't think—that's why I'm askin'."

Fair enough. Jack gave him a kind of knowing smile, and said, "Just between us, I wouldn't believe everything I read in the papers."

On the way up in the elevator, he thought, "Well, you've ducked the question one more time." But how many more times could he duck it? How many more times could he tell people there was nothing to it, or imply that the press was just out to sell papers? He felt that, at any moment now, the truth would be found out, the truth that he himself had been grappling with, and trying to accept, for weeks.

But Christ Almighty, how did you accept such a thing? And if you did, how did you live with it?

The elevator bumped to a halt at the top floor. Just seeing Nancy, bent like a jeweler over an array of slides spread across a light box, gave him a little lift.

"Pictures from summer camp?" he said.

She looked up from the hand-held magnifier. "I didn't hear you come in." She smiled. "I was so absorbed in these terrific pix."

"Oh yeah?" He took the magnifier and studied the same slide she'd been looking at. What he saw was a complex network of fine black lines, set against a pale purple background.

"Looks like tree branches, in winter." He looked up. "But I guess it's not." Their faces were only inches apart.

"You're right," she said, "it's not."

He could feel her breath on his face.

"It's a neuron, magnified four hundred times. The things that look like trees are dendrites."

"I should have guessed."

She didn't move away, and neither did he.

"Dendrites funnel electrical signals to the cell."

He watched the way her lips moved.

"Enough signals and the neuron fires."

"That's obvious."

Should he kiss her? The place was wrong, the time was wrong . . . but the opportunity was here. He had one arm resting on the back of her chair.

"Then what happens?"

She took a breath. "The neuron emits its own electrical pulse, down—"

He kissed her, lightly, quickly, one hand resting against her back.

She didn't respond to it. But he had hardly left her time to. She was looking at him very seriously.

"—down something called an axon . . . Do you need to know more?"

"No," he said, leaning forward to kiss her again. This time her lips came up to meet his. His hand slipped up to gently cradle the back of her head; her hair felt like silk, fine smooth silk, in his hand. If only this weren't happening here, now, he thought . . . if only he could roll back time, to last night in his apartment. There, they had no reason to stop, and nothing to interfere.

She took her lips away from his, and dropped her eyes. The dull white glare of the light box lit her face from below, and suddenly made him want to look away. The light was disconcertingly flat and empty. He straightened up, unbuttoning his overcoat, and saw Sprague standing directly across the hall, in the open doorway of his lab.

How long had he been standing there?

An earthenware jar, with a silver handle, dangled from two of his long, bony fingers, and he looked, to Jack, like some awful parody of a kid with his beach pail. He lifted his chin and the jar in unison, as if in greeting.

"Afternoon, Dr. Sprague," Jack replied, as much to alert Nancy as anything else. She instantly returned to sorting slides on the lightbox. "Is it okay if I ask what's in the jar?" He wanted to gain her a couple more seconds to compose herself.

"Of course you may," Sprague said, coming across the

hall. Jack noticed he was careful to keep the jar from swinging. "It's all that's left—and in some respects all there ever was—of a male homicide suspect." Sprague rested the jar, gingerly, on Nancy's desk. "It's his brain." He smiled, wolfishly, and a vision of sweetbreads, as Mam had sometimes served them when he was a boy, flashed across Jack's mind; when he'd gotten older, and discovered what they were, he had steadfastly refused to eat them. "It's part of my research on cortical abnormalities," Sprague explained.

"Part of your research is about to escape," Jack said, pointing out a loose clamp hanging from the lid.

"I know," said Sprague, "it's broken. So is my scale—I lent it last week to one of those idiots downstairs and now I could swear it's off. I'm going down to weigh this specimen now. Why don't you come? I don't think you've ever seen very much of the institute."

Jack had never known Sprague to be so affable. "Sure. I'll just leave my coat up here." He turned his back to Sprague while taking it off, hoping to catch Nancy's eye, but she resolutely refused to look up from her work.

"Come on." Sprague gently lifted the jar from the desk, but instead of heading for the elevators, went straight to the opposite end of the corridor, where a steel door was marked with a red-and-white sign that said FIRE EXIT ONLY—ALARM WILL SOUND. He turned the handle, then butted it open with his shoulder. No alarm went off.

"Can't stand to wait for the elevators," Sprague said, "so I neutered the alarms."

Jack followed him into a cold, concrete stairway. They went down two flights, Sprague carrying the jar upraised like a lantern to keep it from banging into the iron handrail, and then in through another "neutered" door. The stench was overpowering.

"It's worst at this end," Sprague said. "The ventilation system blows everything this way before it goes out of the building."

It smelled like a zoo that hadn't been cleaned in years—a noxious mix of animal and chemical odors, fermenting in a contained space. There were long rows of metal cages, stacked on top of each other, and in them a veritable menagerie—rats, pigeons, dogs, cats, snakes, monkeys; the monkeys reached out through the bars as Jack passed, one of them succeeding in snatching his sleeve.

"Whoa there," Jack said, yanking the cloth away from the tiny, grasping fingers. The monkey screeched—in disappointment?—then fixed him with a baleful look. Sprague was already at the far end of the room, leveling accusations at two young men in filthy lab coats.

"Its tolerance can be disturbed by anything greater than eight pounds. What the hell did you weigh with it—an elephant?"

"We don't have any elephants," said the one with the brown beard; the other's was black. "We used it for a couple of snakes."

"Pythons?" Sprague shot back.

"Garden-variety stuff, no more than five or six pounds at best. Hello," he said, extending a hand to Jack. "Bill Potter."

His hand was grimy, and slightly damp.

"Vladimir Cazenovia," said the one with the black beard, in an accent right out of a Cold War spy movie.

"Jack Logan."

Both of them suddenly stopped to appraise him. Sprague, noting it, barreled ahead.

"I assume your own scale is in working order again—"

"It is."

"Then I want to reweigh a specimen and see how it checks out against my first measurement."

"Feel free. Caz and I have work to do." Potter and Cazenovia ambled off to a table in the corner, covered with a Plexiglas shield, and sat beside it on two high metal stools.

"Incompetents," Sprague muttered under his breath. He drew from a lower shelf a clean metal tray with its own weight calibration etched into the rim, then undid the clamps on the jar. There was a label on the jar, a white sticker with something typed on it, but Sprague had turned it so that Jack couldn't make it out.

"Ever seen a brain?" he said, removing the lid.

"Nope."

"Then you're in for a treat." He said it as if he meant it. After rolling up his sleeve, he reached into the jar and scooped out the contents—a wet, quivering lump, mottled gray and pink; Jack felt a slight twinge of nausea.

"It's fresh as can be," Sprague said, holding it up to the light. "Normally you have to wait a couple of weeks for it to solidify the way you want, but I wanted this one as close to the actual death as possible." To Jack's horror, he inhaled deeply, as if savoring a bouquet of roses. "This one's rather special."

He placed it on the tray, waited a few seconds for it to settle, then bent, with his glasses on the end of his nose, to study the exact measurement. While he made a note of it on a pad taken from his breast pocket, he asked Jack if there was anything new to report, any sensations, problems, physical or psychological effects.

The day before, in all its awful glory, reared up again, but *what* could he actually confess to? To playing so badly at the show that he'd had to be replaced (a short, and temporary, leave of absence)? To seeing his mother—his *dead* mother—clapping wildly from a nonexistent seat? To getting a back rub from Nancy Liu—and waking up hours later to a bizarrely real *wet dream*?

"Well?" Sprague said, still making notes on his pad. A dog barked, twice, from one of the cages at the far end of the room.

"Nothing much." He pretended to be interested in the notes Sprague was taking. "What are you recording?

"Color, texture, anomalies." Sprague pulled a set of stainless steel calipers from the hip pocket of his lab coat. "You didn't answer my question, and you haven't been looking good lately. Is something affecting you that you haven't told me about?"

Jack was torn between his reluctance to appear like he was falling apart, and a growing need to unburden himself, to spill everything—no matter how crazy it sounded—and let Sprague attempt to make some sense of it. Too much was happening to him, and too fast, and he was increasingly unsure he could control it. But should he confide in Sprague? Was he the best—or the worst—person to turn to?

"Nothing I haven't already mentioned, to you and to Nancy Liu—the trouble sleeping, the aversion to bright lights. That cold, metallic smell once in a while."

"Nothing more?" Sprague was holding the calipers, pincers open, to both sides of the brain on the scale.

"I lost my job." There—he'd confessed to something.

Sprague looked at him over the top of his glasses.

"Temporarily," Jack added. "But I've been so out of it, ever since that episode with Garcia, I've been playing every third note wrong."

The dog at the far end barked again, and a second dog picked it up, yapping excitedly.

"What happened with Garcia," Sprague said, slowly, deliberately, "may have revolutionary consequences. The whole world may change as a result of the research we're doing here. *The whole world.* I'm sorry you've lost your job for a few days, but the trade-off, to my mind, seems more than worth it."

Why did Sprague always have to get him wrong? "I wasn't saying that," Jack replied. "I'm glad I could save the guy's life . . . It's just that I'm having trouble dealing with . . . all those consequences you mentioned."

Sprague removed the calipers, and in an awkwardly paternal gesture, put one hand on Jack's shoulder. "That's why I'm here," he said. "To help you deal with them. To help you discover the source, and the extent, of your unprecedented powers. It's fortunate—*amazingly* fortunate—that you and I have found each other. You may be the only person in the world capable of doing what you do, and I may be the only person capable of understanding it."

The two dogs had been joined by a chorus of others, and the monkeys were chattering loudly and swinging from the bars of their cages. Potter and Cazenovia had gotten up from their stools and wandered over to see what was wrong.

"Did you remember to bring me your birth certificate?" Sprague said, glancing over Jack's shoulder at the growing commotion.

"I don't have it. Mam—my grandmother—does. I can go out there tomorrow and fetch it."

"Good," Sprague said, distractedly. "Do. What's wrong with those goddamned animals?" he shouted at the other two scientists, who were standing in the midst of all the turmoil, looking puzzled.

"Got me," Potter said, lifting his hands. Even the pigeons were flapping their wings. The stirred-up air was making the lab smell worse by the second.

Jack felt a shiver—a reaction to the awful odor?—pass down his spine . . . and he noticed a low buzzing in his ears. He almost felt a little faint.

"Somesing has disturbed zem," intoned Cazenovia, turning slowly, mystified, in the aisle.

"Brilliant," Sprague muttered. He shoved the calipers back into his pocket. "I've got one other thing to discuss with you," he said to Jack, "but this is clearly no place to do it. We'll go back upstairs."

The buzzing in his ears was more persistent now, like static. And he thought, beneath it, he could detect a voice, straining to be heard.

"You'll have to help me with this," Sprague said, "it's settled." He slipped his hands under the brain on the scale, in preparation for lifting it. "Hold the jar over here."

As the wet mass was gently separated from the tray, Jack could swear he heard a voice, still indecipherable, whispering in his skull. Male this time, and guttural . . .

A dog let out a yowl like a wolf baying at the moon.

"Hold the jar over here," Sprague repeated insistently.

Jack lifted the jar, the label turned away, and held it out toward Sprague. The preserving solution—formaldehyde?—sloshed around inside it.

"Hold it *still*," Sprague admonished him.

Jack was trying, but he felt more faint all the time, and the voice was growing louder. At the moment Sprague slid the brain down into the dark interior, the voice broke through the barrier of static, hissing, almost spitting, one word in Jack's ear: *Diablo!*

And Jack knew, without even looking at the label, whose brain was in the jar.

chapter eighteen

WHEN DAWN BROKE, he was sitting at the card table, sipping a cup of decaffeinated instant. He watched, silently, as lights went on, here and there, in the apartment building behind his. Around seven or so, a woman with nothing on scampered up to her open window, threw it down, and scampered away again. At eight, the elderly twins turned on their TV set, and the heavyset writer settled into her desk chair. At eight-thirty, the gay dancer lifted his shades and did some warmup exercises.

His own bed was rumpled, but not slept-in. He'd lain down, playing Coltrane over the headphones for a while, but closing his eyes was an invitation to trouble. Thoughts came . . . and possibly worse. He'd gotten up again.

Not that that had stopped them; all night he'd sat brooding over the events of the past few weeks. Nothing in his life was the same anymore—his old girlfriend was gone, his job was in jeopardy, Mam's health was worse (when he'd called about his birth certificate, her voice had been alarmingly weak and paper-thin); everything in his life felt as if it was coming apart at the seams, and he feared, most of all, that his mind might be following suit.

Now *that* was a conundrum worth puzzling over: how did you decide, with a mind you weren't sure was sound anymore, if your mind was still sound? Talk about a dog chasing its own tail. Saving Adolph Zakin, he felt now, had cracked open some sort of door in him; saving Ruben Garcia (though what for, now?) had kicked it open completely. What that door was, where it had come from, and what was likely to pass through it next—none of that was clear to him. But the possibilities—hadn't he already *seen* his mother? *heard* Garcia?—made his mind do backflips and his heart beat harder in his chest.

In the vacant space—you could hardly call it a yard—between his building and the next, a dog chased a pigeon off a packing crate. He glanced at his watch—nine-twenty. If he was ready to abandon all hope of sleep, he could head out to Weehawken now.

He abandoned all hope.

Outside, the cold air actually made him feel a little better, momentarily clearing his head and lungs. It would take about an hour, but he decided to walk to the Port Authority bus station. What else did he have to do today?

On the way down, he took Columbus Avenue, and browsed in the trendy shop windows as he went. Most of them had some sort of Christmas trappings—red-and-white candy canes, glittering ornaments, colorful lights. It occurred to him that he hadn't bought anything for anyone, and then it occurred to him that aside from Mam and Clancy, who else was there to buy for? For some reason, he found himself staring into a toy store window where they had one of those inflatable figures, about four feet high, that has sand in the bottom and rocks back and forth when you punch it. He'd had one of a clown when he was a kid; this one was a smiling doctor, in a white lab coat. Lab coats made him think of Sprague, and Sprague made him think of Nancy. Wouldn't she think it was fun to have her very own Sprague to punch in the nose whenever she felt like it?

He went inside, and once he'd made sure it came in an uninflated state, bought it. The thought of giving it to her made him smile now and then, all the way to the bus station.

The ride out, against the morning rush, was relatively quick and painless. Had it been longer, he might almost have fallen asleep—the combination of the long walk to the station, the warmth of the bus, and the humming of the engine made him feel pleasantly drowsy and light-headed.

He got off the bus one stop early, to enjoy a short walk along Boulevard East. On his right, about a hundred feet down and the same distance over, ran the steel-gray Hudson

River. At an observation point, Jack stopped and, resting his elbows on the rail, looked out, over the blackened piers that jutted from the New Jersey side, and across the water to New York . . . where everyone went to get famous, even if only for fifteen minutes. Sprague, he reflected, had offered him his fifteen minutes the day before, and he had refused. Everything had already been arranged—he was to appear in a live interview with Bonnie Robb on the local newscast—but Jack had said no as soon as Sprague had brought it up. "Why?" Sprague had demanded, and even Jack had had to think about it before he knew.

"Because I'm not some performing seal," he'd said. "If I go on that show with you and Zakin, I'll feel like some freak, some stuntman who brings people back from the dead when he hasn't got anything better to do. And I'll feel like a fake too—I still don't know exactly what I can and can't do, and neither do you. But that's not what channel four will say; I've seen those shows. If they don't decide to expose me as some sort of fraud, they'll have me sounding like the Messiah before they're through. And if *that* happens, we'll have every nut-case, and every terminal hospital patient, in New York calling in."

"We already have had a few of those."

"I rest my case."

"Then let me make mine. No, we haven't ascertained all that you can do, or, for that matter, how you do it. Can you restore life after it's been gone for hours, or even days? Can you actually cure people of terminal ailments? Do you have to be in physical contact for your powers to work? No, we don't know those answers yet. But we're getting there; every test we do, even if it proves negative, eliminates one more possibility —and eventually we'll arrive at the right tests, and the right answers. In the meantime, maybe we *can* offer hope to people who are dying, or who feel there's no meaning to life as we live it."

"You mean people like Ruben Garcia?"

That had stopped him for a moment. He'd licked his lips, as if wondering what Jack might know, before saying, "Garcia has since died."

"And he was a suspected murderer?"

"No, I don't know what gave you that idea. He's a suspected homicide *victim*."

Had Jack gotten it wrong? "Be that as it may, he's dead now. And that was his brain we just weighed downstairs."

Sprague hadn't bothered to deny it.

"So what good did it do for me to save him? What good does it do for me to save anyone? We're all going to die one day—we're *supposed* to die, for God's sake! Who am I to go running around changing things, bringing back one guy and letting another one rot, making life-and-death decisions over people I don't even know, thwarting, for all I know, some kind of divine plan?"

"Maybe you *are* some part of a divine plan," Sprague had retorted. "Did that ever occur to you—that what we're uncovering at the institute is something that's now *meant* to be uncovered, and broadcast to the world?"

If what he'd wanted was to unsettle him, he'd succeeded. Jack felt like he'd been rocked back onto his heels.

"I won't press you about the show next Tuesday. Just give it a little more thought . . . And I still want that copy of your birth certificate."

His birth certificate . . . and whatever clues *that* might provide. Jack watched now as a huge ocean liner slowly made its way down the river and out to sea. What would there be on his birth certificate to interest Sprague? Mam had asked him why he needed it, and Jack had said he wanted to get a passport. That, of course, had prompted her to ask where he was planning to go, and Jack had had to make up something about a possible trip to Mexico with his friend Vinnie, from the show. Fortunately, by now she'd probably forgotten everything about the cover story, and if he was lucky, the birth certificate business, too. She'd said it was probably stashed in a trunk in the attic, and he'd go up there and find it on his own. Mam would just think he'd come for a visit.

A young Hispanic couple, holding hands, joined him at the observation rail, and Jack bequeathed it to them. He thought again of the inflatable toy he was carrying for Nancy. He walked the two blocks to the house, and when he got there, carted the empty garbage can away from the front curb—pickup was still apparently on Friday morning—and dragged it around to the side of the house. A lace curtain was pulled back as he did so, and he saw Clancy looking out.

"Morning, sir," Jack called. "Part of our new sanitation policy—replacing the can."

Clancy dropped the curtain, and by the time Jack came around to the front, he had left the door open.

"Keep your voice down," he said from the kitchen. "Mam had a bad night, and she's still sleeping."

Jack hung his coat on a peg in the hall, went back to the kitchen where Clancy was sitting at the table with the *Bergen Record* spread out in front of him and a mug of instant coffee, the spoon sticking out, in one hand.

"The water's still hot; make yourself some coffee if you want."

Jack did, while Clancy rustled the pages of the paper, then pulled out one of the dinette chairs with striped yellow seats and sat down.

"She had a rough night?"

"Yeah," Clancy replied, taking the spoon from his mug and dropping it on the paper. "When she wakes up, I think I better run her over to the clinic."

"What'll they do?"

"Who knows? Something . . . then send me a bill." He sipped noisily from his mug. "What's up with you?"

Jack left out everything of consequence, told him the show was still hanging in there, that work was fine, that he was even thinking of taking a little vacation in Mexico. Clancy looked as though this was the first he'd heard of it.

"Didn't Mam tell you I was coming out today? I need my birth certificate for the passport office."

"Oh, yeah," Clancy said, leaning back in his chair. "I remember now." He shook his head. "The days all run the hell together now; I don't know if it's Thursday or Friday till I look in the paper. And then, when I do, I think, 'So what?' Makes no difference what day it is. I've got nothing to do."

Jack had heard this lament before . . . and again he suggested Clancy find some hobby he'd enjoy, or look up some other retired workers from the plant and see what they were up to, or find a part-time job that wouldn't interfere with his Social Security benefits. But Clancy had an excuse for every suggestion, a reason why none of it would ever work, and Jack knew, at heart, that Clancy was afraid to leave Mam alone in the house, or for that matter, attended by anyone but himself. But while Clancy was taking care of Mam, who was taking care of Clancy?

"Is that all you're having for breakfast?" Jack asked. "Why don't you let me make you some eggs or something?"

"Nah, I'll do that later, after Mam wakes up. Here," he said, sliding one hand under the outspread paper, "have one of these." He pulled out a half-empty package of Stella D'oro Breakfast Treats.

"I knew something was missing," Jack said, with a laugh. As long as he could remember, Stella D'oro cookies had been a part of Clancy's day. As a boy, Jack had never understood how Clancy could eat them—they had no goop, and weren't nearly sweet enough. "Tell me something," he said, fishing one of the cookies from the box. "Did you always keep these around because you knew I wouldn't raid them?"

"What? These?"

"Because if you did," Jack said, "there's something you should know." He crunched loudly into the cookie. "I like 'em now."

Clancy gave him a level stare, then slowly smiled. "I got 'em," Clancy said, "'cause they were cheap." Looking down to brush some crumbs from the front of his cardigan, he added, "I never even knew you didn't like 'em." He looked up. "Ask Mam if you don't believe me."

"I will," Jack said, "just as soon as she wakes up."

"Well, don't you be the one to wake her. If you're going into the attic, don't make a racket."

"I won't." Jack got up without pushing his chair back, lifting one leg over it. He was anxious to begin the search, and not only for the birth certificate: he wanted to see if there was anything else—photos in particular—of his mother up there, anything that might confirm, or help him to understand some-how, what he thought he'd seen and heard. He crept up the front stairs to the second floor, past the ticking grandfather clock. The moon above the churchyard showed three-quarters full. At Mam's door, which had been left a few inches ajar, he glanced in. But all he could see, without moving the door and risking a loud creak, was the foot of her bed, piled high with comforters. He put his ear to the crack, but he couldn't hear a thing . . . only the ticking of the clock on the landing.

At the far end of the hall, outside Clancy's bedroom, there was a trapdoor in the ceiling, with a braided rope hanging down. Jack gave it a gentle tug, which accomplished nothing, then a less gentle tug, which did: the door dropped down, and Jack made sure it came slowly, noiselessly. He opened out the folding metal stairs, which were attached to its upper surface, and, holding the handrail, climbed up. Dust coated his finger-tips, and the musty cold smell that he remembered from his boyhood, from those rare occasions when he would accompany Mam up here to collect the Christmas tree ornaments or the rotating fan, came back to him in a rush. The attic had always been something of an adventure . . . and at the same time vaguely frightening. Even now, he was glad to find the hanging cord for the overhead light and switch it on; uncovered, the bulb threw a bright, stark light around the cluttered space. The walls were slanted like the roof of the house and between the exposed beams lay gray woolly beds of insulation. As a boy, he had always been deathly afraid of stepping into one of them and falling into a gray, suffocating nowhere land. He thought, for a second, of that night in Garcia's cell, but just as quickly suppressed it. He had more immediate things to think about.

Like where to start looking for the birth certificate. Amid the rest of the junk—the worn-out armchairs, the lampshades, the Christmas boxes, a broken TV set with the antenna sticking straight up—there was a pile of battered old suitcases and a scratched-up steamer trunk. Looking at them, Jack thought it might have been easier, after all, to go the City Hall route, and ask them to dig out a copy of his birth certificate. But he'd come this far, and he'd at least take a shot at unearthing it.

Unzipping the suitcase on the top of the stack, he found it filled with faded linen tablecloths and curtains and pillow-cases. The one underneath it was crammed with old clothes. Why had Mam even bothered to keep this stuff? Lifting the second suitcase off the stack, he cleared the top of the steamer trunk, flipped the latches, and raised the lid. More old clothes, with the same aroma of mothballs, but these were neatly pressed and packed, with tissue between the layers. They were women's clothes, but clearly not Mam's. There were fringed skirts and leather vests, and bulked beneath them, a cloth jacket with white vinyl sleeves. Carefully, Jack removed the jacket from the trunk and held it up to the glaring light. It was very familiar: the navy blue wool, the white piping. On the back, above the school emblem of a snarling wildcat, it said "Weehawken High" in white felt letters, and then "'65."

It was a senior class jacket, the kind Jack had worn too, but this one was smaller, and quite a bit older. This one, he knew, must have belonged to his mother. Along with everything else in the trunk. That would explain why Mam had preserved it all so carefully; these weren't just old clothes. These were memories . . . all she had left of her daughter. For Jack, it was like hitting the mother lode.

Hardly taking his eyes off the open trunk, he dragged one of the armchairs over beside it. He tossed the plastic cover aside, releasing a sudden cloud of dust, and once it had dispersed, sat down. He took the top layer of tissue paper out of the trunk and laid it down on the wooden floorboards. Then, one by one, he lifted the garments out, holding them up in the light, studying them as if he were an archaeologist cataloguing the contents of some ancient, just-discovered tomb. In a way, he thought, that's just what he was doing—rifling the tomb of his mother, to uncover a past that was his own. He studied each piece of clothing for clues; what did the color say about his mother's personality? What did the shape and size say about her body? Why, he wondered in passing, had Mam chosen to select and preserve these particular items? He felt as if he had been presented with a wealth of information, which he had only to properly decode.

There were other things in the trunk too; on the right side, he found a high school yearbook and quickly flipped to the photos in the back. His mother, Mary Elizabeth Logan, had her head tilted back and she was smiling so widely it looked as if she was about to dissolve into laughter. It was a nice photo, but unusual: all the other faces, lining the page above and below her, were more composed, sober. Mary Elizabeth looked as if she thought the whole thing was a joke and she couldn't begin to take it seriously.

Below the yearbook, there was a trophy from a Girl Scout summer camp, a framed diploma, and a red velvet jewelry box. Jack lifted the box out as if it were made of eggshells, and rested it on his knees. He nudged the chair around so that the light from the ceiling fell directly on it, then pried the box open. It wasn't locked, but just sticky with time and disuse. A paper clipping fluttered against the raised lid. It was from St. Ignatius Church, the church Mam and Clancy still attended, and had been neatly scissored on all sides. Flattening it against his palm, Jack saw that it was a special plea to the parishioners to include in their prayers "Mary Elizabeth Logan, victim of a tragic accident, and the unborn child she carries."

Unborn child? Jack sat perfectly still in the chair, trying to absorb it. Unborn child? His mother was pregnant again at the time of her death? He had always been given to understand she had died only a week or two after his birth. Could it have been later than that? How much later? Was he six months old? A year? *Two years?* How far back, he wondered, could children normally remember? Was it possible *he* could actually *remember* his mother, if only he tried hard enough? He could understand why Mam and Clancy might not have mentioned to him that she was pregnant again at the time of her death— what good would that have done—but why hadn't they leveled with him on *when* she died? What difference would that have made?

Listlessly, he dropped the clipping back into the open lid of the box. With one hand, he rummaged through the jewelry inside—beads and barrettes, thin gold necklaces, oversized earrings with feathers attached. A lot of Indian-looking stuff. He half hoped, half feared, he would come across the blue and silver bracelet he thought he'd seen on the wrist of the apparition. But if such a thing ever had existed, it didn't now—at least not in this box.

He closed the lid and put the box back into the trunk. He had lost his taste for exploration today. All he wanted now was to find the birth certificate—if it was even up here—and go back to New York. He filled the steamer trunk with everything he'd taken out, and looked around for any likely place Mam might have stored the papers.

Mam, who'd lied to him about something as important as when his mother had died.

He went through another suitcase—Clancy's old work clothes—and two cardboard cartons filled with cheap glassware and cutlery. He was about to call it a day when he noticed a metal footlocker with BROOKLYN NAVY YARD stenciled on the side. It was peeking out from behind a stack of folded-up tray tables. Should he bother? Clancy, in his youth, had worked at the Navy Yard; the locker probably held his old tools. He was debating what to do when Clancy himself spoke from the hallway below.

"You still up there?"

"Yes." Jack crept to the open hatchway.

"You've got a cold draft blowing down here," Clancy said, still trying to keep his voice low. "I don't want Mam catching a chill."

"Sorry. Fold up the stair for me, and close the door. I can let it down again from this side."

"You sure?"

"Sure." He'd check the footlocker, and *then* call it quits.

Clancy closed him in. It *was* getting cold up here. Jack pulled the foot locker out into the light and shook it; it didn't clang the way it would have if there had been tools inside. If anything, it sort of rustled, as if it did indeed hold paper. Maybe the certificate *was* in here. Talk about the last place you look, Jack thought.

He tried to raise the hasp, but saw then that it was locked. It occurred to him that he could drag it downstairs and go looking for the key with Clancy—or he could look for something to pry it open with then and there. In the box that had held the cutlery, he found a stained old soup spoon with a strong but narrow handle. Wedging the handle under the lock, he pressed outward. At first, the spoon bent, then the lock did. Jack pressed harder, and the lock, already rusted through, disintegrated. Squatting on his heels, he raised the lid, which came up with a rough grating sound, and saw all kinds of papers and documents and receipts loosely jumbled together. Success at last? The first slip he read was a pay stub from April 1956. The next was a Blue Cross form. He started to sift through a lot of it, giving each piece a quick glance before putting it aside. At the bottom, he spotted a manila envelope, with the clasp sealed. He undid it, and poured out the papers inside. These were newspaper clippings, yellowed with age, and roughly torn from wherever they'd been printed. He carefully unfolded a couple, spread them out on the floor, and leaned back to read them in the light falling over his shoulder. The first, probably from the *Bergen Record*, said "Logan Baby Born: Mother Removed from Life-Sustaining Equipment." And the second, which looked as though it had come from some tabloid, had a photo of Jack's mother—the very picture that had run in her yearbook—under a larger photo of a squalling newborn in the arms of a black nurse. The caption read "Jack Patrick Logan, delivered yesterday, getting a lungful of life at last." But it was the headline that knocked Jack backwards, off his heels and onto the dusty wood floor.

MOTHER, DEAD FOR MONTHS, GIVES BIRTH TO SON— MIRACLE BOY APPEARS NORMAL, SAY DOCS!

chapter nineteen

"YOU HAVEN'T SEEN my red shoes, have you?" Nancy asked, from the bottom of their bedroom closet.

"Nope."

Her sister was as helpful as ever.

"You didn't borrow them by any chance, did you?"

"Nope." There was a loud snap, from her chewing gum.

Nancy crawled out again, wearing only a slip, her hair pulled back and held by an elastic band. "You know where else they could be? And don't say nope."

Her sister opened her mouth, about to say just that, then amended it to "Try under my bed. I *might* have seen them there."

Under Linda's bed, Nancy found not only the red shoes she was looking for, but the leg-warmers she thought she'd left at the skating rink.

"How does all *my* stuff wind up under *your* bed?" Nancy said, holding up her discoveries.

"You're careless." She turned a page of *People* magazine.

Nancy got up and continued dressing. The wedding was only an hour from now. Then there was the reception and dinner, and finally, dancing, for the select friends of the bride and groom, at the Underground. Nancy didn't often go to clubs and discos, and she was looking forward to going to this one.

"Who's taking you tonight?" Linda asked.

"Nobody." Nancy unfastened her hair and fluffed it out with her fingers.

"Nobody? Not even Phillip Chen?"

"Chen's meeting me there."

"So Chen's taking you."

"He's *meeting* me," Nancy reiterated—though Chen was probably looking at it the same way Linda did.

"That why you're wearing your red silk dress, with the slit up the side?"

Nancy had pulled off the dry cleaner's plastic and was turning the dress on the hanger, looking for flaws. "I'm wearing the red silk because the only other decent dress I have, you borrowed two weeks ago and forgot to—"

The phone rang, and Linda picked it up. "May I ask who's calling?" she said, in an overly sweet tone. "One minute, please." She extended it to Nancy, with an interested smile.

"Chen?" Nancy whispered.

"You'll see."

"Thanks." Nancy took the phone, said, "Hello?"

It was Jack. "Hope I'm not catching you at a bad time," he said, "but you know how many Lius there are in the phone book? Took me a half hour to find you."

"How did you?"

"I remembered you lived on Chatham Square. That narrowed it down a lot . . . Who was that who answered?"

"My sister."

Linda mouthed "Who is this guy?" and Nancy fluttered her hand in dismissal. Why was he calling? she wondered. She glanced at her wristwatch—it was five-fifteen, on a Saturday night.

"How are you doing?" she asked, for want of anything better to say.

"Good . . . fine." He seemed to be searching for words himself. "Listen—I know it's kind of last minute, but I was wondering if you were free tonight—for dinner, a movie, anything? I'm sort of at loose ends, and I'd like to get out of the house." Then, perhaps realizing he hadn't issued the most flattering invitation, he said, "I'd like to see you."

It was just what she wanted to hear, and just when she didn't want to hear it. Her sister was studying her face as if it were a hieroglyph.

"Tonight, I'm afraid, isn't good," she said. She explained about the wedding—"it's one of my oldest friends, from grammar school"—and the dinner, and the party afterwards. He left a long pause when she'd finished.

"What time will that party end?" he asked. "I'm a real night owl, and I could catch up with you afterward."

Why was he being so persistent about this one night? "I don't know," she said. "It's at the Underground—some of the people from the wedding are going to meet there, in something called the Torch Room, at eleven. It'll probably run pretty late."

"Great," he said, "I'll meet you at the Underground. I've been there before, and I know where the Torch Room is. I just really need to see you tonight."

There was something funny about his voice, Nancy realized; he was acting very chipper and upbeat, but it didn't sound convincing. He sounded . . . desperate, as though he didn't want her to know how much he needed this. Her mind was racing; should she just agree to it? What would she do with Phillip Chen?

"Is that okay?" Jack asked, eager but, again, a little strained.

Her sister had decided this was all much more interesting than *People* and was waiting anxiously for the full scoop.

"I guess so," Nancy said. "Sure. I can meet you there." Maybe Chen didn't consider it a date, either. "Anytime after eleven."

She had hardly hung up before her sister pounced. "It's a friend, just a friend," Nancy insisted as she flew into the rest of her clothes. "Don't try to make some big deal out of it." But Linda loved it anyway, feeling she'd glimpsed the outlines of some red-hot romantic triangle. She could hardly wait for the next installment.

For that matter, neither could Nancy. She ran out the door, still buttoning her coat, and got to the church in the nick of time. Why did tonight have to be the night Jack needed to see her? Chen was already there, and yes, he was holding a place on the pew for her. He helped her off with her coat, complimented her on her dress. He was such a nice guy, Phillip Chen; she'd known him since grammar school too. They'd even made out a few times in the eighth grade. But now he'd come back to New York, armed with an MBA from Wharton, and he seemed determined to put the rest of his life in order—

and that included a wife, from the old neighborhood, to help him set up a proper Chinese household. Nancy knew that, if she ever came around to marrying him, he'd want her pregnant one week later.

The bride, Amy Wong, was marrying an Italian guy, whose family lived on Mulberry Street, so the guests on either side of the aisle were an interesting mix—mostly Chinese on Amy's side, mostly Italians on Battaglia's. Phillip leaned close to Nancy, and asked if they were Mafia. "If they are," Nancy whispered, "they're not very good at it—the Battaglias live in a third-floor walk-up, and from what Amy tells me, Joey could barely scrape together the money for the tuxedo."

"What's he do?"

"Something in an art department, for a magazine. *Esquire*, I think."

That gave Phillip plenty to think about: *Esquire*, on the one hand, sounded fairly respectable. But art department sounded, well, dubious. And not having money for your formal wear, that plainly spelled trouble. Phillip worried for a second about Amy's choice, before pondering again his own.

Nancy left him to it, looking around to see who else was there, smiling at some friends, exchanging a few words with the chubby young woman beside her, who turned out to be one of Amy's distant cousins. She was wearing very wet, very purple, lipstick, and said she worked "in the fashion industry." Nancy didn't pursue it.

The wedding itself was standard-issue Catholic—Amy, never the prettiest girl in her class, looking radiant in a long, white dress; and Joey, whom Nancy had never seen in anything but the funkiest sort of clothes, in a black tuxedo. It was only when he turned, to escort his bride down the aisle, that Nancy saw he was wearing a brilliant diamond stud in one ear.

The reception and dinner were across the street, in a common room owned and operated by the church, and the two families had apparently decided to team up on the cooking; there was a long buffet table laden with the most eclectic cuisine—mountains of crispy spring rolls, beside a steaming tureen of lentil soup, next to a tray of fried shrimp, beside a lasagna easily a yard long and a yard wide. In her own informal survey, Nancy noted that the Italians ate chiefly the Chinese food, and the Chinese ate chiefly Italian. She wondered whether it was just to be polite, or because they enjoyed the change of pace. Phillip ate so little she asked if he was feeling all right.

"Oh yes," he said. "I'm just a little run-down, I guess. I stayed at the office till ten last night." He smiled and took her hand. "But I can't complain; they warned me in business school it would be like this."

Nancy smiled too, and wondered how to diplomatically extricate her hand. Phillip wasn't squeezing, or even really holding on to her; his hand was simply resting on hers in a kind of easy, proprietorial way. Which almost made it worse.

"Look—they're bringing out the cake," Nancy said, freeing her hand to gesture toward the kitchen doors. Phillip turned in his seat. What, Nancy said to herself, was she going to do at the Underground?

Amy cut the cake, Joey fed her a piece—of course too big, and she nearly choked—and a lot of flashbulbs went off. Nancy ate her own piece of cake while Phillip was still scraping the icing off his.

"Why are you doing that?" she said.

"It's pure sugar."

"That's what you need—to give you a little boost."

"Why would I need a little boost now? The wedding's over."

"What about the Underground?" Nancy blurted out before she could stop herself. Maybe he hadn't known?

But he had, and looked slightly disappointed in her. "Did you want to do that?" he asked.

"Didn't you? Look—if you're too tired, I understand. Your hours have been killing lately. I'll be all right—I can tag along with some of the others." Was she sounding genuinely concerned for his welfare, or eager to be rid of him? "Really, I don't mind going with the others."

Phillip looked at her with even greater affection. Apparently he thought she was trying to let him off the hook, at the expense of her own happiness. He picked up his fork, mashed it into the icing, and cleaned his plate. "There," he said, dropping the fork again, "I can dance all night now. Let's go."

Great, she thought; she'd certainly aced that one. On the way over, they shared a cab with the woman from "the fashion industry" and two others; when it stopped at the end of a dismal West Side block, and the cabbie said "Five-fifty," Phillip looked surprised.

"We're there?"

The others were already piling out.

"The Underground," he said, "this is it. Five-fifty."

Phillip paid the fare, without asking anyone else to chip in, which was classy of him, Nancy thought. The club had no marquee, or sign, or anything. There was just a velvet rope, stretched in front of a narrow set of cement steps leading straight down; the brick walls were splattered with graffiti. Nancy had been to various clubs before, so she knew you couldn't expect much from the outside. But this one *really* looked forbidding. Poor Phillip—he still looked like he couldn't believe it.

The doormen, who must have been feeling unusually kind-hearted that night, let them all in without any wait. Just inside, a girl on a stool collected ten dollars per person, and said, "The check room's that way." It was lucky she did—the lighting was very dim, and there were corridors and staircases going off in all directions.

"What *is* this place?" Phillip asked.

"It *was* a tunnel, or a railyard, or something like that," Nancy said. "My sister's been here. She said it goes all the way under the Hudson River."

Phillip still looked puzzled, and not pleased.

"It's all underground, and underwater," Nancy said, trying to make it sound interesting and fun. "Pretty amazing, huh?"

"Yeah," Phillip said, "amazing."

They checked their coats, and wandered off into what turned out to be an arcade decorated with framed photos, for sale, of naked women wearing dog collars, leashes, and chains.

"Did you already get Amy and Joey a wedding present?" Nancy asked, and Phillip said, "Yes, why?"

"Because I thought if you hadn't, maybe one of these . . ." In the one they were looking at, a blond woman was on all fours, with her leash fastened to a clothesline.

"Want to find the Torch Room," Nancy asked, "where we were supposed to hook up with everybody?"

"Fine with me."

"Let's try that direction." Taking *his* hand now, she led

him, in his nice blue suit and yellow silk tie, out of the arcade and toward the pounding thrum of the music. They passed through a stone archway, guarded by a plastic mannequin with glowing red eyes, down another set of steps, and into what looked to Nancy like . . . nothing she'd ever seen.

It was a vast cavernous hall, with a high, vaulted stone ceiling, eerily lighted by blue and red spots, and echoing loudly with the blasting beat of the music. In a sunken area that ran the length of the room, hundreds of dancers writhed around, twirling and gyrating, and crashing into each other. Above them, behind an iron railing that ran along both sides, onlookers drank, and smoked, and watched the dancers appraisingly. The decibel level was excruciating.

"I can't believe this," Phillip shouted over the music—Michael Jackson, Nancy could now make out—"it's like a cross between Grand Central Station and—"

"—and hell."

Phillip looked at her, and nodded. "You said it."

At the far end of the room on the left, there was a metal scaffolding, three stories high, with a bar on every level; at the far end on the right, a raised area lighted only by torches affixed to the walls. Nancy pointed to the torches, and Phillip gestured, as if to say "lead the way."

To get there, they had to walk along behind one of the iron railings, on a narrow strip already packed with people. Nancy had to weave her way through the crush of bodies, black guys in berets and artfully torn T-shirts, white guys in loosened ties trying to look "downtown," girls with so much eye makeup they looked like raccoons. The smell of smoke, from cigarettes and joints, hung heavy in the air. Where the walkway ended, there were three carpeted steps up, into what was comparatively an oasis of peace and quiet.

"Welcome to the Torch Room," said a tall black waiter in a Carmen Miranda–style turban. "Can I get you a drink?"

It was like a sudden intrusion of sanity. "Yes, please," said Nancy. "A vodka and tonic."

"Make it two," Phillip said.

The turban whirled away, empty tray held high above his head.

"Hey, Nancy, come on over here." It was Amy's older sister, who'd been maid of honor, calling from a Victorian settee. Phillip and Nancy went over to join her.

"Is this place something, or what?" Susan said; somewhere along the way she'd changed from her wedding outfit to a leopard-print miniskirt.

"It's something all right," Nancy said, then told her how she and Phillip had described it.

Susan laughed, and clapped her hands together. Her boyfriend, sitting beside her in an oversized jacket, pretended to laugh too. "That's great," she exclaimed. "Hell!"

And from here, in the Torch Room, it looked even more so; Nancy could hardly take her eyes off the vista that extended out behind the sofa Susan was sitting on. There was another iron railing, about waist high, with two huge stone angels, kneeling and weeping, at either end; between them, and going out as far as the eye could see, into an absolute blackness, was an enormous, vaulted tunnel with two of the original train tracks—the wooden ties, the gravel bed—still embedded in its floor. The tracks emerged from right under the Torch Room, and traveled out, in parallel lines that appeared to converge hundreds of yards off, under the last of a series of rusted steel trestles, bathed in a pale blue light. Beyond them lay that yawning, and impenetrable, darkness.

There was something almost hypnotic about it, and Nancy stood, staring, until she realized the turbaned waiter was hovering beside her, with her drink on the tray.

"Oh, thanks." Phillip had apparently already paid him. "And thank you, Phillip." He was stirring his own drink with the plastic swizzle stick.

A few of the people in the room started to applaud as Amy and Joey arrived—others, who were no part of the wedding, looked confused. Joey was still in his tuxedo, but Amy had changed into a fuchsia Danskin and a leather skirt. She was smiling broadly, receiving kisses on the cheek, fluttering her hands like a flapper doing the Charleston. Susan said, "Boy, is she blitzed." With Joey in tow, Amy made the rounds of the Torch Room, kissing and hugging and waving; Nancy could swear she embraced a couple of people she'd never ever seen before. When she got to Phillip, whose family had known hers all the way back in Taiwan, she gave him a big, sloppy kiss, ruffling his hair, before turning to Nancy, bleary-eyed, and saying, "Hope you don't mind."

"Be my guest," Nancy replied.

"He's just *so cute*," and she kissed him again, Phillip blushing furiously. Joey, standing just behind her, took it all in good humor. His bow tie was hanging undone now, and someone had passed him a joint.

"How ya doin', Nance." He offered her the joint. "Wanna hit?"

"No, thanks. I'm doing fine already," and she rattled the ice cubes in her glass.

"Yeah, well, not as fine as Amy's doin'." Amy had just slumped onto the sofa, with her chin resting on her sister's shoulder. "She's gonna be sick as a dog tomorrow."

"Are you going on a honeymoon?"

She suddenly knew, without looking, that Jack was there.

"Nah, not yet. We're still savin' our bread up to get a better apartment. The way we figure it . . ."

Joey went on to describe their future plans, while Nancy slowly turned in place to look for Jack. Phillip, fortunately, was talking to Amy and her beau.

Jack, leaning against the bar in a white shirt, open at the throat, and a pair of black jeans, motioned with one hand as if to say "You want to come over here, or do you want me to come over there?" A girl beside him at the bar was giving him the once-over, without his knowing it.

Nancy gestured to him, palm up, to stay where he was. Joey was explaining the difficulties of getting what they really wanted—a Soho loft—at a price they could ever afford. Nancy briefly commiserated then excused herself. Phillip turned as she left, and she said, "Be back in a minute—I see someone I know," and scooted across the room.

The girl at the bar had apparently just said something to him because Jack was saying, "Once or twice—but not for a long time." Nancy figured it must have been some variation on "Come here often?" and felt no compunction about cutting in between them.

"You look good in red," Jack said to her, leaning down to brush her cheek with his lips. The girl at the bar got the message, and pushed off. "Who's the suit?"

"The who?"

"The guy in the blue suit."

"His name is Phillip Chen."

"Is he your date?"

It was all very friendly, but still, there was something about the questions that Nancy didn't like. "No, not really, but he is a good friend of mine . . . I told you I had plans tonight, and you said that it didn't matter, that you wanted to see me anyway."

Jack understood the reproach in her voice, and said, "You're right—I'm sorry. Forget I said it." There was a pause, and then he said, "Well?"

"Well what?"

"Will you forget I said it?"

"Of course," and she laughed. "I didn't realize it had been a question."

"In this place that's easy—it's almost impossible to hear anything."

"Looked like you could hear that girl proposition you just fine," Nancy said, with a smile. For a second Jack pretended not to understand, then he smiled too. "She was my cousin," he said, and Nancy replied, "Now we're even."

Phillip was watching them, from across the room, and Nancy said, "I think I'd better introduce you."

"I promise to behave."

"You better."

Phillip pretended to be deep in conversation with Susan Wong's boyfriend when they approached, and Nancy had to touch him on the sleeve. "Phillip, I'd like you to meet a friend of mine from the institute, Jack Logan."

They shook hands. "Oh—so you work at the Institute for Abnormal Psychology," Phillip said. This seemed to come as a relief.

"Sort of."

This made him less relieved.

"I'm actually one of the guinea pigs."

This caused him real consternation. "You're a patient there?"

"Not exactly," Jack said, and laughed. "I mean, I didn't ax-murder my family or anything."

"Jack is Dr. Sprague's pet project," Nancy cut in, before things took a turn for the worse. "Sprague thinks he might have some unusual psychic abilities."

That didn't seem to help much; now Phillip probably

thought he'd shaken hands with Houdini. "Unusual abilities?" he said, looking to Nancy for confirmation. "Like bending spoons, or reading minds? That sort of thing?"

Oh God, Nancy thought; this was not going the way she'd hoped.

"Precisely," Jack said. "I bend spoons with my brain waves. What do you do?"

"I work for Salomon Brothers." And then, in case it wasn't clear, he added, "It's an investment banking firm."

"Yes, I know that," Jack said. "I had a girlfriend who dated a guy who worked there."

"Oh, who?" Phillip twitched his head, as if something had just tickled him behind the collar.

"You wouldn't know him; he left, and now he just raids companies on his own."

Nancy looked more interested to hear this than Phillip. Who was this girlfriend, and when had Jack stopped seeing her? Had he stopped?

"Most of the work I do involves defending companies against raids," Phillip said, running one finger around the neckline of his shirt. He twitched again, and looked behind him.

"Is something wrong?" Nancy asked, and Phillip said, "I could swear someone had just blown on me."

"Wishful thinking," Jack said, feigning a good-natured smile.

This was never going to work, Nancy thought; she had to get them separated. "Who wants the first dance with me?" she said, coquettishly. "It's up for grabs."

Phillip hesitated, as she might have guessed he would; she'd never seen him dance in his entire life. For that matter, she'd never seen him run. Jack slipped his hand around hers and said, "I'll take it. Excuse us, Phil."

Phillip, still looking puzzled, watched them walk away, toward the maelstrom of the dance floor. Damn, he thought, I should have spoken up faster. At least she wouldn't be with *him* now. He loosened his tie, and rubbed at the back of his neck. What a lousy night this was turning out to be—he could have stayed at the firm and picked up a couple of hundred extra brownie points. Instead he was standing alone in the middle of some abandoned subway tunnel, or whatever the hell it was, with an overpriced drink in his hand. What a waste of time. He shook his head ruefully, and lifted the glass to his lips. When he tried to drink from it, he found something foreign—definitely not an ice cube—brushing up against his lips. He lowered the glass, looked inside. Oh . . . it was just the plastic swizzle stick. He fished it out of the glass, and only then discovered that the stick had been bent into a perfect circle, one end stuck neatly inside the other.

"You said you were going to behave," Nancy shouted, moving in place on the crowded dance floor. There was barely room to turn around.

"I did."

She shook her head. "I'd hate to see you misbehave."

"You sure of that?" he said, leering at her.

She didn't even try to make a comeback to that one; the music was so loud it was nearly impossible to be heard over. It was almost entirely percussive now—just the racketing beat of drums and bongos and what sounded like hollow sticks pounding on a log. The dance floor was a writhing mass of flailing limbs and bouncing bodies. She was sorry she hadn't left her drink in the Torch Room; the glass was almost empty, but there was nowhere to put it down.

Jack, as if divining her thought, said, "Want to get rid of that?"

She nodded.

He took it from her hand, and with one big sweep of his arm, swung it over the heads of the people around them and deposited it on top of one of the black floor speakers.

When he turned back to her, he smiled, and then, almost as if he'd suddenly received some startling piece of news, stopped smiling. He stopped dancing too, and simply stared over Nancy's head.

"Jack?"

He was still staring, and Nancy spun around to see at what. With the strobelights flashing overhead, it was hard to make out anything very clearly; the other dancers jerked about, looking like the flickering images in a nickelodeon. Still, there didn't seem to be anything very unusual about any of it.

"What is it?" she said, turning back to Jack. But he was moving past her now, insinuating himself between the other couples, making his way toward whatever he'd seen. Nancy followed in his wake, dodging and weaving and accidentally stepping on toes; one guy, whirling like a dervish, managed to clomp her good on the shoulder, before spinning off again into another orbit.

Jack was rooted to a new spot now, and looking around in all directions. At least *he* could see over everyone's head, Nancy thought; she could barely see three feet in front of her. She tugged on his sleeve and shouted, "What are you looking for?"

"I . . . don't know," he said. "I could swear . . . I could swear . . ."

"Swear what?" The percussion had been joined by voices now, screaming to "do it, do it, do it to some-*body*."

". . . I'd seen her."

Who? Who could have given him a start like that? That girl he'd mentioned to Phillip, the one who'd dated a banker? If that's who it was, the relationship must have been a whole lot more serious than she'd thought.

"Jack—can we go and sit somewhere?"

He was still craning his neck to see around the dance floor, but Nancy was able to guide him gently up the steps, across the walkway set off by the iron railing, and into the first quiet place she could find, a dark little chamber filled with over-stuffed furniture and a monstrous reproduction of one of those Easter Island heads. A guy with his hair in a ponytail was lying on a hassock with his feet against the wall, while his girlfriend rubbed his stomach. Another couple was making out in the corner. It was the best she'd be able to do.

"Let's sit down for a second," she said, and Jack flopped onto a beaten-up love seat. "Now tell me, first of all, who you thought you saw out there."

"If I told you, you wouldn't believe me."

"Why wouldn't I believe you?"

"Because *I* don't believe me . . . What I thought I saw out there, right in the middle of the dance floor, was my mother." He looked over at her, levelly. "Now—tell me you believe me."

Nancy took a second to recover, then said, "You mean your mother isn't dead, after all?"

"She is."

"What?"

"Dead."

Now Nancy really was lost.

"She was dead before I was even born," Jack said, earnestly. "Dead for months." He took her hands and squeezed them. "You know how Sprague wanted me to get him my birth certificate? Well, I went out to my grandparents' place, yesterday, to look for it. In the attic I found a bunch of old newspapers; I've got them at my apartment now. I can *show them* to you. It was kind of a famous case at the time. My mother was killed in a car accident, while she was pregnant, but they somehow managed to keep her alive, on respirators and all, for five more months, until I could be safely delivered." He was desperate for her to believe him; she could see it in his eyes. "My grandparents never told me, they didn't see any reason for me to know something so terrible. My mother'd been tripping; one newspaper said they found everything from alcohol to acid in her bloodstream when she died." His eyes dropped for a moment as he said, "Now I know why Clancy's always acted the way he has about it. But the point is, I was born of a dead mother."

"And now," Nancy said, trying to take this all in, "you think you've seen her here at the Underground?" Where was the logic in that?

"I do . . . and it isn't the first time." He explained how he'd seen her from the pit, at the theater. "That was the night I was relieved of my duties there."

So now *that* made sense . . . or at least it accounted for his having screwed up badly enough to get the boot.

"And I think she's been to my apartment."

But the rest of it, this whole hallucination story, seeing his dead mother—this was definitely trouble; this was someone coming seriously unhinged, right before her eyes. And why, *why* did it have to be Jack?

"I know what you're thinking, I know it sounds crazy; I didn't want to tell you for just that reason. But I'm not making it up. I'm not imagining it. It's happening, I tell you . . . and I don't know how."

The boy with the ponytail rolled off the hassock and onto the floor, laughing. His girlfriend rolled with him.

"That's why I needed to see you tonight . . . I didn't want

you to hear it all from Sprague, or some other way. I wanted
to be the one to tell you myself."

Nancy was trying to forget this was Jack she was dealing
with, and imagine instead that this was just a clinical case she
had to handle. What did her textbooks say about dealing with
delusional systems? How would her professors want her to
talk to him, reassure him, address his fears? God, she needed
to be away from him for a few seconds, to formulate a plan of
action. If only she could call Sprague . . .

"Jack," she said, as calmly as she could, "I've got to go
back to the Torch Room for a minute; I want to tell Phillip to
leave without me. Okay? Then I'll come right back here, and
you and I can go somewhere and talk. *Really* talk. Is that
okay? Will you wait here for me?"

He nodded, mutely, and let his fingers trail off of her as she
left. Though the Torch Room was only a few hundred feet
away, to get there she had to fight her way through mobs of
people—the club had been getting more crowded all the time
—and without Jack leading the way, it was slow going. Several times guys asked her her name, or if she wanted to dance,
or if they could buy her a drink, or, once, take her home that
night; more than once, she had to shake a hand free or veer to
the left when going right would have been shorter. When she
got up the steps to the Torch Room, she saw Phillip, sitting
down now, head down, in conversation with the girl from the
fashion industry. At least he hadn't been standing around by
himself. He looked up only when she got right in front of him,
but made a point of not standing. That was very unlike him;
he must really be mad, she thought. Nancy crouched down,
said, "Phillip, I need to talk to you for a second." She glanced
pointedly at the fashion industry, but she wasn't about to
budge. "In private." She drew him away from the sofa, to the
middle of the room. He still wasn't looking her in the eye; a
bad sign, if ever there was one.

"None of this is what you think it is," she said, "but I don't
have time to explain. Jack Logan is a very special case at the
institute, and he's got a very big problem tonight. I have to
stay with him awhile, and be sure he's okay. Do you understand?" She was starting to feel like a Ping-Pong ball between
these two. "You don't have to wait around for me," she said,
"I'll be all right. And thank you, Phillip, for being my escort

tonight." She tried to make it sound light but sincere.

Phillip wasn't that easily placated. "That's it?" He looked at her, his face, usually so impassive, a mixture of hurt and anger. "You drag me down here, and then you dump me for this maniac?" He debated saying something about the swizzle stick; decided against it. "Just tell me one thing, Nancy. Was this a setup?"

"I don't know what you mean." Lord, this was just what she hadn't wanted to get into, a debate.

"Had you and this guy arranged, ahead of time, to meet down here? Was that why you were so willing to let me off the hook, up at the wedding dinner?"

One thing you could say for Phillip, Nancy thought—he's no fool. But then, neither was she. "No way, Phillip—this was just an unfortunate coincidence. All I can—"

"Now what's he want?" Phillip was looking behind her. Nancy turned.

Jack was coming up the stairs, glassy-eyed, muttering something. Oh, Christ, Nancy thought—now it was all going to hit the fan for real. Jack was brushing past the turbaned waiter, who gave him a second look, and heading toward them. But it didn't seem to be them he was looking at. Phillip, as if sensing something was really wrong, sidled in front of Nancy. Jack kept coming.

"Something the matter?" Phillip said, almost as a challenge, when Jack got within reach. But Jack acted as if he hadn't even heard him—or seen Nancy. "Did you want to do another of your Uri Geller stunts?" He held up the plastic straw from his drink. What, Nancy wondered, was *that* supposed to mean?

Jack, staring fixedly over the railing at the end of the room, said, "Wait—please wait for me," and then, without taking his eyes off whatever he was looking at, said to Nancy, "Don't you see her? There—between the tracks."

Nancy quickly glanced where he was pointing—just beyond the flickering light of the torches, somewhere in the tunnel—then back at Jack. The buttons on his shirt were open halfway down his chest, and she could see he was breathing heavily.

Phillip had turned and looked too, seen nothing. "Hey, Jack," he said, adopting a more conciliatory tone, "why don't you sit down and take a break? Why don't we all just—"

Jack didn't wait for him to finish. He said, "Yes, I'm coming," but not to Phillip or Nancy, and walked toward the railing. Before anyone could stop him, he had swung one leg over the iron bar, and then the other. Spreading his arms wide, he leaped from the floor of the Torch Room, and down onto the open train tracks. A few people noticed what he'd done, thought he was drunk, laughed. Susan Wong, standing not far off, said, "Who is that guy?"

Nancy ran to the railing. Jack was about eight feet below her, still crouching on the gravel road bed. The old steel rails ran along both sides of him, under the huge trestles, and on into the blackness of the tunnel.

"Jack!" Nancy called down. "Jack! Wake up! There's nothing there, Jack!"

"Go for it, man—go for it." A wiseguy with a Prince Valiant haircut.

"What's he doing?" The girl who'd tried to pick him up at the bar.

"The guy's stoned." One of Joey's ushers.

There was a crowd assembling at the railing now, some just curious, some egging him on. Jack stood up, brushing the grit and pebbles from his hands. He paid no attention to the catcalls, or to Nancy. Slowly, but purposefully, he set off down the tracks, his white shirt a pale blue in the spotlights that illuminated the first hundred yards or so of the tunnel. Phillip said, "I'll go get a bouncer or someone."

But Nancy was afraid there might not be time. She looked hurriedly to either side, where two stone angels, holding torches of their own, guarded the tunnel entrance. Behind each one of them, and above the train bed, ran a cement catwalk, no more than a couple of feet wide. It wasn't much, but it was better than trying to jump the railing.

She ran to the base of one of the angels, climbed up onto it, and edged around until she had reached the catwalk it protected. Susan Wong shouted, "What are you *doing*?" Nancy didn't know any more than Susan did; she just knew she had to get to Jack, and bring him to his senses, before something terrible happened.

There was a brief, unnerving moment when she had to let go of the statue, and step down onto the catwalk. She knew it was all psychological, that the pathway was sufficiently wide to walk on—that's why it had originally been put there, for Christ's sake—but only if you didn't *think* about it too much. The flickering light from the Torch Room bathed everything in an uneven orange light, which made depth and distance even more difficult to judge. She flattened herself against the wall, getting a feel for the gritty cement beneath her feet, and threw a glance at Jack. He was passing underneath the second of the huge steel trestles now. If he was saying anything, he was too far away for her to hear it. The brick wall behind her was surprisingly warm and dry. Pipes behind it?

"Hey, lady, what the fuck do you think you're doing out there?"

It was the black waiter, with the leopard-print turban. He was swinging one leg over the iron railing of the Torch Room, just as Jack had done.

"I'm a doctor; that's my patient out there. I'm going to get him."

"No you ain't. *I'm* going to get him. You're going back into the club."

Nancy didn't feel like arguing with him. She had her balance now, and with her hands still resting slightly against the warm brick, she moved off down the catwalk.

"Shit," the waiter said, when he saw her inching away. He stood on the ledge of the Torch Room, wondering what to do, which lunatic to collect first.

Phillip's face appeared in the crowd just behind him. His mouth was open, but he was speechless. Amy and Joey were leaning over the railing as though this was the best, and most unexpected, wedding entertainment they could ever have dreamed up. Never in her life had Nancy felt so exposed, so afraid, and curiously . . . so alive.

The waiter jumped to the tracks below, missed his footing, and sprawled forward. "God*damnit*!" He rolled over, holding his ankle. "God*damn*it. I'm gonna *kill* that sucker when I catch him."

Nancy tried to increase her speed. But as she got farther away from the Torch Room, the light grew dimmer, the air and walls colder. Jack was weaving back and forth across the tracks now, but not as if he was disoriented; it was more as if he was looking for something, or someone. At some point,

Nancy thought, she was going to have to climb down off the catwalk and onto the floor of the tunnel itself. Was there a set of stairs ahead, or even one of those steel ladders like you see on swimming pools?

The waiter was up now, but hobbling. He threw a finger at Nancy as he passed down the middle of the tunnel, shouting, "Get on back! I'll do this!"

But Nancy kept on. Jack was under the third trestle now; its huge rusted bulk hung high above him, like an iron bone in the rib cage of some monster. Nancy thought for a second of Pinocchio, swallowed up in the belly of the whale.

The waiter was hollering at him now. "Hey you! Hey! Where you think you're going?" His words echoed around in the barreled vault of the tunnel with a hollow, ghostly sound, which seemed to have its effect on the waiter, too. When he shouted again, it was less strident, almost friendly. "Hey you, hey buddy—why don't you come on back? Come on now—come on back."

Either the roadbed had been rising, or the catwalk descending, but the distance between the two was no more than a yard or so now. Nancy scanned the gravel for any obstructions, then jumped down onto the tunnel floor. The waiter wheeled around when he heard her land.

"You too now?" But he didn't seem unhappy to have her there. "What exactly is wrong with this dude?" Jack was still way ahead of them, almost entirely beyond the reach of the blue spotlights.

"He's hallucinating," she said, picking her way across the train tracks.

"Yeah? And what else? Watch out there," he said, pointing to a splintered tie. "Is he dangerous?"

"No. I don't think so."

This didn't seem to reassure him.

"Not if I'm there," she added.

"Then you *be* there."

They picked their way between the tracks, keeping Jack just within sight.

"What's your name, anyway?"

"Nancy."

"Lionel . . . You got balls, you know that?"

"Thank you, I guess." They were both, she noticed, speaking in low tones, leery of creating any more echoes, affected by the increasingly eerie atmosphere. Nancy looked back for an instant, toward the Torch Room; it looked like a stage set from here, raised up above the level of the tunnel floor, framed by the stone angels, lighted by the orange flames. Dozens of people were packed against the railing.

Only in this case she and Lionel and Jack were the show.

Jack was beyond the spotlights now; all she could see of him was the faint glow of his white shirt.

"You know where this tunnel ends?"

Lionel, still limping a little from his fall on the tracks, said, "No idea. I been *told* it hooks up to some underground railyards. But I gotta believe there's a gate, or a fence, or *somethin'* that's gonna stop him. How could the club have got a permit here if this thing was still opened up to hell and gone?"

How could they, Nancy agreed; there had to be a fence, or a wall of some sort, to seal it off. And it had to appear soon . . . because if the tunnel got any blacker, there'd be no way to see Jack, much less catch him.

"Mother?"

Could she have slipped past him?

"Are you there?" He curled his fingers around the silver meshwork of the cyclone fence; it was the highest one he'd ever seen, like a backstop at a baseball diamond. It rose almost to the ceiling of the tunnel. "Are you there?" he repeated.

Why would she have abandoned him now? Why would she have led him all this way, just to desert him at a dead end?

He shook the fence, but it was so huge, and so high, it barely rattled. The only light came from a single white bulb, mounted in a circular metal fixture directly overhead. There was no gate, or opening, of any kind. He leaned forward against the fence, resting his forehead on the cold metal. "Mother," he murmured, "is it really you? Or am I crazy?" With his eyes closed, he rolled his head, back and forth, against the fence. "What is *happening* to me?"

". . . Jack . . ."

His eyes sprang open, his fingers clutched the metal grillework. There was a shadowy figure off to his right, on the other side of the fence. He stumbled across the tracks toward her, mumbling, "Wait! Don't go!"

She was standing only a few feet back from the fence, in a gloomy pocket near the wall. Her dark hair nearly concealed her face, but still she looked to be no more than nineteen or twenty years old. She was wearing a blue jacket, with white vinyl sleeves, and Jack knew, if she turned, he would see "Weehawken High" on the back.

"Jesus . . . it is you." He could hardly believe his eyes. "Come closer."

But she stayed where she was. "You come to me," she said. Her *voice*—it ran through him like a lightning bolt. It was the most beautiful, most foreign, most familiar sound he'd ever heard.

"How can I?" He shook the fence. "How can I?"

"You want to, you can." She turned on her heel, and sauntered off, slowly. The jacket read "Weehawken High."

"No! Wait! Don't go!" He shook the fence fiercely, and suddenly realized it had given way, peeled loose from the wall. It didn't leave much of a space, but if he pulled it back as hard as he could, and wedged himself against the wall, there'd be just enough room to get through.

When he turned sideways, his back to the cold bricks, he saw two figures coming down the tunnel toward him. One was Nancy, that much he could tell, but the other . . . the other was astonishingly tall, and dark. He had to squint before he could make out the turban that created the illusion of such height. It was that waiter, from the Torch Room. Together, he knew they would try to stop him. Which he could *not* let happen, not when so much was at stake. There wouldn't be time to make them—to make *Nancy*—understand.

But they must suddenly have seen him. Nancy cried, "Jack! Wait for me! I want to help you!"

It was like being tugged in two directions at once, Nancy pulling him back toward the club, his mother luring him deeper into the tunnel. He had to hurry.

Pushing the fence back with all his strength, he squirmed through. The fence snapped back with an angry clatter. Nancy and the waiter were running toward him, stumbling over the train ties and loose stones.

"Go back!" he shouted. "Go back!"

"No . . . wait . . . *please*." Nancy came to the fence, gasping for breath. "Jack . . . don't go any farther. There's nothing out there . . . Please come back."

The waiter hobbled up, favoring one leg. "Listen, dude— you keep goin' and you're gonna get arrested, and *I'm* gonna lose my job. Okay? So be nice and come on back to the club with us, and I'll get you a free drink, anything you want, on the house."

Nancy was pleading with him with her eyes, and he was afraid that if he looked any longer, he might give in. "Go back," he said, softly, and turned away. When he heard the waiter say, "Shit, how'd he get through here?" he set off down the tunnel at a slow jog. He still had to be sure not to overpass her.

The roadbed was curving now, and gradually descending. A couple of times he almost lost his footing. There was no sign of his mother, anywhere. But he knew now that she would not have deserted him, that she would be waiting for him, somewhere ahead. Far behind him, he could hear the screeching sound of the metal fence being scraped against the brick wall. He ran faster.

And suddenly found himself at the end of the curve, standing where the tunnel, like a river flowing into the ocean, opened onto an underground cavern so vast he was momentarily stunned. A subterranean railyard, acres and acres of it, criss-crossed by a thousand tracks, filled with the abandoned carcasses of locomotives and passenger cars and, stacked like shoeboxes three or four high, gray container cars that said ALLEGHENY or ATLANTIC TRANSPORT on their sides. They looked, in the dull uneven glow of the light bulbs strung sporadically overhead, like huge, sleeping insects, their black steel glinting like the carapace of a beetle, the muted orange of the passenger cars like the back of a ladybug. Nowhere, in all this enormous space, was there any life or movement.

How, Jack wondered, would he ever find her in here?

He wouldn't, of course—she would find him . . . just as she had been doing.

He left the overhang of the tunnel, and descended to the cluttered plain before him. Once down among the tracks and railroad cars, he found it even darker, more forbidding. The cars loomed above him, blocking the light, casting deep shadows. He entered a sort of aisle, between what looked like they'd once been coal trains, and stopped when he saw something, fast and dark, flash across his path. A cat, down here? He bent down, to look under the car where it had disappeared. At first there was nothing, but when he said, "Hey, kitty," snapping his fingers, he saw a lot of squirming between the tracks, and heard not a meow but a squeaking sound—*many* squeaking sounds. And glimpsed the snap of a black, whiplike tail.

Jesus—it's rats. A whole nest of them, crawling all over each other. He quickly stood up, and looked around for something he could use as a weapon, just in case he needed one. A stick, a pipe, a broom handle—anything. He glanced up, toward a passenger car parked at the end of the aisle he was in, and saw, behind one of its smudged windows, the pale silhouette of a face . . . perfectly still, in profile. The train said MONONGAHELA RAIL AND CARGO, in faded white letters, on the dull-red side.

It was as much of an invitation as he was likely to get. There was a scuttling sound from the rat's nest beneath the train, but nothing came out to molest him. The face in the window stayed just as it was.

The only entry to the car she was in was at the rear. He went to it slowly, gripped the handrail; the rusted paint flaked off on his hand. He swung himself up, onto the corrugated metal steps, and took hold of the door handle. Holding his breath, he pushed in on the door; it rattled slightly, but didn't budge. He pushed again, and this time it creaked back a few inches. How the hell had his mother gotten this open? Or had she even needed to?

He put his shoulder to it, and gave the door a shove. It grated against the floor, then suddenly gave way, swinging back with a *bang* against an interior wall, and carrying Jack halfway into the car. He stumbled against the back of a seat, and regained his balance.

His mother, seated about ten rows ahead, didn't move, or turn around.

The interior itself was murky with shadow. Some of the seats faced forward, some of them back; all were tattered and beaten-up. Between them, there were little tabletops: on one, to Jack's right, there was a filthy old folded newspaper. This must have been a dining car.

The only sound was his own labored breathing.

"Mother . . . I'm here," he said, as if she could possibly not know it. But he felt he had to say something, had to speak to her before she somehow vanished again. "I want to talk to you." He took a step toward her, but she still didn't turn. He went from row to row, holding the iron handle on the back of each seat, until he was just behind her. Her hair was neatly parted, right down the middle, and glistened as if it had just been washed. Her arms were resting on the table in front of her.

He knew now that the chase was over. He slid into the seat facing hers. They sat, silently, like two travelers thrown together at the same table, not knowing where to begin.

Her eyes were downcast. She had long, full lashes. She seemed, though he didn't dare reach out to touch her, as substantial, as *real*, as he was. And so *young*. He couldn't get over how young she was—how much younger than *he* was. Somehow, it seemed easier to overlook the fact that she was dead than that she was so much younger; it was as if his mind, having accepted the impossible, had balked at going even one step further. It couldn't quibble with what patently could not be, but the evidence of his senses—what he saw sitting passively on the cracked leather seat—*that* it could contest, and would. His own mother could *not* be seven or eight years younger than he was!

She moved her hand on the tabletop, as if to brush away some crumbs. Not that any morsel of food would have escaped the rats, Jack thought, not after all these years.

"I thought I'd never catch up with you," he said.

She didn't reply.

He looked around at the dark and dilapidated car. An open suitcase, empty, hung forlornly from a luggage rack overhead. He tried again.

"You picked quite a place to finally get together," he said, and to his amazement, she smiled, just like a teenage girl might do.

"Yeah, well . . . I didn't really plan it this way."

She was talking to him! They were actually sitting together, talking now, in one place; she wasn't moving away, or disappearing, or leading him on. That alone exhilarated, and frightened, him . . . because now they were truly, somehow, in league.

"What *did* you plan?"

She hesitated, then shrugged. She was slender, but the big shoulders of the jacket bulked her up. "None of this . . . I never planned on anything that happened to me." There was a resigned, even wistful, tone to her words. "Let the good times roll . . . isn't that what you musicians say?" Her eyes came up to meet his now, and again, it was as if he were looking into some strange sort of mirror, seeing some bizarrely altered reflection of himself. There were the same deep-green eyes, the same dark eyebrows, the same wide mouth, with the tiny lines at either corner. But this was the face of a pretty—*very* pretty —young woman, someone who could have been his sister, his *younger* sister, and everyone would have noted the striking resemblance. For a moment, Jack felt as if that's who she was, and he was overcome by a sudden rush of tenderness and solicitude. He could almost *feel* his brain grappling with the possibility, liking it, battening onto it as an explanation for all that had come before. If only this were his long-lost sister, then other things, some of them at least, might fall into place, might start to make sense. If only the whole situation could be rethought with that as the essential premise . . .

But of course it couldn't. A sudden shiver snapped him back to reality. For the first time, he realized how cold it was. He buttoned up the open front of his shirt.

"You were at the show," Jack said, "last week."

She nodded her head. "Front row seat."

"What'd you think?"

"Didn't you hear me clapping?"

Of course he had; he could hear it even now, that endless, hollow, rhythmic rapping of the rolled program in the open palm. "And you were at my apartment, later that night." Exactly *when*, he silently wondered?

She gave him a sly smile. "You got my card."

The program.

"Were you shocked?"

Was he? She asked him almost playfully, as if it had been a prank and she was anxious to know how it had turned out. "Yes," he said, "when I figured out it had been you."

She looked pleased.

"But why were you there? Or here—tonight?" There was so much he needed to know, he didn't dare lose this opportunity. "And how? How can you do this? I found a bunch of old newspapers, in the attic in Weehawken—Mam and Clancy had stashed them away—I read about what happened to you, the accident, the stuff after—"

She had turned her head toward the window as he spoke, gazing off at whatever could be seen through the cracked and dirty glass.

"—the respirators, the brain scans. How they managed to keep you alive, all those months, until I could be safely delivered. Do you *remember* any of that? Were you aware of what was happening? I couldn't tell from the articles—the guy who was driving the car, who died in the crash; was he somebody special to you, or just a friend?" He wrapped his arms around himself, to try to get warm, then asked what he'd been waiting to ask all his life. "Was he my father?"

"Is that all you wanted to know?" she said, bitterly. "Jesus, you sound like Clancy. He'd stand by the hospital bed saying, 'Who did it? Who did it?' Like whoever knocked me up was somehow responsible for turning me on to drugs or putting my face through that windshield."

There *was* something about that in one of the articles—how she'd been thrown through the glass and onto the hood of the other car. But here she looked completely unhurt.

"Like, what about *me*?" she said. "How do you think it made *me* feel to have my whole life cut short like that? To just have everything taken away from me in about three seconds flat? And all because some guy behind the wheel couldn't handle a couple of downers?" She looked over at Jack, in her eyes a deep-seated and lingering resentment. But surely not against *him*? "And yes, that guy driving the car was your father. Or at least probably."

Schmidt, Edward Schmidt. Jack had read it in the papers.

"Though you don't look anything like him," she said. "Lucky for you."

Jack didn't know what to think or feel anymore; he'd just discovered who his father was, after a lifetime of wondering, and then lost him again in the very same breath. It was as if he'd caught a puff of wind.

"Did you love him?"

She twisted her face, as if surprised at him. "Jack . . . and by the way, I'd never have named you that . . . he was just some guy who'd been nice to me. There was little enough of that around that house."

"Even from Mam?"

"Mam wanted a good, sweet Catholic daughter," she said, ruefully, "and instead of seeing me, and loving me, for who I really was, she spent all her time pretending I was that same little girl who'd taken communion at St. Ignatius. The strain on both of us," she said, with a sad smile, "was pretty incredible."

"Clancy, I guess, was even worse."

She chuckled, softly. "You could say that. Though I'll say this much for Clancy; he knew who I was . . . You know what I used to call him? The Pope. It started out as Pop, of course, but then when I got to around fourteen or so, and he was always telling me what I could do and where I could go and when I had to be home, I started calling him Pope because of all the bull. Clancy didn't like it, but Mam," she said, smiling mischievously, "she thought it was an absolute *sacrilege*." Jack found himself smiling back, and feeling such a jumble of emotions, he could hardly make sense of anything. There was joy, the indescribable joy of finding his mother at last; there was relief, and sadness, excitement and curiosity—and above all, a warm and growing sense of complicity. His mother's eyes were sparkling with laughter now, and Jack began to laugh too—a giddy release of all the pent-up emotions inside. His mother leaned forward, across the table, laughing merrily, and that made Jack laugh even harder, more convulsively. Her expression urged him on, her fingers extending toward him. The bracelet! He saw it now, the blue stones and silver band, just peeking out from the sleeve of the jacket. He was so happy, so exhilarated—everything was going to be all right now, all his questions were going to get answers, all his fears were going to be allayed! Even if he'd wanted to—and he didn't—he couldn't have stopped the laughter; it came over him in waves, shaking him, taking him over. And his mother, leaning ever closer, leaning so close he could see the moisture on her lips, the tip of her tongue, egged him on, laughing herself, nodding her head as if to say *yes* to all that he was wishing.

Her hand came closer still, the fingers outstretched—the fingers were white, dead-white, in the gloom of the train car. The nails were pale, and slightly pointed. He lifted his own hand onto the table, and slid it slowly toward his mother's. The touch of her skin was warm, and soft, and she gently covered his hand with hers.

"Feels good, doesn't it?" she whispered.

He nodded.

"Feels right," she said.

He closed his eyes, in complete agreement, and felt her squeeze his hand more firmly. My God, she was *there*, in every way—now he had even felt her flesh. He wanted to reach across the table and hug her, hold her face between his hands, feel *her* arms wrapped around *him*. It felt as if some sort of electricity were coursing up his arm. He caught his breath, hoarse from the laughter. Opening his eyes, he saw her face, framed by the upraised collar of the jacket. He was about to say, "It *is* right," when he felt, beneath his feet, a slight but sudden tremor in the floor of the car. The shadows shifted over by the door. There was the squeak of rusted metal, and a long sinewy arm lashed out, gripping the handrail. A moment later, the waiter in the turban had hauled himself into the open doorway. Jack's mother didn't even turn around.

"Don't move," the waiter said. Nancy appeared behind him.

His mother's fingernails dug into the back of his hand. She began, before his very eyes, to fade away.

"Jack!" Nancy elbowed past the waiter, and hurried down the aisle. "Jack, *please* . . ."

His mother's eyes were the last thing he saw, glittering like green coals in the dimness . . . Nancy knelt beside his seat, grabbing the hand his mother had just relinquished.

"Thank God we found you—when we got to the end of the tunnel, I thought it would be hopeless. But we heard you laughing, and Lionel saw you, sitting by yourself in the window of the train, and . . ."

Jack could still feel the scratches that his mother had left. Nancy was still talking, talking the way Jack had been laughing, just to release all the tension and the fear. The waiter, his turban askew, was leaning against the wall, exhausted, and staring at them both as if they'd just escaped from a mental ward. Jack felt increasingly cold, and lonely.

And he missed his mother now, more than he ever had in his life.

chapter ⤚ twenty

"This is what we call the 'green room,' even though it's brown. Help yourself to the refreshments." She waved one hand at the coffee urn and the sticky pastries wrapped in cellophane. "I believe you've already met Mr. and Mrs. Zakin."

"No, but we've spoken on the phone," Sprague said, striding over to the low sofa they were sitting on. "I'm Dr. Orson Sprague!" He shook Adolph Zakin's hand. "And this," he said, turning toward Jack, "is Jack Logan."

"Yes. We know," said Mrs. Zakin.

"Of course you do," Sprague said, laughing and hitting himself on the forehead with the heel of his hand. "Of course." He was a lot more nervous than he'd expected; he'd have to calm down, or he'd say something equally stupid on the air.

Jack, meanwhile, had stopped dead in the doorway. He and Adolph Zakin were exchanging a long, and no doubt meaningful, look. Sprague would have to ask Jack later if he'd been able to read Zakin's thoughts, or if he'd felt anything special. Jack told him everything now, and complied with all his wishes.

"Listen," Bonnie Robb said, having performed the introductions, "I've got another segment to do first. So please, make yourselves comfortable, and if there's anything you need, just ask Ellie." Ellie was a shy, skinny teenager who was probably working as some sort of intern.

Jack came into the room, nodded to Mrs. Zakin, shook

hands with her husband. "It's good to see you looking so well."

Zakin held on to his hand. "It's good to feel so well," he said, a slight tremble in his voice. "It's good to be alive." He squeezed Jack's hand between both of his own.

Sprague made a mental note of it: "Ask Jack if physical contact with Zakin excited any peculiar recollections of the previous experience." He was going to have so *much* to ask Jack after this show was over, and so much more to do, what with the other interview requests, the random calls, the inquiries from—

"Uh, excuse me," said Ellie, hovering at his side. "Would you like to go into makeup now?"

"Makeup?"

"Yes, well, most of our guests get a little makeup, for the camera—otherwise they kind of shine."

Was he perspiring, and more than the others? "If you think so . . ."

"It's just down the hall—we've already done Mr. Zakin."

Well, that was a relief.

"And we'll do Mr. Logan next." She smiled, sheepishly, at Jack. Did this guy always get a reaction like that, Sprague thought?

"Just follow me." Ellie led the way to a tiny room with a barber chair, where the makeup person—watching the show on a portable TV—asked Sprague to take off his glasses.

Sprague hated having his glasses off, even for a second; he was so blind without them, he felt unprotected and vulnerable. Nonetheless, he surrendered them, and took a seat in the chair. She tucked a large, paper bib into his shirt collar and over his shoulders. He could hardly make out his own features in the mirror that faced him.

"My name's Antoinette."

"Dr. Orson Sprague."

"What kind of doctor?" She was dabbing at something in her hand. "Close your eyes."

"Doctor of psychoneurology." Something touched his face —something damp and cool—and he jumped.

"Ooh, sorry—I didn't know you were so touchy. It's just a little base." She touched him again, under the eyes, with what he now knew was a damp sponge. The TV on the countertop was burbling something about a traffic tie-up on the FDR.

"What are you doing on the show?"

Sprague didn't know quite how to take this—was she questioning his *right* to appear, or in what *capacity* he was appearing? He said he'd be discussing his work at the Institute of Abnormal Psychology.

Antoinette went on swabbing his face with the sponge; it was a very peculiar, and unpleasant, sensation. "Oh, now I've got it—it's about that story I read in the *Post*. That old man—he was in here ten minutes ago—who came back from the dead. Wooh"—she did a little shudder—"that stuff scares the pants off me . . . But where's the guy who actually did it, the one who brought him back?"

"He's in the green room."

"I can't wait to see him. Last week I did Don Johnson, and this one's got me even more rattled than that . . . Was what he did just a fluke, or can he do it all the time?"

"That's what we're trying to determine." Now she was coating his neck with the same disgusting stuff. "Please be careful of the tie." It was a Liberty of London, thirty-five dollars, and he'd bought it expressly for this show. She said nothing, but ceased work on his neck.

"Now don't jump, I'm just gonna put a little liner around your eyes. Otherwise, they won't even show behind the glasses."

He endured this too, thinking about other things to distract himself—the newspaper clippings, for one. On Monday morning, Jack had barged into his office, without even calling ahead, and tossed them onto his desk. "Your birth certificate?" Sprague had asked, and Jack had said, "These are even better." He'd been right. Sprague had wanted the certificate so that he could identify the attending physician and see if there had been anything unusual about the birth—these articles had answered that question right off the bat . . . and at length. They even named the physicians in charge, a Dr. Prescott and a Dr. Mehta. Sprague had pored over the stories, while Jack sat slumped in a chair. When he'd finished, he'd had so many questions, so many fresh leads to pursue, he didn't know where to start. But he did know he was on to something: what had puzzled him all along was that there seemed to be nothing in Jack's past to account for his possessing any unusual powers, nothing in his medical history or family background —unless it had something to do with that anonymous father— to suggest an origin for his death-defying feats. Now there was.

Nothing explicit, nothing crystal clear, but something.

"Tilt your head up, please. Keep your eyes closed." She was dusting his face with some sort of powder—he had to stifle the urge to sneeze—then running her finger along the inside of his collar to release the paper bib. The TV anchor was listing what was coming up in the next half hour—a movie review, the weather update, a look at far-out ski fashions for the winter season, and an exclusive interview with "a young man with some extraordinary lifesaving powers—and a theater celebrity whose life he saved. Stay with us." Theater celebrity, Sprague figured, was their way of implying a Broadway star would be coming up, and not some rich old man known only to the producers and other theater owners. Nor did he fail to note that he himself had been left out of the equation altogether.

"That's all," Antoinette chirped. She patted the front of his new paisley necktie. "And the tie's as good as new."

"My glasses?"

"Oh." She reached around to the counter and handed them to him. He slipped them on and regarded himself in the mirror: he looked like he'd just spent a week in the Caribbean. That, or his ancestors had been Cherokee.

"Where do I go now?"

"Just back to the green room. You can tell Ellie I'm ready for the miracle man now."

That would be the last thing he'd say.

In the green room, Jack was leaning forward in his chair, talking to the Zakins. It all looked very cozy. Ellie said, "You'll be on in about ten minutes," to Sprague, then told Jack it was his turn for makeup. Looking no more pleased than Sprague had been at the prospect, Jack dutifully followed her out of the room.

"So," Sprague said, rubbing his hands together nervously, "you've made a full recovery then, have you?" There was another TV in this room, also tuned to the show in progress.

"We believe so," Mrs. Zakin replied.

"Your doctor?" Sprague asked, though he had no knowledge of New York's cardiac specialists.

"Dr. Levy, Abraham Levy."

He nodded, sagely.

"At Doctors Hospital," Mrs. Zakin added.

He nodded again, as if to confirm that too. A silence fell upon the room, and Sprague busied himself at the coffee urn. The weatherman was predicting snow.

"I don't know why they bother," Zakin said. "They have no idea what the weather's going to be. Totally *unscientific*."

Sprague turned toward the set.

"I hope your work is more reliable."

Sprague felt himself challenged. "I take every precaution," he said, "to make sure my experiments, and results, are sound."

"Not easy," Zakin said, bluntly, "considering what you're experimenting with . . . How do you get a fix, in some institute, on life after death, on a person's soul? What do you study?" Perhaps realizing his tone had been more pugnacious than he'd intended, he said, "Seriously, what have you been looking at? I don't know how you'd get a handle on this. Seems so . . . ephemeral."

"In some ways it is," Sprague said, warming to the topic, now that he felt his authority was no longer being questioned, "and in others, not at all. True, we have yet to pull up an image of the human soul, much less follow it in transit between this world and the next—should there prove to be a next—but there are always quantifiable factors we *can* identify in the laboratory setting." He began to outline some of the experiments he'd done with Jack, and hint at some of the findings, when Bonnie Robb popped in the door, listened for a second, then said, "Whoa! Save all that for when we're on the air! I want you to be fresh. Where's Jack?"

"In makeup," Ellie said.

"Okay, you bring him into the studio when he's ready." Then, to Sprague and Adolph Zakin, she said, "Ready when you are. We might as well get you two seated on camera."

Sprague felt his heart race in his chest, now that the moment had come. Mrs. Zakin patted the back of her husband's hand as he got up. "Break a leg," she said, and he smiled.

Robb led them down the hall and around the corner. She

stopped at a swinging door with a lighted ON AIR sign above it; when the light went off, she took them through, and into the studio itself. They had to circumvent the backdrop of some set, and step over several thick black wires coiled across the floor. She walked them up to a raised wooden platform, carpeted in blue, on which four swivel chairs were arranged in a semicircle; the backdrop here was a stylized skyline of New York. A scruffy guy wearing a headset and consulting a clipboard said, "Sprague?"

"Yes?"

"You're there," and he pointed to the chair on the end.

"Logan?"

"He's coming," Bonnie said.

"Then you're Zakin," he said to Adolph. "Please take the second chair from the right."

When they were seated, the scruffy man came around behind them and attached lavalier microphones to their neckties; Sprague watched with dismay as the little teeth of the microphone clamp bit into the raw silk. "Hide as much of the cord as you can under your jacket," the man said, and Sprague tucked the black wire under his suit coat.

Sprague had never been in a TV studio before, and he was amazed to see how *tacky* it all looked up close. He'd seen this program on television and never thought twice about it; the set looked fine, even rather sleek. But sitting there, under the banks of overhead lights (only a few of which, he was thankful, were turned on—it was already quite warm underneath them) everything seemed bleached out, stark, vacant. The blue carpeting, particularly near the edge of the platform, where presumably the camera wouldn't pick it up, was frayed and worn; the backdrop of New York was just a thin scrim, and, toward the bottom, again where the camera wouldn't intrude, it ended abruptly in a rumpled heap. The stems of several of the flowers in the bowl that rested on the glass coffee table were held erect by twisted strands of wire.

When Jack was brought in, he was seated in the chair next to the one Bonnie Robb was going to occupy. He was wearing blue jeans, neatly pressed, a black blazer, and a white shirt, without a tie. Sprague had hoped he would be better dressed. The floor manager, as Sprague now took him to be, attached the microphone to Jack's lapel, then asked each of them, starting with Sprague at the far end, to count to five. Apparently, he was testing their audio levels. He listened carefully, then mumbled something into the little microphone that was positioned in front of his mouth and connected to his headset. He nodded, moved the microphone on Zakin's tie a little higher up, then asked him to count again.

"Okay?" he asked whomever he was talking to in the control room. "Okay." He turned to Bonnie, conferring with one of the cameramen, and said, "We're one minute away."

Sprague felt his heart do another leap in his chest—one minute away!—but Robb acted as if she had all the time in the world. She finished whatever she was saying to the cameraman, laughed, strolled up onto the platform. Her own microphone was draped across the arm of her chair. She fastened it to a flounce on the bodice of her dress, crossed her legs, and leaned back as though she were waiting for nothing more than a manicure.

"Thirty seconds," said the floor manager. One of the two cameras, large, black, and mounted on a rolling dolly, moved forward, focusing on Robb.

"Twenty."

"Don't worry about looking at the cameras," Robb said to the three of them, "we'll take care of that. Just keep your answers brief and to the point, and don't be afraid to show emotion."

What was *that* supposed to mean, Sprague wondered—did she expect someone to cry?

"Ten." The rest of the overhead lights suddenly came on.

Robb, however, remained unconcerned. She touched her blond hair to see that it was all in place, straightened up in her chair, balanced her small clipboard with its list of questions on her knee; she smiled, but not so brightly as to diminish the seriousness of the story she was about to introduce, and looked into the near camera.

The floor manager held up one hand with the fingers spread, lowered his head in concentration, then pointed his index finger directly at Robb.

"The word *miracle* is often overused," she said, speaking straight into the camera lens; a tiny red light shone just above it. "We say it's a miracle if the train's on time, or the whites come clean in the wash. But *real* ones, real honest-to-God miracles, occur very rarely." She left a beat, then said, "One occurred just three weeks ago, in the Broadway theater district—where miracles are prayed for every night."

Mounted on a wall bracket off to his right, Sprague noticed a TV monitor, which suddenly cut from the head-shot of Bonnie Robb, to an exterior view of the Empire Theater, with its marquee advertising *Steamroller*. It was night, and a well-heeled crowd was leaving through the flung-open double-doors.

"It was a little after eleven that night when Adolph Zakin, owner of the nation's third-largest theater chain, was leaving the opening-night performance of the new musical *Steamroller*. I myself was there to cover that premier performance."

Sprague suddenly sat up straighter in his chair. Did she have footage of the actual event? Why hadn't she told him if she did?

The scene on the monitor cut abruptly from a long shot to a closeup of Bonnie Robb, standing in her coat in the middle of that opening-night throng. She was clearly setting up, saying something that had not been recorded, glancing behind her to see what the background would be.

"We were preparing to shoot an introduction to my review of the show," continued the voice-over, "when something went wrong." On the monitor screen the look on her face changed to one of uncertainty, then concern; she was trying to see something off to her left, bobbing on her tiptoes to see over the crowd.

"Adolph Zakin had stepped back to clear our camera shot, slipped off the curb, and fallen into the street—and directly into the path of an oncoming limousine." The monitor showed only random moments of the drama: the chauffeur gesticulating wildly, the spotlights turning on the flatbed truck across the street, and then, after the camera had apparently been lifted over the head of the man holding it, a wobbly shot of a young man in a long tweed coat, bent down over something in the street. Zakin. His wife was kneeling on the other side, pleading, frenzied. My God! Sprague thought—they've actually got it. He glanced over at Jack, who was also riveted to the scene on the monitor. Had he known about this film? No, it wasn't possible—not from the stupefied look on his face.

Zakin was squinting at the monitor, as if unable to see it very clearly, as if unsure he wanted to see it at all.

"At the time our camera recorded these brief glimpses—and we apologize for the picture quality—we didn't know we were possibly filming a miracle in progress." The shot moved to the front of the limousine, the shining chrome and grille-work—the cameraman must not have known exactly what he was getting—then back, in a sweeping motion, to Jack, who was now pounding Zakin's chest; Mrs. Zakin was trying to stop him. The picture stopped, then resumed, at a point possibly a minute or two later, with another overhead shot of Jack straddling Zakin's prone body, his chest pressed flat against the old man's, his hands clutching his shoulders.

"Mr. Zakin had suffered a major cardiac arrest after being jolted by the limousine; the man seen here, attempting to revive him, is Jack Logan, a musician in the show."

It looked like a still-life, Jack simply pressing himself, rigidly, against the inert body beneath him. But then, something stirred—one of Zakin's hands, resting on the pavement. The fingers twitched, spasmodically. Jack, the tails of his overcoat flung wide, slowly rolled to one side, his eyes closed, his breath clouding in the air. Zakin shivered, from head to toe, then rose up on one elbow, looking totally disoriented. His wife instantly gathered him into her arms; someone in the crowd moved and blocked the camera. The monitor Sprague was watching suddenly switched to Bonnie Robb, live in the studio again.

"A minute later, an ambulance arrived and took Adolph Zakin to St. Luke's-Roosevelt Hospital. Today"—a shot of Zakin on the monitor now—"he is our guest. Mr. Zakin—you said then, and you have repeated since, that you *died* that night, and were brought back to life. How do you know you weren't simply resuscitated by one of the more orthodox measures Jack Logan took, such as pounding your chest?"

"Because . . . because I wasn't." He looked as if he hadn't fully recovered from what he'd just seen on the monitor. "I didn't know that film existed."

"We didn't either," she assured him, "until we took a quick look through the archives just before the show."

Now *that* was bullshit, Sprague thought.

"But tell us what you experienced that night, after you were struck by the car."

"Nothing," Zakin said, "at first. Blackness . . . I died."

The camera, Sprague noted, was staying close in on him.

He went on to describe what were, to Sprague, the already familiar details—the sensation of traveling toward a bright, hot light, the searing intensity of it, the weightlessness, the sense of release. "And then, just as I was about to pass straight into that light—it was changing shape all the time, by the way, you could almost say *beating*—this man sitting next to me now"—and he banged one hand on the arm of Jack's chair—"came up out of nowhere, from somewhere behind me, and put his hands on my shoulders."

Sprague perked up in his chair.

"What did he do then?" Robb asked.

"I don't remember all this very clearly," Zakin said, "but I do remember turning, to face him. It was good not to be looking at that light for a second. He put one hand over my eyes, and it felt terrifically hot, almost electric. I told my wife later that I felt like I'd been soldered back together again, body and soul."

The camera had cut to Jack now, sitting very still in his chair. "Jack Logan, Broadway musician," Bonnie Robb said, with great intensity, "*did* you bring a dead man back to life?"

The camera held on Jack's face as he tried to find an answer.

"What *happened* that night?" she prompted him again, urging him with a flip of her hand to answer quickly.

"I think Mr. Zakin knows as much about it as I do . . ." he said, hesitantly. "I saw him slip off the curb, and the limo pull in . . ."

But this wasn't what Robb wanted to hear. "Yes, we know —we *saw*—all that," she interrupted. "But, in your own words, tell us what you *did*, once you got down on the street with Adolph Zakin . . ."

Jack appeared uncertain of what to say, what he could add to Zakin's account, that would also satisfy Robb. He looked across to Sprague, as if for help, and Sprague leaped in.

"It's a difficult experience for Mr. Logan to recount," Sprague said. "He appears to go into—"

"Let me introduce you to our viewers," Robb interjected.

She gave his name and credentials. "Now, what were you saying he goes into?"

"A sort of trance state," Sprague said, happy to have heard his own billing. You never knew who watched these shows, and what kind of grants they had it in their power to dispense. "What he does—the powers he is able to employ—are difficult to describe, much less to verify."

"But would these powers include the ability to bring someone back to life?" She was determined to get an affirmative answer to that, on the record, and from someone other than Zakin.

Sprague, after a moment's thought, decided to give it to her. "Yes . . . they would."

Robb sat back in her chair, having cleared at least that one obstacle. "What proof do you have, other than what happened to Mr. Zakin?" Now she could show her investigative skills.

"I have personally witnessed the case of a suicide, a man who had ingested a lethal dose of Pavulon, who was resuscitated with no other intervention than what Jack Logan was able to do, with his bare hands."

"Is that what we're talking about then," Robb said, to both Sprague and Jack, "the laying on of hands, what the faith healers have been claiming to do all along?"

"No, that's not what I do," Jack said, roused now to his own defense. "I'm not a faith healer. I never claimed to be. I can't cure people." He stopped short, about to go on, but not sure if he should; his own vehemence had surprised him.

Robb, of course, was delighted; she'd finally gotten a rise out of the star witness, and she wasn't about to let it subside. "What *are* you then? What can you do? According to Dr. Sprague here, you've—for want of a better word—*resurrected* one man who'd killed himself, and saved another who'd died of a massive heart attack."

"But that's not *curing* people, that's not *healing* them. That's what I wanted to say on this show. That's why I agreed, finally, to come on." He stopped again, bent forward in his chair, looking so earnestly into Bonnie Robb's face that her prosecutorial zeal was nearly quashed.

"Go on then," she said, "say what you came on to say."

Jack's head was lowered; he didn't even dare look over at Sprague, for fear he'd disapprove of what he was about to say.

And ever since the weekend, when he'd decided he would need Sprague's help from here on in, he'd tried to do nothing to displease him. "I came on," Jack said, suddenly realizing he had better look up for the camera, "because I didn't want people watching the show to get the wrong impression... I didn't want them to think some guy was posing as some sort of..." He searched for some way to end the sentence, some way not to say the word he had in mind.

"Some sort of what?" Bonnie asked.

"Some sort of, well, like a... Messiah."

Oh, that was *good*, Robb thought.

Jack hastened to explain himself, to put that unfortunate word choice behind him; even saying it, he felt, was somehow wrong, and he was afraid it would be all people would remember of the interview. "In Mr. Zakin's case, or the other one that Dr. Sprague mentioned, I *was* able to do something —I *think*—to help them. I'm not being evasive when I have a hard time explaining it. I don't honestly know yet what I do, or how I do it; that's why I'm at the institute, under Dr. Sprague's supervision—to find out. But in the meantime— and this is what I really wanted to say—people who are ill, or desperate, or who just lost someone, they shouldn't think that there's some miraculous answer out there, some cure-all. Already some people have called the institute and asked for help, and I need to say to those people, I'm sorry, but I can't help you. Not yet. Not now. Not while—"

"You mean you might be able to—or willing to—in the future?" Robb interjected.

She'd broken Jack's stream of thought, his concentration. "I'm not saying I wouldn't, if I *could*, but—"

"When do you think you *will* be ready?"

"It's not a question of being ready, it's a question of... of *understanding* first, exactly what's going on, and not offering people in need of help some kind of hope that isn't there."

Off camera, the floor manager was signaling the remaining time. Thirty seconds? Fifteen? Jack wondered if he'd made his point sufficiently, if he should try to clarify it one more time.

But Robb didn't let him. She turned to Sprague and said, "Do *you* think he's ready, right now, to start saving lives, to bring people back to the world of the living?"

Sprague was caught a bit off-guard; he'd been so intent on

what Jack was saying. "I believe," he said, "that Jack Logan has some extraordinary powers, and that, if the institute can find enough time and money"—no use missing the opportunity—"to develop them, they will prove to be an enormous boon to all mankind. I also—"

"Pardon me, but we've only got a few seconds left, and I want to ask that same question of Adolph Zakin."

"Yes?" He looked confused.

"Do you think Jack Logan is ready to start bringing people back from the dead?" she repeated, anxiously.

Zakin glanced over at Jack, as if not sure what he could say now without appearing disloyal. "I only know what he did for me."

"And what he did for you—you've already said it—was bring you back to life. Right?"

He looked back at Robb.

"Right?"

That man with the headset was making some other time signal with his hands. Zakin held Robb's gaze, and said, simply, "Yes." He was not about to deny the greatest gift he'd ever been given. "Yes."

chapter twenty-one

IT WAS HARD to tell if Jack was awake or asleep. The only light in the room came from the illuminated face of the clock, and the flashing red light on the answering machine. At midnight, the last call had come in—from an elderly man, with some sort of kidney disease in a hospital bed in Westchester. He'd still been talking when the machine cut him off.

Jack was lying very still now, one arm draped across Nancy's bare abdomen. She wanted to get up and go to the bathroom, but if he was asleep, she didn't want to disturb him. She turned her head on the pillow and looked at him; his eyes were closed. Gently, she lifted his arm away from her damp skin and rolled to the side of the bed. When she stood up, she felt her skirt and stockings, all knotted up, on the floor beneath her feet. So much for the stockings, she thought.

In the bathroom, she waited till she'd closed the door before turning on the light. It was so harsh and bright she had to close her eyes for a second to shut out the glare. Well, she thought, waiting for her eyes to adjust, she'd done it now— and squinted at herself in the mirror above the sink. There were smudges under her eyes where the makeup had run, and several stray hairs were pasted to her cheek. Her bra, still strung on one shoulder, trailed down her back; in their haste, they'd never even gotten it completely off. Now she removed it and tucked it over the towel rack. She rinsed her face and wondered if Jack would mind if she used his toothbrush—and figured that, after all that had already gone on between them, it couldn't really matter.

But then—what did? Did what they'd just done *matter*?

For once in her life, she knew, without a doubt, that it had. She didn't have to convince herself. She *knew*.

After the TV show, which she'd watched on a portable TV at the institute, she'd met him at the Olympia. He was still all keyed up about it, relieved that it was over—and that he'd fulfilled his obligation to Sprague—but worried that it hadn't gone the way he'd hoped. "I said what I'd set out to say, or at least most of it, but I don't think that's what people will have heard—I think they'll have heard Zakin saying 'Yes, he brought me back from the dead.' That's all I think they'll have come away with." Nancy didn't know what to say to that—because, basically, she thought he was right, that his high-minded appeal for forebearance and understanding had fallen on deaf ears. Zakin's testimony was what they would re-member of that show—and the flurry of phone messages on his machine that night had borne her out.

At his apartment, after, there'd been no talking, no delay; he'd flipped the lock on the door, turned to her, and kissed her. They'd fallen back onto the bed, still kissing feverishly, groping at each other's clothes. She turned her head now and in the mirror she could see a slight purplish mark on her neck; she had felt his teeth there when he'd come. Her sister, she knew, would spot it on her at fifty paces.

But what time was it now, she wondered? The clock had been turned away from her, and her watch was somewhere on the bed or the floor, in that tangled heap of clothes. Her ear-rings were missing too—when had she taken them off?

When she turned off the light and went back to the bed, Jack said, "Hi."

She laughed, softly. "Hi," she replied, and laid down be-side him, on her stomach. She propped her elbows on the bed. "You know it's ten after two."

"I was just wondering that."

"Isn't your family going to be frantic?" His hand lightly rested on the small of her back.

"I already took care of that."

"How?"

She hadn't intended to tell him this, and she still wasn't sure it was such a good idea. But she'd already started, so she finished. "I called them when the show was over and told them I'd be working late at the institute, and might just stay the night there instead of going home and then back again first thing in the morning."

"And they bought it?" He stroked her back gently.

"Of course they bought it. They trust me."

With his fingers, he traced a small circle at the base of her spine. "So do I," he said.

The circling motion made her skin tingle.

"I mean that," he said. "I swore, after breaking up with my last girlfriend—"

"Stephanie?"

"Yes . . . How'd you remember that?"

"Women remember such things."

"I'll keep that in mind . . . Anyway, the point is, I swore to myself I'd never trust anybody again. I'd never leave myself open to that kind of hurt again. And now, here I am, with you." He shook his head on the pillow. "When you came back with me from the Underground, and I showed you those clippings, and explained to you about my mother . . . I knew how crazy it all sounded, but I knew I had to tell you; I knew that I *could* tell you."

God, what a night that had been: Jack nearly in shock on the cab ride uptown, then, once they got to his apartment, positively manic, throwing the clippings at her, waving a rolled-up theater program—saying something about its having belonged to his mother—insisting she *believe* him. It had been the scariest night of her life.

And now, here she was, in bed with him . . . and not scared in the least.

His fingers traced a larger circle, grazing the top of her buttocks.

"I knew I could tell you anything," he said, "and no matter what, you wouldn't run away from me, or laugh, or hate me for it. I knew I could chance it again, with you."

She wanted to reply, to say something tender and reassuring, but words were the last thing on her mind at that moment. His hand had gradually eased itself down, until he was brushing, back and forth, across the cheeks of her ass. She felt as though her skin were catching fire. When he trailed his fingertips even lower, into the crevice between her legs, touching the insides of her thighs, she dropped her head, her hair hanging down onto the rumpled sheets.

"I gather you trust me, too," he whispered.

She laid herself flat against the sheet, her eyes closed, her head turned toward the door.

She felt him stir on the bed beside her, then place both of his hands on her buttocks. He was straddling her, as she had once done him, that night she had massaged his shoulders. He was kneading her flesh between his fingers, and gradually opening her, more and more. He gently urged her legs farther apart.

"I wish there was more light," he said, "to see you by."

He slipped his hands around and under her, lifting her ass in the air.

"I wish there was more light," he repeated, pulling her back against him now. "I wish . . . there was . . . more light . . ."

Nancy had no need for light; at that moment, she felt in need of nothing.

At the front desk, Tulley seemed to pay no attention to the fact that they had come in together.

In the elevator, holding hands, Nancy said, "With Sprague, we'd better be more circumspect."

"We're not there yet," Jack said, glancing at the lighted panel above the door, then pulling her toward him. "We've got three more floors." He put one arm around her waist, almost lifting her off her feet, and kissed her. The elevator bumped to a halt, one floor below Sprague's, and Jack had just let go of her when the doors slid open.

Sprague was standing there, his hands thrust deep into the pockets of his lab coat, his feet tapping with impatience. His eyes flicked from one to the other; Nancy blushed and looked down at her feet. Jack wanted to tell her to look up and brazen it out. But it was already too late.

"Morning," Jack said. "I thought you always took—"

"The stairs? I saw the elevator was coming up."

The doors started to close automatically. Jack pressed the OPEN button. But Sprague stayed where he was.

"I was coming upstairs to wait for you both," he said. "I had no idea I'd be so fortunate as to catch you together."

Jack didn't like the sound of that "catch you together."

"Come out—I have something to show you."

They stepped out of the elevator and followed Sprague down the hall. As they passed the steel doors behind which the lab animals were kept, Jack caught a faint whiff of that terrible stench he remembered from the week before. To his relief, they stopped at another door, on the opposite side of the hall, and Sprague pulled a large key from his pocket.

"I've been working on this all night, for the past two nights," he said, jiggling the key in the lock, then pushing the door open. "It's lucky I remembered it was here."

He flicked on the lights and ushered them into the room. There was a battery of machines—to Jack, it looked sort of like the control panel in a recording studio—set up on one side of a floor-to-ceiling glass wall. On the other side of the wall, where the lights had not yet been turned on, there was a large cylinder, no less than eight feet long, and painted a pale robin's egg blue.

"It's a holdover from the hippie-dippy days," Sprague said, with some disdain, "but I should be grateful it was never dismantled."

"What is it?" Nancy asked.

"Before your time, perhaps." He turned on the lights on the other side of the partition. "It's a sensory-deprivation tank."

Jack went to the glass and looked through. The cylinder was resting on two or three wrestling mats, and bolstered on all sides by cinder blocks. At the near end, two black hoses and several orange wires protruded from the shell, snaked their way across the linoleum-covered floor, and disappeared under the base of the room divider. Clearly, they hooked up, somehow, to the array of instruments in the control room.

"As soon as you showed me those newspaper articles about your birth," Sprague said to Jack, "I knew I would have to put you into the trance state again, to see what, if anything, we could dredge up. I wanted to regress you as far back as possible." He came and stood just behind Jack, his reflection appearing, ghostlike, in the glass. "But I was never satisfied with the results we achieved upstairs. I always felt we had only scratched the surface of your potential." He smiled and lifted his chin toward the cylinder. "Then I thought of this."

"Why will this be any better?"

"For one thing, we'll deprive your senses, just as the name of the thing implies, of all external stimuli; you'll be able to concentrate entirely on your inner vision. Second"—and here he sounded particularly triumphant—"I have taken some pains to create, in terms of water temperature, salinity level, et cetera, a close facsimile of the fetal environment."

Jack turned to face him directly. Sprague's eyes were bloodshot, no doubt from his round-the-clock labors, but he seemed terrifically pleased with himself.

"It'll be close as we can get to a womb," Sprague explained. "Possibly that will help you to recall, or even recreate, what may have transpired during those formative months of your embryonic life."

"If I was just an embryo," Jack said, "how could I be thinking, or noticing, anything—much less remember it now?"

Sprague's good humor abruptly vanished from his face; he hated to be challenged. "Don't question what you do not understand," he said. "At only seven weeks after conception, you had hands that moved, and clearly defined fingers. The bones of your skull were already growing together to protect your incipient brain. At fifteen weeks, your sensory organs were almost completely formed. At sixteen, you were moving actively inside the womb; you had a mouth, lips, and eyes that could *see*. No one knows—least of all you—precisely what a human being is capable of, at *any* stage of its development. Let us not close our minds to any possibilities."

Jack glanced over at Nancy, who shook her head as if to say "What did you expect?"

"Sorry," he said, to placate Sprague, "I'll keep my mind open."

"Good. Then we can go forward with this right now."

"You mean, you want me in the tank now?"

"I already told you, I've been up for two nights just getting it prepared. I didn't do all that just for the hell of it. Nancy," he said, turning to her, "take off your coat, for God's sake. I'll want you to help me monitor the various readings. We're going to be recording all the usual things, and several others in addition. Jack, you can come with me."

He opened a door, also made of glass, at the far right side of the wall, and strode into the tank room. The air was warm and humid. "I want you to take a look at this first," Sprague said, "so you can see what we're doing."

Jack stepped up after him, onto the wrestling mats. Sprague slipped his fingers into a small indentation on the top of the cylinder, then slid back a hatchway about three feet long. The inside of the tank smelled to Jack like the seashore.

"The water in there is about twenty inches deep," Sprague said, "and the salinity is enough to keep you afloat without touching the bottom. You see that black disc in the side wall, near the top?" He pointed to something that resembled the mouthpiece on a telephone receiver. "That's a two-way microphone. You can hear us; we can hear you. The sockets you see around it"—there were three—"are for the heart and brain-wave readings. The electrodes I attach to you will have jacks at the other end; you simply stick the red jack in the red socket, the blue jack in the blue, the black in the black. Get it?"

"Sounds simple enough."

"Good. Get undressed."

"What?"

"Get undressed. Let's get started."

Jack glanced at the glass control booth, to see if Nancy could hear what Sprague had just said. She appeared to be trying not to laugh, so he assumed she had. Sprague caught his glance, and said, "Please—let's not be ridiculous. Do you want me to tell Nancy to turn around?"

She did, without Sprague's asking.

Jack took off his clothes, laid them on the wrestling mat. "Everything?" he said, stopping at his underpants.

"I think you'd be very uncomfortable in there with those on."

Jack stepped out of them, and Sprague removed from the voluminous pockets of his lab coat a roll of surgical adhesive tape and several of the electrode wires, which he attached, like leeches, to Jack's chest and temples. Finally, he added a thin pair of rubber ear muffs, which he fitted securely over Jack's entire ear.

"Now," Sprague said, "if you will step into the tank, gently—I don't want you to disturb the water any more than necessary—we can get things underway."

Jack was almost glad to get into the tank; it had felt awfully strange to be standing there stark naked, with Sprague taping wires to him and Nancy keeping her back turned. (At one point, she had peeked over her shoulder and smiled.) The water was quite warm, and the bottom of the tank slippery smooth. Jack held onto the edge of the hatchway as he lowered himself in.

"Before you lie back," Sprague said, "stick the jacks in the sockets."

He watched as Jack did so, then, satisfied, said, "Lie down now."

Hesitantly, Jack lay back in the tank, allowing his legs to come up off the bottom, his head to rest in the cushion of salty water. As soon as he was lying flat, buoyed up in the center of the tank, Sprague said, "Fine—are you comfortable?"

"Yes," Jack said, the water sloshing gently up onto his chest and under his chin. It drummed softly against the rubber sheaths covering his ears.

"And you can hear me fine?"

"No problem."

"Then I'll close this now."

Sprague slowly rolled the hatchway closed, shutting out the light. Jack found himself plunged, suddenly, into an absolute and total blackness. His first thought was that this was what it must be like to be buried alive, to see the lid of the coffin closing. But far from feeling "sensorily deprived," he felt himself instead keenly aware—of the warm, salty water bathing his limbs, of the gentle drumming sound in his ears, of the rich, deep blackness surrounding him. All his senses seemed to have been put on alert, alive to every nuance in his sealed environment, anxiously striving, in one way or another, to *perceive*.

He had only been in the tank a minute or two—or at least that was all it seemed—when he heard Sprague's disembodied voice, speaking to him in the darkness. "If you can hear me," the voice said, clear but with a tinny electric edge to it, "say yes."

"Yes . . . I can hear you," Jack replied. He licked a speck of salt from his lips.

"Good," he heard Sprague saying, as if to himself, "the sound quality's fine." There were a couple of taps, and clicking noises, and then Sprague said, "Jack, I want you to do the standard entry to the trance state. I'll count off the numbers for you; then, once you're under, we'll take it from there. Are you ready?"

"Ready."

"One."

Jack rolled his eyes up, toward the top of his head.

"Two."

He closed the lids.

"Three."

He exhaled slowly, and let his eyes, beneath the closed lids, relax and drop to the normal level. As he did so, he felt his whole body also relax, trained to it now by frequent repetition. He let his limbs float free, and languidly, in the water, and his mind, in its own way, do the same . . . float away, free of his body . . .

In the control booth, Sprague flicked off the outgoing microphone; he would still be able to hear any sound from inside the tank, but Jack would not be disturbed by any noises he or Nancy made. Quickly, he pointed out to Nancy where the various controls and meters were, and told her what to keep track of. She seemed to have already figured out most of it; grudgingly, he admitted to himself that, as lab assistants went, she was smarter than most. In fact, if he came right down to it, she was the smartest he'd ever had.

And judging from what he now knew was going on with Logan—his initial suspicions, that day he'd seen them huddled over the light box, had been correct—she was also the most alluring. So they had a love affair going? That was something he'd have to think over, at a less critical time. One way or another, there would be ramifications to it, for good or ill, and he would have to keep as well apprised of it as he could. He might even be able to work it to his own advantage, somehow.

"The readings," Nancy said, "are just beginning to slow down."

"How much?"

"Still within normal range." The heartbeat was approaching what would, under most circumstances, be the sleep state. But it was, as usual, the electroencephalograph readings that worried her. His brain activity had, for a brief time, soared;

then, as she had now seen on these tests several times, it had begun its inexorable dip, toward the region where it had no business being. She had, from the very first, been alarmed by this precipitous decline But now—especially with last night behind her—she felt terrified. Sprague glanced over at the meters, drummed his fingers on the top of the console; then, apparently, he decided it was time to begin guiding Jack wherever he wanted him to go. He put a finger to his lips, to indicate Nancy should no longer speak to him, then flicked his microphone back on. Whether it was intentional or not, his voice dropped a register, and took on some of that mellifluous quality Nancy associated with FM disc jockeys.

"Jack . . . I want you to remain utterly relaxed, totally at ease, and attend only to the sound of my voice." For the next few minutes, he recited all the standard instructions and questions, and received from Jack the expected, monosyllabic replies. For Nancy, it was eerie to hear Jack's voice issuing from the microphone speaker; because of the tank, it had a hollow, almost sepulchral tone to it.

"Jack . . . I want you now to think back, to when you were six years old, and in the first grade . . . I want you to think about something you liked about that, anything at all, and tell me what it was."

Sprague was just fishing, Nancy knew, asking any old question at all, on his way to the stuff he really wanted to know. Jack was saying something about a tetherball game, played in the schoolyard, and Sprague was just waiting for him to finish. The second he had, Sprague asked him to think back even further, to when he was three or four, and to tell him now something he remembered from those years, good or bad, it didn't matter, just something from the time before he had even gone to school. There was a longer pause, during which Nancy could swear she heard the gentle sloshing of the water in the tank—looking out at it, it was hard to believe that Jack was floating, naked and in a trance, inside it—and then Jack said something about Mam and a Ferris wheel, and swaying in the air, high above the beach at Asbury Park. This seemed to interest Sprague a little bit more, and he asked Jack to tell him why he thought this had made such a strong impression. "What is it," he said, "you remember most about that ride on the Ferris wheel?"

"I remember most . . . the dusk,'" Jack said. "It was the end of the day. I was looking out, over the ocean, at the horizon . . . It was the first time I'd seen something like that."

"Like the horizon?"

"Yes . . . you could actually *see* the way the earth curved . . . the way the light was fading away at the edges . . . the way . . ."

Sprague waited, then asked, "The way what?"

"The way it . . . reminded me of something . . ."

"Reminded you? Of something from even earlier in your life?"

Nancy knew, though she was afraid to look, that Jack's EEG line would be rapidly flattening out . . . if it hadn't already. She looked—and confirmed her worst fears. She tapped Sprague on the shoulder and pointed to the printout; Sprague seemed totally unsurprised.

Returning to the microphone, he asked again, "What did the sight of the horizon, at dusk, remind you of, Jack?"

"Of . . . I don't know . . . somewhere I'd been already . . ."

"But you said you'd never seen anything like it before."

"Not, you know, in real life . . . not since I'd been born . . ."

The blackness in the tank had yielded, gradually, almost imperceptibly, to a somber gray. At first, Jack had thought his eyes were simply becoming accustomed to the dark, but then he had realized that even with them closed, the same gray light, cloudy and roiling, filled his vision. It was like wandering through an immense steam bath, without walls, without boundaries of any sort, seeing no one, but aware, nonetheless, of not being alone.

Aware, in fact, of multitudes.

But wherever he looked, the shapes—faces?—which had almost coalesced, seemed instantly to evaporate again, into the same gray, misty vapor The vapor seemed *composed* of those evanescent forms, of their strange and unspoken longings. He felt, as he passed through it, that the mist fairly clung to him, with invisible fingers, and parted only reluctantly. He knew what he was looking for, and knew, as well, that it would be looking for him.

When, he wondered, would they meet?

Sprague's voice came to him, over the tank speaker,

sounding as it would on a transatlantic call—muted, submerged, oddly delayed. "Jack," he was saying, "where are you now? Tell me what you're seeing, where you are."

How could Jack answer? What could he say? Ever since that day he'd pulled Freddy Nunemaker from the sand heap, he'd thought of this place, when he thought of it at all, as "where you go after." He'd never formulated it more than that, never tried to attach any other name or explanation to it. And now, with Sprague asking him to name the place, he found himself unwilling to say even that. It wasn't just "where you go after," but also, and he now understood it more fully than ever before, as the place—

"Did I pick better this time?" The voice and the face materialized at the same moment, out of the mist in front of him.

Jack didn't understand.

"In the train car, you said I'd picked a strange place to meet . . . is this any better?"

He was still trying to get over her sudden appearance, and Sprague was saying, distantly, "Jack, can you hear me?"

"Yes," he replied, "I can hear you."

His mother grimaced; her expression said "Why is he bothering us?"

"Then tell me what's going on."

"Tell him you went to visit your dear old mom," she said, and Jack wondered, suddenly, if Sprague could hear her voice, too.

"Can he—" he started to whisper to her, but she shook her head, smiling, and said, "No, not unless I really wanted him to. I'm dead, remember?"

"What was that?" Sprague asked, anxiously. "What did you start to say?"

"I'm where you think I am," Jack said, "doing what I have to . . ."

Sprague switched off the outgoing microphone, and slammed his fist against the console. "What the hell is that supposed to mean?" He swiveled in his chair, toward Nancy. "'Where you think I am, doing what I have to'—what *is* all this cryptic bullshit?"

Nancy kept her head down, said nothing; with Sprague, she'd learned the hard way that it was best simply to let the storm pass. If you tried to calm it, you'd only get drenched.

It was Jack she was worried about—she was fairly confident no physical harm could come to him, floating serenely in the sensory-deprivation tank, but she wasn't at all sure about the psychological effects he might sustain. How many times could he make this bizarre, unnatural journey—wherever it was he actually went, however it was he actually got there—and still return unscathed, unaffected?

Over the intercom speaker, she heard him say "Not until now," and wondered, with a shiver, who he was talking to.

"But now you do?"

He looked around again, trying to pierce the veil of mist. "I know that this is where I must have been." It was, in some ways, familiar to him now; it was "where you go after," where he'd come to fetch Nunemaker, Zakin, Garcia. But it was also unfamiliar—the white light, which beat so relentlessly, was nowhere to be seen. To the extent he could determine direction at all, it was somewhere off to his right, and above him; from that direction, he could sense, through the passing vapors, a faintly warming glow. But nothing more than that. He had the vague, ineffable feeling of having arrived in some sort of limbo.

"We were here together, a long time ago," his mother said, wistfully. She wasn't wearing the high school jacket this time; she had on a simple summer dress, with fabric straps that tied over her bare shoulders. Jack didn't remember it among the things he'd found in the attic trunk.

"I didn't know whether I wanted to stay here, or leave," she said, absently brushing her hair back, over her shoulders. "I didn't know what I could expect."

"What you could expect, if you left?"

"If I died, outright. If those . . . if *they* had let me be one thing or the other."

Dead or alive, Jack took her to mean.

"I'm sorry," he said.

She shrugged, and gave him a sad smile. "Not your fault, God knows." She laughed, harshly. "Nothing you could do about it," she said, looking him up and down. "You had no more on you then than you do now."

For a second, Jack had no idea what she meant; then, with

another horrid shock, he realized that he must be appearing to her naked, just as he was in the tank. He looked down at himself, and saw that, like the spirits that he had encountered here before, his flesh was both visible and strangely transparent. He tried to cover himself with his hands, then wondered if his hands couldn't be seen through as well. He felt foolish even trying to hide himself, and his mother laughed at his attempt.

"I was wondering when you'd notice," she said. Throwing her head back, she laughed again. He wanted to laugh with her, but was still too embarrassed.

"Is there anything I can do," he said, "to—"

"Cover yourself?" She paused, as if contemplating it, then said, "I don't think so . . . you come here with whatever you have, or don't have, on your back."

"But you," he said, "each time I've seen you, you've had something else on, even things that I've seen in the trunk at Mam and Clancy's."

She was nodding her head, as if pleased that he was so perceptive. "That's different," she said. "*I'm* different, in case you haven't noticed."

Suddenly, she was wearing the blue-and-white jacket with "Weehawken High" on the back.

"I am no longer bound . . ."

Then she appeared to him in a tie-dyed shirt, and a pair of feather earrings.

" . . .by the boring conventions . . ."

A red sweater and blue jeans.

" . . .of everyday life. I can wear anything I wore . . ."

A ski parka and boots.

" . . .and even *be* anything I was."

A little girl, with green eyes and short dark hair, stood in front of him—she looked to be six or seven years old. A butterfly pin was clipped to her plaid jumper.

"For grammar school, I went to St. Ignatius. Did you know that? I hated the uniform, and I always wore this," she said, displaying the pin, "just to be different."

Jack was dumbfounded.

"The thing about the spirit is," the little girl went on, rubbing one shiny black shoe on top of the other, "it can look like anything it was in life, from the second you started to the

second you died. It's all the ages you were, and no age at all.
That's what I call the good part."

"What's the bad part?" Jack asked, numbly.

"It can't ever change."

Jack was confused. "It just did."

She wagged her head from side to side, chin down, like a
little girl refusing to take her nap. "No it didn't. Just the way
it *looked* changed. *It* stayed the same."

Jack followed, and yet he didn't; he felt that his mind was
about to explode, with all that it was being asked to grasp. He
didn't even know who, or what, he was talking to anymore—
a little Catholic schoolgirl, fresh from catechism class, or an
elusive young woman, with a tragic past. An elusive young
woman who'd once carried him in her womb.

"Mother," he said, feeling ridiculous addressing a six-year-
old that way, "I need to—"

"You *don't* need to call me Mother," the girl interrupted.
"Call me . . ."

And she changed again, before his very eyes, into the
young woman in the summer dress.

". . . Eliza. That's what I liked my friends to call me, at the
end."

"Eliza, then—I need to *know* what's happening to me. I
need to know what *I* can do, and how." The vapors seemed to
grow thicker between them, her figure somehow to recede. "I
need to know what's *happening* to me."

In the control room, Sprague howled with frustration—
he'd been hearing one-half of the conversation all along, the
enigmatic apologies and queries, the comments on what *she*
—presumably his mother, that's what he'd called her at one
point—was wearing, the puzzling question "What's the bad
part?" He was overhearing all the critical questions, but none
—*not one*—of the critical answers. And *now*, the most important information of all was about to be transmitted, and
again he was locked out, unable to hear it, unable to glean for
himself what he'd worked so hard to uncover.

Nancy could see him debating whether to cut in, through
the intercom, or not. And she knew he was afraid that if he
did, he might break the trance, or interfere with what little he
was getting. But there was something else, something that had

just begun to show up on the cardiograph readings, that she wanted Sprague to know, right away.

"I think you should look at this," she said. "This hasn't ever happened before. His heart rhythms have slowed, even more than usual. It's almost as if the machine is having trouble reading them."

Sprague, still itching to interrogate Jack, cast a distracted eye over the charts.

"I don't know if it's a mechanical defect, or if something is wrong with Jack," Nancy said, and Sprague actually began to focus in on the data, "but either way, I think it's clear we should stop the experiment now."

Sprague was rubbing his lower lip between his fingers.

"Shouldn't you begin the instructions to break the trance state?" Nancy urged. "I think it's very clear that—"

"Nothing will be stopped, until I say so." Sprague's eyes flashed behind his spectacles. "Is *that* clear?"

"What's happening to you?" she said, echoing his question. "That's easy—you're waking up."

He'd never felt more like he was living in a dream.

"You've figured out that you're not *like* all the rest of those people, the ones who mind all the rules and do what they're told..." She seemed, as she spoke, to be moving backward, away from him. He started to follow her. "You've figured out you don't belong with them."

"Where do I belong then?" But she didn't answer. She seemed to have wrapped herself in a shroud of mist. As best he could tell, they were moving away from the source of light and heat. How slow, or fast, they were going, he had no way to gauge. He only knew that, as he traveled, he felt increasingly cold, and inconsolable.

"You belong," she finally said, "with me," and sighed, sadly. "I'm the one who made you what you are, who gave you these special...gifts."

The mists were beginning to boil around them now, a dark and turgid stew of movement.

"I died, giving you life...and I gave you something more." Her voice was earnest, but her features, behind the mist, were unclear. "I gave you a piece of my spirit, Jack—a piece of my life...and a piece of my death." Out of the swirling cloud of vapor, her arm extended, the blue-and-silver bracelet dangling from the wrist. He reached out, to take her hand, but her fingers remained tantalizingly beyond his grasp.

"You were born opened up, to the whole universe—and I saw to it you stayed that way."

The fog around them grew denser and more agitated, and he suddenly became afraid of losing his way in it. He clutched again at her extended hand, and this time she let him grasp her fingers. He felt himself drawn, with extraordinary power, into her embrace; her eyes were blazing green, with delight, and her teeth sparkled white as she laughed. Over her shoulder, far behind, but growing closer all the time, he could now make out a churning bank of thick black cloud, rolling in place like a monstrous wave, seething like a storm held in check on the horizon . . .

"You have to stop it, now!" Nancy insisted. "If you don't, I will."

Sprague was scrutinizing the charts, running the paper strips back and forth between his fingers. The brainwaves had done just as he'd expected; he'd learned not to be surprised by this. But the heart readings . . . they made no sense at all. The rhythm had slowed, altered, then slowed some more; just when it appeared it would come to a stop, it had suddenly been punctuated by a strong, regular beat again . . . with a murmur effect after. It was as if the heart were beating in syncopated time, as if one rhythm were gradually subsuming another, as if, in fact, there were *two* hearts beating on the single chart . . .

"Are you going to stop it?" Nancy said, rising from her stool.

. . . as if there were *two* hearts beating, one growing stronger, the other weaker; Sprague gazed out in wonder at the pale blue tank. My God—what did he have inside of it now? He suddenly jumped up out of his chair and made for the glass door.

"What are you doing?" Nancy shouted.

"Don't touch anything!"

He threw the door open, and ran into the humid room. The wrestling mats squelched beneath his feet. His fingers scrabbled at the indentation in the hood of the tank, then he caught hold of the hatchway and slid it back.

Jack was curled, in the fetal position, his head awkwardly twisted up and out of the water. His eyes were open, staring blankly, unfocused. He was breathing, but low, and stertorously.

And he was alone in the tank.

Sprague looked wildly around the room—had something escaped when he'd opened the hatch?—then back inside, at Jack. His eyes had narrowed, against the intrusion of the light, and his left hand, held until now as if it had been clutching something, suddenly relaxed.

Damn, Sprague thought—*damn damn damn*. He'd come so close, closer than ever before! But what would he have in the way of proof? Nothing, again. Absolutely *nothing*.

Nancy was standing beside him now, looking tense and terrified. Logan's eyes were fully closed. "Jack," Sprague said, tonelessly, and with some reluctance, "I'm going to bring you out of the trance state now..."

chapter
twenty-two

"How long will it take?"

"Just two days. By Friday morning, your new phone number will be in operation."

"And the one I have now," Jack asked, "will be working until then?"

"Yes."

He figured he'd just do as he'd been doing, and leave the answering machine on. "Okay. Thanks," and he hung up. By the end of the week, he'd be free of all the unsolicited calls. And he'd only give out his new number to the few people who needed to have it, and whom he could trust.

But what should he do now? Nancy wasn't coming over till seven o'clock, and it was only two now; outside, it looked cold and gray. Still, anything was better than hanging around the apartment, practicing scales and wondering if he should give Bert a call to ask about his job. He figured he'd go over to Riverside Park and get some fresh air.

In the downstairs foyer, he stopped to collect his mail—a couple of Christmas catalogues, a Con Ed bill, and two letters with return addresses he didn't recognize. He was checking to see if they were really addressed to him when a man in a brown tweed jacket and an ascot pushed the door open and said, in an English accent, "Jack Logan, I presume?"

Jack hesitated.

"Geoffrey, with a g, Mansfield—from the *Investigator*." He put out his hand and Jack reluctantly took it. There was a camera slung over his shoulder.

"I've called for you at the Institute of Abnormal Psychology, and I'm afraid that got me nowhere. And answering machines I find so off-putting—I thought I'd just come 'round and see if I could catch you in your very lair." He smiled, not very convincingly, and with one hand tried to brush down his thinning hair. "Windy out today—reminds me of home."

"What is it you want?" Jack said, stuffing the mail into the pocket of his overcoat. "I'm on my way out."

Mansfield was not a man to be easily deterred. Still smiling, he said, "Just a few minutes of your time, Mr. Logan. Your story, as it's been presented in the *Post*, has interested me, but I don't feel—to be perfectly honest with you—that it's been accorded the kind of attention which, if what's been said is true, it truly warrants."

Jack pushed past him, and out of the door. Mansfield pretended to have been holding it open for him.

"Nothing personal," Jack said, over his shoulder, "but I'm really not interested in any more stories about me." He walked quickly away. "Sorry to have wasted your time."

"But you haven't," Mansfield said, scurrying up to walk beside him. "This was all entirely on my own initiative. I don't hold *you* responsible for what *I* decide to do."

He'd had his phone number changed; now, Jack wondered, would he have to move? The camera was bobbing against Mansfield's back.

"What I'd *like*, if you could just spare me the time—and I'd be very appreciative if you could—is to talk to you, in *depth*, about these unusual talents of yours. I want to know what you *think* about them, and who the real Jack Logan *is*. I'm not interested in some superficial, sensationalistic rehash of what's already been said—I want *your* words, and *your* thoughts, on what's been happening. I want, and I believe the *Investigator*'s readers would want, to know exactly—"

Jack stopped, turned, and put up his hand. "I meant what I said. No story."

Mansfield, his mouth still open, looked as if he was just waiting for Jack to finish, before going on with the rest of his pitch.

"No story," Jack repeated, to forestall him. "Now if you want to walk around after me, there's not much I can do about that. But it's not going to do you much good either—I've got nothing else to say, about any of this."

"But I can promise you—"

"So with all due respect—"

"—that your story will be told—"

"—bug off."

Mansfield's mouth shut, then seemed to set itself rigidly into place. He glared at Jack. "I'm giving you one last chance," he said, between barely parted lips, "to cooperate with this. The story will be written, one way or the other, and I can promise you," he said, repeating his earlier phrase in a more sinister tone, "it will be better for you if you'd gone along." His hair, what there was of it, was blowing wildly about his head.

Jack couldn't believe the guy was threatening him now. "See ya around," he said, and turned away. As he walked down the block, he could swear he felt Mansfield's eyes boring a hole in his back.

The park was just what he needed—sparsely populated, with a strong wind blowing off the Hudson. He went past the barren trees and brown earth, down to the waterfront. He headed south, toward the boat basin, and when he got there, turned up the collar of his coat and took a seat on an empty bench. His thoughts skittered from his encounter with Mansfield to the TV show with Robb, from Nancy to Stephanie (shit, what if she showed up now, walking Kurt's dog for him?), from his mother to Mam. Christmas was right around the corner and Mam and Clancy would be expecting him; he didn't look forward to it. Especially now, with Mam so unwell.

He was still wrapped up in his thoughts when someone else took a seat, at the other end of the bench. An elderly man, incongruously dressed in a bulging down coat and a stocking hat. At first Jack took no notice of him, then realized, when he looked again, that it was actually a *young* man sitting there. He'd been fooled by the drawn features of his face, the lack of any hair poking out from the hat, and the slow, fragile way in which he'd sat down. When their eyes met, the man nodded, and Jack nodded back.

"Beautiful here, isn't it," the man said, looking out over the gray water and the boats bobbing along the piers.

"Yes . . . it is."

"Ever since I was a kid, I've found the sight of water—an ocean, a river, a lake—soothing. The bigger the body of water, the smaller my own problems seemed to be in comparison."

Jack knew what he was talking about—he had always enjoyed such vistas himself, and felt that they somehow put things in his own life into perspective. But this guy looked as if he should be studying nothing less than the Pacific.

"My name's Baldwin," he said, "Adam Baldwin," and he waited, as if Jack might possibly recognize it.

"Jack Logan."

"I know."

"It took Jack a second to grasp what he'd just heard, then, suddenly, he felt a steel gate drop somewhere deep inside him. This wasn't just some stranger sharing his bench—this was another setup, or another needy case, or even, could it be . . . "You're not from the *Investigator*, are you?"

"The what?"

"The tabloid."

"No."

"Are you a reporter?"

"No."

"Then how do you know me?"

"I don't. I saw you on TV the other day. I went to your building, to try to talk to you, but you were just leaving, with that man carrying the camera."

"And you don't know him?"

"Never saw him before in my life . . . I *will* admit that I trailed you here, which wasn't easy." He smiled weakly. "You walk pretty fast, and I walk pretty slow—these days."

"Why did you?" Jack asked, though he already knew. He knew from the sad but eager look in the man's eyes, from the dead-white pallor of his skin, from the hairless skull he knew was concealed beneath the stocking hat with the bright red pompom dangling forlornly from its top. He knew, and his heart virtually contracted in his chest.

"Because I'm dying," the man said, "and because I thought you might be able to help me." He looked down, and then away again, off across the river. They sat in silence as a couple of kids raced past on beaten-up dirt bikes. "I know it's asking a lot," he said, "but I'm sort of beyond being polite these days. It's one of those things I can't afford anymore."

"What's wrong?" Jack asked, gently, though he dreaded to hear the answer. This guy looked to be more than a few years older than *he* was.

"Cancer of the brain," Baldwin replied. "Inoperable." He sounded quite matter-of-fact about it. "My wife spoke to the Institute of Abnormal Psychology after we first heard about you. We never heard back."

Exactly how many calls had there been like this, Jack wondered? What was Sprague doing with them all? What *could* he do?

"I realize you've probably been inundated," Baldwin said. "Still, after seeing about the ten-thousandth specialist last week, and hearing the same prognosis—which is, basically, forget it—I thought I'd take a chance." Seeing that he had engaged Jack's attention, and even his sympathy, Baldwin slid a littler closer to him on the bench, and recounted the history of his disease.

Jack, as he listened, could not get his mind off the fact that this ravaged man, with possibly only days left to live, was somewhere close, *very* close, to his own age. It brought home the horror, and the sadness, of it so much more strongly, made him feel some aching sort of bond with him. When Baldwin reached into his back pocket and pulled out his wallet—"I want to show you a picture of my baby girl"—Jack almost begged him to stop. But the picture was already out, and Jack was holding it in his fingers. A young woman, in a hospital bed, beaming and holding a ruddy-faced baby.

"She's gotten a lot prettier than that since then," Baldwin said. "The baby, I mean."

"Your wife's pretty too."

Baldwin took the picture back, gazed at it, then replaced it in his wallet. His motions were all slow and fearful, the motions of an elderly man afraid of breaking fragile bones. "It's as much for them, as myself, that I want to live," he said. "As much for them, as myself."

"If you saw that television show," Jack said, having to restrain himself from resting one hand on Baldwin's shoulder, "you know that I can't *cure* people. Whatever I *can* do, it isn't that."

"How do you know?" Baldwin replied. "Have you ever tried?"

"No . . . I haven't."

"Then you don't really *know* that you can't. What if I believed that you could? And asked you to try it on me?" He looked over at Jack, his eyes filled with pathos, and challenge. "What if *I believed*," he said, urgently, "and what if that was enough—all you ever needed, in fact—to *heal*? What if that was true, and just another miracle—like the ones you've already performed—was waiting till now to happen? What if all you'd ever needed was someone who *believed*, in his heart and in his soul, that you could do it?" His eyes glittered, brightly, feverishly, as if all the life that was left in him had fled there. He reached up and plucked the stocking hat from his head. The skull was bony, and dotted in several places with discolored patches and a light furze of hair.

"Put your hands on me," Baldwin pleaded. "I *believe* that you can heal me."

"Adam, please, there's nothing—"

"Don't tell me there's nothing you can do." He clutched at Jack's hands, lying restive in his lap. "You *can*. You *can*." He bent his bare head down toward Jack's hands. "You have nothing to lose—and *I* have nothing to lose. Do it—please, do it. I *believe* in you, I *believe*." His head was bent, as if in prayer; the knobs of his vertebrae poked up from his neck. "I *believe*," he was muttering, over and over again, "I believe."

A middle-aged nanny, pushing a stroller, gave them an odd look as she passed. Jack, as much to get it over with as to console Baldwin, lifted his hands and placed them, like a benediction, on top of his bowed head. He held them there, for a few seconds, feeling the skin, still warm from the hat, and the few prickly hairs. Baldwin had fallen silent, but when Jack started to take his hands away, he grabbed them and rolled his skull, hard, against them, as if to cover every inch with the healing powers they contained. When he'd finished, he slipped his hat back on, with his head still lowered, before slowly sitting up again. He took a deep breath, and sighed.

"If you want to know if I feel any different," he said, evenly, "I don't. But I'm not disappointed, because I didn't expect to. I knew I wouldn't jump up feeling great again. I believe that what you've done will show up slowly, over the next few days, or weeks. I believe you've set in motion the healing process."

He was talking to himself, and nothing Jack could say would make any difference.

"I believe in what you've done for me . . . I believe in what you've done . . ."

The boats bobbed at the ramshackle wooden piers and Jack sat quietly, measuring the depth of the emptiness he felt inside.

chapter ~ twenty-three

"IF THEY PLAY that goddamned 'Ave Maria' one more time, I'll bomb that station."

Cazenovia lifted his head out of the tank and looked at Sprague. "It's because of Christmas . . . only four days away."

Sprague gave him a disgusted look. "You think I don't know when Christmas is?"

Cazenovia tugged on his short black beard.

"Have you finished with the camera yet?"

"Almost."

Cazenovia's head disappeared again, into the emptied sensory deprivation tank. There were a few small noises—screws being turned, wires threaded—then his head appeared again. "Done." He clambered out, and onto the wrestling mats. "Everysing now is done."

Sprague looked around the room with satisfaction, but a lingering sense of uncertainty too; was there anything he'd forgotten? At all four corners of the windowless chamber, on poles that stretched from floor to ceiling, he had installed—or rather, Cazenovia, the technical genius, had installed—infrared video cameras; they were capable not only of rolling continuously, but—in the event of any sort of motion occurring within three or four feet of their stationary field of vision—popping a bright flash and taking a still image of whatever had been fleetingly caught. Another such camera—but without the flash attachment—had just been mounted inside the tank itself.

Strapped to each of the corner poles, beneath the camera,

was another device that also served two purposes; Sprague was very pleased that he'd thought of this. The thermistors, which were roughly the size and shape of large cucumbers, were programmed to record any change in air temperature, and any alteration in the room's air flow. If something passed by them, even if it could not be seen by the cameras, the thermistors would record its presence.

Finally, above the glass wall that separated the control booth from the tank chamber, there was a supersensitive, two-way intercom speaker. The radio was playing on it now, carrying more of that Pavarotti Christmas crap; but later, it would be used to carry voices—and other sounds, in frequencies not normally heard—between both halves of the laboratory.

Cazenovia wiped his hands on his rumpled trousers, and said in his fractured English, "I must have to be leaving now. Everysing is done."

"What about *testing* it all," Sprague said, "to see that it's all been done properly?"

"I must have to be leaving now," Cazenovia repeated. "I come tomorrow if you vish to test." He stood around, waiting for something.

"Well, if you're going, go," Sprague said, impatiently.

"Ze money?"

"You want me to pay you for something when I don't know if it works yet?"

Cazenovia, who'd been holding his hand out, put it down. "Ze money tomorrow zen?"

"Yes, tomorrow—*provided* it all works right."

Grumbling in whatever language it was he spoke, Cazenovia slouched out of the room. And Sprague was left wondering how he could test all this apparatus without him.

It was ten o'clock at night, too late to call Nancy over to the institute. Nor, for that matter, would he even know where to find her. He had his suspicions—he could probably call Logan's place and get her in two seconds—but he wasn't yet prepared to let them know that he knew about their little romance. He snorted. The two of them were, in some respects, a team now, and he would have to keep in mind that whatever he told, or showed to, one, was no doubt instantly transmitted to the other.

Given that, maybe it was better if Nancy *didn't* know anything about these modifications he'd just made. No use alerting, or alarming, Logan.

His mind returned to the immediate problem: to test all these new devices, he needed to create noise, and motion, and some degree of body heat inside the tank room. He could do it himself, of course, but then he wouldn't be able to monitor everything from the control booth. If only that damned Cazenovia hadn't been in such a hurry to leave . . . what, after all, did a gnome like that have to get back to? His rats, and pigeons, and . . . Sprague smiled with glee at having so effortlessly hit upon the solution.

He hurriedly passed through the control room, and across the hall. He put his ear to the steel door of Cazenovia's lab, before unlocking it and stepping inside. There was an idle fluttering of wings in several of the darkened cages, a rustling in some others. The smell was as bad as always. But at least no one was there—Cazenovia had gone home, and Potter was nowhere around. Sprague felt a little like a kid in a candy store: what animal should he take? He paced, quietly, up and down the moonlit aisles. The pigeons stirred, flapping their wings—but pigeons were such filthy, and stupid, birds. What if he took one and it simply perched on top of one of the cameras and stayed there? The snakes, which slumbered, glistening, like lengths of rubber hose, were out of the question —too difficult and dangerous to handle. The same for the rats. From the far end of the room, he heard a bark—a dog might be just the ticket. He was hoping it might be a fairly friendly specimen, when his sleeve suddenly caught on the edge of a cage. He reached around to free it, and felt his fingers clenched by something tight and pincerlike. He jerked his hand away and whirled around. The creature screeched and leaped to the back of the cage.

A monkey, he thought.

The animal leaped again, to the front of the cage, flattening himself against the grillework, chattering wildly.

A rhesus, if Sprague remembered correctly from his own animal experimentation days. Of the genus *macaca*. The animal threaded his arm through the bars, fingers extended.

And very cooperative, as Sprague recalled.

He lifted the cage by the steel handle at its top, and carted it out of the room. The animal, perhaps pleased by the novelty of the excursion, stayed silent. Sprague locked up Cazenovia's lab behind him, and returned to the tank room. On the way in, he used his free hand to slam off the radio.

But how best to release the creature? Propping the glass door to the control booth open with the floor bolt, he took the cage to the far corner of the room, behind the sealed sensory-deprivation tank, and in one swift motion lifted the front bars away. Before the monkey could grasp that he was free, Sprague scuttled out of the room, closing the glass door and kicking down the floor bolt to lock it.

Done.

Sprague sat down, triumphant, and watched as the monkey, with some initial trepidation, ventured out of the cage. Looking all around, with his white-hooded eyes, he acted as if he thought at any moment some greater trap was about to be sprung. His tail, about two feet long, rose up above his body and coiled in the air. When he turned and saw the pale blue tank, he stopped in his tracks, to assess what it might be.

Ah yes, thought Sprague, take your time—I have plenty to do in here. Rolling up the sleeves of his lab coat, he went about flicking on the various monitors and recording devices. Yes, yes, much to do in here; it was no easy thing to devise an experiment which would, if successful, register the presence of a human soul. Trapping it, of course, would be better, but as yet Sprague had no idea how to go about that; he didn't know enough about its properties. Soon, he hoped he would. But for now, he'd have to be content to record some visual, auditory, thermal, or kinetic evidence of the spirit, and then throw *that* in the teeth of his detractors . . . and he knew exactly whom he'd throw it at first.

The day before, Frelinghuysen, vice-chairman of the institute's board of directors, had called him in and waved Arlette Stein's latest article at him; she'd given her own account of Logan saving Garcia. "What on earth are you up to, Sprague? This has always been a reputable institution; we do real science here. You're turning us into some sort of media sideshow with all this stuff about bringing people back from the dead. I'm telling you now, I want it to stop."

Sprague had retorted with something about the freedom of the press, and their instinct for what was genuine news, when Frelinghuysen held up his hand to stop him.

"You've done solid research over the years, Sprague. And I'd hate to have to move for your eviction from the institute. But I'm not sitting still for this resurrection nonsense."

Sprague had not recanted, but he hadn't put up a fight, either; better, he thought, to bide his time and later surprise them with something irrefutable.

Surprise the *world*, for that matter.

The rhesus had prowled, on all fours, over to the tank, then climbed up onto it. In no time, he'd found the indentation for the hatchway, but his fingers were neither large enough, nor strong enough, to pull it open. He was getting bored trying.

Flicking on the two-way intercom, Sprague said, "Don't worry, my little friend—we'll soon have more interesting things for you to do." The monkey looked up, toward the speaker, then spotted Sprague behind the glass. He stared at him with eyes as black as obsidian.

Yes, yes, much more interesting... Sprague checked to see that the thermistor calibrations were all correctly synchronized. All four registered the temperature in the room at exactly 80.1 degrees Fahrenheit, with no appreciable air movement. Sprague had covered even the ceiling vents with plastic garbage bags. The monkey suddenly turned, and a split second later the thermistor closest to him showed a tiny blip on its meter, indicating a transient air current. Cazenovia had done his job well, so far. But there was still the video element to check.

On top of the console, Cazenovia had balanced an old Sony portable TV. When Sprague turned it on, the screen was broken into four separate squares; Cazenovia had originally used it to observe the behavior of rats at four different parts of a maze. Now, Sprague saw four different views of the tank room, and the monkey inside it. With a little fine tuning, the picture, still black and white, came in much more clearly. The only thing left to do now was test the whole system, to see how it would work in actual operation.

"Lights out," Sprague said over the intercom, as he darkened the laboratory except for the dim violet light around the control console. The monkey sitll showed up tolerably well on the portable TV. "But what we need is *movement*."

Sprague turned on the radio again, tuned it to the first rock 'n' roll station he could find; what he wanted was cacophony.

And that was what he got—screeching guitars, pounding drums, a lyric having something to do with nuclear destruction. The monkey shrieked and leaped off the tank, then raced to one of the steel poles on which a thermistor and camera were mounted.

"Yes . . . climb it, if you like," Sprague said, under the crashing music. "Let's see how sturdy everything is."

The monkey leapt halfway up the pole, swung himself around it in the dark. The room was very nearly pitch-black —what kind of night vision did the animal have, Sprague wondered? Enough, apparently, to find its way to the top of the thermistor, and perch there, with its tail wrapped tightly around the pole. The music blared, and the monkey held fast.

"You'll need to move around a bit more than that," Sprague muttered, and flicked the music suddenly off. The monkey waited, tensely, as if expecting it to blare again, then cautiously began to explore his surroundings again. With one arm, he reached up to the bottom of the camera, mounted just above his head, and delicately probed the metal corrugations of its underside.

Sprague could only make out the creature's movements by watching him on the TV monitor; the infrared camera at the opposite end of the chamber carried an unobstructed, but remote, view of him. Still, Sprague thought, if he could get an image, even this clear, of the visitor Logan last entertained here, it'd be more than anyone else had ever done. If he could *see*, or in some way simply *detect*, the presence of that spirit Jack had claimed was his dead mother—dead now for well over twenty years!—wouldn't that set Frelinghuysen back on his heels! Wouldn't *that* make the scientific establishment sit up and take notice! Sprague, Dr. Orson Sprague of the Institute of Abnormal Psychology, would become the man who was singlehandedly responsible for opening *this* world onto the *next*, for extending humanity's frontiers further than they'd ever been. He would wield an influence, in the course of human history, greater than that of Darwin, Marx, and Freud, combined!

Provided his linchpin didn't slip.

He sat back in his chair—the monkey was contentedly grooming itself at the moment—to think about that linchpin once again. When Jack had been lifted, wet and naked, out of the tank, he'd been very slow to come around, very disoriented. His account of his mother's physical transformations, of her strange words to him, of their journey together toward a black and churning horizon, had been garbled and confused, contradictory and elliptical. It had taken Sprague at least a couple of hours to calm him down and get it all straight. And after managing that, he had seen no point in telling him about the two heartbeats, one subsuming the other, that had shown up on the electrocardiograph; it would only have served to alarm him all over again. He had told Nancy, later, that it had been nothing more than a technical glitch in the machine, which he had already corrected. But there was no telling if she'd believed him.

There was a bright popping light from the tank room, and Sprague looked up to see the monkey leaping away from the camera he had just clambered onto. He landed on the floor, chattering loudly, and raced across the room to the opposite pole; shinnied up that and rested, once again, on top of the thermistor. Sprague checked the thermistor's meter, and saw that the monkey's body heat was rapidly raising the temperature inside the container. Everything, Sprague reflected, was working admirably.

And then, just as suddenly, it wasn't. While looking at the reading of the thermistor the monkey was sitting on, Sprague noticed that another of the devices, fully fifteen feet away, had suddenly registered a small but significant air movement. It could have been a breeze, of course, set up when the monkey flew through the air, but as Sprague watched the tiny arrow, like the indicator on a speedometer, it didn't decline; instead, it increased, just slightly. Something was stirring up the air at the far corner of the lab; Sprague glanced at the four squares on the TV monitor, and saw nothing but the empty chamber, and the monkey on the pole.

But the monkey was staring in the direction of that third thermistor, too, and holding himself perfectly still—almost as if he was hoping to remain unnoticed.

Was there some sort of draft in there, some way for air to flow in, or out, that Sprague had not anticipated?

The last thermistor, nearest to the control booth where Sprague was sitting, suddenly registered its own marginal air current. But again, without any heat equivalent. The monkey, which was now looking in *that* direction, screamed, and flew off the pole. He raced the length of the lab on all fours, the whole time turned in sort of a three-quarter fashion, as if to see over his shoulder. He had no sooner arrived at the far corner of the lab than he spread open his jaws and bared his teeth. But at what? Sprague couldn't see a thing on any of the infrared monitors. The monkey reared up on its hind legs, took a vicious swipe at nothing but air. He backed up against the wall, then took off again, screaming, and flailing his tail.

"What the hell is going on in there?" Sprague said, aloud. The monkey was now racing around and around the lab, sometimes swinging himself by the metal poles, frequently stopping to lash one arm, viciously, at whatever he believed was chasing him. The themistors were all registering the violently disturbed air now, and if Sprague had not been able to see for himself the direction in which the monkey was fleeing, he would have been able to discern the clockwise movement just from the sequential way in which the four thermistor meters were waxing and waning. The cameras were functioning equally well; each time the monkey passed closely enough to trigger their flash response, a bright light went off, and the monkey, even more panicked, would race away, running around and around the tank room, scampering over the wrestling mats, sometimes over the tank itself, looking everywhere, anywhere, for some sort of refuge from his unseen pursuer.

How long, Sprague wondered, should he let this go on? The devices were all, more or less, working properly—but this bat-shit monkey was getting so agitated now he might somehow damage one of them. The experiment should probably be stopped, the monkey pacified—somehow—and put back in his cage and returned to Cazenovia's lab. But Sprague was not exactly anxious to go into that tank room and try to *catch* the little fucker just now. He was likely to get bitten, clawed, or worse. As a first step toward calming the creature down, he deactivated the flash response on the four video cameras. But that didn't seem to slow him down a bit; he was still running, from something else. Sprague sat back, puzzled, and looked again at his array of instruments—and saw now something he had missed before. The temperature readings, also recorded by the thermistors, were all exactly three de-

grees below where they'd begun; he hadn't seen it initially
because the change had apparently come suddenly, and so uni-
formly, throughout the room. It was very odd for it to have
happened at all, much less in that uniform way.

There was a crash against the glass and Sprague jerked
back in his chair. The monkey was flattened against the glass
wall, his hooded eyes wide with terror, his mouth open,
spraying foam and spittle; he was balanced, precariously, on a
tiny ledge in front of the control room, his fingers pasted
against the window. He was screaming, over and over and
over again, trying desperately, it seemed, to press himself
through the glass and into the dimly lighted chamber where
Sprague was sitting. His tail, curled around behind him, was
thumping against the glass, too. Sprague knew the glass
would hold, but still, instinctively, he drew back. The monkey
screeched, his fingers slipping and sliding on the smooth
glass, trying to gain some purchase.

Could it be, Sprague thought, that even without Jack
Logan here, he'd managed to tap into something extraordinary?

The monkey stopped screaming. He seemed almost to
cough, then turned his head slowly to the left. He caught his
breath, and screamed again; it seemed to Sprague that he was
trying to turn his head back to the right again, as if he were
trying to resist some opposing force. His jaws kept snapping,
and biting, at the air. His tiny ears lay flat against his skull.
The head kept turning, inexorably, to the left. The monkey
was now looking back over his shoulder, the tendons in his
throat taut and bulging. Just when Sprague thought he could
turn no farther in that direction, the head whipped around
again to the right. Then the left. Then the right. The head was
twisting back and forth, more and more rapidly, the eyes wide
open but strangely blank, the screeching altogether stopped.
The thing could no longer catch its breath. The head lashed
left, then right, then left, each time a little farther around, far
as it seemed possible to go, until suddenly it spun so hard to
the right that there was an audible crack and it just kept going
. . . all the way around to the front again. The head drooped
backward, on the stalk of the neck, as the arms fell listlessly
from the glass. A second later, the creature toppled into

a little furry heap on the floor. On the TV monitor, it looked like an empty hand puppet.

The temperature in the room had dropped another three degrees. Sprague tried to compose himself by making a note of the change, and then by checking the other instruments. The air movements, recorded by the thermistors, appeared to have stopped. He glanced at the monitor again: the monkey lay just where it had fallen, below the window of the control booth. He felt he should go in and retrieve it.

What had done that to the creature's neck?

He turned on the lights all over the laboratory, and looked slowly around. The only movement was a tiny ripple in the plastic bag that covered the ceiling vent. And then, even that stopped. The instruments registered no further changes. He stood up, looked around again. As a scientist, he should examine the monkey's remains as quickly as possible, to determine exactly what had happened. (What did he mean, exactly what had happened? He *knew* what had happened—its neck had been broken. What was he trying to tell himself—that this had somehow been accidental? He'd seen it, though he couldn't believe it, with his very own eyes.) But there was nothing in the laboratory—at least nothing he could *see*—that might have caused it. And if there *was* . . . well, a monkey was one thing, and he was quite another.

He strode purposefully to the glass door, kicked up the floor bolt, and threw it open. The air was appreciably cooler than that in the control booth. The monkey lay a few feet to his left. He walked over, crouched down beside it. It had landed on its back, with its arms oddly folded across its abdomen; the fur on its chin and chest were matted with blood and spittle. Perhaps he should first put on some rubber gloves, Sprague thought—this was likely to get messy.

The lights went out, all over the lab, and the hair on the back of Sprague's neck suddenly stood on end. Still kneeling, he whirled around, staring into the darkness of the tank room. Over the intercom, he heard a woman's voice say, "I hate monkeys."

He crawled a few feet away from the dead animal, toward the sensory-deprivation tank. It was then he realized that the violet light above the control console was on. Behind the glass, smeared with the residue of the monkey's ordeal, he thought he saw something move, something that was standing in the shadows of the room.

"But then, it wasn't monkeys you were after, was it?"

It was a *young* woman's voice, almost girlish. And so—now that his eyes had become accustomed to the light—was the figure lurking in the control booth; it was a young woman, as best he could make out, with long dark hair. She was wearing some sort of jacket.

"You were after me, I think."

Sprague's mouth was so dry he couldn't speak.

"Do I have to introduce myself?"

"No, no . . . you don't," Sprague croaked. "I know who you are. You're just as Jack described you." He swallowed, hard.

"So are you," she said, and laughed, merrily.

His back was pressed against the cool, curved surface of the tank. "I never expected to raise you so easily."

"*Raise* me?" she said, teasingly. "Where did you think I was—hell?" She laughed again, while Sprague slowly got to his feet.

"No, of course not," he said, "I didn't mean that—it was just a figure of speech. I didn't mean—"

"I know what you meant," she reassured him, "don't worry about it."

Her figure seemed to fade in and out of view, its outlines never entirely clear. It was, Sprague thought, like addressing a hologram. "You were here once before, weren't you," Sprague said, "in the tank with Jack."

"That tank?"

"Yes," Sprague said, resting his fingertips on the top of the cylinder. "I was able to detect your heartbeat."

She paused, as if considering how to answer, then said, "I wasn't with Jack; he was with me. And neither one of us was in that tank."

Sprague, emboldened now by the continuing exchange, said, "Where were you then, if not here?"

"Oh, Christ," she sighed, "I expected more than this from you." To his amazement, she slumped into the chair at the control panel. "Maybe I was wrong."

She was either swiveling in the chair, or coming in and out of focus again.

"I'm doing you a big favor, you know."

"You are?"

"By appearing . . . even as much as I am. By all rights, you ought to be dead first."

"But Jack can see you all the time."

She snickered. "Ah, but Jack's a special case, isn't he? Jack's got talents."

"That's what I want to know about," Sprague breathed, "his talents . . . your talents . . . the afterlife." He could hardly believe he was talking to a spirit, that all his work had finally brought him to this astonishing encounter. But what should he be saying? What could he do to make the most of it? His mind was racing, trying to grapple with all the possibilities. And how—*how*—could he salvage some sort of *proof* of what he'd done?

"What Jack can do," she finally said, "he can do because of me. I kept him alive in my body, and now he, in a way, keeps me alive in his. These little forays you've been arranging for him, into the Other World, they've brought us very close together again."

Sprague, still trying to figure out what he should be doing, said, "Glad to have been of help."

"Oh, you've been more help than you know," she said, "only not everyone's so happy about that."

"Who's not happy?"

"Oh, all the usual suspects . . . the ones who died in the last ten minutes and haven't yet accepted it . . . the ones who think they shouldn't have died at all . . . the ones who think the dead should stay that way and the living ought to stay where they belong. In other words," she summed up, "all the usual narrow-minded fools."

"Is there something I could do," he said, "to make it up to them, something that would convince them that my intentions were never to . . ." He trailed off, in the face of her renewed laughter. What had he said that was so funny? Her teeth, in the violet light, appeared to glow red. "Why are you laughing?" Sprague said, angry despite himself.

For one split second, her face seemed to change utterly— to flatten out, her eyes to sink deeply into their sockets. She stopped laughing, and leaned forward.

"I'm laughing because you're so damned anxious to please

the dead, and you don't give a shit about the living, Sprague. Don't *you* think that's funny?"

"No."

She chuckled softly, but with no real mirth. "Well, I do . . . it's probably why you were chosen in the first place."

"Chosen? For what?"

"For immortality," she said, grandly. "For making the discovery that will rock the world. Haven't you felt it all along, Sprague? Haven't you known it, in your heart of hearts? Haven't you always been sure that you were the one?"

He didn't know how to react—was she being sincere, or simply taunting him?

"No, I mean it," she said, as if intuiting his doubts. "You want proof of the Other World, and I'm the one who can give it to you. Proof," she said, rising from the chair, "that you can *see . . .*"

The jacket seemed to dissolve before his very eyes—her shoulders showed naked through the glass.

". . . and touch . . ."

She turned fully toward him, her bare breasts gleaming in the violet light.

". . . and offer to the world. *This* world."

She was leaning forward on the console, her long dark hair slipping over her shoulders and swaying, gently, in front of her breasts. Her lips were parted; in her eyes was an invitation. She paused, expectantly.

Sprague slowly moved away from the tank. Was she really going to wait there for him? His shoes squeaked as he stepped off the mats. Was she really going to give him all she'd promised?

"There's just one thing you'll have to do for me," she said, almost in a whisper.

He approached the open door to the control booth.

"You'll have to make sure Jack keeps coming back." Her eyes were following him, though her head didn't turn.

He entered the booth. She was arched over the console, entirely naked. She cocked her head now in his direction. She looked real enough, *substantial* enough, to touch, and *feel*.

"Jack's the key," she said. "He must keep coming back." With one finger, she flicked off the violet light.

"Can you promise me that?" she said, from the pitch darkness.

"Yes," Sprague said, "anything, I'll do anything you ask, but please . . ." He put out his hands, the fingers extended, and plunged toward her. He felt nothing, then something—the back of the empty chair. "Please," he said, "don't go yet—I've waited so long, there's so much I still need to know. Please don't go yet." He waited in the blackness, his heart pounding fiercely, his hands clutching the back of the chair. There was no sound, no movement—no sign of another's presence. "Please," he said, but there was no reply. "Please."

He didn't know whether to feel desolate or elated— crushed at her disappearance, or exhilarated by her promises. He bent forward, to grope for the light switch, and only then became aware of not being alone. He felt a light pressure against his upper back, as if someone were leaning over him. Two arms snaked their way around his shoulders. Something soft, and very wet, nestled against his cheek.

"You're here," he whispered, not yet daring to turn around. "You're here."

The lips nuzzled his cheek again; they were stickily wet, and clinging.

Slowly, slowly, he straightened up, feeling the weight of her—her bare breasts?—pressing between his shoulder blades. But as he turned, so, apparently, did she—he could feel her still pressing against his back, her arms still entwined around his neck. "Please," he said, "let me touch you . . . let me turn on the light and look at you." He turned again, but she still remained behind him. It was as if she was playing some childish game with him.

You want to play a game, Sprague thought? Is that what you want? Then I'll play along, my own way.

Turning again, he swept both of his hands across the top of the control console, batting the central light switch on. The room blazed white with light.

There was no one in front of him, no one behind. He glanced down at the arms sill wrapped around his neck—they were thin and wiry, covered with black hair. The front of his lab coat was stained with blood. Dangling over his shoulder, warm and wet, was the lifeless head of the monkey. Sprague shuddered with disgust, pried the creature off his shoulders, and threw it against the glass wall. It crumpled in a heap atop the console.

Over the intercom, he heard, so faintly it might have been coming from another world, a young woman's laughter.

chapter twenty-four

THE CALL FROM Burt, the contractor, had come in the nick of time. The last of Jack's guitar students had just stuck a note to his mailbox saying he'd decided to take up drums instead, and Jack was wondering if it was time to bite the bullet and get in touch with the guy who booked musicians for the bar mitzvah and wedding circuit. He was about to go looking for the number, when he decided to check with Registry first and see if he had any messages.

He had one, from Burt, and called him back immediately.

"What did you do," Burt said, "change your home phone number? I called there first and they said it was no longer in service."

"Yeah, well, I was getting some calls I didn't want to take, and I just decided to get an unlisted number."

There was a slight pause, then Burt said, "From people who wanted to talk to an angel? I saw that other article in the *Post*, the one about the guy who tried to kill himself—Garcia. Are you still doing all that?"

Jack didn't know how to answer; he didn't want to lie to him, but he didn't want to say yes either. He was afraid if he did, Burt would think he was still too crazy to return to the show. "It's no big deal," Jack said, "I go in once or twice a week for some tests."

"But you're still pulling that con?" Burt persisted, though good-naturedly.

Jack figured it was too late now to retract it. "Sort of," he said. Now he'd be playing the bar mitzvah circuit for sure. "How's the show going?"

"Getting by, getting by . . . So tell me, in general you feeling any better?"

"Yeah, I'm okay," Jack said. "I just needed a little rest. I've got things pretty much under control now."

"Enough so you think you could play the show again?"

Jack could hardly believe his ears. "Oh yeah, definitely," he found himself burbling. "That'd be no problem. I'd really like to be playing the show again." This was too good to be true.

"Then why don't you come down tonight? Come a little early—a couple of the numbers in Act Two have been trimmed, and I'll show you the changes. Other than that, it's the same old drill."

"Great—I'll be there." He wanted to kiss the receiver. "And Burt—thanks. Thanks a lot."

"Forget it."

"I won't."

Man, what a narrow escape, Jack thought; another five minutes and he'd have been booked for a wedding reception in New Jersey.

Around six-thirty, he pulled the Fender Strato-caster out of the closet and took the subway down to the theater. None of the other musicians were there yet. Burt was in his office—a dank little cell across from the locker room—buried in paperwork. When Jack said hello, he jumped in his chair.

"Jesus, you startled me," he said, stubbing out his cigarette and looking up. "Musicians never show up early for work."

"You told me to, so you could show me the changes," Jack reminded him.

"Oh, yeah, right," he said, leaning back in his chair and giving Jack the once-over. "You look okay—you sure you feel okay?"

"Feel fine."

Burt seemed to take him at his word. He riffled through the clutter of papers on his desk, pulled out a dog-eared score. "I marked the changes—I'm sure you'll see how they work."

Jack took the score, glanced at some of the cuts. They'd lopped about ten minutes out of the act. "No problem," he said, then, when he'd caught Burt's eye, added, "I appreciate the second chance."

"Hey, I already told you," Burt said, quickly looking away, "don't thank me."

And for the second time, Jack felt that he really meant it, that he really *didn't* want to be thanked.

"I told your sub to clear out the locker," Burt said, his head bent low over the timesheets. "Go on and get settled again."

It was almost as if Burt was feeling *guilty* about it. Jack waved good-bye with the score, not that Burt noticed, and went back to the locker room. Vinnie and Haywood had checked in, and were dumping their stuff. When they saw Jack, they hooted and hollered. Haywood stuffed a toothpick in his mouth, and Vinnie, taking out his trumpet to empty the valves, said, "About time! About time! I didn't know what else we could do to your sub."

"What do you mean?"

"We put tacks on his chair," Haywood broke in, "gum in his score, I gave him a toothpick I'd stuck in the soap in the men's room. I tell you, there was no way to get the message to that dude."

Was *that* what Burt had been feeling guilty about—that the sub had been tormented by his friends? "Well, whatever you guys did, thanks—it worked."

Catalano, Van Nostrand, and the rest of the band drifted in; over the backstage intercom, the stage manager gave the ten-minute call.

"You see the changes in the second act?" Vinnie asked.

"Yes," Jack said, distractedly, "Burt marked my score." But something else was different too: there was a short, dark-haired girl stashing her coat in what used to be Veronica Berghoffer's locker. Jack gestured at her turned back and asked Vinnie, in a low voice, who she was.

"Name's Miranda something. She replaced Veronica right around the time you left."

"How come?"

Vinnie shrugged, bent down to untie his shoes in preparation for playing the show. "Veronica was acting pretty spacy. She told Haywood she was having trouble sleeping, couldn't concentrate. I don't know what she's doing now." He sat back up. "Why? You planning to give it another try with her?"

Jack let it pass. Burt appeared in the doorway, clapping his hands together and telling everyone to get a move on. They filed through the narrow passageway into the pit and set up. When Consuela stepped to the podium and rapped her baton, Jack had to look up at her; she was staring straight back at him. She gave him a little nod—a warning?—and lifted her baton for the downbeat. Jack studied the score sheet in front of him as if his life depended on it.

The first act went off without a hitch. The more he played, the better it felt. After an especially tricky passage, Vinnie even gave him a thumbs-up sign. The girl who'd replaced Veronica had noticed he was new, and smiled his way. Funny, Jack thought—for all she knows, *I'm* the sub.

During the intermission, Jack trailed back to the locker room to horse around with the other musicians. He was introduced to Miranda, who said he seemed to be doing an amazing job for his first time out. Vinnie said, "This is the guy who *wrote* that riff in the middle of the factory scene. He's the *original* lead guitar." Miranda apologized, and Vinnie went on, "Logan was with this show when it was a standing-room-only, smash hit."

"It was?" Miranda asked, incredulously.

But Jack couldn't bear to see someone so misled. "This show has been on the ropes since the out-of-town tryouts," he said. "And from the look of tonight's house, it's due for a knockout punch pretty soon."

"You mean it's going to close?"

"This show's been closing ever since it opened," Haywood threw in from the other end of the bench.

"Yeah, but tonight the place sounds like an empty warehouse," said Catalano. "You see all those empty seats?"

Jack had counted fourteen in the first row of the mezzanine alone. It would be just his luck, he thought, to get called back to work on the eve of the show's closing.

"Time to make music," Burt called into the locker room. On their way out, he touched Jack on the elbow and said, "Stop into my office after the show, will you?" Before Jack could ask why, he took off after Van Nostrand, saying something about skin books in the pit.

Why did Burt want to see him, Jack wondered? Had Consuela complained about him again? How could she? His playing, he knew, had been fine; he hadn't missed a cue, or a note, all night. He took his seat in the pit feeling distinctly unsettled again, and told himself to forget about it or he *would* start blowing his cues. Maybe it was just some union regulation, some employment form that had to be signed—yeah, that was it, he tried to persuade himself, just one of those papers Burt had been shuffling around.

Still, he had to concentrate doubly hard on the rest of the score, especially the newly trimmed sections, in order not to make any mistakes. He wanted to be able to present himself to Burt with an absolutely unblemished performance behind him. And as far as he could tell, when the curtain finally came down, he'd done just that.

While the other musicians went about collecting their stuff from the locker room, Jack knocked on Burt's open door. He was sitting behind his battered, gray metal desk, talking to a woman whose back was to the door. "Logan," he said, and the woman turned, "I want you to meet—"

"Arlette Stein," Jack said. He remembered her from that night he'd saved Garcia.

"That's right—we met a few weeks ago." She didn't bother to elaborate. "Burt was nice enough to provide me with a house seat for tonight's performance," she said, "and the opportunity to talk to you after the show."

Jack looked coldly at Burt, who ducked his gaze. No wonder he'd been acting so guilty.

"We both thought there might be an interesting story in your returning to the show," Arlette continued, oblivious to the silent exchange. "You know, something like 'Broadway Gets an Angel with *Real* Wings,' something like that. The first thing I—"

"Is that what you thought?" Jack said to Burt, ignoring Arlette altogether. "Is that why you called me back to the show—so you could get some free publicity? Maybe keep it afloat at least through the holidays?"

"Jack," Burt replied, raising his hands from the desk, "I swear to you, I called you back for the same reason I hired you—you're the best lead guitar I know."

"That's right," Arlette interjected, looking from one to the other, "Burt was just telling me that—"

"The best lead guitar who could get a plug for *Steam-*

roller," Jack retorted, bitterly. "From now on, why don't you just take out an ad?" And he turned and stalked across the hall to the locker room.

"Hey, Jack," Vinnie said, already prepared to go, "a bunch of us are gonna get together on New Year's Eve and watch the ball go down in Times Square, then go back to my place to party. Barbara told me to be sure to ask you to come."

Jack yanked the lock off the handle of his locker, and grabbed his coat from the hook.

"So what do you say? If you want to skip Times Square and just come to the party afterwards, that's okay, too."

"I'll let you know," Jack said, and strode out of the room.

"Merry Christmas to you, too," Vinnie called after him, sounding bewildered. Jack heard him ask someone, presumably Haywood, "What's eating him?"

But Jack still wasn't out of the woods. Arlette was at the backstage door, with her note pad out, talking to Gus. When she spotted Jack, she abruptly turned away from him, and said, "Burt told me you'd be coming this way."

"Good old Burt."

"Listen—I'm sorry if you feel you've been taken advantage of, but why don't you use my story to set the record straight?"

"The record doesn't interest me anymore. The record's whatever you people at the newspapers and TV want to make it. Now if you'll excuse me . . ." He tried to get around her, but she quickly moved to block him. He stopped dead, clenching the handle of his guitar case.

"That's not true, what you said about the record," Arlette argued. "It's only when our sources aren't upfront with us that things get wrong, or maybe misrepresented. As a reporter, I stand behind everything I write."

"That's probably the best place *to* stand," Jack said, and feinted to the left; Arlette subtly moved in that direction, and Jack dodged around her to the right.

"You didn't sign out," Gus sputtered as he hurried through the backstage door.

"Do it for me." And he was out in the backstage alley, in the cold night air.

The other theaters were just letting out, so his chances of hailing a cab were nil. Holding his guitar upright against his chest, he weaved his way through the crowds, and over to the Eighth Avenue subway stop. On the ride uptown, he tried to forget about Burt, and Arlette, and the whole business—he wondered briefly if he could afford to quit the show altogether—and concentrate instead on what was ahead of him that night. Nancy was coming over; they had planned to celebrate his return to the show and, even though Christmas was still two days away, exchange presents. Best of all, she'd told her parents that she'd be spending another night up at the institute.

They had until the next morning. It was just too bad he didn't feel like celebrating.

Five minutes after he got home, Nancy buzzed from downstairs. She came up the stairs carrying a wicker picnic basket and a plastic shopping bag. "Like my matching luggage?" she said, when she saw Jack standing in the open doorway to his apartment.

"Very smart." They kissed at the threshold, then he drew her inside by pulling one end of her scarf.

"Whoa! Don't you even want to know what's in the basket?"

"Sure," he said, wrapping an arm around her waist and kissing her again. "I can't wait."

When their lips parted, she said, "I'll say." She pretended to push him away. "But at least let me get my coat off."

Underneath, she had on a pair of black slacks and a loose white sweater. "So how'd it go?" she asked him, over her shoulder, as she took the basket over to the bed and flipped up the lid. "Were those friends of yours—Vinnie and Haywood—surprised to see you?" She had taken out a white tablecloth, with a red tiger embroidered in its center, and thrown it over the comforter.

"Yes," Jack said, "they were."

Now she was taking out plates—real china dessert plates and teacups—and setting two places.

"How big were those changes they'd made in the music?"

"Not very."

"Could you start some water boiling?"

"I could." He went into the tiny kitchenette and put the kettle on. When he came back, he saw that she had put out several different kinds of cake and fruit.

"You want to tell me what's going on?"

"Not yet," she said, carefully removing from the bottom of the basket an elaborately decorated teapot. "Could you fill this with the hot water?"

"Yes, ma'am." He did as he was told, and when he returned there were two lighted candles on the bedside table and the lamp had been turned off.

"Now?"

"Yes, if you'll take a seat."

Cautiously, so as not to upset the crockery set up on the mattress, he sat down across from her, cross-legged just as she was.

"What time is it?" she asked.

He looked at the lighted clock behind him. "Ten of twelve. Why?"

"It should be midnight. But then it should be New Year's Eve, too."

"What are you talking about?" he said, with a laugh.

"I'm serving you the traditional Chinese foods of good fortune for the coming year. We should start with these." She passed him a bowl full of dumplings. "Your chopsticks are on your napkin."

He took several and passed the plate back.

"These are called *jiaozi*. I made them myself. They're supposed to be eaten precisely at midnight."

They were soft and warm, and filled with spicy ground meat. Jack couldn't believe she'd gone to so much trouble for him. While he ate, Nancy poured out the tea. "This tea is called *yuan bao cha*, and it's also considered 'lucky'—its name has something to do with silver ingots."

The tea was sweet and fragrant, and it was accompanied by several other lucky foods—rice cakes whose roundness symbolized peace and harmony, date cakes, and a platter made up of peanuts—"they're associated with longevity"—lotus seeds, and other dried fruits. "This combination platter," she said, "is something called—and don't even try to remember it—*zaoshengguizi*."

"And what does that mean?"

She laughed and said, "Funny you should ask. Roughly translated, it means 'to soon realize the birth of noble sons.'"

Jack laughed too, and toasted her with his teacup.

"Yeah, well, that had better be a joke," Nancy said. "I had a hard enough time explaining to my parents that I'd be staying overnight at the institute again."

"Would it be easier," Jack volunteered, facetiously, "if I spent the night at your family's place? I could just as easily catch a train *down*town after the show."

Nancy gave him an overly sweet smile. "It's very kind of you to offer, but I don't think so."

A silence fell. Jack sipped the last of his tea from the little china cup. "This was incredibly nice of you to do," he said.

"My pleasure."

"I mean it." Quickly clearing the dishes from the bed, he rolled over beside her. "I think this was the nicest Christmas present I ever got."

"But this wasn't your actual present."

"It wasn't?"

"No. Look under your pillow."

He reached under the pillow and pulled out a small wrapped box.

"I put it there while you were boiling the water. Go ahead —unwrap it."

He tore off the paper. *"The Wizard of Oz,"* he said, reading from the front of the videotape, "the original, unedited 1939 film classic."

"I thought, since we always refer to Sprague as—"

"I know what you thought," he said, "because great minds think alike. Look under *your* pillow."

She did, and pulled out the package Jack had hidden there before going to the theater. When she unwrapped it, she still wasn't sure what it was. Jack helped her to remove the cellophane and shake out the uninflated toy. "Where's the nozzle?" he said, turning it over.

"There."

"Shall I do the honors?"

"Please."

"This may take a minute or two." Halfway through blowing it up, he stopped and said, "I should have had Vinnie do this. Guitar players aren't known for their breath control." Nancy was leaning back against the headboard, watching with delight as the figure took shape. When it was fully inflated, and Jack stood it up beside the bed, she laughed and said, "I recognize the white lab coat."

"But have you ever taken a punch at it?"

"Are you kidding? Of course not."

"Then this is your chance," and he poked it in the nose. It rocked way back on its base, then just as quickly rocked forward again. "This is to help you get rid of your aggressions."

"Let me at it," she said, getting to her knees on the bed. "Take *this*, Sprague," and she socked it to the floor. "And *this*," when it teetered back up again. Jack took a swipe too, and it spun away from the bed. Nancy took one last lunge, missed it, and ended up half on the floor. Jack dragged her back up onto the bed.

"Whew. I don't think I realized the full extent of your pent-up aggression."

Nancy sighed and lay back against the pillows. "I have," she said, "and let me tell you, it's no fun."

. Even in the flickering candlelight, Jack could see a pensive expression steal across her face. He lay down beside her, on his back. "If it's really that bad," he said, "why don't you quit?"

"And leave you to his kind ministrations?"

"I can take care of myself."

"Can you?" she said, turning her face toward his. She looked as if she was debating what to say. "You didn't see yourself after you came out of that sensory-deprivation tank. I did." Should she tell him, now, about the terribly altered heart rhythms? "And there's something else you don't know— something Sprague has tried to pass off to me as a mechanical malfunction. I checked the machine later, on my own, and it's working fine."

"What machine?"

"The tank-room cardiograph. Your brain waves did all the usual, impossible things, but your heart joined in this time. The machine acted as if it was recording two entirely different heartbeats . . . only the first one, the one you started out with, almost got lost in the second."

"What are you saying?"

"I'm saying, your heart nearly stopped—and even then Sprague wouldn't stop the experiment."

"And where did this second heartbeat come from?" Jack

asked, though there was only one possible answer.

"I don't know . . . you tell me."

And he knew she was thinking the same thing.

"Jack—I think you're putting your life in danger every time you make these journeys now. I thought it was dangerous right from the start; now I think it could be deadly. Sprague's completely consumed with it. He thinks you're his ticket to a Nobel Prize, and he won't stop at anything anymore." She found his hand on the mattress and took it in her own. "You've got to stop, before something terrible happens. You've got to stop traveling between this world and that other one . . . before you get trapped there for good."

They lay quietly beside each other, Jack haunted by all that she'd just said. No, he hadn't seen himself dragged from the tank—but he could remember that overwhelming sensation of loss, of having been drained, down to the marrow, of something essential, something vital. In his heart—his nearly stopped heart—he had felt an almost unbearable loneliness, a sense of despair that had washed over him, again and again, like a rolling, black wave, until, in the light of the lab, with a blanket wrapped around him, it had slowly, but even now not completely, receded.

And yes, inextricably bound up in that despair, there had been a thread of pure and simple fear—Nancy wasn't wrong. He had felt it himself, that sense of growing menace. But should he allow it to stop him in his tracks, forego his newfound powers, and desert the mother he had only just discovered? Was that the sane thing to do—or merely the cowardly?

"Can we get under the blankets?" Nancy said. "It's getting chilly in here."

"You're right. It is."

They pulled their legs up, then crawled under the quilt; the white tablecloth, with the embroidered tiger, still lay on top of it.

"You never told me the significance of the tiger tablecloth," Jack said, as Nancy nestled her head in the crook of his arm.

"It was given to me as a child. The tiger's supposed to ward off evil spirits."

"Then maybe we should leave it on tonight," he joked, but Nancy didn't seem amused. He gathered her closer. One of the candles on the bedside table blew out. "Must be a draft in here."

"Must be," Nancy said, slipping one hand between the buttons of Jack's shirt. "Just look at our inflatable Dr. Sprague."

Jack glanced across her, at the blow-up toy. It was rocking, with its bright red nose and its painted-on glasses, back and forth on its rubber base, almost as if, it dawned on Jack with a sudden slight shiver, almost as if it were being purposefully rocked by some unseen hand.

The other candle abruptly sputtered out, throwing the room into total darkness. He could still hear the rustle of the rocking toy, as he drew the white cloth, with its guardian tiger, up and over Nancy's shoulders.

chapter ∼
twenty-five

HE AWOKE, ALONE, to a ringing telephone. He picked it up and mumbled, "Hello?"

"This is the operator. Will you accept an emergency call from a Mr. Clancy?"

"Mr. Clancy?"

"Jack, it's me," he heard Clancy saying in the background.

"Will you accept this call?"

"Of course," he said, sitting up. The tablecloth, with the red tiger, had been tucked around him. "What's up?" he said. "Did you lose my new number?"

"Yes. I don't know where Mam put it..." There was something subdued, but urgent, in his voice. "Jack, Mam's in the hospital. St. John's."

The same hospital Jack had been born in.

"That's where I'm calling you from."

He swung his legs off the bed; his clothes lay in a heap on the floor. "What happened?"

"I don't know, for sure...somebody'd called her, she was talking on the phone, next thing I heard was her lamp hitting the floor. Maybe she'd done that on purpose, so I'd hear it downstairs. She was hardly breathing at all when I got to her..."

"And you took her to the hospital?"

"The ambulance did. She's in Intensive Care now."

Jack didn't know how to ask the terrible question that he had in mind. But Clancy guessed it.

"The doctors say..." He stopped for a second, unable to

speak. "The doctors say . . . it's going to be hard to hold her."

"I'm coming right out," Jack said. "Just wait there. I'll be there in an hour."

He leaped out of the bed and flew into the clothes he'd had on the night before. In the bathroom, he rubbed some cold water over his face, and read the note Nancy had left stuck to the mirror: *Merry Christmas,* it said, *see you on the 26th.* She was going to an uncle's place, with her family, for a couple of days.

Outside, he flagged down a livery service car and offered the guy thirty dollars, all he had in his wallet, to drive him to Weehawken.

"Forty and I'll do it."

"Thirty's all I've got. Take it or leave it."

"I'll take it."

He was at the hospital forty-five minutes after Clancy had called. There was a small waiting room, across the hall from the Intensive Care Unit. Clancy was sitting on one of the green plastic chairs, his elbows resting on his knees, one foot tapping nervously. When Jack sat down beside him, he simply said, "They're in there now, the doctors."

"They say anything else?"

"Not yet." Clancy was wearing one of his threadbare cardigans and a pair of baggy trousers. "Half the time I don't know what they're telling me anyway." He ran his hands roughly over his face, as if he was trying to wash this whole thing away.

"Can you tell me again what happened?" Jack said. He needed to hear it once more, now that he was fully awake.

Clancy listlessly recited the details of the morning, the medication he'd brought in to Mam in her bedroom, the coffee and cookies he'd had for breakfast, the call she'd gotten just before collapsing. "By the time I got up there, she was half out of the bed, the lamp on the floor, the telephone too . . . For a second," he said, scrubbing the sides of his face again, "I thought she was already gone."

"Who was it on the phone?" Jack asked, merely to fill in the picture, merely to know everything there was to know about such a fateful moment.

Clancy had to think. "Somebody I didn't recognize . . . sounded like he was *British*." He shook his head. "Who would

Mam know, who'd sound like he was British?"

"Didn't he give his name?"

"He did, but I didn't bother to remember it. After I found her, I just told him to get off the line, I had to call the hospital."

An Irish accent, Jack might have understood—some obscure relative, from the old country. But British? It was just one of those things he might never know the answer to.

The door to the I.C.U. swung open, and a doctor, about fifty-five or sixty, with a jaunty bowtie above his white coat, came out. Jack stood up and introduced himself.

"Ian Prescott," the doctor replied, looking him fixedly, almost appraisingly, in the eye.

"How is she?" Clancy asked, with trepidation, from his chair.

"Not good, I'm afraid," Prescott said. He drew up a chair, and Jack sat down too. "With the one lung gone," he explained, "the other has been working overtime for years now. I don't know how much longer it can carry the burden."

"Well, can't you do some sort of transplant—I read about 'em all the time," Clancy put in, "or use some kind of machine to breathe for her?"

"There are other complications," Prescott said, in very sober tones, and by the time he had finished outlining them, Jack knew what he was trying to say, that it was just a matter of hours—a day or two, at best—before Mam would pass away.

Clancy simply got to his feet and said, "I'm going in to see her now." Prescott didn't stop him. "The head nurse will keep an eye on him," he said to Jack.

"Is there anything we should be doing?" Jack asked, helplessly.

"Everything that can be done, we're already doing," Prescott said. Then he added, "You know, it's a funny thing—I had a call about you, just the other day, from somebody named Sprague. In New York."

Jack was speechless, then remembered that Prescott's name had appeared in one of the articles he'd found in the attic.

"I was doing my residency here when your mother was brought in. I wound up helping with your delivery."

"What did you tell Sprague?"

"Nothing much he didn't already know; he'd scoured the back issues of all the local newspapers. You were rather a celebrated case, you know, in your time."

So Jack had gathered, from the clips that he himself had seen. But did Prescott know anything of his *current* celebrity?

"I asked him why, after all this time, he was so curious about it now," Prescott volunteered, "and he said you were a patient of his."

"What kind of patient?"

Prescott appeared surprised by Jack's question. "Psychiatric," he said, "but nothing serious. He told me he was just checking up on some unusual background information you'd included in your medical history. I assured him," he said, with a slight smile, "that it was all true. He said he'd wanted to hear it from the horse's mouth."

"And that's it, that's all he said?"

Prescott shrugged. "It's all I remember. Oh, he asked after Dr. Mehta, who'd been truly in charge, and I told him Mehta had left the hospital fifteen years ago and gone somewhere in India."

Sprague was thorough; Jack had to give him that. And he hadn't given the real reason for calling—that was a blessing. Prescott, apparently, did not read the *Post*.

"I've got other patients to look in on," Prescott said, "but I'll be here all day. When your grandfather comes out, you can go in for a few minutes—just try not to disturb her." He stood up and, before going, said, "It's nice to see you turned out so well."

Even now, Jack thought, even here, with Mam gasping for breath across the hall, it was the unnatural turn his own life had taken that rose up, out of nowhere, to haunt him. Nancy's words from the night before came back to him, too, and he experienced again that tremor of fear. For a second, he felt, in the pit of his stomach, that same gnawing emptiness, that same strange sense of having almost . . . disappeared.

An orderly went by, pushing a rattling cart of linens and equipment.

But could he just turn his back on the whole bizarre business? Turn his back and walk away, pretend none of it had ever happened? Sure, Garcia was dead anyway—but that wasn't his fault. And Zakin, Adolph Zakin was alive and well

—that was definitely a victory. It was even possible—who knew anymore?—that he'd helped that guy in the park, that Adam Baldwin. Maybe there *was* some power in his hands . . . some power he could use, now, to help Mam.

When Clancy came out a few minutes later, his eyes red-rimmed, his face a pallid gray, he said, "I told her you were here—you ought to go in now. The nurse said you could have five minutes."

Jack put a hand on Clancy's shoulder as he sat down, then crossed the hall to the Intensive Care Unit. At first, he was surprised at the dimness of the lighting, then he passed into the brilliant glare around the nursing station. A heavyset nurse, wearing the kind of peaked hat he didn't think they wore anymore, said, "Mr Logan?"

"Yes."

"The last bed on your left. Five minutes, no more. Keep your voice down and don't do anything to agitate her."

There was a drawn curtain on one side of her bed, a wall on the other. On the curtained side, there was a battery of machines and an IV unit; on the other, a single, straight-backed chair. Jack pulled the chair closer to the bed and sat down.

There was almost no sign of Mam; almost no sign of anyone at all. The crisp white sheet that covered the bed showed only the slightest elevation where she lay beneath it; her frail limbs made nothing more than wrinkles in the sheet. The top half of the bed had been raised slightly, and a clear plastic sheet—an oxygen tent, Jack remembered from a previous episode, years before—had been draped over it. Mam's face appeared sunken and faded, far away, behind the plastic scrim. There was a low but constant whooshing sound, from the oxygen compressor.

Jack guessed where her hand lay, under the sheet, and gently placed his own on top of it. Her head turned, just a little, on the pillow. "Don't try to talk," he said. "Just rest."

But her head shook, ever so slightly, and her hand stirred. He inched the chair even closer, and put his face up to the tent. A pale green tube had been inserted in one of her nostrils, and a couple of black wires—Jack was reminded of Sprague's lab—trailed from somewhere under the sheet and into the monitors ranged around her.

"The doctors said you should just lie still," Jack repeated, "to recover your strength."

But Mam would have none of it; she knew better. He sensed she wanted to tell him something. And behind the plastic curtain, he could see her lips moving. But the sound of the compressor was too great for him to hear her. He leaned his head against the cool plastic, and said, "Mam, I'm sorry —you'll have to say it again." And then he heard, "*Investigator.*"

He sat stockstill in the chair.

"Called . . . about you."

Mansfield—that bastard. His was the British accent Clancy had heard.

"Said you had . . . powers." It was meant, Jack understood, as a question. But what exactly—and how much—had Mansfield told her? "Is it true?" she asked, in a ragged whisper.

Was *what* true? Had Mansfield told her about Zakin? Garcia? The TV appearance Jack had made? How had he even found her?

"Mam . . . I don't think now is the time—"

Her hand slipped out from under the sheet, and, with surprising vigor, clutched his. He looked down at her bony, but tenacious fingers.

"Jack . . . tell me," she said.

And he did—everything that he believed Mansfield already knew, and might have told her himself. Then he told her about the experiments that were being done at the Institute of Abnormal Psychology, and his own mixed emotions about them. When he paused for a moment, hoping he had satisfied her curiosity, she squeezed his hand again and said, *"How?"*

"How do I do it?"

She nodded, once.

The moment of truth had come, the moment he'd feared and at the same time secretly hoped for—the moment when he could tell Mam that he knew all about his own miraculous birth, and that he believed it was connected to his equally miraculous abilities. There might not *be* another time in which to do it—and it was absolutely *vital* that she know.

"Mam, remember when I came out to Weehawken and said I needed my birth certificate to get my passport?" He explained the real purpose of the search, and told her about the newspaper clippings he had discovered in Clancy's footlocker. When he thought she had understood, and accepted, that revelation, he took a deep breath, put his own hand on top of hers, and said, "There's something more."

The nurse poked her head around the partition, silently assessed the situation, and said, "Not much longer, okay?"

Jack nodded, and when she left he said, "There's something else I think you *must* know, something I think will make you very, very happy."

Mam waited, absolutely still, while he found the words.

"In that Other World that I've been telling you about, those who have gone before us still live. In that Other World, Mam, I have seen, and I have talked to, my mother—your daughter —Mary Elizabeth."

There was no sound now but the steady pumping of the air compressor, the faint rustle of the oxygen tent. Mam's hand seemed, in some subtle way, to relax beneath his, her shoulders to fall. A pinging noise, rhythmic and mechanical, began to emanate from one of the machines beside her bed. Suddenly, almost in that same instant, there was the sound of rubber soles squeaking hurriedly across the floor. The nurse reappeared: "You have to leave, immediately." Another nurse came up right behind her, pushing a trolley; Jack stood up, moved out of the way. Over her shoulder, the head nurse said to him, "Please leave the I.C.U." She was yanking the sheet back. Dr. Prescott sped past him. Jack retreated into a patch of shadow, just to one side of the curtained partition. Prescott was bending over the bed, issuing instructions to the two nurses. A second doctor appeared, went to the other side of the bed. Mam was lost, made utterly invisible, by the sudden crush of bodies around her. There was a flurry of activity— urgent conferrals were held, a syringe was filled, administered. More instructions flew back and forth; some sort of device—it looked like the two halves of a cantaloupe—was removed from the trolley and put to use. Heads kept turning, from the bed to the bank of monitors and then back to the bed again. There were bleeps and whirrings, buzzes and gasps from the host of instruments. But after several minutes, the commotion gradually subsided; the mechanical noises began to abate, except for one steady high-pitched whine, and the hands of the doctors and nurses ceased to fly about. It seemed as if they had run out of things to do. Prescott stood up straight again, with his hands pressed to the small of his back. The head nurse still hovered, doing something Jack could not make out; the other nurse began replacing things on the trolley. Even the high-pitched whining stopped. The second doctor said to Prescott, "Sorry, but this one was a long shot to begin with." None of them realized that Jack was still there, in the shadows to one side of the curtain.

"I'll leave it to you then," Prescott said to the head nurse. "I'll go out and tell the Logans." He turned to leave, and saw Jack. He paused. "Have you been there the whole time?"

"Yes."

"Then you know. Your grandmother has just passed away."

Jack said nothing; he stepped forward and around to the side of the bed where he'd originally been sitting. The head nurse looked at Dr. Prescott; he gestured at her to let him be. Jack pulled the chair away from the wall, drew it up to the bed.

Don't think it's over yet, Mam. I'm coming for you. He took her hand between his own, then bent his head over it. *I'm coming.* In his mind's eye, he *summoned* this time, he didn't wait for it to appear, the image with which these journeys usually began—the mountain of sand, the red-steel scaffolding, the hot, bright, summer sun. He turned his inner vision toward that bright and burning sky, and willed himself to travel up toward it. There was a cold, metallic smell in the air, and a faint breeze that slowly turned to wind, a wind that bore him up and carried him toward the light. A vague babble of voices, that he had come to expect, assailed him on all sides. *I'm coming, Mam—wait for me.* All around him the landscape had faded to a vast, unyielding white; the heat was growing more intense by the second. The very air seemed to pulse, rhythmically, with a huge and invisible energy; out of it, as if suddenly carved from light, Mam appeared. She was facing the other way, but when Jack called to her, she turned, puzzled; her gray hair blew gently about her face, her skin had a kind of hectic flush to it. Though twenty or thirty feet appeared to separate them, Jack extended his hand to her, and in that instant the gap was closed. Mam allowed him to take her hand, but when he said, "Mam, come with me," and tried to

lead her back in the direction she'd just come, she resisted.
Her head kept turning toward the bright and beating light that
had appeared, and was growing ever closer, in the distance.
"Don't look at the light," Jack told her, but Mam, shaking her
head, said, "I must." Jack tried, with his other hand, to shield
her eyes from it, but Mam seemed to be able to look right
through him. "Mam, we need you," Jack said. "Clancy needs
you. I need you . . . come with me, Mam . . . come with me."
The light was becoming steadily more intense, the air around
them more agitated. Jack himself found it harder and harder to
keep his eyes from the light, and at the same time felt a rising
surge of fear within him; he did not want to pass through that
burning beacon again. He did not want to feel its scouring
fire; this time, he feared, he would not survive it. It would
consume him, utterly, and strand his soul in the Other World
—just as Nancy had predicted.

The winds around them began to whirl like a maelstrom.
Jack released Mam's hand, and clutched her frail shoulders
instead. "We love you," he said, "you don't have to die . . . not
yet." But Mam fixed him with a serious and troubled gaze.
"We love you," he repeated, imploringly.

"Then let me go," she said, searching his face as if for the
last time. "You have to let me go, Jack."

"No—I don't," he replied, tears springing to his eyes. He
sounded, even to himself, like a petulant child. "I *love* you."

"I know you do," she said, with a sad but radiant smile.
"That's *why* you must let me go. This is not for you to decide,
Jack—this is God's will."

The light beat, like crashing cymbals, in the air around
them.

"It doesn't have to be," he said, softly, though he knew the
battle was already lost.

"Yes," she answered, gently removing his hands from her
shoulders, "it does."

She turned again toward the great and pounding light, and
Jack could not resist looking too. In its shimmering heat there
appeared to be a multitude of beings, all indistinguishable,
and a chorus of voices, all unintelligible. Even Mam, con-
fronted with this wonder, hesitated, staring in awe at the
boundless light.

"God will wait," Jack whispered, just behind her.

Mam tilted her face, her eyes closed, up and into the blaze . . . but did not move.

"God will wait." Was she faltering? Would she return with him, after all? The air around them wildly swirled, hot and dry, like the wind off a desert. "Mam . . ." Jack breathed, lifting his hand to touch her shoulder.

"Mam," came the reply, out of the very heart of the light. One shape, out of thousands, had coalesced, one voice became intelligible.

"Mary . . ."

Her face floated, long hair streaming, in the boiling light. "Mam, hurry . . . I cannot wait for you here."

"Mary, darling . . . yes, I'm coming." Mam lifted her arms toward the light, and was borne up into it, effortlessly, like an ash rising from a fire. She disappeared into the massive, amorphous light. Mary Elizabeth disappeared too, but not before Jack heard her voice calling out to him, calling him to join them.

Already, he felt the powerful magnetic pull of the light, and with it the diminishment of his will to resist. Another few seconds and he would willingly give himself over to it, close his eyes and drift, as Mam had done, into the embrace of that terrible brightness. It would be so easy, so very, very easy, to give up the fight and simply let it happen. And he would not be alone there! He'd have Mam now, and his mother, and he would be scoured, inside and out, by that living flame, reduced to cinders, made whole, obliterated, born anew, forgotten, purified, rendered no more nor less than what his heart in life had made him . . .

The light was shining directly into his eye; his lid was being held up with one finger.

"Can you hear me?" Prescott was saying.

The light shone now in his other eye. It was pitifully feeble compared to the light he'd *been* looking at.

"My God, you should feel his skin," Prescott was saying to someone. "It's like he's turned to ice."

"Do you want to give him an injection?"

"I don't know . . . I thought he'd just fainted."

A hand was pressed to the side of his neck.

"His pulse is a little slow, but otherwise it's all right."

Jack rolled his head and managed to say, "I'm all right."

He looked up and saw Prescott, and the head nurse, hovering above him. He was lying on the floor. "What happened?"

"You fainted, and fell out of the chair," the nurse replied.

"How do you feel now?"

"Cold," Jack said, "but okay." With a hand from Prescott, he sat up. His eyes were now level with the mattress on Mam's bed. Her hand, the one he'd been holding, had been tucked under the sheet; it made a little bump, the size of a snowball.

"Can you stand up?"

"I think so." Carefully, testing his balance, he got to his feet. The wires and tubes were no longer attached to Mam; the monitors had been turned off, too.

"Have you told Clancy?" Jack said to Prescott.

"Yes. I was with him when you collapsed in here." He looked Jack up and down. "You seem all right now—are you?"

"Yes, yes, I'm okay." Folding both arms around himself to warm up, he walked slowly past the semicircular counter of the nursing station, and out into the hall. Clancy was waiting for him.

"They told me you—"

"I fainted," Jack said. "I'm sorry. I'm all right now."

Clancy, clearly overcome by it all, stood silently, rooted to the spot. There was some small commotion down the hall, at the general nurses' station.

"I think we should go home now. There's nothing else we can do here." Jack took him gently by the arm, and led him away from the I.C.U. As they passed the nurses' desk, he heard the name "Logan" repeated twice, insistently, as if someone were trying to find them.

"We're the Logans," he said, stopping.

A man with thinning hair and an ascot wheeled around. "Remember me? They're telling me your grandmother just died in Intensive Care."

Mansfield.

"Can that be?" he went on, in his clipped British tones. "I mean, with you here to save her?"

Jack slugged him in the face so hard he was carried halfway over the nurses' desk, before slipping back down again, unconscious, in a heap on the floor. His legs stuck straight out, like stilts.

"If he wants to press charges," Logan said to the two stunned young nurses, "you know where to find me."

Then he led the bewildered Clancy over to the row of elevators, and took the first one back down.

chapter twenty-six

"THAT MUST BE them over there."

"You want me to get closer?"

"No, just pull up to that bend, and park."

Tulley maneuvered the old Chevy Cavalier to the spot Sprague had indicated, and stopped. About a hundred yards away, on a slight rise, ten or twelve people were gathered at an open gravesite. A priest, bareheaded, in a long, black overcoat, was saying some words. The sky, gray and thick with clouds, threatened snow any moment.

Sprague, also sitting in the front seat, had to look past Tulley's barrel chest in order to see anything. "Push your seat back," he said. Tulley fumbled for the catch, then reclined. Now Sprague could see Jack, in the same tweedy overcoat he always wore to the institute, standing at the foot of the grave, head bowed, hands clasped. Sprague felt like a hunter who'd successfully tracked his quarry. It hadn't been easy.

For one thing, his home phone number had been changed, and though Nancy no doubt had the new one, she was away for the holidays at some damned relative's. Sprague had then called the theater where *Steamroller* was still running, found out Jack was back in the band, and had left a message for him with someone backstage. Logan had either not gotten it, or not bothered to reply. Sprague was at his wits' end when that Prescott character had called him from St. John's Hospital. He said he'd found out Dr. Mehta's forwarding address in India, "if you still want it, that is."

"Yes, of course I do," Sprague had replied, "though I seem

to have lost track of the patient in the meantime."

"You mean Logan? He was out here just three days ago." And then he'd explained about Jack's grandmother. "In fact, I thought you should know he took it rather hard." He told Sprague that Jack had clutched his dead grandmother's hand, mumbling intensely to himself, and a minute later had fallen in a faint to the floor. "He was stone-cold, too, if you can believe that. I've never felt anyone—anyone alive, I mean— who was that cold."

"And what about his grandmother?" Sprague shot back. "Did she revive?"

"What?"

"Did she revive, come back to life? What happened to her?"

"What do you mean, what happened to her? She was dead. She stayed that way." Prescott had sounded unsure of Sprague's sanity now.

"Oh . . . yes," Sprague had replied, getting control of himself again. "I'd only thought . . ." The hell with it, how could he ever explain it away? "And Jack Logan—he recovered his senses?"

"Yes, completely, as far as I can tell." He still sounded uncertain about Sprague. "Can I give you that address for Dr. Mehta?"

Sprague had taken it down and thanked him; then before hanging up, he'd asked if Prescott had any idea where to find Logan.

"No idea," Prescott had said. "I expect he's been helping his grandfather with the funeral arrangements and all that. There's only the two of them."

It had taken Tulley a half hour on the phone to track down the funeral parlor, and get the time and place of the actual ceremony. It now looked to be drawing to a close.

The priest had closed his book, and the onlookers had stepped back from the sides of the grave. The casket was being lowered, slowly, into the hard, ice-covered ground. Must have been hell, Sprague thought, on the gravediggers.

"You gonna get out?" Tulley asked.

"Not yet," Sprague said, "not until it's over."

* * *

When the casket rested at the bottom of the grave, Jack stepped forward, after Clancy, and Mam's only sister, to toss a flower on top of the polished mahogany lid. All through the ceremony, he'd been carrying on an imaginary conversation with Mam, telling her how much he loved her, telling her that he would do his best to look after Clancy, telling her, most importantly, that he understood what she had said, and silently revealed to him, in the Other World—that death was neither to be feared, nor tampered with. That it was God's will, and not his. That his powers, however great, and wherever they'd come from, were at best a form of meddling, and at worst a contravention of some Divine plan. It was all, at last, settled in his mind, and it felt right. The questions he'd been wrestling with for weeks had been answered, and the fears that had steadily been gathering strength within him had been eased. Now, as his own flower came to rest with the others, he said his last good-bye.

Clancy was standing, staring into the grave, as if asleep on his feet. He'd been that way ever since the hospital; Jack had been commuting between Weehawken and New York the whole time. With the funeral costs and everything else to contend with, Jack had decided to stay with the show as long as it lasted; he was in no position to pass up a weekly paycheck. (Burt had sworn not to pull any more fast ones.) The priest had put a hand on Clancy's shoulder and was talking to him in a low voice. The others were quietly dispersing. Jack took the opportunity to step away from the grave and look around. That same car he'd noticed earlier, the old Chevy, was still parked in the gravel drive. As he watched, the passenger door on the far side opened, and a tall man got out and turned around. Jack could hardly believe his eyes—it was Sprague. And now Tulley, from the driver's side. They saw that he had spotted them, and waited there. Jack looked over to see that Clancy was still being taken care of—Mam's sister, Irene, was with him too—then cautiously descended the slippery hill, balancing himself with the gravestones as he went.

Sprague came around to the back of the car, a rolled-up newspaper in his hands. Tulley leaned, arms folded, against the driver's door.

"We came to pay our respects," Sprague said as Jack approached.

Tell me another one, Jack thought.

"We appear to have arrived a little late."

"Yes," Jack said, "the funeral's over."

"So we see . . . so we see."

"What *did* you come for?"

Sprague paused, rapping the newspaper in the palm of his black leather glove. "You're not an easy man to reach these days. Did you get the message I left for you at the theater?"

"Yes. I did."

"Ah . . . then why didn't you come to the institute?"

"Because," Jack replied, "it's over."

"What is?"

"All of it . . . the experiments, the hypnosis, the cardiographs, the tank. I can't do it anymore."

"You mean because you failed to save your grandmother?"

Jack caught himself before answering. "What do you know about that?"

"Everything," Sprague said, smugly. "Dr. Prescott and I have been in constant communication."

"Then you know that I tried, and failed," Jack said, seeing a perfect way out.

"Yes. You failed—once. That doesn't mean you won't succeed the next time."

"There won't be a next time," Jack said, shaking his head. "I'm telling you, it's over."

"And I'm telling you," Sprague said, stepping closer and lowering his voice, "it's not. You think I came this far, only to stop short on the very threshold of confirming my discovery? You think I'm going to throw away a lifetime of work, all because *you* haven't got the *guts* to see it through?" He rapped the newspaper harder against his glove. "You know what *I* think, Logan? I think you're trying to cut me out of this. I think you're trying to run the whole show by yourself now." He snapped the newspaper open and showed the front page to Jack. "Did you think I wouldn't see this?"

It was a copy of the *Investigator*. Under a headline that read "Miracle in the Making?" there was a picture of Jack, on a park bench, pressing his hands to the bared head of a man in a down coat.

"Are you a faith healer too, now?" Sprague taunted him. "Is that a lucrative sideline you wanted to explore?"

Jack had grabbed the newspaper away and was quickly scanning the text. The byline, of course, was Mansfield's, and yes, he had Baldwin's name there and quotes from him too. "'I believe that he has healed me,' confided the terminally ill young ad man. 'I can feel the process already.'" Had it all been a setup, after all? Or had Mansfield simply followed Jack into the park, taken the pictures with a telephoto lens, then paid off Baldwin for his story?

Sprague was watching him with icy eyes. "First time you've seen it?" he said, scornfully. "Jesus, spare me the surprise. I suppose you don't know he died on Christmas morning, either, at New York Hospital?"

Jack let the tabloid fall away. All he could think of was the fervency with which Baldwin had murmured "I believe . . . I believe" on that bench in the boat basin. What good had his believing done him? What good had Jack done him?

"Oh, so you *didn't* know," Sprague said, registering his sudden dismay. "Well, perhaps now you'll put away these notions of faith-healing, and put yourself back under my supervision, where you belong."

Jack was dimly aware of Tulley, circling around behind him.

"We can straighten all of this out," Sprague went on, calmly, but with a clear undercurrent of menace, "on the way back into the city. Why don't you just get into the car, Jack, and we'll return to the institute."

Tulley was right behind him now, so close that Jack could feel his breath, clouding in the cold air, on the back of his neck. He slapped the tabloid back into Sprague's hand and said, "Don't even think about it." Tulley had taken hold of his left elbow.

"About what?" Sprague replied, putting on a big false smile in case anyone should be watching.

"About getting me into the car. 'Cause if I have to, I'll take out both of you—you first, and then"—shoving his elbow back, hard, right into Tulley's solar plexus—"*him*." Tulley coughed, and doubled over.

Jack turned around, patted Tulley on the back, and started to walk away. The priest and Clancy and Irene were all looking down at them from the gravesite. Jack heard Sprague saying, "No, no, not now," to Tulley, "not with all of them watching."

Jack climbed back up the hill, just as the first flakes of snow began to fall. *First Mansfield, now Tulley,* he thought, with a wry, sad smile. *I'm going from savior to prizefighter in record time. What*, he wondered, *would Nancy say?*

Then, turning up his collar against the falling snow, he offered up a silent prayer for the soul of Adam Baldwin.

chapter
twenty-seven

THE FORECAST FOR later that night, New Year's Eve, wasn't a good one. Heavy rain, possibly turning to sleet and snow. In self-defense, Nancy had opted for the layered look —a cashmere sweater over her blouse, a pair of leg warmers over her jeans, and a raspberry-red ski parka, with a hood that folds out of the collar, over everything else. She felt prepared for anything.

Out on the street she realized it was lucky she was. People were already acting crazy, weaving down the street in paper party hats, shooting off bottle rockets, shouting "Happy New Year!" out the window of passing buses. One guy she passed was leaning against a lamppost, retching between two parked cars. And it was only ten-thirty. Times Square at midnight was going to be a zoo.

Nancy crossed over to Mott Street and waited outside one of the most popular Peking duck restaurants until a cab pulled up, then jumped in before anybody cowering inside the restaurant had a chance to come out.

"Broadway and Forty-fifth Street, please."

The cabbie finished scrawling something on his route record, then slammed the meter back on and took off with a jolt. This, Nancy thought, is a man who's not happy about working tonight. But then, who in his right mind would be?

Only Sprague. And she wasn't so sure what mind he was in. When she'd put on her coat to leave the institute at six-fifteen that evening, he'd looked surprised.

"Where are you going? Two new specimens have just arrived."

"I have to go now," she replied. "It's New Year's Eve, you know."

"What's that got to do with it?" He sounded so much like Scrooge she'd half expected him to add, "Bah, humbug!"

"I have a date."

"'A date,'" he mimicked, sourly. "I don't have to ask who with. Jack Logan, I'm sure."

It was the first time he'd acknowledged knowing about them.

"Yes," she'd admitted, glad to have it all out in the open now, "it is with Jack. We're meeting at the theater after the show, and we're going to go over to Times Square to watch the ball drop." It was about time Sprague heard how normal people lived their lives.

"Well, isn't that nice . . . young love. Please give your boyfriend my regards, will you. Tell him, if there's anything you haven't already told him, that the institute goes on without him." As she waited for the elevator to come up, he'd shouted down the hall after her, "Tell him he can rot in hell!" Strangely enough, after three days of studious silence, the curse had come as something of a relief.

A light film of wet flakes was starting to paste itself to the window of the cab. The cabbie muttered, "Shit," and turned on his windshield wipers. "You want me to try to get closer than this?"

They'd gotten as far as Fortieth Street, but traffic was totally gridlocked: the cab was wedged between two idling buses, and a cop, armed with a whistle and a flashlight, was trying, unsuccessfully, to clear the intersection. Some of the streets had been blocked off altogether, to free up Times Square, and traffic was being rerouted.

"No, that's okay. I'll get out here." She paid the driver and got out of the cab, right in the middle of the stalled street. The sidewalks, even in the cold and snow, were packed with revelers; there were hordes streaming out of the huge, triplex movie theaters and mobs swarming in and out of the fast-food joints. Senegalese street peddlers were hawking umbrellas and noisemakers and fake Cartier wristwatches from the top of cardboard boxes; a woman with a megaphone was distributing

Watchtower booklets and warning that the end of the world was near. A zoo, Nancy thought, would have been a kind way to describe this scene.

Though the theater was only a few blocks away, it took her nearly a half hour to get there. By the time she did, she could see that the show had already let out—the front doors were wide open, all the lobby lights still on; she went around to the backstage door and found Jack and his friends in the locker room. Jack gave her a big hug, and introduced her to the guys she'd heard so much about—Vinnie and Haywood (whom she'd met, for two seconds, the night Jack had first invited her to see the show), Van Nostrand, Catalano. All but Van Nostrand had girlfriends with them.

"So—we ready to move now?" Vinnie asked. "Remember —anybody gets separated, just meet up back at my apartment —"

"*Our* apartment," his girlfriend—or wife—put in, rolling her eyes.

"Yeah, right—*our* apartment," he said, throwing one arm around her, "anytime after a quarter of one or so."

"Gotcha," Haywood said, impatiently. "Come on already, or it's gonna be next year before we get out of here."

They poured out the backstage door, past Gus, who was working his crossword puzzle like any other night of the year, and into the backstage alley. The wet snow was still coming down in lazy swirls. Haywood's girlfriend, a pretty black woman, rail-thin, with big gold hoop earrings, looked none too happy. "Don't worry about it," Haywood said, reading her mind. "I'm gonna buy you an umbrella."

Out on the street, they tried to stay together, but the crowds were so thick, and there were so many umbrellas already up, and police barricades to get around, that it was a constant struggle. Jack, with one arm firmly wrapped around Nancy's shoulders, almost seemed to be purposely hanging back.

"Don't you want to keep up with your friends?" Nancy asked.

"To tell you the truth," he said, leaning down and kissing her ear under the flap of the hood, "not really. We can catch up with them at Vinnie and Barbara's. When the ball comes down, I want to be alone with you."

"Alone?" Nancy said, smiling and taking in the mob crushing in on them from all sides.

"Yeah, well," he said, laughing, "alone as we can get."

Getting separated from the others wasn't very difficult. At the next corner, Jack pulled her by the arm, and she was swept through a revolving door and into the brightly lighted interior of a McDonald's. "How much time have we got until midnight?" he asked.

"About thirty minutes."

"Good. Don't tell Vinnie—he made his special chili for later on—but I'm starved. I need a burger and fries now."

"You're gonna brave that mob?" There seemed to be more people inside the McDonald's, pressing toward the front counter, than there were outside. The air in the place was oppressively hot, and smelled of sweat and grease and wet clothes.

"I'm gonna try. You want anything if I make it?"

"No, not for me. I'm going to wait outside for you. It's so much more peaceful out there."

He watched her thread her way back to the door, then made his own way toward the counter. When he got there, the only thing they had ready to go were Big Macs, so he had one of those, a large order of fries, and a Coke. Rather than try to juggle it all outside, he found a spot at a side counter and wolfed it down then and there. A clock above the breakfast menu said ten to twelve.

He used some paper napkins to dry the snow off his hair, then went outside to get Nancy. He figured she'd be waiting right outside the door, as he'd never be able to find her if she'd gone any farther, but to his surprise she wasn't there. The noise level was already so deafening that calling out for her was fairly pointless. Next door there was a video arcade; could she have gone in there to get warm?

The arcade was as packed as the McDonald's; rows and rows of beeping, clanging pinball machines, Pac-Mans, Donkey Kongs. Rap music was blaring from the overhead speakers. He went from row to row, looking for her raspberry-colored parka, but he didn't see it anywhere. And after a couple of minutes, he knew she couldn't possibly have taken refuge in there. Even the McDonald's had been better than this.

So where was she? He went back outside, checked the McDonald's again, then looked at his watch—it was only four or five minutes till midnight. Damn—if he didn't find her soon, they'd miss watching the ball drop together. It was already lighted—a great big glowing apple—perched on top of the Times Tower. A happy, drunken, stoned crowd was surging and swaying beneath it, waving at the TV cameras, blasting plastic horns. Where the hell was Nancy?

Maybe, it occurred to him, she'd hooked up again with Vinnie and the gang and been lured off to wherever they were standing. But how was he supposed to find them then? In this crowd, you couldn't see more than two or three bodies ahead of you. He was torn between hanging around the McDonald's, waiting for her to return, and going off to find her—impossible as that seemed.

A panhandler, swathed in the bubble-wrap used for mailing packages, accosted him with an empty paper cup. Jack dropped a quarter in just to get him to go away.

He'd started out surprised; now he was growing concerned. It was so unlike Nancy to just wander off and get lost in the crowd. She hadn't been all that enthusiastic about going to Times Square in the first place. Why would she go off on her own, into that crazy mob scene? Maybe something had happened to her, though he couldn't think what; there were cops, some of them on horseback, all over the place.

Several colored spotlights began to play up and down the Times Tower. The golden, glowing apple quivered at the top of its perch, then slowly, with the crowd chanting off the seconds, started its descent. Jack leaned back against the plate-glass window of an electronics shop and watched it fall. Hats and hands and umbrellas were waving wildly, jubilantly, in the air. The snow was drifting down now in thick, white flakes; anywhere other than New York, it would be making a beautiful white blanket. When the apple hit the bottom of its slide, there was an eruption of noise and light, horns honking, spotlights turning, music blasting from a hundred portable radios. The crowd started singing, in ragged unison, "Auld Lang Syne," and from the direction of Forty-second Street a police siren *whoop-whoop-whooped* its way eastward.

What the hell should he do now? If Nancy wasn't with Vinnie and the others, she wouldn't know where to go. She'd never been to Vinnie's apartment and Jack hadn't given her the address. *Why* hadn't she come back to the McDonald's? Short of going back to his own apartment, on the chance that she would try to meet up with him again there, there was only one thing he could think of: maybe she'd left a message of some sort on his answering machine, telling him where she'd gone. He fished his last quarter out of his pocket, found an empty phone booth in the back of the video arcade, and called his machine. It picked up on the first ring, which meant someone had left a message. He signaled it with the beeper, waited while it rolled back, then heard "Welcome home, Jack. This is Dr. Sprague."

Sprague, on New Year's Eve?

"In case you're wondering what happened to Nancy Liu, she's here, with us, at the institute. I think, if you're concerned about her welfare, you should come over yourself, alone, as soon as you get this message. We'll be expecting you."

Jack hung up the phone, stunned, and sat there until a Puerto Rican kid rapped on the glass door with a quarter.

"You done?"

Jack nodded, and left the booth. He didn't even hear the clanging of the pinball machines all around him. All he could think of was the message he'd just heard; how had Sprague gotten her to the institute? And who had done it? Sprague had said "us": he must have meant himself and Tulley. He wouldn't dare involve anyone else. Jack looked at his watch. It was a quarter after twelve. They couldn't have had her at the institute for very long; the message must have been left only minutes ago. That was the one thing, it suddenly occurred to him, that worked in his favor; Sprague was expecting him to have to travel all the way home before getting the message, and then come back across town and down again. He wouldn't be expecting Jack for a while yet. Jack might be able to surprise him . . . if he hurried. Any other plans would have to be made on the run.

He bolted out of the video arcade but was instantly stymied by the crush of people outside. He collided with a huge guy in a Villanova sweatshirt who said, "Hey man, where the fuck you think you're going?" Then, trying to get around him, banged into a blue police barricade that he hadn't seen. He had to get out of Times Square—then he could worry about finding a cab to get him uptown.

Making his way across to the East Side, through the pandemonium, was impossible; instead, he started to fight his way north. Twice he had to step over people who had fallen down drunk on the sidewalk; once he edged too close to a cop's horse and got smacked in the shoulder with its nose. Everywhere, he was caroming off bodies, knocking into umbrellas, wedging himself between couples, skipping back and forth between the curb and the sidewalk. By the time he got to Forty-eighth Street, it was possible again to run, dodging and weaving, through the late-night revelers. But the pavement was slippery with the wet snow, and occasionally he had to grab hold of a street sign to regain his balance and catch his breath.

A cab—he needed to find a cab. But on New Year's Eve, in the snow, he knew he had a better chance of finding a camel. At a streetlight, he had an idea: there were limos all over town that night, and when they weren't transporting whoever had paid for them, they were idling outside nightclubs and restaurants. He looked up at the street sign; he was already at Fifty-second. He knew where to go. He ran east, to the "21" Club, and sure enough, it looked like a limousine convention outside. It took him only two tries before a driver accepted twenty to drive him up to the institute.

"Make really good time," Jack said, "and I'll make it twenty-five!"

It was a long, silver limo, with a TV and a bar in back. But Jack played with none of the toys. What he had to do, while the car sped, silently, through the snow-covered streets, was come up with a plan of action. But not knowing what kind of danger Nancy was in made it very tough. Just how crazy was Sprague? How far would he go to get Jack back where he wanted him? Pretty damned far, Jack thought; abducting Nancy was already a criminal offense. And it showed he knew how involved Jack was with her—at least that little mystery had now been cleared up, once and for all.

"What side of the street do you want?" the driver asked.

"Right side, about halfway down the next block."

"Nobody coulda made better time."

"I got ya," Jack said, taking a twenty and a five from his

wallet, then leaning forward and handing them through the little glass panel behind the driver's head.

"Have a happy New Year." He snagged the bills between two fingers.

The car slid to a halt—up here the street was nearly deserted—and Jack jumped out. Aside from the lights that were on in the first-floor reception area, the building was dark. But that still told him next to nothing; Sprague did all his work on the upper stories, in the rear. Was he in his own research lab, or back in the tank room, one floor below? Jack sidled up the front steps, staying out of sight, then peered in through the iron bars on the door. The reception area was empty; Tulley, thank God, wasn't at the desk. He tried the door; it was open. So far he'd guessed right—they didn't expect him yet. He ducked inside, and made for the security desk. There were three small TV monitors, one labeled ELEVATOR. Jack flicked it on, saw the interior of the elevator car. More importantly, he saw that its doors were open and it faced a fire extinguisher. That meant it was on the fifth floor, where the tank room and the animal labs were located. He flicked off the monitor again. Since he couldn't punch the elevator button without alerting Sprague and Tulley to his arrival, he took the back stairs instead, praying that Sprague had left the alarms on the upper floors neutered. When he got to five, he put his shoulder to the door, turned the handle, and pushed. It opened with a grating sound, but no alarm.

The smell, however, was as bad as ever. The door opened into the back of the animal lab. The four long rows of cages, running the length of the room, glinted blue and black in what light managed to filter through the steel mesh on the windows. Jack left the door open behind him—for all he knew, he'd need it later—and crept up one of the aisles. As he passed one of the dogs' cages, the animal inside—a collie—started to bark. Jack stopped, whispered, "It's okay, boy, it's okay," and for a moment the dog did stop. But the second he moved on, the barking started again, louder; the dog was even beating its tail against the side of its cage, thumping the metal like a drum. The other animals were awakened by the noise: the pigeons started warbling and flapping their wings; the monkey gibbered and rattled his bars; the rats began madly scurrying in circles. The whole lab, it seemed, had erupted around Jack.

He was just a few feet from the hall door when he heard
footsteps approaching from the outside. He turned quickly and
retreated to one of the aisles. But the tails of his overcoat,
flapping behind him, somehow snared one of the cages, and
brought it crashing down onto the floor. The top of the cage
flipped off, just as the door to the lab flew open and the
overhead lights came on. Jack, crouching down below the
level of the cages, held his breath and waited.

"Who's in here?"

Tulley's voice—he would recognize it anywhere.

"Potter? Cazenovia?"

Jack inched back down the aisle.

There was a long pause, then Tulley said, with tremendous
satisfaction, "So it's you, asshole. You made good time."

Jack was eye to eye with a batch of hamsters.

"Sprague wants you."

He could hear Tulley's shoes squeaking, slowly, across the
floor. Jack ducked around to the back of the aisle.

"But I want you first."

Jack flattened himself against a stack of cages. What
should he do now? What *could* he do?

"Come on, asshole . . . come on out."

Tulley was pacing back and forth across the front of the
room. Jack could tell from the way his voice moved.

"I ain't got all night."

He should create a diversion, Jack thought . . . something to
get Tulley's attention long enough for him to sprint for the
door to the hall.

"Your girlfriend don't either."

Jack's heart nearly stopped at the mention of Nancy.

"You know, she's not bad-lookin', for a Chink."

He was coming down the aisle now, the one in which Jack
had knocked over the cage.

Jack fumbled at the latch of the cage behind him, then
swept out the pigeons inside it. Two of them shot up toward
the fluorescent lights in the ceiling. There was a loud, but
muffled, *pop*, and in the same instant one of the birds exploded in a puff of feathers and blood. Spattered bits of it
rained down on Jack.

"Target practice," Tulley joked.

Jesus Christ—he had a gun. Jack remembered what Nancy

had told him when he'd first come to the institute—that Tulley was an ex-con Sprague had given a job to.

"And I see you."

Jack turned his head slowly, and saw that Tulley was aiming the gun at him, from about ten feet away, through the back of the empty pigeon cage.

"So just get up . . . and keep your hands where I can see 'em."

Jack stood, holding his hands out at waist level, palms up.

"You ain't so tough now, asshole, now it's just you and me." The gun was a gleaming black, with a gray funnel that Jack took to be a silencer, fitted over the front of the barrel. "No more cheap shots, like that one you took out in Jersey."

Tulley was standing with the gun trained casually on Jack's abdomen, his stumpy legs held far apart. Behind him Jack thought he detected something, on the floor, move.

"Wouldn't I like to waste you," Tulley said, apparently weighing his chances of getting away with it.

"Could be kinda messy," Jack said, just trying to buy some time. Behind Tulley, he saw that movement again—something black and green, slithering toward them both.

"Messy's no problem," Tulley said, "not with Sprague around. He can make anything disappear."

It was a snake, a big one—it must have been in the cage Jack had knocked over. Jack pointed to it with one finger and said, "You ought to look behind you, Tulley."

"Yeah, right—what kind of dumb shit do you take me for?"

The snake raised its head, tongue flicking, just behind Tulley's left ankle—it must be hopping mad, Jack thought, after the tumbling it took.

"So don't believe me . . . it's your ass," Jack said.

The snake drew its entire length into a loose coil and hissed malevolently. Tulley heard it and glanced behind him.

"Fuck!" He jumped back, swinging the gun around. Fangs bared, the snake leaped at his calf; Tulley shot, and a piece of the linoleum flew up in splinters. Jack grabbed the empty pigeon cage, smashed Tulley in the back of the head with it; he spilled over, the snake still hanging on and lashing in the air. "Get it offa me! Get it off!" Jack vaulted over them, the snake's tail smacking the bottom of his shoe, and ran for the door. The other animals were shrieking and banging and fluttering in their cages. He slammed off the light switch and yanked the steel door shut. The noise died the second the door was closed; with any luck, Jack thought, Sprague might not have heard any of it.

He quickly crossed the hall to the tank room, inched that door open. There was a short entryway, then the control booth; Sprague was bent over the instrument panel, utterly absorbed. Jack had closed the door behind him, and thrown the bolt from the inside, before Sprague heard him and turned around.

"Oh. It's you." He said it quite matter-of-factly, as if nothing out of the ordinary were going on. "Tulley was supposed to let me know when you got here."

"Tulley's busy."

Sprague gave him a long, level look. "I won't ask you what that means, because I don't really give a damn. What I wanted was to get you to the institute—and now I've done that."

"And I want Nancy."

"And I've got her."

"Where?"

Sprague smiled, slipping his hands into the pockets of his lab coat. "That all depends."

"On what?"

"On your cooperation." He sighed and sat down again in the swivel chair at the control panel. "I'm sick to death of tracking you down, Logan. My time is precious, and that's a waste of it. I'm about to make history here, and I can't have you obstructing my progress."

"You wouldn't be able to make *anything* if it weren't for me."

Sprague nodded, and with one hand fiddled with a fat orange cable that trailed across the controls. "For now, that's true. But it won't always be that way."

Though the tank room wasn't lighted, Jack could see, in the reflected glow from the control booth, that some things were different in there—poles were set up at all four corners of the room, and next to the tank, there was a chair, with something draped over it.

"I need to secure your sustained cooperation," Sprague

went on, "for at least another month. I need you to live here, at the institute, and accede to whatever experiments I request ... including, of course, repeated trips to what you call the Other World."

"I've already told you, I won't do that anymore. Under any circumstances."

Sprague held one end of the orange cable, with a silver prong, between his fingers. "Of course you will ... starting tonight. Because if you don't, you'll never see Nancy Liu, alive, again ... You don't believe me." He idly fitted the silver prong into a round socket on the control board, then looked up at Jack and smiled. "Would you like to know what I just did?" he said.

Gradually, the things draped over the chair outside had begun to take shape: they were clothes—jeans, leg warmers, a raspberry-colored ski parka.

"I just sent eleven hundred volts into the sensory deprivation tank. And guess who's inside it."

Jack waited ... waited for Sprague to say it was all a joke —a terrible, unconvincing joke; that Nancy was safely ensconced in the office upstairs; that the orange cable he'd just plugged in was simply something harmless—a microphone connection, or an EKG hook-up. But Sprague didn't say anything; he just sat there in the swivel chair, smiling madly, then pulled the plug from the socket again. "I think ten seconds is more than sufficient. Her heart surely stopped after three or four." He looked at Jack appraisingly. "Don't you have work to do?" He cocked his head toward the tank room.

She couldn't be in there, Jack thought; even Sprague, more insane than he'd ever imagined, couldn't have gone as far as that. But then he looked at her clothes again, and remembered what Tulley—armed—had warned in the animal lab. Without a word, he turned and charged through the open glass door to the other room. *Please, God, don't let her be inside the tank.* The orange cable slithered across the floor, up and onto the wrestling mats, then in through the slightly opened hatchway. He knocked the chair aside—all of her clothes were there, down to a pair of socks and lacy panties—and yanked the hatch open the rest of the way. Nancy lay in the water, on her back, her eyes closed, her mouth set. Her bare shoulders were oddly raised; then he realized that her arms had been drawn—

tied?—behind her. The orange cable disappeared into the dark, salty water.

"We won't bother to hook you up to the monitors on this trip," Sprague announced, over the intercom. He was sitting at the control panel, in a pool of pale violet light; he had also, Jack noticed, closed and bolted the door between the chambers.

Jack grabbed the orange cable, jerked it out of the water; he wrapped the loose end once around his wrist, then pulled on it as hard as he could. There was a fast rattling sound— the glass in the observation window shivered—and the rest of the cable came bursting out of the wall. Pinning the end with the plug beneath one foot, he snapped the cable upward, ripping the plug off.

Sprague looked surprised. "Good thinking," he said. "But shouldn't you be on your way?"

Jack threw off his overcoat and kicked off his shoes. "I'm coming back," he said, ominously.

"Not alone, I hope."

Jack clambered rapidly into the tank—there was barely room for the two of them in there—and lay down beside her, on his back, in the water. His clothes were quickly saturated and clung to his skin. Nancy's naked body was buoyed up, so that she floated half on top of him. He slipped one arm down and around her, the water sloshing against the curved walls of the tank, the fluorescent tube in the ceiling of the lab swimming in and out of view. Suddenly, the light switched off, and the room was plunged into blackness. Nancy's skin felt as cool and smooth and lifeless as marble.

Jack closed his own eyes and breathed deeply. There wasn't a second to spare. He had to banish all thoughts of Sprague, and Tulley, and concentrate—*concentrate*—on making this journey. *Nancy*, he thought, *Nancy* . . . The blackness in the tank faded to gray, then to white. He felt like a rocket bursting from its launch pad, gathering power and speed and direction . . . the red-steel scaffolding, the mountain of sand . . . the increasing heat, and brilliant light . . . the wind, with its babble of urgent voices, rushing past his ears. *Nancy, where are you? Where are you now?* At even the thought of losing her, his heart felt as if it would break in his chest. He hurtled forward, trying to *see* in the searing light, to find a shape in the shapeless void. The voices in his ear assumed a greater urgency, a low moaning, an almost coherent pleading. *Nancy, no—don't have gone on without me*. As the light grew more and more intense he could discern the vague and beating outline of its source. But nothing—not a sign—of Nancy anywhere. Was he doing something wrong? Was it already too late? He called for her, with all his mind and all his heart, but only the beacon—the white-hot, burning light—became more clear to him. He would have to pass through it again, if he ever hoped to find Nancy and return to the living world with her. He was so close now he had to shield his own eyes with his hand, and brace himself for the blazing immersion. The wind had risen to a deafening shriek. He gave himself over to the terrifying light, and once again he felt himself scalded and purified, torn apart and strangely made whole, buffeted and drowned and cleansed and clarified.

But unlike before, there was a rawness, an anger, to the light that embraced him; he felt, more than ever, the magnitude of his transgression, the enormity of his trespass. And in his heart he knew that, if he were allowed to escape alive this time—alive in the sense that the world understood it—it would be the last time such grace, or mercy, would be extended to him.

He found himself expelled, reeling and drained, into that vast and mist-filled terrain; he could hardly tell if he was walking, or floating somehow. But Nancy, he knew, had to be near; she might even be concealed in the vapor that swirled right before his eyes. He opened his lips, parched and numb, to call out for her, but before he could even utter her name, he felt a hand slide deftly into his. His heart leapt with joy. "Nancy!" he breathed. The vapor shaped itself into a face, a long, pretty face, with dark hair streaming to either side. The eyes that gazed so deeply into his were the green of emeralds bathed in light.

"I knew you'd be back."

"Mother . . . I—"

"I know why you're here . . . Let me help you."

He felt her grip tighten on his hand, felt himself drawn through the parting mist. They were moving, rapidly, away from the light, away from the heat. He no longer knew what to do; his mother—Eliza?—was smiling confidently, urging him on, nodding assurances. But something was wrong, something made the blood in his veins grow cold. Though there was no way of knowing for sure, he felt—instinctively —that he was traveling farther and farther away from wherever Nancy might be. The air was becoming thicker, and colder, all the time, the mist more clinging, almost damp to the touch. He felt, as he had once before, a growing and inconsolable emptiness within him. He wanted to resist, but didn't know how.

"Mother—this isn't right," he mumbled. "This is not where I'll find her." He tried to withdraw, to pull back, but there was nothing to hang on to, no ground to dig his heels into. "I have to go back," he said, "I have to go back."

"You *are* going back," his mother said, "back where you belong."

"No," he said, shaking his head and trying to concentrate, "no." He found it increasingly hard to collect his thoughts. "There's very little time, very little time."

His mother laughed, and even tossed her head at this. "Time is the one thing we've got plenty of."

His eyes, more accustomed to the dimness now, were able at last to pick out a feature in this landscape—a line of demarcation, a bank of boiling black cloud that formed, at the very limit of his vision, a writhing but stationary horizon.

"Time won't matter to you here," his mother went on. "What's a day, or a month, or a year, when you chalk it up against eternity?"

"But I'm going back," he said, struggling to catch his breath, "going back, with Nancy."

"Are you?" she said, her voice suddenly turning bitter and cold. "Are you? That's what I thought too—after the accident. I thought that I was going back. But I never did." The black rampart was growing closer all the time. "I was only kept alive for *your* sake . . . I was just the egg that hatched you . . . I was used as your fucking *incubator*."

Her fingers fastened like talons around his hand. She seemed to be draining the strength—the very life—right out of him.

"How do you think that felt? Lying there in that hospital bed, month after month, so you could grow, while I withered? How do you think I felt about that?" Her eyes blazed with a green fire. "And then, when you were big enough, and strong enough, to cut it on your own, they ripped the tubes and wires out of me like I was some fucking appliance that nobody needed anymore . . . They never even fixed my broken nose."

The bank of clouds was rising above them now, curled at the top like some miraculous wave that never fell. There was a strong, cold metallic odor in the air, and a noise that sounded like a million voices wailing incessantly, all at once. Jack tasted despair, as distinctly as if it were wine he'd just drunk.

"But I never hurt you," he said, the words falling like ashes from his tongue. "I always loved you."

She threw back her head in what he first thought was laughter, but became, instead, a harrowing scream. "Is this what you loved?" she said, lowering her face again, utterly transformed. The nose was smashed flat, a bloody smudge across her face; her eyes were blackened, sunk deep in their sockets; her flesh was raw, and gouged with shards of glass. "Is this what you loved, Jackie boy?"

Her arms snaked around him, astonishingly strong, and her body rubbed up against him. Her face was only inches away. "Is this what you loved?" she whispered, through broken teeth and torn lips. "Show me."

She bent her head—there was a gash in the crown of her skull as if it had been cleaved with an ax—and pressed her open lips to his. He felt her tongue, like a living icicle, probe and scour his mouth. She tasted of blood and agony and rot, but he was powerless to resist her; he was unable even to move. She put her hands, cold and hard, against his face, and seemed to suck the breath right out of his body. *This*, Jack thought, through the terrible and overwhelming sadness, *is what it is to die*. He felt his strength ebbing like a tide, washing up and into the mighty black wave that towered above him; it was like a wall of water, but made of dust, shadow . . . and something else that he could not discern. It changed its shape and texture constantly, flickering like flame, rising like smoke. As he watched it, hypnotized by the swirling facade, his mother's grasp gradually lessened, her lips came away, she faded back, and into the roiling wall of darkness. It was *then* he saw what else it was made of. Faces, and bodies—more than he could ever have imagined—rising and falling, twisted and contorted, screaming and pleading and weeping; he saw mouths, open, and eyes, staring; he saw arms reaching out and legs kicking wildly. Bodies merged, and disappeared, and appeared again; he could see them, and see through them, at the same time. The wall went on as far as he could see, stretching away, curved like a crescent moon, rising up toward a black and starless sky, falling away toward... what? His eyes were drawn, almost against his will, to the foot of the wall, or where the foot should have been; instead, he saw a vast and bottomless swirling, a black miasma that seemed to drop away forever into... what had his mother said, *eternity?* His own feet were balanced on the very brink of the precipice.

"Jackie boy, come and join us." His mother's voice somehow spoke within his head; her face remained, green eyes glittering, in the seething wave. Other faces beckoned him too—men and women, of all ages, all colors. *"Sí—ven con nosotros"* suddenly echoed in his head, and he thought he saw, in the tortured blur, the grinning face of Ruben Garcia. *"Ven con nosotros."* "Come and join us, Jackie boy." He couldn't take his eyes from the wave, and in his heart he felt such a killing sadness, he had no desire to. If this was death, if this was oblivion, then why go on? "Come and join us." If this was what it all came to in the end, how could he find the courage to face another day? Why, if this was waiting, should he try? "What's a month, or a year, or a century, chalked up against eternity?" Despair engulfed him like a billowing, black shroud. He stared, lost and empty, into the endless wave, and the burning green eyes of Eliza; his feet teetered, on the insubstantial edge of the chasm. Having glimpsed eternity, he could not go back. That much he knew. "Come and join us, Jackie boy." There was only one thing left for him to do, and that one thing was as easy as giving up, as falling forward... into that awful canyon that boiled up before him. "Yes," he sighed, and stepped forward.

His foot encountered nothing—only air, cold as ice—and the wall suddenly disappeared. In front of him, all he could see was a pale film, gray and translucent.

"Don't look anymore."

The voice was Mam's.

"It's hell you were looking at—not eternal life."

His eyes had been covered by her hand; he could feel the warmth of her palm on his face.

"Come to us, Jack!" his mother snarled, her voice reverberating in his head.

"Ven con nosotros!"

"Close your eyes," Mam said.

He did as she told him—he had no more strength left to resist, or even wonder—and felt himself borne helplessly backward, away from the angry wall.

"Come to us! Come to us, Jackie!"

Eliza's voice, spitting with fury, echoed still . . . but more faintly.

He knew, without looking, that he was traveling at an amazing speed; the air was noticeably warmer, the crashing tumult of the wave receding.

"You mustn't come here again," Mam was saying. "You mustn't do this, Jack."

But he'd had to, he'd had to come—there'd been a reason, a reason he was struggling to remember.

"You've come too far. You've seen what you never should have."

"I had to come," he whispered, "there was someone here . . ." *Nancy*, he remembered. He'd come for *Nancy*.

He opened his eyes—they were no longer covered by Mam's hand—and in that instant saw, carved from the gray mist, the figure of Nancy. Mam was only a disembodied voice, saying "Take her and go—go now! Jack—you haven't much time!" Her tone was filled with great love and enormous alarm. "Go!"

He called to Nancy—she turned, naked and bewildered—and on seeing him receded farther into the mist. "No, Nancy! No—!" The distance between them closed rapidly. There were tears, he could see now, streaming down her face. She put up her hands against him.

"No!" she cried. "Don't come any closer!"

"*Why?* I came here for you!"

"*You put me here!* It is because of you that I'm here! I'm *dead* because of what you do!"

"But I can save you! I can save us both!"

She spun around, her body a mix of flesh and vapor, light and shadow. Her shoulders heaved; she wept hysterically. There was no time to reason, or persuade. They'd both been so long in this Other World it might not even be possible to return to the living world anymore. He threw his arms around her, clutching her from behind. "I can save us." Was it true? "Keep your eyes closed—come with me."

With all the strength he had left in him, he held her fast, and concentrated his thoughts. The mist flew past them, the air grew hotter. The light, the beating light—they'd have to go through it. He spread one hand across her face, over her eyes, and braced himself again. A second later, they were swallowed up—immersed in the blazing beacon—then shot out, breathless, into a flat black sea. He was holding her tight, half on top of him; water—rife with salt—sloshed up over his chin, into his mouth. He couldn't breathe, and had to let go of her. She was sputtering, too, her chest heaving; they were lying together, on their backs, in a watery grave.

The tank.

Jack's mind sprang awake; they were back in the lab, they were both alive. Did Sprague know it yet? He must; he undoubtedly had the intercom on. "Nancy," Jack gasped, "are you all right?"

She coughed, said, "I think so."

"Then you've got to get out, quickly. Get out of the tank."

"I can't . . . my hands, they're tied behind me."

Jack slipped his hands under her, found her wrists; they were bound together, with what felt like one of the electrode wires. He tried desperately to undo the knot, but in the dark, underwater, it was impossible to get untied. The air in the tank was so hot and heavy, it was almost as hard to breathe as to move. And even under their loud and labored breathing, he thought he could hear—yes, it was getting louder all the time —that fearful howling of the damned.

"Hold your breath," he said. "I'm going to turn you over."

He took hold of one elbow, and flipped her facefirst into the water. He fumbled again at the knot; then, forcing her wrists even more tightly together, he dragged the wire, with sheer force, over and off of her hands. She jerked her head up into the air, banging it hard against the top of the tank.

"Get out! Get out!"

The howling echoed, like a pack of baying hounds, in his head.

She struggled to her feet, still gasping for breath, and clambered out of the tank. As soon as her feet had cleared the hatchway, Jack sat up himself, threw his arms out of the tank. He was halfway out, when he felt his foot snatched from below by an icy hand.

"Come to us, Jackie!" he heard from inside the tank.

He looked in horror back into the water, where Eliza's face—still mangled and bloody—beamed up at him, green eyes shining. He jerked his foot away, then smashed it down, into that wide and smiling mouth. He felt nothing but the slippery bottom of the tank. Spilling out of the hatchway, he landed on his hands, next to the overturned chair and Nancy's scattered clothes. There was a pale red glow in the room, emanating from the poles, and from the control booth where Sprague was still sitting. Nancy was at the glass door, naked, struggling to pull it open.

"Knew you'd do it," Sprague said, over the intercom, when he saw Jack scrambling to his feet, "though you certainly took your time."

"Jack! Help me with this," Nancy cried.

He staggered across the room to her, his sopping clothes stuck to his limbs. The door, he could see, was bolted at both the top and bottom. "Open it up!" he shouted, and Sprague laughed.

"In the middle of an experiment?"

"The experiment's over!"

"Hardly," Sprague countered. "I had a deal, with your very own mother; I keep you coming back, she gives me all the proof I need to confirm my discoveries."

Jack slumped against the bolted door; Nancy had dropped in a heap beside it. The air in the room was becoming strangely agitated; Jack could feel a cool breeze ruffling his hair, making the wet sleeves of his shirt snap and billow around his arms. He knelt down next to Nancy; drew her, shaking, into the protection of his embrace. Against his back, he could feel the cold hard steel of the pole Sprague had installed there. In his head he heard, again, that plaintive howling, that unearthly tumult, growing louder; then Nancy raised her head, as if she had heard it too.

"What's that?" she moaned.

He drew her closer. "Hold on to me, no matter what."

The noise, like the breeze, was emanating from the tank; it echoed and reverberated, like a monstrous choir clattering up from the bottom of a well. The tank itself shook and shivered, *boomed* as if sledgehammers were being swung against its interior. The breeze became a wind, cold and metallic, pouring forth from the open hatchway and gusting, in slow, powerful circles, around the room. *Hell is coming after me*, Jack thought. He looped one arm around the steel pole—was that a camera mounted on it, above his head?—then back around Nancy; he locked his legs around her too.

"Your mother's as good as her word," Sprague said, his head bent over the panel, his hands flying to various controls. "The dead you can do business with."

Totally, uncontrollably, out of his mind. Jack watched as at first a fine tendril, and then a denser coil, of gray vapor slipped from the hatchway of the tank. It rose, as smoke would do, up to the ceiling of the lab, but instead of hitting the ceiling and then thinning out, it seemed to continue, inexorably, to rise, dissolving all sign of the ceiling itself. More and more of the mist followed, moving in sluggish circles all around the perimeter of the room, gradually obscuring those dimensions, too. There were lights—flashbulbs?—popping at frequent intervals, photographing, if anything, nothing Jack could see. Before his eyes, the walls and ceiling of the lab had virtually disappeared, replaced, he now could tell, by that vacant gray terrain of the Other World. Sprague would be seeing it—the place Jack went on his journeys—for himself at last. Jack glanced up and to his left, where the booth had been.

Sprague was sitting, slack-jawed, in a pool of violet light. The observation window shimmered, like a screen suspended in midair, in front of him.

"Is this the deal you made," Jack shouted, "to be swallowed up alive?"

Sprague, still riveted, said in a monotone, "What is this?"

"The Other World, Sprague! Don't you recognize it? It's come to see you!" Nancy huddled closer in his arms, twisting her face against his chest.

"The Other World," Sprague slowly repeated, awed, almost mesmerized. The back wall of the booth had disappeared, too . . . and in its place, Jack could dimly make out a distant but roiling bank of clouds.

"And this," Sprague intoned, as if to himself, "is where the soul goes after death."

"No," replied a woman's voice, young and taunting, "this is Disneyland."

His mother was hovering, only partially visible, somewhere between the tank and the observation window. The outlines of her body faded in and out of view, etched in red by the ultraviolet lights. "You wanted proof. Now you've got it . . . all you could ever want."

The wind in the room had gathered speed, and the black wall behind Sprague had grown perceptibly higher . . . and closer.

"Jackie here doesn't seem to like it." Her head turned toward Jack and Nancy. "He keeps leaving us." She gave him a sad, reproachful smile. Even in the sunken holes of her skull, her green eyes glittered brightly. "You know the way too well, Jackie . . . I think you'll keep leaving us as long as you have a living body to return to."

Jack stared back at her mangled face, her long hair streaming in the wind.

"But that won't last forever," she said, teasingly, and turning her gaze back toward Sprague. "Nothing does . . . except, of course, eternity."

Behind him, the boiling black wave had surged even closer; Sprague seemed to sense it at last, and tearing his eyes away from Eliza, turned slowly in his chair. The wall spread itself above him like a vast, black waterfall, growing higher and wider all the time.

"See anyone you know?" she said to Sprague, and in that instant the face of Garcia, and then Tulley—Tulley!—materialized in the midst of the seething wall. Their hands lashed out, with half a dozen others, to clutch at his arms, his legs, the hanging tails of his lab coat. He clung frantically to the sides of his chair, screaming, "Logan—help me! Help me, Logan!"

"Glad to," Eliza replied, and moving effortlessly through the glass of the observation window, pried his fingers from the arms of the chair. "Logan!" he screamed again, flailing wildly, as the greedy hands from within the wall dragged him into their embrace. "Logan!"

Jack watched in horror, his arms wrapped fiercely around Nancy, as Sprague was tossed, turned, and finally, as if being dunked by an irresistible force, utterly submerged in the cascading wave. Eliza turned in place, smiling widely through her broken teeth, and said, "Nothing lasts forever, Jack..." Laughing now, she threw out her arms and was sucked backward into the swirling blackness. As she was, the wind rose to a deafening roar; the observation window shivered, and just as Jack ducked his head on top of Nancy's, it exploded into a thousand pieces, sending shards of glass whistling past them, into the mist. When he dared to look up again, the wave was gone, and the gray vapors that had filled the room were thinning out, shimmering like heat waves...evaporating. The walls and ceiling of the room reappeared. The wind abruptly died down. Nancy cautiously raised her head to look around.

"Is it over?" she asked, in a small voice.

Her clothes, and the overturned chair, lay scattered across the wrestling mats.

"It's over."

"And we're alive?"

Jack laughed softly. "We're alive."

Her body gradually unclenched itself. She surveyed the entire lab. "Where's Sprague?"

Jack let his legs stretch out before him. *Where was Sprague?* He expected to find his body on the floor of the control booth, below the shattered glass. His soul? He hoped never to see that again, as long as he lived...and longer.

"He's gone," he said, stroking Nancy's hair. "We're safe now. Everything's okay."

Epilogue

DOWN THE BEACH, she could hear children laughing while they played in the surf. Twice the lifeguard had warned someone on a raft to come in closer to shore. Discreetly, Nancy reached under herself and adjusted the bottom of her bathing suit.

This was the tiniest bikini she'd ever, under any circumstances, dared to wear; Jack was the one who had spotted it, in the window of a boutique in the hotel lobby. Half an hour later, he'd given it to her, wrapped in tissue paper, on the balcony of their room.

"You must be kidding," she'd said.

"When in the islands . . ."

"In that case, I should go topless."

"Just be sure to wear plenty of sunblock."

Smiling, she rolled over onto her stomach, and looked out to sea. The water was deep blue, dappled with whitecaps; the sky, except on the horizon, bright and untroubled. On the horizon, there was a faint line of clouds, and even from here she could see that rain was falling. Something about it made her stop smiling and want to look away; she did.

The beach, a broad arc of white sand, was sparsely populated. There was a rocky promontory at one end, dotted with tidal pools, and several kids were busily exploring it. She wondered what had happened to Jack.

She crossed her forearms and laid her head down on them. The smell of hot sand and suntan oil . . . there was nothing like it, she thought, for sheer relaxation. It was almost enough to make her forget for a little while what had happened to her back in New York. Almost... but not quite. Nothing, she reflected, would ever do that completely. Though Jack, God knows, was making a valiant attempt.

It had been his idea to blow the money from the *Investigator* on this trip. *Steamroller* had closed, to no one's surprise, and Nancy, of course, was without a job; even her classes were still on holiday break. After they'd arranged to sell their story to Mansfield, Jack had said, "Leave the rest to me," and the next thing she knew, he had two tickets to St. Thomas.

As far as her family knew, she was there with her friend Amy, from NYU. (Her sister, she was sure, hadn't fallen for it.) She was due back in just two more days, and dreaded the thought.

She felt some sand kicked up onto her shins and heard Jack whistle and say, "Hey, baby, where'd you get that Band-Aid you're wearing?"

"An old boyfriend bought it for me—don't let it worry you."

He flopped down next to her on the beach towel. In his hand, he had a rolled-up newspaper.

"You got it?"

"Fresh from the mainland."

She slipped on her sunglasses and quickly flattened out the paper. The top headline was something about an extraterrestrial's New Year's resolutions, but below that it read *"Investigator Exclusive: False Messiah Causes Bizarre Death of World-Famous Doctor."*

"I didn't cause it," Jack observed.

"Don't be so modest."

There was a grainy photo of Jack, clearly cropped from the pictures that had been taken on the park bench with Adam Baldwin, and a smaller snapshot of Sprague, taken from one of the institute catalogues. The story, written in Mansfield's inimitable overheated style, went on to describe how "Jack Logan, a Broadway strummer who once laid claims to extraordinary powers of healing and even resurrection (see the December 27 issue)" had inadvertently, "but tragically nonetheless, brought about the deaths of a security guard, one Randall Tulley, and the world-renowned brain specialist and staff member of New York's prestigious Institute of Abnormal Psychology, Dr. Orson Sprague."

"He'd have liked his buildup," Nancy said.

"Wait'll you see how I wind up."

"I can't wait."

While Jack idly brushed the sand from the back of her thighs and traced the line of her bikini bottom with one finger, Nancy flipped to the inside page where the story continued. There was another photo, of a big black tank that bore no resemblance to the one in the lab, and a caption that read "The sensory-deprivation tank which led to the bizarre and untimely death of neuropsychologist Dr. Orson Sprague."

"This tank," Nancy said, "it's nothing like the one at the institute."

"What did you expect," Jack said, insinuating one finger under the elastic of her suit, "accuracy?"

"Get out of there," she said, flicking him away. "There are children on this beach."

She went on reading; according to Mansfield, Sprague had died of electrocution, while attempting to wire the tank for further experimentation with "the guitar-playing charlatan, Jack Logan." Jack, apparently, had duped the "trusting, but hopelessly naive, scientist into believing in his self-professed powers, and even in paying for them."

"So far, you're not coming off very well," Nancy commented.

Jack laughed. "I guess he can't forgive me for slugging him at the hospital."

"Or for making him cough up fifteen hundred for this exclusive."

"You're right. He told me he'd been slugged plenty of times."

There was a lot about Jack's "malicious chicanery," and Mansfield's own clever sleuthing. In the end, Jack was cast as a shallow but repentant cad, now piecing together a living as a guitar instructor in a shabby Upper West Side studio, and "rummaging forlornly, for solace and understanding, through the broken rubble of his forgotten Catholic faith."

"I'd like to see rubble that isn't broken," Nancy said aloud.

"Oh—so you're done. Still want to go out with me?"

She pushed the paper away and laid her head back down on

the towel. "I guess . . . provided you're through with all this chicanery."

"Through," he promised. "If that article doesn't put a stop to the Jack Logan story, nothing will."

But would it? She closed her eyes and listened to the lifeguard's whistle. By publicly exposing himself, by openly admitting to an elaborate hoax, Jack had hoped to kill the story once and for all . . . to put it all behind them, for good now. Nancy prayed that it would do the trick.

The lifeguard's whistle blew again. Then she heard him say something, though she couldn't make out the words, over his bullhorn. There were shouts from down the beach, a woman's voice raised in alarm. Nancy lifted her head. "What's going on?"

Jack was already sitting up. "I don't know. It's down by those rocks."

The lifeguard had called everyone in from the water, and bounded off his stand. He was racing down the beach, his feet kicking up little bursts of white sand.

"Maybe I should go see what's going on," Jack said.

A flicker of fear coursed through Nancy. "He'll take care of it," she said, as casually as she could. "I'm sure it's nothing." She put her head back down on the towel, as if to prove it. Far off, she could still hear the growing commotion.

Jack waited another few seconds, then said, "I'm gonna see what's up." He patted her on the behind as he got up, then walked quickly away. There was a knot of people—several adults, some kids—gathered by the promontory. *Please*, Nancy thought, *please don't let it be what I think it is*.

She saw Jack, as he drew closer, begin to jog.

Please—no.

The lifeguard was kneeling now, by something on the sand. A woman in a straw hat whisked the children away, shooing them up the beach. Nancy couldn't stand not knowing anymore; she stuck the *Investigator* under the towel so it wouldn't blow away, and got up. Now she could see that the lifeguard was bent over a body—it looked from here like a little girl—and giving her artificial resuscitation.

Jack was watching from a few feet away.

She glanced out to sea for some reason—the rain clouds were coming closer, drifting in toward shore.

She stepped off the towel—the sand, cooled by the breeze off the water, was comfortably warm underfoot—and moved slowly down the beach. She was torn between wanting to know exactly what was happening, and not wanting any of this—why here? why now?—to be happening at all. When she was a few yards away, she saw that the lifeguard was pressing the girl's abdomen—she was blond, about nine or ten years old—and blowing into her open mouth. Coming up beside Jack, she slipped her arm around his waist and said softly, "How did it happen?"

"She was playing in the tide pools around the rocks," he said, still staring intently at the straining lifeguard. "She got hit by a wave, pulled under . . . as far as I can tell."

There was a young Filipino woman, in a brightly flowered bathing suit, kneeling on the sand, utterly silent, squeezing her hands together. The nanny, Nancy thought? Another woman stood beside her, one hand clutching her friend's shoulder.

The lifeguard leaned back, winded, and felt the girl's wrist, again, for a pulse. His face was red from exertion. The little girl, wearing a yellow swimsuit with tiny blue fish all over it, lay flat and still as a stone.

The lifeguard mumbled something to the kneeling woman. "I'm sorry," it sounded like, "I don't think . . ."

Nancy felt Jack's body stiffen. "Jack," she said, "you can't . . . she's gone . . . there's nothing you—"

"I can try." He lifted her arm away from his waist. "I have to." He touched the lifeguard on the shoulder, said, "Please— let me." The lifeguard, looking exhausted and confused, moved aside. Jack knelt beside the girl, in his turquoise Jams and sunglasses; put his hands on her narrow shoulders. He said something, so softly it couldn't be heard, then leaned forward, pressing the girl's body against his.

The Filipino woman, terrified, tears welling up in her eyes, looked across him, to Nancy. Nancy nodded at her, reassuringly, and held up one hand to signal patience. She knew where he was going, even if she could never know how he traveled there, and she knew the dangers he faced.

The storm clouds had spread, like a fine black veil, across

the entire horizon now. A strong wind had kicked up off the water.

Where was he right now, she wondered? What was he seeing? Had he found the little girl? His back was tense, but he didn't move; he almost seemed to have stopped breathing. His brain waves, she knew, would have dropped off precipitously by now; his body temperature would be eight or ten degrees below normal. It was his heart she worried most about—what was his heart doing? Was it beating strongly, regularly—alone? Were the souls of his mother, of Tulley, of Sprague, aware of his coming? Were they—she felt a shiver descend her spine—lying in wait for him?

A big drop of rain, cold and solitary, skidded down her arm.

Jack's shoulders, tanned and gleaming, strained over the girl's body; all but her legs and feet were obscured. How much longer could he risk being there? Was he being held, against his will? Was he still searching for the soul of the girl?

The Filipino let out a squeal. "Her foot!" she screamed. "It moved!"

Nancy looked down; both feet were moving now, the heels arching, the toes stretching up. Nancy heard a gurgling sound, and a wet cough; the girl was coughing, and spitting up water. Jack's shoulders visibly relaxed, and he rolled, listlessly, onto the sand beside her. The lifeguard jumped over him, raised the girl's head; she was coughing, and crying, and dribbling water. Nancy dropped beside Jack: "Are you all right? Can you hear me? Are you all right?" She snatched his sunglasses away.

The storm clouds passed directly overhead, throwing a deep gray shadow over his face.

"Jack . . . Jack . . ." His eyes were closed, his mouth slack; his skin felt like ice. "Jack . . . please . . . Jack, can you hear me?"

Another drop of rain landed square on his forehead, trickled down onto the bridge of his nose. His eyelids twitched, and his head stirred, almost imperceptibly, on the sand.

"Yes, yes," Nancy heard herself saying, "yes, you're alive, you're alive, Jack . . . yes."

He opened his eyes, just as the rain began to fall in earnest.

She leaned over him to protect his face. He said something she couldn't make out; she leaned closer.

"Piece a cake," he whispered, slipping his fingers, so gently she hardly noticed, back under the bottom of her bathing suit.

DOWN RIVER

STEPHEN GALLAGHER

Johnny Mays. Imagine the moral conscience of a selfish child in the frame of a plain-clothes cop. The city: his playground. We, the city-dwellers, his toys.

And Johnny never had a toy he didn't break.

But now Johnny's dead, isn't he? He started something and pushed it too far. Now they're fishing for his body at the foot of a dam and Nick Frazier has been left behind.

They'd been friends once, a long time ago. Nick had even hoped he might save Johnny. But by Johnny's reckoning, Nick had betrayed him.

As Nick goes looking for answers, people start dying – dying in a sequence that is leading straight back to Nick Frazier. And when they haul Johnny's car – his empty car – from the lake, the truth becomes clear.

Johnny Mays is back. And he's baying at the moon.

'Puts its author on an equal footing with the best of British horror'

Kim Newman, *City Limits*

POST A LITTLE HAPPINESS

Post·A·Book

A Royal Mail service in association with the Book Marketing Council & The Booksellers Association.

Post-A-Book is a Post Office trademark.

MORE HORROR TITLES AVAILABLE FROM HODDER AND STOUGHTON PAPERBACKS

STEPHEN GALLAGHER

☐	49178 1	Oktober	£2.99
☐	42268 2	Valley of Lights	£2.50
☐	51112 X	Down River	£3.50

JAMES HERBERT

☐	03045 8	The Fog	£2.99
☐	49355 5	Haunted	£3.50
☐	02127 0	The Rats	£1.99

STEPHEN KING

☐	05769 0	Pet Sematary	£3.99
☐	41739 5	Misery	£3.50

DANIEL RHODES

☐	49478 0	Next After Lucifer	£3.50

All these books are available at your local bookshop or newsagent, or can be ordered direct from the publisher. Just tick the titles you want and fill in the form below.

Prices and availability subject to change without notice.

Hodder & Stoughton Paperbacks, P.O. Box 11, Falmouth, Cornwall.

Please send cheque or postal order, and allow the following for postage and packing:

U.K. – 55p for one book, plus 22p for the second book, and 14p for each additional book ordered up to a £1.75 maximum.

B.F.P.O. and EIRE – 55p for the first book, plus 22p for the second book, and 14p per copy for the next 7 books, 8p per book thereafter.

OTHER OVERSEAS CUSTOMERS – £1.00 for the first book, plus 25p per copy for each additional book.

Name ....

Address ....

....